# Vanished in the Crowd

**Also by Rhys Bowen and Clare Broyles**

The Molly Murphy Mysteries

*Silent as the Grave*  *All That Is Hidden*
*In Sunshine or in Shadow*  *Wild Irish Rose*

**Also by Rhys Bowen**

The Molly Murphy Mysteries

*The Ghost of Christmas Past*  *The Last Illusion*
*Time of Fog and Fire*  *In a Gilded Cage*
*Away in a Manger*  *Tell Me, Pretty Maiden*
*The Edge of Dreams*  *In Dublin's Fair City*
*City of Darkness and Light*  *Oh Danny Boy*
*The Family Way*  *In Like Flynn*
*Hush Now, Don't You Cry*  *For the Love of Mike*
*Bless the Bride*  *Death of Riley*

*Murphy's Law*

The Constable Evans Mysteries

*Evanly Bodies*  *Evan Can Wait*
*Evan Blessed*  *Evan and Elle*
*Evan's Gate*  *Evanly Choirs*
*Evan Only Knows*  *Evan Help Us*
*Evans to Betsy*  *Evans Above*

# Vanished in the Crowd

Rhys Bowen
&
Clare Broyles

MINOTAUR BOOKS
NEW YORK

This is a work of fiction. All of the names, characters, organizations, places, and events portrayed in this work are either products of the author's imagination or used fictitiously.

First published in the United States by Minotaur Books, an imprint of St. Martin's Publishing Group

*EU Representative:* Macmillan Publishers Ireland Ltd, 1st Floor, The Liffey Trust Centre, 117–126 Sheriff Street Upper, Dublin 1, D01 YC43

VANISHED IN THE CROWD. Copyright © 2026 by Janet Quin-Harkin (writing as Rhys Bowen) and Clare Broyles. All rights reserved. Printed in the United States of America. For information, address St. Martin's Publishing Group, 120 Broadway, New York, NY 10271.

www.minotaurbooks.com

The Library of Congress Cataloging-in-Publication Data is available upon request.

ISBN 978-1-250-39935-9 (hardcover)
ISBN 978-1-250-39936-6 (ebook)

The publisher of this book does not authorize the use or reproduction of any part of this book in any manner for the purpose of training artificial intelligence technologies or systems. The publisher of this book expressly reserves this book from the Text and Data Mining exception in accordance with Article 4(3) of the European Union Digital Single Market Directive 2019/790.

Our books may be purchased in bulk for specialty retail/wholesale, literacy, corporate/premium, educational, and subscription box use. Please contact MacmillanSpecialMarkets@macmillan.com.

First Edition: 2026

10  9  8  7  6  5  4  3  2  1

*This book is dedicated to the brave suffragists
who went before us and paved the way.
Without them we would not have the right to vote.
May we follow in their footsteps
and raise our voices for the rights
of women the whole world over.*

# Vanished in the Crowd

# ✺ One ✺

New York
Monday, September 20, 1909

"Mama, you'll never guess in a million years!" My adopted daughter, Bridie, came flying into the house like a miniature tornado, her schoolbag knocking the newspapers from the hallstand as she hurtled toward the kitchen. I had just settled my ten-month-old baby, Mary Kate, into her high chair, where I was trying to persuade her that pureed carrot was edible. The result so far was that both Mary Kate and I were liberally spattered with orange daubs.

"Holy Mother of God!" I exclaimed. "I thought that school was teaching you to behave like a young lady. What has made you charge in like the cavalry?"

Usually her excitement had something to do with her best friend, Blanche. It ranged from *Blanche has a new dress made of raw silk* to *Blanche is going to Paris*. Blanche, as you may have guessed, led a very different life from our own, in a mansion on upper Fifth Avenue, while our abode in Patchin Place, a quiet backwater in Greenwich Village, was somewhat humbler.

I looked up expectantly at Bridie. "Well?"

"You know the big celebration?" she said. "The Hudson-Fulton parades?"

Who didn't? The whole city had talked of nothing else for weeks. The city was already filling up with visitors from all over the world. It was to be a joint celebration of three hundred years since Henry Hudson had discovered the river named after him and one hundred years since Robert Fulton had invented the first commercial paddle steamer, thus making commerce on the river possible. There were to be two weeks of parades, starting on September 25, some through the streets of the city and one grand naval parade with replicas of Hudson's and Fulton's ships, naval vessels from the American navy, and vessels from nine other countries. Since the aim was to promote international peace and prosperity, I thought it rather ironic that the ships were all armed to the teeth with impressive guns—the German dreadnoughts trying to outdo the English battleships and the American warships trying to outdo both.

"How could I not?" I replied. "Your poor father has been tearing his hair out, trying to make sure everything is safe and secure." As the New York head of the newly founded Federal Bureau of Investigation, Daniel was tasked with providing security to the various foreign diplomats, heads of state, and military personnel during their time in New York.

"That's good," she said, still breathless. I suspected she had run all the way home from school. "Because I am going to be in one of those parades." Bridie attempted to be a fashionable young lady, but when she was excited she reverted to the giddy, unrestrained excitement of a girl.

"You are?" The parades were one week away and there had been no mention of this before.

She nodded. "Miss Allen told us about it today. We had a special assembly. It's the historical and cultural parade. There are floats showing educational progress in America."

Bridie went to an expensive school for young ladies, paid for by my friends Sid and Gus, who lived across Patchin Place. Sid and Gus, whose real names were Elena Goldfarb and Augusta Walcott, were women of private means who broke all the rules of society and did whatever they pleased. This ranged from going to Paris to study art to turning their sitting room into a yurt and eating Mongolian food. Life across the street from them was never dull.

"And you're going to be on one of these floats?" I interrupted before she could go on. I had never learned to be patient, I'm afraid.

She nodded. "It's a float showing education for young women. It's going to say FUTURE WOMEN OF NEW YORK: A BRIGHT AND PEACEFUL FUTURE FOR OUR NATION."

"That's grand," I said. "But why have I only heard about this just now? I thought everything had to be approved by the committee and was in place weeks ago."

"It was," she said. "Another ladies' academy was supposed to be on the float. A more important school than ours. But their principal is very forward thinking, and very much in favor of the advancement of women. She wanted to have girls standing at a blackboard on which there was a complicated math equation and other girls at a table doing a chemistry experiment, as well as girls painting and reading. The committee got wind of it and said absolutely not. Girls were to be shown as future homemakers, raising intelligent and educated children. So this principal said, 'Not my girls. They are going to change the world.'"

She paused, catching her breath. "So she withdrew from the parade at the last minute and we were asked instead."

"I'm pleased for you," I said, although privately I agreed with the principal. "So I take it you'll not be doing science experiments either?"

Bridie giggled. "No. Some of us are going to be sitting around someone who is giving a talk on health and nutrition. Healthy bodies, healthy minds. And others are going to be dancing, cooking, and mending. But it doesn't matter. Twelve of us were chosen and I was one of them."

"Wonderful," I said, trying to make my face show only enthusiasm when in reality I was worried.

"You don't seem really happy for me," Bridie said.

"Oh, I am. Honestly, my darling. It's just . . . well, you probably know that money is tight at the moment, so if you're all going to have to have expensive costumes made for a parade that is less than a week away . . ." I couldn't finish the sentence. I didn't want to say that she couldn't take part.

"Oh no. Not at all," Bridie replied. "As soon as Blanche's mother heard that Blanche is going to be in the parade, she said she'd have identical white dresses made for all of us. She has a seamstress that can do it quickly. Wasn't that kind of her?"

"It was. Blanche's mother is always very generous."

"So you don't have to worry about a thing." Bridie gave a little sigh of happiness. "A new dress and thousands of people seeing me in a parade! How could anything be more perfect?" She paused, smiling down at Mary Kate now, who had stopped eating and was staring up at Bridie in absolute fascination. "Did you understand that, Mary Kate?" Bridie said. "I'm going to be in a parade."

Obviously Mary Kate had no idea what a parade was, but she gave a grin, revealing her new teeth. "Bye-bye," she said.

This, we had worked out, was not saying goodbye but her version of Bridie. My son, Liam, now almost five, had been playing out in the back garden. Hearing Bridie's voice, he now came in.

"Bridie's home!" he exclaimed, flinging open the door.

I took one look at the muddy shoes, hands, and knees and stopped him. "Hold it right there, boyo. You get yourself cleaned up at the outside tap before you come and hear your sister's news."

"I'm going to be in a parade, Liam," Bridie called after him. "One of those big parades."

"On a boat? A navy boat?" He paused in the doorway. He had lately become obsessed with ships.

"No, silly. On a float."

He looked puzzled. The only float in his vocabulary was a root beer one.

"It's like a big, decorated platform pulled by horses, going down Fifth Avenue," I explained. "We'll go and watch her and cheer."

"And guess what, Mama!" She was off and dancing around again. "Some girls will have hoops. We are supposed to roll them to each other in a ladylike manner . . ." She paused. "Oh Lordy. I hope I don't lose mine and it rolls off the float."

"I expect some kind spectator will retrieve it," I said. "And you'll be practicing a lot first."

She nodded. "There will be more girls walking beside the float carrying banners with our school's name on them." She broke off as something else occurred to her. "Oh, and I forgot to tell you. Blanche's mother is paying for the dresses but we have to have matching shoes and little crowns of flowers on our hair. We have to buy those ourselves. The shoes are from Lord & Taylor on Broadway. They are white patent with a little bow at the toe. Really pretty. Miss Amelia showed them to us today so we'll know which ones to buy. And she suggests white silk stockings to go with them, as the skirts show our ankles. Maybe we can go to the store tomorrow? And the crowns are being made for us. They have little rhinestones in them so they'll sparkle. Of course, we'll have to curl our hair the night before. Blanche is going to have a beauty stylist come to the house that morning. Oh gee whiz, I hope it doesn't rain!"

As she spoke I was doing mental calculations about how much a pair of good shoes, silk stockings, and a crown might cost. Bridie seemed oblivious to the fact that money might be a concern right now. She was proving she was a true fourteen-year-old by forgetting to be sophisticated, grabbing two slices of bread and slathering them liberally with jam.

"Go easy on that, young lady," I said. "We have to make that one jar last till the end of the month."

She froze, looked up in surprise. "Mama, why are we suddenly so poor? Papa has a good job, doesn't he? Everyone was very excited for him and he was written about in *The New York Times*."

"He does have a good job," I said. "And very good prospects for the future. The only thing wrong is that he's been working for nearly three months without a paycheck."

"He's not going to get any money for what he's doing?"

I gave a sad little chuckle. "Oh yes. It's a good salary, actually. Better than what he earned with the police. And the money has been approved by Congress. It's just that the wheels of government grind slowly, it seems. It takes time to go through the various budget departments and for somebody to set up actually paying him. When it finally comes in, all will be fine. He'll be getting a big chunk of back pay. It's just that now we're trying to be frugal."

Bridie nodded and solemnly scraped some of the jam back into the jar. "It's a pity you can't go back to work," she said. "When you were a lady detective you earned money, didn't you?"

"I did," I said. "But I have a small baby and a young son who need me."

"You've got Aileen," she said.

Upstairs I heard Aileen singing as she tidied. Yes, I was lucky to have a cheerful mother's helper like her, but I found myself wondering how long we could go on paying her with no money coming in. Then I corrected myself. I was worrying too much. We surely had enough savings in the bank to tide us over.

Bridie tucked in to her jam sandwich. I started to prepare tonight's liver casserole. It was lucky some cuts of meat were still cheap because there were now only a few coins in my purse. Confound that Daniel Sullivan, I thought angrily. I didn't ask him to take this new job. He was doing just fine with the police and we could eat better than liver and onions.

"So do you miss it?" Bridie looked up.

"Miss what?"

"Do you miss working? Being a lady with a business? Independent?"

I considered this. "Yes. I do at times. When we had that problem at the movie studio and they asked me to go undercover, I truly enjoyed it. It made me realize what I'd given up, although I do love my home and my family."

Bridie made a little grunting noise as if she didn't agree with any woman being content with motherhood. "When I finish my studies at Vassar I'm going to be an independent lady," she said. "I can't decide whether I want to be a scientist or a writer or maybe even a lady detective."

"You're a lucky girl." I looked at her, mouth jammy at the sides and crumbs on her chin, and had to laugh. "You've the whole world of opportunities ahead of you. And at the right time too, where there are so many new discoveries every day: electricity, telephone, moving pictures . . ."

"Oh yes," Bridie said. "I'd forgotten that one. I might want to be an actress. I never really got a chance to try it out properly. That movie studio didn't call me back for another role in the summer like they promised they would."

"I'm afraid the movie studio was in turmoil after all that happened," I said. "I wonder if they will ever get back on their feet again with nobody to run it."

Bridie nodded sadly. "It's too bad. Then I could have given you the money for our food."

I felt a tear prickle at the back of my eyes. "Oh, sweetheart, I wouldn't have wanted to take your money. No, don't worry. We'll be doing just fine, I promise."

I felt guilty that I had involved her in our present condition. As I threw the onions into the frying pan, a thought suddenly occurred to me. I had money that would tide us over. I had been paid for my work at the movie studio and had stashed those five bank notes away for a rainy day. And now that rainy day had come, sooner than I had expected.

Bridie glanced up at the clock. "I must go and tell the ladies across the street!"

"I don't know if they'll be too excited," I said. "Oh, they'll be happy for you, but they are not big fans of the celebration, as you know. When the parade committee was announced and the city was represented by a hundred and fifty men, it was bad enough. Not a single woman to give her input. Then when the suffragists asked to march and were turned down, they were not pleased."

Bridie stared at me, taking this in. "That was another reason that the principal of that other school withdrew," she said. "She's also a suffragist." She paused. "I think I'll be a suffragist when I leave school. It's not right that women can't vote, is it?"

"No it's not. But there are some women in the world doing amazing things, in spite of all the opposition," I said. "Madame Curie, for example."

"Oh yes. We learned about her," Bridie said. "She won the Nobel Prize. But she can't vote either, can she? And when her papers were published they had to have her husband's name on them. It's simply not fair."

"I agree. And I'm glad that your generation will do something about it," I said. "Now go and pick up those things you knocked over in the hall and then come and have a cup of tea."

"Can't I go over to the ladies' first?" Bridie asked. "I'm dying to tell them."

"They've been busy getting ready for guests, like everyone else in the city," I said, "so perhaps you should not interrupt them."

"They've got guests staying with them?"

"They have," I said. "They are hosting fellow Vassar alumnae who will be taking part in the parades, and also Gus's cousin from Boston, I believe. I'm sure we'll be invited to meet them when they've settled in."


I went through the normal evening chores, trying to keep worry at bay while I waited for Daniel to come home. I let him eat his dinner in peace, waiting to find the right time to bring up our money situation. I understood that the poor fellow had been working hard all day, making sure security was in place for the parades as well as the big civic receptions that included various heads of state. So I sat patiently watching him eat his liver and onions, which he did without complaining. When he'd finished his plate he actually said, "That was good, Molly. We should have liver more often."

Which just goes to show you never know what a reaction will be. I poured Daniel a cup of coffee, cleared away the plates, went up to read Liam his bedtime story, made sure Mary Kate was sleeping, and checked on Bridie's homework before I joined Daniel in the parlor.

"Daniel," I said. "We had liver tonight because I'm running really short of money. This can't go on."

He sighed. "I know. I've written to Mr. Fitch again, explaining our plight. We should hear something soon."

I fought back my rising temper. "And how soon is that? When we're close to starving? When I put the children out on the street to beg?"

He put down the paper. "Molly, aren't you being a trifle overdramatic?"

"Perhaps I am," I said. "But I need more money right now, Daniel. Can you go to your bank tomorrow and take out some of our savings?"

To my horror his face actually turned bright red.

"What?" I asked, a feeling of dread creeping over me. "We don't have money in the bank? I was sure we had savings."

"Well, you see," he began, averting his eyes from my glare, "I've been paying the five agents working for me out of our savings."

"You've been paying five salaries for three months?" I demanded. "Daniel Sullivan, you want your head examined."

He looked embarrassed. "There's no reason they should not be paid on time, and as their boss I felt responsible. They have families to feed."

"And we don't have a family to feed?" I could hear my voice rising. "You didn't think to discuss this with me first? To ask my opinion on whether we should empty our savings account?"

He looked away. "I didn't want to upset you or cause you worry," he said. "I was sure the money would come in and I could replace it—"

"Without my knowing?" I finished the sentence, still glaring at him. "Is that how our marriage is to be, Daniel? I'm just the little woman at home and you make the decisions about what to do with our finances?"

"Look, I'm sorry," he said. "I thought I was doing the right thing."

"What you should be doing is going down to Washington and thumping on someone's desk until they write you a check. What if some bigwig suddenly decides that the Bureau doesn't need a New York office after all and you're let go? And we're out hundreds of dollars?"

"Molly, that won't happen," he said. "It will all come right in the end. It's just that these things take time."

"And while we wait, your family will be reduced to eating bread and jam," I snapped. "And liver."

"But I liked the liver," he said, then flinched as if I might hurl the pillow I was clutching in his direction. "I'll try and do something about it, Molly," he said. "I promise you I won't let my family starve." He gave a small sigh. "The trouble is I'm already run off my feet right now. I'll be in the middle of something and get a message from the mayor that he'd like to go over plans for the handling of carriages and automobiles at his reception and then from the German ambassador concerned about who will be guarding his battleship."

"As if a ship with that many guns can't guard itself," I said. "As it happens, I do have small savings of my own I was keeping for a rainy day. Those can get us through a few more weeks, but I'm not paying your employees."

"I can't let you use your savings, Molly," he said.

"We could always ask your mother for a loan," I said in a measured tone. Daniel's mother was, thankfully, involved with the Hudson-Fulton festivities in White Plains, otherwise we would have had the expense of hosting her as well. Although where we would put her these days escaped me. Our little house was nearly overflowing. But, luckily, the parades were not confined to Manhattan. There were to be parades all the way up the Hudson, both naval and land, continuing for weeks into October. We received daily letters from Mrs. Sullivan about how grand their parade was to be, and I will confess I was just as glad to have her stay at home. I didn't mention this to Daniel; instead I said, "I'm sure she'd be delighted to help with our current economic crisis."

"Absolutely not!" His face turned red again. "We are not letting my mother know our current predicament. I've said I'll sort it out and I will."

I suppressed an urge to grin. That was exactly the response I knew I'd get. Now he really would have an incentive to get that pay!

## Two

We didn't see anything of Sid and Gus until Wednesday of that week. I had to restrain Bridie several times from knocking on their door, reminding her that they were getting ready for their guests and it wasn't proper to barge in uninvited. I happened to see one guest arrive. Judging by the number of valises and hatboxes she brought with her I thought this might be Gus's cousin from Boston. The Boston Walcotts were known to be members of high society, and money was not lacking.

However, on Wednesday afternoon Gus knocked on our front door, to be greeted by excited whoops from both Liam and Bridie. I was alone with those two, Aileen having taken Mary Kate out in her buggy to do the vegetable shopping and Daniel working, as usual. His hours had become longer and longer since this whole performance started. He'd come in, grab a bite to eat, and then be off again, sometimes late into the evening.

"Well, isn't that a warm and wonderful welcome," I heard Gus's voice say. I had been in the kitchen, making a suet pudding. I wiped off my hands, hurriedly removed my apron, and came out into the hall.

"I wanted to come and visit you but my mother wouldn't let me," I heard Bridie complain. "She said you were busy with lots of guests."

"That is true," Gus replied, "but we are never too busy for our dear neighbors. I came to invite you over for tea to meet them."

"Is there cake?" Liam asked.

"I'm not sure you're included in the invitation, young man," I said, but Gus laughed.

"Of course he is. And yes, there is cake. Come on." She glanced back at me. "You'll have to meet my cousin, for which I apologize in advance. She's very much an old-school Boston Walcott and you'll see why I fled from my home as soon as I could." She fell into step beside me. "I received the request to stay with us out of the blue. She has friends appearing in a parade and wants to watch. She heard I had a charming little house nearby and since funds were tight for a poor single lady like herself she hoped I could find a small corner for her." She glanced at me and rolled her eyes. "I could hardly say no, could I? She's a fearsome spinster so don't be surprised if she finds everything wrong with you."

"But you have more than one guest staying?" I asked. "Sid mentioned fellow Vassar alums?"

"That's right," Gus said. "There were supposed to be two of them, but only one has shown up so far." I saw a worried frown cross her face, but she went ahead and opened their front door for us to enter. I heard the sound of voices coming from the front parlor. Since Sid and Gus had the habit of turning that room into something else—it had recently been a movie studio and then a Japanese shrine—I presumed that it had gone back to normal sofas and chairs in honor of the guests. Gus went ahead of us.

"Here they are," she said. "Molly and Bridie dying to meet our guests and Liam dying for cake."

I entered the room and saw Sid, actually wearing a respectable burgundy dress for once, perched on an upright chair. A slim, serious-looking woman with round spectacles was sitting on the sofa, and in the armchair sat a large, imposing woman in a black dress with beaded shawl. Her back was ramrod straight. Her hair was piled into an impressive coil in a rather old-fashioned style. There was some resemblance to Gus in that round face, but the look she gave me was so haughty that I froze on the spot.

"Cousin Prudence, Miss Anne Johnson, allow me to present our neighbor Mrs. Sullivan, her daughter Bridie, and her son Liam."

"How do you do," I said, giving a meek bend of the head. The thought raced through my mind that I was glad my mother had not named me Prudence. I'd never have lived up to the name.

"Sullivan?" Cousin Prudence intoned. "Irish, I suppose, with all that red hair?"

"Quite correct," I said. "I'm from County Mayo."

"And your husband?"

"Was born in the city here. His mother resides in Westchester."

I saw a flicker of approval—or was that surprise in the fact that she lived in an affluent part of the world? "And his father?"

"Passed away a long time ago. He was a detective with the New York Police, as was my husband."

"He's also passed away?"

"Oh no. I meant he's no longer a policeman. He is now attached to the federal government."

She made a disapproving noise at this. "No good can come of that," she said. "They should learn to let the states get on with it. I resent people deciding that what's right for some backward Southern state is right for Boston."

"Do sit down, Molly dear," Gus said. "I'll pour you a cup of tea. And, Liam, come into the kitchen with me so that we can find you a pastry, fresh from the bakery."

Liam needed no more urging. Bridie stood uneasily near the door until I patted the sofa beside me. "Come and sit with me," I said. "And when Miss Augusta returns you can tell the ladies your good news."

"Good news?" Sid asked, looking at her expectantly. "You did well on the literature paper you were working on?"

"I did," she said. "But this is much more important." She glanced over at the door, willing Gus to return.

"How old are you, young lady?" Cousin Prudence asked.

"Fourteen." It came out as barely more than a whisper. Obviously she found Cousin Prudence as intimidating as I did.

"Speak up, child. I cannot abide those who mutter and slur their words. If you've got something worth saying then say it."

"I'm fourteen," Bridie said, louder this time.

"And she goes to a distinguished academy for young ladies here in the city," Sid said, "where she is excelling in her studies. We expect her to follow us to Vassar one day."

The disapproving grunt was repeated. "I don't hold with all this education for girls," Cousin Prudence said. "Gives them ideas. Makes them discontent with the life that women should be leading. Wives and mothers. That's what we're bred for."

"Surely you must realize that women can contribute more than mere motherhood." The other woman, Miss Johnson, had sat silent until now. "I must inform you that women are contributing to research in many fields—designing contraptions for the home to make life easier for the housewife, finding new cures in medicine, and making great strides in the sciences." She leaned forward. "Why, the other lady we are expecting to stay here is most respected in scientific circles. Before her marriage she was becoming a leading authority on viruses."

"Viruses?" Cousin Prudence asked, now peering through her lorgnette. "What in heaven's name are they?"

"From what I understand they are tiny invisible organisms that are responsible for many sicknesses," Miss Johnson said. "They infect our bodies, apparently. Willa Parker and her husband did experiments on how viruses can replicate themselves in the body. Before their marriage they published a paper together that took the medical world by storm. Now, of course, she is expected to play the wife and mother, as society demands, while he goes on with his research."

"And quite right too," Cousin Prudence said. "All this work outside the home is not good for the female constitution."

Gus returned to the room, carrying a cup and saucer. "Here is your tea, Molly dear," she said. "Milk and sugar as you like it. And Bridie, if you'd like milk, you know where to find it in the kitchen."

"No thank you," Bridie said. "I want to stay and tell you about my good news."

"Of course you do," Sid said. "Go on. We're all ears."

Bridie went quite pink with everyone's eyes on her. "My school is to be part of the historical and cultural parade," she said. "We're on a float about education for women."

"How very exciting," Gus exclaimed. "Well done. What will you be representing?"

"Oh, just ourselves," Bridie said. "The theme is 'Healthy Bodies, Healthy Minds.' There is a lecture on nutrition and we will be exercising. And wearing new dresses." This last part seemed the most important, I gathered.

"Definitely new dresses," Gus said with a smile. "And who is providing these dresses? Does your mother have to make them?"

"Oh no. Blanche's mother is providing them," Bridie said. "A dressmaker came to school to take our measurements a few days ago. Which is good because we don't have much money right now, as my father is still waiting for his pay packet and we are quite poor."

"Bridie, we don't discuss such things," I reprimanded her, feeling my own cheeks turning red.

She blushed too. "Sorry, Mama. It's just Aunt Sid and Aunt Gus are like family."

"Anyway," Sid said, rapidly changing the subject, "we have good news too. We shall also be part of one of the parades."

"But I thought they turned you down?" I said.

"As Vassar graduates for the historical parade, yes, they did. However, we are smarter than a committee of men, you'll be pleased to know. Maud Malone has managed to get a float designed as Mount Olympus in ancient Greece into the carnival parade. So she invited us to be on it. We'll be going as Greek goddesses." She chuckled.

"And which shall you be?" I asked.

"We haven't decided yet," Sid said. "If Miss Johnson agrees, perhaps we shall be three Muses. What do you say, Anne?" Miss Johnson nodded seriously.

"Or the Fates." Gus smiled. "With our one eye shared among us. But the important thing is that we'll be on a float. Part of the parade."

I hadn't thought it meant so much to them, but obviously it did.

I did not want to outstay our welcome when Sid and Gus had visitors to entertain, and to be truthful I found Cousin Prudence heavy going. Several times I had to bite my tongue not to give a rude answer to her. When I got up to leave and collected Liam from the kitchen, Sid came with me.

"Thank you for coming," she said. "You can see that we're finding this not exactly easy. And we're rather worried about our other guest."

"The one who hasn't arrived yet? The scientist?"

"That's right. She should have been here three days ago but we've heard nothing from her."

"You said she's a mother now. Perhaps her child had a last-minute illness."

"Perhaps," Sid said. "Except that her husband telephoned last night, asking to speak to her. He was concerned that we had not seen her. He believed her to be staying with us. He was quite rude about it, actually."

"Holy Mother of God," I exclaimed. "If he doesn't know where she is, what can have happened? Has she far to come?"

"From Philadelphia," Sid said. "Not exactly the ends of the earth. Perfectly good train service."

"How worrying for you," I said. "There's not much you can do except wait for her, is there?"

"We are going to make some calls on friends of ours," Sid said. "Other paraders." She seemed to give a significance I couldn't make out to that word. She paused. "Willa is planning on parading with us, so perhaps she may have decided to stay with one of the other women involved."

"Involved in the parade float?" I asked.

"Yes, and—"

"Could we have some more tea, Miss Elena?" Prudence called from the sitting room.

"I'll tell you about it later," Sid said hurriedly, giving me a quick peck on the cheek and Liam a pat on the head as she walked with us to the front door. When we were outside she said softly, "Can we talk to you about it, Molly? Perhaps tomorrow?"

I nodded, and she continued.

"Gus and I think she may not want to be found."

# Three

Thursday, September 23, 1909

The streets were full of pedestrians, automobiles, wagons, and taxis as I left home to go shopping the next morning. Men were perched high up on Jefferson Market, stringing it with wire, and passersby looked up curiously.

"It's the new lights for the celebrations," one man said knowledgeably, shading his eyes with his cap as he peered up. "They say there won't be a dark corner in the city!"

*They might be excited about the celebration,* I thought sourly. *They hadn't had to buy their child new shoes and stockings at Lord & Taylor.* Bridie and I had made the purchases and she was giddily excited about the parade. But I wondered if I had made a mistake. If Daniel was going to receive his pay this month as he hoped, then fifty dollars would see us through splendidly. But the worrying thought would not leave me alone. Suppose he didn't? Suppose I had spent money on frivolities that we would need next month for food?

I determined to keep to a low budget and hope for the best for now. A chicken could last us all week as a roast, then a casserole, and then a stew with dumplings. But the dratted butcher was taking advantage of the crowds and a scrawny chicken was selling for twice the price. I settled for a ham bone with precious little meat on it, thinking I could make pea soup. That and some fresh bread could keep us full for several days. No Sunday roast for Daniel. Maybe that would help him understand the difficulty of our situation.

I couldn't be too angry at him though. It was quite a noble thing to do, making sure that the families of those men under him did not go hungry. In fact, it was the sort of thing I might have done. I allowed myself a small smile as I made my way into a long line outside the baker. Did married people take on one another's traits? Would he be making impulsive decisions and I be the one scolding him for his lack of sense? My smile soon faded as I saw that the baker had also raised his prices. HUDSON-FULTON SPECIAL read a hand-lettered sign in the window.

"It's highway robbery!" the woman behind me complained. "I can't wait until all these people go back to where they came from."

"It will get worse before it gets better," said her companion, who was tightly holding the jacket of a little boy determined to run off down the street. "The celebration doesn't start until Saturday. I wonder if there will be space to walk out our own front doors."

My mood was restored when I finally reached the counter and the shop assistant charged me the regular price for my loaf of bread. "Local prices for regulars," she said with a wink as she handed the warm loaf across the counter to me.

As I turned into Patchin Place a man was walking up the alley to Sid and Gus's door. I hurried forward, hoping it was our friend Ryan, a playwright and charmer who made any occasion more lively. But it wasn't Ryan. The man standing at their front door wore an ill-fitting black wool suit with a soft fedora. I looked at him with some curiosity, I confess, as he rang the bell, but decided to mind my own business as I walked up my own front steps. I had just put my shopping bags down in the kitchen and gone back to properly close the door when I heard shouting.

"I know she's in there. Open the door." The man pounded on Sid and Gus's front door so violently I thought he might make a dent. I waited, peering out of my door, wondering if anyone would appear from their house. Then, as he pounded again, I decided to take the matter into my own hands.

"Excuse me," I said, crossing the little place. "I am a friend of this house. Could I ask who you are looking for?"

"I'm looking for my wife." The man turned and fixed me with a belligerent stare. "She told me she was coming to stay with her friend Mrs. Walcott."

"Miss," I corrected. "You must be Mr. Parker."

"Dr. Parker," he corrected me automatically.

"Dr. Parker," I went on, "I spoke to Miss Walcott last night and she was very concerned that your wife hadn't arrived yet. In fact"—the thought came to me as I spoke—"Miss Walcott was planning on calling on some friends this morning to ask if anyone in their group had seen your wife. If you come back this afternoon she may have some news for you."

"I had never heard of this lady until weeks ago," he said accusingly, stepping back to get a view of the upper windows. "How do I know my wife isn't here? Look, there is someone in the window upstairs." It was true the curtain had moved. Someone must be home. To tell the truth, I would not put it past Sid and Gus to hide a wife from a belligerent husband. But they had seemed worried as to her whereabouts as well. He resumed his pounding on the door. "Willa! Willa, come down here this instant. I order you!"

Just then the door flew open and Gus's cousin Prudence stepped out. "What on earth is the meaning of this racket?" She fixed us both with a frosty stare.

"I'm looking for my wife." The man hesitated. Cousin Prudence was a commanding presence. "And she was supposed to be staying with the Walcott person here."

Prudence stepped forward again, causing the man to step back onto the pavement. She pulled herself up to her full height and looked down at him. "If you have been so careless as to lose your wife," she said, "it is not the concern of this respectable household, led by Miss Augusta Walcott, of the Boston Walcotts," she said in ringing tones. "Miss Walcott," she continued, "is not at home presently. She has gone out. I am the only person here." The man was shocked into silence and stood, his mouth gaping slightly. Prudence was not ready to give up the battle yet. "Would you like to search me," she continued, "to see if I have hidden your wife somewhere on my person?" And she held her impressive arms wide. All the bluster went out of the man. He took his hat off and gave a small bow.

"I'm terribly sorry," he said in a soft voice. "I'm just very worried about my wife. We have a little boy at home. What do I tell him?"

"I'm sure Miss Walcott will do everything she can to help," I said, softening at the mention of a child. "She is not a kidnapper, I can assure you. Are you sure that your wife came to New York?"

"I took her to the train station myself," he said, clearly making an effort to be calm. "She wrote to tell me that she had arrived. That's why I was so confused when I telephoned and she was not here. I had to get on a train and come right away."

"I promise you I will inform my cousin of your visit as soon as she arrives," Prudence said stiffly, still holding her arms out as if blocking Dr. Parker physically from the door. "She will be in touch with you with any information that she has obtained."

"Will you be staying on in the city, Dr. Parker?" I asked. "Or returning to Philadelphia?"

"Staying on, of course, until I locate my wife." He snapped out the words.

"Where are you staying, then?" I asked. "How shall we know where to locate you with a message?"

"I don't know yet." The man wiped his eyes tiredly. "It seems that every hotel in the city is full. I have some acquaintances among the professors at NYU. I'll see if one of them can put me up." That explained his appearance. The ill-fitting thick suit and soft hat were the mark of an academic of some sort. I remembered that we had been told he was a scientist. "I will come back this afternoon to see if Miss Walcott has any news for me." He raised his hat, gave a stiff little bow in Prudence's direction, and walked off down Patchin Place toward the Jefferson Market building.

Prudence and I stood staring after him for a few moments. "Really," she said dismissively. "I had heard that New Yorkers were ill-mannered. And a medical man as well."

"Well, he's from Philadelphia," I volunteered. "And I believe the 'doctor' refers to an academic degree rather than a medical one."

"Pshaw." She tossed her head, throwing out the exclamation of disgust. "No one in Boston would behave in such an uncouth way. Why he practically accused me of kidnapping his wife." A peal of laughter made me look up. Sid and Gus were just turning in to Patchin Place. They had on their best society ladies' costumes, but Prudence's lip still wrinkled in disgust as she saw them walking arm in arm.

"Pshaw," she said again, turned, and walked back into the house.

"Molly, I'm so glad you're here," Sid said as they dropped arms and hurried up to me. "We wanted to talk to you."

"Did you find out something about Willa Parker?" I asked.

"No, nothing." Sid's face fell. "No one knows what's become of her, and that's why we thought—"

"Dearest, let's just discuss it before we get Molly involved." Gus put a hand on Sid's arm and Sid stopped speaking. A look passed between them.

25

"Well, Dr. Parker was just here and as rude as you said. He accused your cousin Prudence of kidnapping his wife."

"Prudence?" Sid let out a peal of laughter. "Prudence a seducer of innocent young wives?" She doubled over.

"And you, Gus," I went on. "He was peering in the windows and yelling as if you had her hidden in there."

"How unpleasant." She wrinkled her nose. "And how did you get involved, Molly?"

"I just heard him shouting and came outside to investigate," I said. "That reminds me. I have the groceries out on the kitchen table. I must put them in the icebox." A thought struck me. "I've got to pay the ice and the milk man today," I groaned, more to myself than to my friends. The savings meant to last the month had dwindled alarmingly. Worry must have shown on my face.

"Is what Bridie said true, Molly?" Gus said. "Are you having some financial difficulties?" My face reddened. I hadn't meant to burden my friends, but I was no good at hiding what I was feeling.

"We'll get through this," I said evasively.

Gus put her hand on my arm and gave it a comforting squeeze. "Could we come by for tea this afternoon, Molly? Perhaps at four?" she said. "We would invite you over, but—"

She was cut off by Prudence appearing on the doorstep. "Does one talk in the street like an urchin in New York? I ask only for information."

"—we want to be able to have a private conversation," Gus finished with a despairing glance at her cousin.

"Of course," I said, wondering if I would need to go out again for more bread or if my budget would stretch to purchasing the pastries that Sid and Gus liked.

"We shall bring over a treat, and you supply the tea," Sid said, anticipating my dilemma, then added, "And we may have an idea that would help."

"Let's talk about it first," Gus said firmly, taking Sid's arm and steering her past the disapproving Prudence into their house with a smile to me of farewell.

I put away my purchases, checked that Bridie had come home safely, and then put a kettle on for tea, putting my best china cups and saucers on a tray. I was quite curious about what they wanted to talk to me about—something for which they were not quite in agreement, it seemed. Sid and Gus appeared on the doorstep at four o'clock just as promised. I sat them in the front parlor, then went to find plates for the French pastries they had brought. As I was serving them, Bridie came dashing down the stairs to meet them, regaling them with tales of the school's preparations for the next day's parade.

"And you must come and see me," she finished. "I will wave like anything!"

"I hope you are not neglecting your studies," Gus said with an indulgent smile. "Remember, you are studying to be someone important in the world."

"Yes, I want to work for women's suffrage," Bridie said seriously, earning herself a beaming smile from the two of them, "and be a professional woman. Is it true that the lady who was coming to stay is a scientist? I've never heard of a woman scientist before except Madame Curie."

"Yes she is." Gus's brows furrowed. "Or was, before she had a child. She and her husband worked in the lab together." She turned to me. "Her husband returned a little while ago to call on us."

"He must have been a bit more polite—I didn't hear any yelling," I said as I put teacups in front of my guests.

"He was indeed more reserved," Sid said. "But he did imply that we had hidden her away somehow. *All you college women*"—she put on a deep voice in imitation of Dr. Parker's—"*are in this together somehow.*"

"In what together?" I asked. "Wasn't she just coming for the parade?"

"That's just it," Gus said, "I don't know. We aren't well acquainted with her. She was a few years ahead of us in school. Her younger sister was in our year but I have lost all contact with her. Someone in the suffrage movement asked us to host Mrs. Parker for the celebration."

"And we feel responsible now," Sid put in. "What if something has happened to her?"

"I don't see how you can be responsible if she never turned up," I said.

"Well, her husband holds us responsible," Gus sighed. "He claims he is going to hire a Pinkerton man to find her."

"There you are, then," I said. "Then she is no longer your charge." I poured out tea, noticing, as I moved behind the little table, a stray wooden block of Liam's. "Did he say anything else about the child?"

"The child?" Gus queried.

"He said their little boy was missing his mother," I went on. "It is rare that a mother will leave a child behind willingly, isn't it? I can see why her husband is desperate to have her found."

"Yes, but what if she doesn't want to be found?" Sid said. "What if it is her husband she is running from?"

I considered this. He had seemed angry and even violent. A woman had little recourse in the law from a violent husband. Perhaps he rarely allowed her to travel and she had decided to use the celebration as a way to disappear for good. But if both parents were now in the city, where was the boy? My detective's mind began to whir. It all was a bit of a mystery.

Sid took a sip of her tea, then put her cup down decisively.

"Now, Bridie says you are in some financial difficulty." She gave me a penetrating stare.

I hesitated and it was Bridie who spoke up first. "We're poor now,

Aunt Sid. We have to ration the jam. And you can't believe what shoes and stockings from Lord and Taylor's cost. It's an outrage." She said this so seriously it made me smile, even though I was squirming with embarrassment.

"Bridie, go up and start on your homework," I said, not wanting to discuss this in front of her.

"But, Mama," she began, then stopped when she saw the look on my face. She rose obediently. Too obediently, I thought, and turned to watch her go. "Tell me later," she silently mouthed to Sid as she stood in the doorway. She froze when she saw my gaze and quickly left the room.

"We are fine, really," I said firmly, turning back to Sid and Gus. "My husband has just done an honorable and foolish thing. When it comes right we'll be rolling in it, but just now we are in a bit of a pickle." It felt like a relief to share with my friends after holding the worry bottled up inside for so long. I recounted the whole business.

"Well, the federal government deserves to be censured," Gus said when I finished. "I shall write to Mr. Fitch myself."

"I hope he will pay more attention to you than he has to Daniel," I agreed with a wry smile. "But Daniel assures me it will all come right within the month."

"Well, we have a way of making it come right this week," Sid said.

I reddened. "Thank you, you are always so kind, but I couldn't possibly take your money. For one thing, Daniel would hate it."

"It's not like that," Sid said, sweeping her hands as if brushing my concerns aside. "It is an extremely logical move." She held up a finger. "One: Gus and I want Willa found. We want to find her before her husband does and ask her if she wants help or wants to disappear." She held up the next finger. "Two: you need some money." And the third. "Three: you are a detective. Ergo," she finished, "we want to hire you to find Willa Parker."

## Four

Late that evening I sat at my kitchen table while I mulled things over. Liam and Mary Kate were safely asleep. Aileen and Bridie were in their own rooms, Bridie no doubt trying on the new shoes and working on hairstyles to best show off the little crown. Daniel, naturally, was still out somewhere, doing whatever he had to do these days. I suspected that included plenty of whiskey and cigars with members of the organizing committee. I needed quiet to think over what Sid and Gus had proposed. I had been polite and noncommittal at the time, telling them I'd have to discuss it with my husband.

"Did Daniel discuss with you his decision to move from the police to this new federal bureau?" Gus asked calmly.

I hesitated. "Not exactly. He sort of presented it as a fait accompli. But I did tell him that I had no intention of moving to Washington. Then he explained it would be to run the New York bureau. It would mean more money, he said, and a chance for promotion in the future. So I wasn't against it. As a matter of fact it occurred to me that he'd be safer in a federal job than chasing gangs and murderers in New York."

"Whether you were happy or not is not the point," Gus insisted.

"He took it for granted that the man makes the decisions. You once had your own detective agency, Molly. You answered to nobody. Don't you miss that?"

"Of course I do," I replied. "But I also cherish my current role as wife and mother. I wouldn't be without Daniel or the children for anything."

"Nobody's asking you to," Sid said. "But you have a sweet little servant girl who dotes on your children. Liam will be going to school in the new year. Bridie helps out in the house . . . sometimes. So you are not tied down in the way that many women are."

"And, Molly," Sid said, leaning across Gus, "we are certainly not doing this as any sort of favor to you. Please don't see it as charity. We need help and you are qualified to help us. What if that man is a wife-beater and Willa has finally escaped from him, only to be found by his Pinkerton agent?"

"Yes, Molly. What kind of man uses a Pinkerton agent to find his wife? He must suspect that she is trying to escape from him."

"I think you are right," I said slowly, "I am just not sure if I am ready to take a case."

"But, Molly—" Gus began.

"Dearest, don't press her." Sid had put her hand on Gus's arm. "Let her think about it." She rose and Gus followed. "I know she'll do the right thing." They had exchanged a look.

"I'll think about it," I promised as I walked them to the door, and then I watched them fondly as they crossed the little court.

And I did think about it, once the house was quiet and I was alone. I toyed with the spoon in my saucer. I had to admit I was tempted. Sorely tempted. I had missed the excitement of having my own job. I had been quite successful at it. Oh, don't get me wrong, there had been danger at times and I'd been scared out of my wits. But there had also been the satisfaction of solving a case, of making it right for people and having them thank me. I was worth something in those days, not just as Mrs. Daniel Sullivan, wife and mother. I was a professional woman, hired to solve mysteries, problems. There was no denying that we needed money at this very moment. Also it would be reassuring not to have to rely on the money Daniel handed me each week. I could have my own savings account—probably not in a bank, as that would require my husband's signature, but hidden in a safe place in the house.

But then came the question of whether or not I would tell Daniel I was going to take on this case. I didn't like the feeling of going behind his back, but he'd gone behind mine when he decided to pay those men out of our savings account. Did two wrongs ever make a right? I shifted in my seat and took a sip of my now-cold tea. If I took on this case, how on earth could I find the time with all that was already happening? Saturday was the big naval parade, with hundreds of ships sailing up the Hudson. I would certainly have to take the children to see that. It was to be a once-in-a-lifetime spectacle. I'd promised Aileen time with her family on Sunday. Then Daniel had mentioned an opening reception on Monday, and Bridie's parade, the historical one, was on Tuesday. I could fit in some time tomorrow but after that the days ahead would allow me little time to escape.

"I'm going to bed," Bridie said, interrupting my thoughts. She had come downstairs in her nightdress. "My schoolwork is all finished."

"Good girl." I rose to give her a hug.

"Are you going to look for the missing woman for the ladies?" she asked curiously.

"I'm not sure yet," I said. "Now, go on up, it's late."

"You should do it," she said. "You're a good detective. You found out who killed the studio directors last summer."

"I'm thinking about it," I promised. "Now go on with ya." She gave me a peck on the cheek.

"Good night, Mama," she said and then walked back up the stairs.

The mention of murder somehow brought a new darkness to my thoughts. Was the missing woman in danger as I sat here and contemplated? I realized time was of the essence. The Pinkerton man would be searching with probably more skills and ways to open doors than I had as a mere woman. There was no way . . . I got up and paced around, finding the silence of the house overwhelming. I wouldn't wait up for Daniel any longer. I'd just go to bed, sleep on it, and come up with a decision in the morning. I stoked the kitchen stove, locked the back door, and went up to bed, leaving the hall light on for Daniel. All was quiet upstairs. I peeked into the children's room. Liam lay curled up, his arm around his stuffed dog, looking positively angelic. Mary Kate lay on her back in her crib, also looking peaceful. I gave a sigh of relief that she had now graduated from breastfeeding to a cup so that I would be freer to go about my business without the need to rush home every few hours. And thank heavens she now slept through the night. *Be grateful for small mercies, Molly.* That's another thing my mother used to say when I complained how unfair it was that the girls at the big house had more clothes than they could ever wear while I had the same dress, which had to be let out at the seams as I grew. At the time I wasn't sure we even had the smallest of mercies, but looking back, at least we weren't turned out of our cottage or dying of hunger in the Great Famine. I smiled as I bent to kiss Liam's forehead and tiptoed out again.

I lay in bed, listening to the noises of the city: the distant pop-popping of an automobile, now ever more common around us. Music from a phonograph, a baby's cry, shouts, a police whistle. All safely far from us in Patchin Place. All the same, I worried whenever Daniel was out late. I supposed his new job was safer, although one of his missions was to break up the new Italian gang that was threatening the city. They had already killed one policeman this year. But this week he was guarding dignitaries. He would be safer, smoking cigars and drinking brandy, even if the hours were quite annoying for a wife.

Annoying hours. I toyed with the words. If I took up detective work again, how could I know what it might entail? My hours before had certainly not been regular. How could I stake out a residence? Follow a person to another borough? *Stupid*, I said to myself. I had a young baby. She and Liam had to come first. *Be content with your current job and leave the missing woman to the Pinkerton man.* I was just dozing off when I heard the front door close quietly, then soft feet up the stairs. Daniel came into the bedroom. I was going to give a loving greeting but heard myself saying, "And where have you been tonight?"

"Oh, I'm sorry. Did I wake you?" he asked.

"No. I was finding it hard to sleep," I said. "A wife worries about her husband's safety."

"I'm quite safe at the moment." Daniel sat on the bed and took off his shoes. "Bored but safe. I've had to listen to more pompous speeches in the last two weeks than in my whole life. Tonight it was a reception at the Hotel Astor, welcoming the representatives from Japan. Long speeches about international cooperation and a bright new future for the world. And a strange Japanese wine to drink that I did not take to."

"Speaking of receptions," I said. "You mentioned there is the official opening gala at the Hotel Astor on Monday. How fancy is it? Am I to wear full evening dress? I might have to borrow something from Gus."

"The reception on Monday?" Daniel had been unbuttoning his shirt. "Oh no. That doesn't include you, Molly. It's men only."

I sat up in bed. "Men only? So this great celebration of New York as a cosmopolitan city at the hub of the world does not include women?"

"There are to be afternoon tea receptions for the wives of

dignitaries," he said, "and women are invited to the gallery to hear the speeches after the dinner. What's more, a woman is actually reading a poem she has written for the occasion. Julia Ward Howe, the famous poetess. Quite an honor, wouldn't you say?"

I didn't say. I lay back in bed, feeling my hackles rising. Not only had the entire planning committee consisted of men, but the suffragists had been banned from marching and now the opening reception would only allow women in the gallery after the main event. We were an afterthought of society. We simply did not matter in the grand scheme of things. I had never felt more drawn to the cause. And then I thought, *I'll show him. I'll show them. I'll take that commission from Sid and Gus and find that missing woman before the Pinkerton man does.* And what's more, I didn't see the need to tell Daniel about it yet.

It took me hours to fall into a fitful sleep. My thoughts kept wandering the streets of New York after the missing woman. How could I find someone in a city this large if she truly wanted to disappear? In my dreams I kept trying to find her, running after a figure who vanished around a corner every time I got near.

I awoke with a headache to find that Daniel had already left. It was not like me to send him off without a good breakfast, I thought guiltily. But then, he was more likely to spend today at receptions and meetings than stalking underworld criminals, so I thought he would survive. Bridie had the day off from school and she left for a dress fitting at Blanche's house only to come home upset and emotional. "I tried on my dress, Mama, and it didn't fit properly. The dressmaker must have taken my measurements wrong. They said they could fix it before Tuesday but what if they can't and I'm the only one who can't be in the parade?"

"I'm sure it will all be just fine," I said, not quite as sympathetic as usual. "Blanche's mother will see that all the dresses are perfect."

"I hope so," she said. "Now I'll be worried until Monday. I won't be able to sleep or do a thing."

*I know how you feel*, I wanted to say but didn't. Having to carry a worry around is a draining experience. Instead I put an arm around her. "We have so many exciting things to look forward to that you'll not have time to think about it. The big naval parade tomorrow, right? We'll go down to the Battery early and get a good place to view the passing ships."

She nodded as if ships could not put the worry from her head.

"Do you have homework to do before Monday?" I asked. "You were mentioning that Latin translation. Now would be a good time to get it all finished."

"All right." She went to walk away, then turned back. "Oh, by the way, Miss Amelia told us that each family has to bring money on Monday to our rehearsal for pastries and lemonade for the morning of the parade."

"And how much would that be?" I noticed the sinking feeling in my stomach.

"Only fifty cents."

I went over to my purse. "I'll give it to you now, just in case . . ." Meaning *just in case there is not fifty cents there by Monday*. Aileen looked on hopefully as I gave Bridie the coins from my purse.

"Could I have my pay for this week and last, Mrs. Sullivan?" she asked. "Only my da's marching with Tammany in the parade and he's had to spend for the costume." She twisted her hands shyly, obviously embarrassed.

"Of course, you must have your wages," I said, trying not to let my face betray my worry as I took five dollars out of my rapidly emptying purse and put them into her hand. "And don't give them all to your family," I added. "Save some. A woman must have her independence."

"That's what Aunt Sid and Aunt Gus say," Bridie put in. "We women must have the vote and our independence." She looked around the kitchen at the sink full of dishes, the baby fussing in my

37

arms, Liam sitting at the table, his face smeared with jam. "Are you an independent woman, Mama?" Her voice was doubtful.

"Yes." I handed Mary Kate to Aileen and brushed the crumbs off my dress. "Yes I am." I didn't bother to put on my coat or hat but marched across the street and rang the bell.

"Molly dear." Sid smiled as she opened the door.

"I'll do it," I said without preamble. "I'll take the case."

## Five

"Excellent." Sid opened the door wider. "Come in, Gus will be so pleased. She has been really worried." But before I could take a step a loud voice boomed out from the interior.

"Elena, our luncheon is waiting."

Sid winced.

"Coming, Prudence," she called, then, in a softer voice to me, asked, "Would you like to come and eat with us, Molly?"

"Really, Augusta, I can't believe how you live now." Prudence's voice could still be clearly heard. "Even that immigrant woman from across the street has a girl to open the door for her. How can you live with no servants at all?" Gus's reply was in a lower tone and I couldn't make it out.

"Oh dear." Sid looked mortified. "I'm not sure you would enjoy our company, Molly." She grimaced. "I have an idea," she went on. "Prudence is visiting friends this afternoon and Gus and I are going to a committee meeting. Why don't you come? Several of the women there are acquaintances of Willa Parker."

"That sounds perfect, shall we—" I started, but Sid winced as another booming, "Elena!" came from the house and there was the sound of a chair being pushed back.

"We have a cab coming at three," Sid muttered.

"I'll be ready," I promised. Sid gave another quick smile and closed the door.

By three I had my unruly hair pinned up under a stiff hat and my two-piece suit on. I hoped I looked presentable if not fashionable. But then I told myself that the sort of women I was going to meet probably didn't care about fashion. That was the problem. When one went with Sid and Gus, one never knew if the dress was going to be silk pajamas or the height of Fifth Avenue elegance.

I was happy to see that Sid, Gus, and Anne Johnson emerged looking much like businesswomen themselves as a taxi pulled up.

"Fifty-First Street and Madison Avenue," Miss Johnson said to the driver as we climbed in.

"Sid tells me you have agreed to take our case," Gus said as we began to inch our way up Sixth Avenue. The streets were so crowded that I was sure it would have been faster to take the El or perhaps even to walk. Slow-moving visitors blocked the sidewalks, gaping up at the towering buildings and the elevated railroad track. Street vendors selling potatoes, pretzels, and hot dogs claimed the outer edges of the streets and the cabs, automobiles, and carriages were forced to squeeze down the center, stopping frequently as large groups of pedestrians surged across the road. "Wonderful. I feel most uncomfortable with her husband coming around, accusing us of spiriting her away. And I must give you this"—she opened her purse and pulled out some bills, rather carelessly—"before I forget."

"Thank you," I said, tucking them away in my own purse. I felt a slight thrill as I did so. This was the first money I had earned by my own efforts since I was married. Then I corrected myself. There had been that business in the summer with the studio. I had needed money then as well, because Daniel had been out of town, leaving me without money. I reflected that I should always have some money of my own tucked away for emergencies.

"How well do you know her?" I asked. "Do you know why she might want to disappear?"

"She was ahead of us at Vassar," Gus said, "so I didn't know her well. We heard through the college newsletter that she had begun a distinguished scientific career. So when she wrote to us, asking to stay during the celebration, of course Sid and I were thrilled."

"I stayed at their house several times," Anne said softly. "When we were at school. But I was really friends with her younger sister rather than Willa."

"Did she mention that she would bring her son with her?" I asked. It seemed to me that a woman running from a bullying husband would not want to leave a child behind.

"No," Gus said. "I think I had heard she was a mother, but she didn't mention a child coming to stay."

To my mind that made it more likely that her disappearance was unplanned.

"Her letter mentioned some mutual friends," Sid put in. "A suffragist leader, Miss Paul, and Maud Malone, whom you will meet today."

"Are we going to a suffrage meeting?" I asked, surprised. "I assumed this was a float committee meeting, if you are to be part of the parade."

"All the ladies on the float are enthusiastic proponents of the cause," Anne said earnestly. "We have a little surprise planned for the organizing committee."

"A surprise?" I raised my eyebrows in inquiry but the three of them just smiled.

"You just come and watch," Sid said, a somewhat wicked grin on her face. She looked at Gus, who smiled as well and then changed the subject. "Have you heard that Julia Ward Howe is reciting an original poem on Monday night but all the attendees will be men?"

"I did," I said, my indignation rising. "I have heard we may come and listen from the balcony if we choose."

"I refuse to listen from a balcony while being denied entrance to the actual event," Gus said hotly. "It's like the servants at home, watching from the balcony as guests came to a ball. Miss Ward Howe is a suffragist herself. I will wait until I have a chance to meet her in person."

I remembered my mission. "So Mrs. Parker is a suffragist too, or at least has suffragist friends."

"That's why we thought you might learn more about her at this meeting," Sid said. "I can't believe she would disappear and not let any of her friends know her whereabouts."

"Unless she has met with foul play," I said. "I will have to ask Daniel if any women have been found dead in the city."

"Oh surely not." Anne turned pale, as if this thought had not occurred to her. She took off her glasses and wiped them with her handkerchief.

"I hope not, but it is an avenue I must explore," I said. "Assuming the worst has not happened, do you know any reason she might have wanted to disappear?"

"Besides her very rude husband?" Gus asked. "Didn't it seem to you that he expected her to be hiding from him?"

"Yes, that's exactly what I thought," I said.

The El thundered by overhead and all conversation stopped as it passed.

"What will you tell Daniel about your investigating?" Gus asked when the sound had died away. "Will he approve of your detecting?"

"I'm not sure yet," I said lightly, staring out of the side window as we turned onto Fifty-First Street. *What am I going to tell Daniel?*

Just past St. Patrick's Cathedral was an imposing marble mansion. The cabbie stopped in front and Gus hopped out.

"This is it?" I had passed this house many times but never thought I would be invited in.

"Who is your friend who is holding the meeting?" I asked as we mounted the steps to the grand front door.

"Mrs. Alva Belmont," Sid said. "Before her divorce she was Mrs. Vanderbilt."

"Jesus, Mary, and Joseph," I exclaimed, "I've certainly heard of her! Isn't she one of the richest women in the city?"

"She is—and since her second husband's death she has been devoting her money to the cause," Anne added as the big door swung open and a butler invited us in with a grave nod of the head.

Gus, suddenly looking every bit the Boston Walcott, handed him her card.

"They are upstairs in the Armory, Miss Walcott," the butler said. "Won't you follow me." We followed him across a grand foyer and up a marble staircase.

The Armory turned out to be a huge, echoing room that looked as if it was taken directly from a castle in Europe. A life-size wooden horse stood in one corner with a full suit of armor astride it, as if a knight from the Middle Ages was riding into the room. Two other suits of armor stood beside it. There was an impressive display of actual arms hung along one wall, from ancient-looking swords to rifles, shotguns, and some sleek very modern pistols. I hoped Mrs. Belmont was the peaceful type. It looked like she could have armed half of the city if she wanted to stage an uprising!

"We hold our meetings in here generally," Gus said, her voice echoing as we walked across yet another vast expanse of marble. "It seats up to two hundred." I could well believe it. "But today we are a smaller group." There were about twenty ladies in the room, some standing around a table with some sort of material on it, some in earnest conversation looking at different documents. I had expected a gathering in a mansion like this to be like a polite tea party. This was more like a war room.

Two rows of chairs had been set in front of a podium. A blackboard behind it held an intricate drawing of a float. A Greek goddess with folded wings stood behind a marble throne. Sketches of smaller ladies in Greek garb standing in front and walking alongside the float obviously represented the marchers in the parade.

"Oh wonderful," Sid exclaimed, walking up to the blackboard. "The float design is complete."

"Ladies, shall we get started." A tall, dark-haired woman who looked to be in her midfifties came out from behind a Japanese screen in the corner. "I am excited to show you the designs." Her clothes and hat looked like they came straight from a window at Macy's entitled "The Modern American Woman." She held herself with a self-assured air that commanded attention. The murmured conversation stopped the instant that she spoke. This was obviously Mrs. Alva Belmont herself!

"Get us some seats, dearest," Gus said to Sid. "I'll introduce Molly to our hostess." Sid turned to do as she was asked and Gus steered me over to the woman who was now arranging papers on the podium.

"Mrs. Belmont," she said as the woman looked up, "I would like to introduce my friend and neighbor Mrs. Molly Sullivan. She is a supporter of ours and we want to get her more involved in the cause."

Was it my imagination or did those perfectly composed features look a little uncomfortable just for a moment? If she did, she recovered herself seconds later. "Mrs. Sullivan, how nice to meet you. Will you be taking part in the parade?"

"No, just cheering from the sidelines." I smiled. "The drawing of the float looks beautiful."

"Yes, we wanted to have a 'Future Women of New York' float in the historical parade but, as Miss Walcott may have told you, it was not approved. So we turned our attention to the carnival parade. If my late husband were still here I would have had more influence, I believe, but as it is, we women have been pushed aside and virtually ignored in all aspects of the planning." She sighed heavily. The women had taken their seats and were looking to Mrs. Belmont expectantly. I excused myself to sit down in the seat Sid had saved. As I turned to go I heard Mrs. Belmont say in a low voice to Gus, "Was that wise? To bring an outsider in at this stage?"

"Mrs. Sullivan is a good friend," Gus said in a similarly low voice, "and she has a purpose for being here I can tell you about later." I took my seat and looked up in time to see Mrs. Belmont nod at Gus, then give a questioning stare in my direction. Our eyes met and she looked away.

"Ladies," she said again, and a hush descended upon the room. "Thank you for coming." She flipped through her notes. "Our agenda for the day is not long. We need to approve the float and the dresses. This"—she pointed to the drawing—"is the float design committee's final draft for approval. Now, I think we have all had a chance to examine it. Do I have a motion?"

A woman in a stiff houndstooth coat rose and said, "I move that we accept the float design as presented."

"Do I have a second?" Mrs. Belmont looked around the room.

"Seconded," another woman said without rising.

"Very well," Mrs. Belmont said. "Discussion?"

"Why are the wings closed like that?" A younger woman seated in the rear rose and peered at the drawing. "I thought they were supposed to be majestically open. Isn't she *Winged Victory*, the goddess Nike?"

"They will open," another woman called, "just as—"

"I should mention," Mrs. Belmont said loudly before the woman could finish, "that we have some guests with us today." The women in front of the questioner turned around and began a whispered explanation that I couldn't hear.

"Miss Walcott and Miss Goldfarb have brought their neighbor. And we have a visitor from Philadelphia." Mrs. Belmont continued, "Might you introduce your guest, Miss Walcott?"

Gus rose, "This is my dear friend and neighbor, Mrs. Molly Sullivan. She is a supporter of our cause and is a businesswoman herself. Stand up, Molly." Flushing red, I rose to a round of applause and curious looks from the gathered women.

"And most of you know our sister activist from Philadelphia, Maud Malone." Mrs. Belmont's voice was warm. "She couldn't be with us at this time, but she sent a friend to support us, Mrs. Harriet Schilling."

A blond woman in a dark high-necked suit with a white jabot at her neck rose to enthusiastic applause. "Thank you, sisters," she said with a shy smile. "The Pennsylvania Women's Suffrage Organization sends its greetings."

Mrs. Belmont applauded with the other ladies and then narrowed her eyes, although she kept a pleasant smile on her face. "There is one more lady I haven't had the pleasure of meeting yet." Her gaze focused on a woman in the back row. I had to turn completely in my chair to see at whom she was looking. The woman's face was shaded by a black bonnet. She was short but strongly built, dressed in severe black like a widow. It was hard to tell her age.

"How do you do. I'm Mrs. Smith." The woman smiled and gave a wave to the group. "Or rather the widow Smith. A sorority sister suggested that I might be of use on the float since I am very handy with a needle." She gave a small, tittering laugh that seemed out of place with her strong build and features. There was another round of applause. The woman raised her head and I caught a glimpse of her face. Mrs. Smith was none other than Mrs. Goodwin, an undercover police detective!

## Six

I saw a flash of recognition on her face as she recognized me, and then it was gone. The simpering smile returned as she gave a slight bow and then sat down. Instantly my mind was full of questions. What was a police detective doing here? I had worked with Mrs. Goodwin before and knew her to be a skillful undercover agent. It was possible that she was a supporter of suffrage. But to find her at a float committee meeting calling herself Mrs. Smith seemed incredible. That and her strange manner convinced me that she was here as an investigator. If so, who was she investigating and why?

Alva Belmont, our hostess, was a very important and well-known woman in the city. Was she involved with a scandal in some way? Or was Mrs. Goodwin investigating this meeting itself and the women in the room? I looked around at the diagram and costume fabrics. There did seem an undercurrent of something more going on, but what it was I couldn't say.

These thoughts preoccupied me as the meeting continued. The float design was accepted and a detailed discussion of the method of construction ensued. It seemed the basics were in place at a warehouse in the north of the city, but the final decorations and mechanics still needed to be finished. The heads of various committees gave their reports. Mrs. Belmont had several dressmakers standing by, and as the voting ended, some women went behind screens to be fitted for their costumes, while others chatted and helped themselves to the sumptuous fare set out on beautiful tables. As soon as we rose, I made a beeline for Mrs. Goodwin, holding out my hand.

"Mrs. Smith?" I made it a question. She took my hand and shook her head slightly, her eyes communicating a warning.

"Yes, I don't believe we've met," she said. "Are you a former Vassar student or a friend of Mrs. Belmont?"

Our eyes locked. She knew full well that I wasn't either of those things. That reminded me that I was also here to investigate. Both of us, it seemed, were here on false pretenses. I gave her a small nod.

"I am a friend of Miss Augusta and Miss Elena, as they mentioned," I said. "Pleased to meet you, Mrs. Smith. I hope you don't suspect that anything will go wrong with their float," I probed, thinking, *Why is she here?*

"I hope not indeed," she said with a smile. "Especially not with the needlework since that is what I am here to aid with."

It struck me that she might have been hired by Dr. Parker. Had he called the police, and had they sent in a woman detective?

"My friends are a bit worried about a member of this group who was meant to be staying with them. I wonder if you have heard of her. A Mrs. Willa Parker?"

"Mrs. Parker?" Mrs. Goodwin's attention had been taken by something across the room.

"Yes, she seems to be missing."

"How worrying. I'm so sorry." She laid her hand on my arm, looking beyond me. "If you will excuse me, Mrs. Sullivan." I looked after her as she walked off. A wave of doubt washed over me. Had it been too long and now my detective skills were dying? Here I was in a room full of women who must have information and my mind was blank as to how I should proceed.

I tried to focus my thoughts. Sid and Gus had said this was to be a float of Vassar alumni, but these women seemed to be from many walks of life. It was hard to believe they were all from that women's college. They were clearly suffragists. At least a quarter of them wore divided skirts or men's trousers, so they were members of the rational dress movement. It seemed incongruous that they were interested in portraying Greek muses and goddesses.

"Molly." Sid was waving from across the room. "You must come and meet Mrs. Schilling." Sid stood with the woman in the dark high-necked suit. Blond curls peeked out from under a houndstooth tourist hat. "Harriet Schilling, meet Mrs. Molly Sullivan." We shook hands. "Mrs. Schilling is also from Philadelphia," Sid said with a meaningful look. "She's just arrived from that city."

"Are you an acquaintance of Mrs. Parker?" I asked, catching Sid's meaning.

"I am," she said, glancing at Sid, "and was she not to stay with you and Miss Walcott?"

"Yes, but we are quite worried," Sid replied with a frown. "She hasn't shown up and we have had no news of her."

"You have not heard from her since you arrived in New York?" I asked Harriet.

"No, I'm afraid not," she said, looking uncomfortable. "We were to meet at this gathering, and as you see she is not here." She turned slightly, starting to walk away. Was everyone going to give me the cold shoulder today? First Mrs. Goodwin and now Harriet Schilling seemed most unwilling to speak to me. But Sid saved the day.

"Don't run away," she said, slipping her arm through the woman's in a familiar way. "We want to know you better. We always make sure our out-of-town sisters feel welcome here. How do you know Mrs. Parker?" The woman still looked uneasy but made no further move to leave.

"We are both wives of professors," she said. "At Penn University."

"That is fascinating, Harriet," Sid said with a wide smile. "I may call you Harriet, may I not? And you must call me Sid. All my true friends do."

Harriet looked startled at this nickname but nodded tentatively.

"And I'm Molly Sullivan," I said, following Sid's lead. "So the wives of professors know each other well?"

She nodded again. "It is a small community. She and her little boy have been at our house for many a dinner while our husbands are off at college meetings or in a research lab."

"I understood she was an academic herself," I said.

"Yes." Harriet's face brightened as she spoke about her friend. "She and her husband met as research assistants for the same professor. She spends almost as much time as he does in that lab or typing up their research for journals."

Sid, now confident that Harriet would not run away, let go her grasp.

"Their research?" I asked. "So she is still a member of the college as well?"

"Not officially," Harriet said. "His name is on the papers, you understand. Otherwise they would not be taken seriously, as things are in the scientific world. But she lives, eats, and breathes that research."

"So she does the research, but he gets the credit?" Sid was incensed.

"I'm afraid that is the way it is in many research departments." Harriet shook her head sadly. "Most of us type up papers for our husbands and correct their spelling and grammar."

"I knew I had a decidedly bad opinion of her husband," Sid said heatedly.

"So you have met Dr. Parker, Miss Elena . . . Sid?" Harriet's face became guarded again. "Is he in the city?"

"Yes, he came to our house accusing us of hiding her," Sid said.

"Which of course we would if she needs hiding. But unfortunately we have not seen her and could tell him nothing."

I took a breath. "You seem like a good friend to her, Harriet—do you have an idea of where she might be?"

Harriet's gaze was wary. "She has family in the city, I believe, but I am not sure of their address." She looked between me and Sid. "Do you have a card, Mrs. Sullivan?" she asked. "I would be happy to ask her to call if I gain any information about her."

I had to admit I did not. "But Sid will be working on the parade float," I offered. "She can pass any information on to me."

Harriet was now edging away from us, clearly wanting to be done with this conversation. "How very nice to have met you." It was a dismissal. She gave a nod and turned away.

"She is definitely hiding something," Sid said too loudly as Harriet walked away.

"Hush, she'll hear you," I quieted her. "How do you know her?"

"I have never met her before but we have mutual acquaintances. Mrs. Belmont said she was sent by Maud Malone though, and that is high praise."

"Maud Malone?" I questioned.

"She is a brilliant suffragist who is leading the fight in Philadelphia and here." Sid spoke with animation. "This float in the parade was her idea."

This heightened my suspicions. "Sid dear, what exactly are you going to be doing in the parade?" I asked, laying my hand on her arm with some trepidation. "It doesn't sound as if you will be merely portraying some Greek goddesses."

She gave a wicked grin, "You'll see."

"Who was that poor woman that you kidnapped?" Gus asked curiously as Sid and I approached the table where she was draping herself in white organza.

"Harriet Schilling, an acquaintance of Mrs. Parker," I said.

"I was helping Molly with her sleuthing," Sid put in. "Mrs. Schilling claims to have no knowledge of Willa's whereabouts, but Molly and I are suspicious, aren't we?"

"If Willa is hiding Mrs. Schilling, she may be protecting her," I mused. "She wouldn't know if she could trust us or not."

"Of course she could trust us!" Sid said hotly.

"She doesn't know us, dearest," Gus said in a placating tone. "Or she would know she can have confidence in us."

"I have an idea!" Sid said with animation. "Molly can secretly follow her when she leaves and perhaps she will lead her right to Willa."

I had some doubts about this plan. "Perhaps she will just tell us where she is staying if we ask," I ventured. But as I looked around the room I realized we were too late to carry out either plan. Harriet was nowhere to be seen.

"Have you two been measured for your costumes?" Anne asked in a soft voice as she came out from behind the screen. "Are we ready to go?"

In truth I had forgotten that Anne was there. Her mousy brown outfit and small face with wiry eyeglasses seemed designed to be overlooked. I had barely spoken two words to her the whole time she had been staying with Sid and Gus.

"I still need my measurements taken," Sid said.

"And I'm wondering if we can add some of this fabric into the petticoat to create a fuller skirt." Gus held up the organza.

"Not a full skirt for a Grecian woman, surely," Sid said as they both disappeared behind the screen.

Anne and I stood there in awkward silence for a moment.

"Do you have a profession, Miss Johnson?" I ventured finally.

"Me?" She seemed taken aback by the idea. "No, I'm not bold enough for that." She returned to silence.

"Do you know Mrs. Parker? Have you met before?" I tried again.

"Yes," she said. "I'm not sure if she would remember me, although

I have stayed in her family's home, many years ago." For a moment there was silence again. We stood there listening to a muffled argument about organza on the other side of the screen.

"We have corresponded by letter, however," she said. Another pause. "We are connected through her sister," she went on, just as I thought it was unlikely she would speak again. "She was at Vassar with us. Winnie Hartman. We stay in touch."

"Yes?" I encouraged.

"Originally, Mrs. Parker and I were both to stay with her sister in their brownstone on Fifty-Third Street, but then I received a letter from Mrs. Parker saying that her sister would be hosting the German ambassador and his wife and suggested we stay with Miss Augusta instead."

"So you know the sister's address?" I asked. Finally I had a lead. The family might know something of her whereabouts.

"I have it in an address book among my possessions in my room. I can look it up for you if you like?" She made this a question. I wondered if Sid and Gus had mentioned my investigation to her. I decided not to bring it up in case they hadn't, so I just nodded.

"Thank you," I said with a smile. "I would like to speak to Willa's family."

"Would you?" She looked surprised. "Well, I will be seeing them on Monday."

"You will?" I looked surprised in my turn.

"Yes, at the opera house gala. They are planning to come for the speeches."

"I thought women weren't allowed at the gala." I couldn't keep the sour note out of my voice.

"Not down on the floor, or at the dinners before," Anne said, making a face in sympathy with my views, "but we can listen from the balcony. I want to hear Julia Ward Howe recite her poem."

"That does sound worth it," I agreed.

"Winnie offered me a place in her box, as a way of apologizing for not hosting me during this trip," Anne said. "I'm afraid I only have one though."

"Did you say they are hosting the German ambassador? The count?" I asked, surprised.

"I believe so. It is someone very important, I believe," Anne said seriously. "The State Department didn't want any other guests in the house for his security."

"I know his security detail," I said with a smile. "My husband is in charge of it." Daniel had mentioned that he could get a ticket for me, and surely he would be able to ask the ambassador for a place in the box since his wife would be up there. It would be much easier to ask about Willa if I was introduced to the family in a social setting. If I just turned up at their house they were bound to be tight-lipped. I said as much to Anne, adding, "If I am able to come, may my husband and I escort you, or will you be joining someone for dinner earlier?"

"I'm quite on my own; I would appreciate that very much." Anne's pinched face had relaxed and her words seemed to come more freely. I recognized that what I had taken for standoffishness was just painful shyness.

Sid and Gus finally emerged from behind the screen, still in animated discussion about the draping of the costumes.

"Of course the Greek goddesses were not concerned about the baring of breasts," Sid was saying.

"I'm not suggesting bare breasts, just that we must make sure our costumes do nothing to shock or offend," Gus replied. "That draping seemed to leave little to the imagination. And the amount of leg that is shown could be rather startling."

"We need to be able to move freely, remember," Sid said. "And not risk tripping over our garments."

She gave Gus a warning frown and Gus strode out ahead of her to join Miss Johnson and me. We were some of the last women to leave the huge armory. I glanced around, hoping to see Mrs. Goodwin again, but she had already left. I tried peeking into the rooms that we passed with open doors. I was longing to have a look around the rest of the house. I was always amazed that anybody lived this way, with butlers and living rooms as large as my whole house. But we were escorted downstairs by a gracious yet stern footman who seemed to have been instructed not to let any ladies wander. We came out onto the staircase and started down it. We crossed the foyer and Mrs. Belmont herself was standing near the door, shaking hands as each lady left.

"Thank you so much for coming," she said as she shook mine. "I will see you at the float construction on Friday," she said to Sid and Gus.

"Will you be there yourself?" Gus said, surprised.

"I like to be hands-on." Mrs. Belmont smiled. "I wasn't born in a house like this, you know." She gestured at the grand entrance. "And I didn't get here by sitting back and letting others do things for me. When I want something done well, I do it myself."

"Hear, hear," Sid said. Just before we turned away, there was a noise upstairs. Mrs. Belmont glanced up the marble staircase and then ushered us out with an imperious smile. The door closed behind us and I paused, thinking. I could have sworn that upstairs, peeking through the rails of the balcony, had been a little boy.

# Seven

I returned from the meeting with some satisfaction. I had set out to look for a woman and I already had snippets of news to go on. I now knew that, though she was a scientist like her husband, he took the credit for her research. I was afraid it did seem that she might be escaping from her husband and her marriage. I was almost certain that someone in that room knew where she was, and now I had a way to meet her parents or her sister. So I had a place to start. *Paddy Riley would be proud of me!* Riley was the detective I learned from when I got my first job in New York, as his assistant. He didn't really believe in women detectives and I had to learn more from observing than from his teaching. In fact, come to think of it, he would never have expressed pride in my work and would probably have told me to go home to my husband.

My husband. That was the problem. As I prepared the children's tea I wondered what to tell Daniel. Would I have the nerve to face him and say, "Listen now, Daniel. There's something you should know. I have decided to go back to my profession and become a private detective again. I have been commissioned to find a missing woman."

The trouble was I couldn't see him replying, "That's just grand, Molly. I'm really proud of you."

No, I'd have to phrase it more delicately than that. Tell him that my friends were so worried about Willa Parker and, knowing I had skills as a detective, had hired me to find her. Wasn't it lucky that I'd be bringing in money when we sorely needed it?

Yes. That's just what I'd say, because he couldn't argue that we didn't need money. My thoughts were interrupted by a wail from Mary Kate and I noticed she had tipped over her dish of bread and milk. Her tray was now swimming in it and milk was dripping onto my clean floor.

"Oh no. You bad girl," I exclaimed, then immediately regretted it. "It's all right. Don't cry. It was an accident," I said. "It was your mother's fault. I should have been feeding you, not leaving you to feed yourself. Here, let's clean you up and get you a fresh bowl."

I lifted her out, sponged her down, then sat her on my lap as I fed her. Balancing work and family was not going to be easy; I could see that.

Aileen had taken Mary Kate and Liam up to get them ready for bed and Bridie and I were settling down to a sparse meal of toasted cheese—the last of the split pea soup, which had lost its appeal by now anyway, was not allowed on a Friday—when Daniel came home.

"Well, that's a surprise." I looked up. "Home before midnight for once. Quite unexpected. Were there no more receptions to go to?"

He frowned. "Look, Molly, I'm sorry I've been gone so much. It certainly wasn't my idea and frankly I'd never have chosen this assignment if it hadn't been thrust on me. Believe me, trying to placate so many different nationalities has been quite wearing. I've had the German ambassador thumping tables all afternoon because his battleship is to go in the parade after the British one and he sees this at the ultimate insult. I had to tell him, politely but firmly, that I am not one of the parade organizers. My only task is to make sure that his ship can proceed without hindrance and his men can goose-step their way down Fifth Avenue."

I came over to him and put a hand on his shoulder. "I'm sorry. I should have realized you're being run off your feet. I'm afraid there isn't too much food left. We just had toasted cheese."

"It's all right," he said. "I did have a substantial luncheon with some of the committee members at the Astor. Fried oysters, then sole in a parsley sauce, followed by apple pudding. Quite tasty."

I didn't say what I was thinking. It seemed like an eternity since I'd had a tasty meal. "So will bread and cheese be enough for you, then?" I asked.

"I wouldn't say no to some pickles to go with it," he said, giving me a smile, "and a bottle of beer."

"The first I can grant," I replied. "But not the second. However, we do have some of your whisky left."

He shook his head. "No, I should save that for a rainy day." This would have been a perfect time to ask Daniel for an invitation to Willa's family box, but as I took breath to speak he pulled out a chair and sat down. "How are you, Bridie? School going well?" He studied her. "Why the long face?"

"We didn't go to school today," she said. "We had to have fittings for our parade dresses, but do you know, Papa, my dress didn't fit me properly. It looked horrible. It made me look as if I had big . . ." She blushed and couldn't say the rest.

"They're going to alter it, Bridie," I said. "I'm sure they'll make it look just perfect."

"That's what you have fittings for," Daniel said. "When I have a new suit made I have to go in a few times for them to tuck a little bit here and let out a little bit there."

"Oh really?" She looked more hopeful.

"Of course. So cheer up. Big day tomorrow, right?"

She nodded.

"I'm taking the children down to the Battery to watch the naval parade," I said. "Sid and Gus have been invited by Cousin Prudence to join them in someone's building in Upper Manhattan, overlooking the river. Another of Gus's family members, I gather. She has them scattered all around. But we weren't included, and I think the Battery should give us a good view if we get there early enough." I paused. "I don't suppose you'll be joining us? I'm not sure about bringing Mary Kate, although I do want Aileen to be able to see it."

I looked at him hopefully.

His eyes had that wicked twinkle in them that I'd found so attractive when I first met him. "I can do better than that," he said. "I've a surprise for you, Molly. I'm to keep an eye on the parade from a police boat and there will be room for my family on board. What do you say to that, huh? We'll be up close to the boats as they pass up the river."

"On a boat, Papa?" Bridie jumped up, ran around the table, and threw her arms around his neck. "That will be spectacular. I can't wait to tell the girls in my class. They'll be so impressed. I don't think even Blanche is going out on a boat."

Daniel looked at me for approval.

"Daniel Sullivan," I said. "Sometimes you do come up on top after all."

"I'm going to telephone her and tell her!" Bridie said, then caught my startled expression. I still regarded the telephone as a contraption only to be used in the most dire of circumstances, but, according to Bridie, the young people used it daily. "May I, Papa?"

"I suppose," Daniel said. "Like as not you will hear only static and have to shout to make yourself heard."

She gave a delighted smile and left the kitchen.

Never one to leave well enough alone, I added, "Of course, I'm not sure we have enough money to take a cab down to the dockside."

I regretted my words as Daniel's expression fell. "It will come any day now, I promise," he said. "If we can just keep our heads above water till this confounded celebration is over I'll even go down to Washington myself and wrestle the money from their hands."

"About time," I said. "But you don't have to worry so much anymore, because I've taken an assignment." I had been cutting slices of bread from the loaf and put them in front of him, along with a slab of cheese. He looked up sharply.

"You've what?"

"You heard me. I've decided it was time I used my talents to help support this family."

"Molly, you're not serious." He was frowning now. "You're the mother of small children, and you've plenty on your plate just keeping this place running. Making our home a happy place. That's where your talents should lie."

I had meant to break this news to him gently, but now I felt my face flushing. "I'll have you know that I am more than just a brood mare. And right now I'm using my skills to put food on our table—something you don't seem to be able to do," I snapped, then took a deep breath and calmed myself down. "Oh don't worry, Daniel. I'm not doing anything stupid or dangerous, but I've been hired to find a missing woman."

"Hired by whom?" He was still looking fiercely at me.

"By our neighbors across the street. This woman was supposed to come to New York to join them on their parade float, but she hasn't shown up and her husband is worried about what could have happened to her."

"Then it's up to her husband to go looking for her, not you and your friends."

I sat down at the table opposite him. "Did it not occur to you that she might be escaping from a husband who abuses her, who beats her perhaps, and that she doesn't want him to find her? That does happen, you know. She might be using this trip to New York as an excuse to make the break from him."

He sighed. "Molly, I don't think this is something you want to get yourself involved in. People's domestic disputes are messy and rarely one-sided. And I should point out that it is perfectly legal for a husband to beat his wife if she has failed in her duties in some way."

"As long as the rod is not thicker than his thumb," I retorted. "Oh yes. I do know that. And that he always keeps children and property in a divorce. The world is not a fair place, Daniel Sullivan." I paused, toying with what I had just said. "I should like to see you try and beat me."

I saw the flicker of a smile. "I wouldn't be foolish enough to attempt that, as you very well know. Besides"—he looked at my flushed cheeks and the smile broadened—"I think I might be the one in danger right now."

It was true that I was the one with the hot temper. Daniel was the calm one. I made an effort to keep my tone even.

"My friends just want to know that the woman is safe, that's all."

"And just how do you intend to do this in a city that's teeming with several million extra people at the moment?"

"Get in touch with people she might know or contact, I expect. I already have her father's address. In fact, if you can get me that ticket you promised me for Monday night, I may be able to sit with her family."

"Her family is wealthy enough to attend the opera house reception?" Daniel asked with surprise. "Surely they aren't attending social engagements if their daughter is missing?"

"That's what I thought," I said, "but it seems they are. Doesn't that seem suspicious? As if they know where she is?"

"That is a bit strange." Daniel frowned. "I'm surprised her father doesn't have the police out looking for her."

"That's what I thought as well," I said. "But I'd also like to know from the police whether any bodies have been found who might match the missing person. It is always possible that she went to the wrong part of the city and came to a bad end."

"Not very likely at this moment, I would have thought," Daniel said. "The place is full of out-of-towners, and with extra police on the beat. She wouldn't have met the wrong type of person unless she'd gone down a back alley in Hell's Kitchen or over on the East River docks. And since she is a friend of your highly educated neighbors, she'd have no reason to venture into less savory parts of the city."

"It's too bad you're no longer with the police department and thus can't check for me," I said. "I could give you the father's name and address."

"If her father has not called the police, he must suspect that she is safe," Daniel said. "He could certainly get them involved if he wanted to if his family has the standing to attend the opera house reception."

"And my investigation?"

"I will give you the ticket I promised and ask the German ambassador's wife to receive you," Daniel said. "I don't think even you can get into much trouble at the premier social event of the year."

"Thank you," I said, ignoring the condescension in his tone. "If you won't ask the police to look into it I thought I might ask Mrs. Goodwin . . ."

His head jerked up. "Mrs. Goodwin. What on earth made you think of her after all this time?"

"Because I saw her today," I replied. "I went with Sid and Gus to a meeting where they were planning their float for the parade."

I saw an eyebrow raise in surprise. "Their float? Your friends are joining the parade? As what, may one ask?"

"Goddesses and muses of Ancient Greece with a temple of Nike," I said. "Since they were not permitted to march in the historical parade as Vassar graduates they decided to join the carnival one later in the week. I gather anything goes that is amusing and entertaining. What could be more entertaining than Gus playing a lyre?"

He didn't reply to this, still considering what I had said. "And Mrs. Goodwin was there, at the planning meeting?" He frowned. "I'm pretty sure she did not attend Vassar nor any other institute of higher education. Where was this meeting held?"

"At the new mansion of Mrs. Alva Belmont on Madison Avenue."

"Mrs. Belmont?" He paused. "How do your friends know her? I didn't think they moved in such exalted circles. They say that new mansion cost a fortune and a half, and now she finds herself a rich widow. You'd have thought the kind of cause she'd take up would be more meaningful than floats for a carnival parade."

"I should think every New Yorker wants to be part of the celebration somehow," I said.

He was still frowning. "I hadn't heard that Mrs. Belmont was, shall we say, progressive in her opinions—a champion of women's rights. But perhaps I am wrong."

"She's green with envy!" Bridie came bursting back into the kitchen. "And guess what else. She has a rotary phone now. She can dial directly. So I'm green with envy about that. Are we thinking of getting one of those?"

"We are not," Daniel said and went on, "Don't you have homework to do, young lady?"

"It's Friday, Papa, and we have the week off regular lessons for the celebration."

"Well then, please go up to your room anyway. I want to talk to your mother."

Bridie looked confused. Her gaze went from Daniel to me.

"Yes, run along, my darling," I said.

She walked past us, then looked back once before she climbed the stairs.

"Let's go into the back parlor," Daniel said. "I don't want little ears listening in to this."

"What on earth is it, Daniel?" I asked.

He said nothing but led the way into the back parlor, closing the door firmly behind us. "Now," he said. "Your meeting today has raised a red flag, Molly. You know very well that the suffragists had petitioned to march in the parade and were denied—rightly so, since this is no occasion for protest and conflict. The aim is to show New York as a modern city of harmony and prosperity. Nothing must allow that illusion to be shattered, and it's my job to make sure it isn't."

He sat down in one of the leather armchairs. Feeling like a schoolgirl about to be grilled, I sat opposite him, presenting him with a blank face.

"So let me ask you. This meeting today, are you sure it wasn't a gathering of suffragists?"

"I expect some of the women were in favor of the cause," I said. "I am myself. But the meeting did no more than approve the costumes for the goddesses and discuss how the statue of *Winged Victory* should be positioned on the float and how her mechanism was going to work when she spreads her wings without knocking any of the women off the float."

"There wasn't an ulterior motive? Are you sure these women are not planning some kind of disruption?"

"Of course not," I said. "It was a good-humored meeting with plenty of jokes about Ancient Greece—jokes that only the highly educated could enjoy. I must confess most of them went over my head." But his question did put a doubt in my mind. There had been an undercurrent that I didn't understand in that meeting; topics that were whispered about just outside my hearing. But I didn't want to share my thoughts with Daniel until I'd had time to make sense of them.

"I suppose that's all right, then," he said. "But hearing Mrs. Goodwin was there makes me wonder whether the police suspect more is going on than meets the eye. They are asking her to keep an eye on these women because they can't be trusted."

"That's not fair," I said. "I'd say these women are completely trustworthy. It's just that their cause is one that men are unwilling to understand. You can't think it right that half the population has no say in the running of our country, or our state, or our city? Half the population, Daniel. Look at the committee for this celebration. All men. Did no one think that women should also be represented and share their ideas? I'd have thought if you left parade design to men you'd have nothing more than rows of men in uniform marching, or perhaps some floats showing the history of warfare and machinery. No man would have thought of goddesses and muses, and yet they are equally a part of our history."

"I don't suppose they would," Daniel had to agree. He looked a little amused at my tirade. "And I do see your point, Molly, but you have to realize that men make the decisions for the household, so when a man votes he is voting for his entire family, having presumably discussed options with his wife."

"Huh," I retorted. "Anyway, I don't know why we are discussing votes for women when all that was being planned was a carnival float full of Grecian goddesses."

"Look, Molly," he said, his voice softer now. "It's my job to keep this celebration secure. If you value your husband's position you'll help me out here. By all means go to these planning meetings with your friends, but keep your ears open for any hint of subversive activity."

"You want me to be your spy?" I asked angrily. "To spy on my friends?"

"It might mean the loss of my job if anything goes wrong with these parades," he said. "I'd be called into public committee hearings to answer for my department. And then where would we be?"

"With about the same amount of money coming in as there is now." I gave him a withering look.

"Let's not touch that again," he said, remarkably calmly. "That will be sorted out and everything will be fine. I just want to know that none of these women are planning to do anything silly or dangerous. Look at their sisters in England. Chaining themselves to railings? Hunger strikes? Even hurling bombs. They've gotten quite out of hand. We can't have that happening here."

"Desperate times call for desperate measures," I said. "But you needn't worry, Daniel. There was no talk of violence or bomb throwing at the meeting today."

"Make sure it stays that way," he replied.

## Eight

After Daniel had fallen asleep I lay staring at the ceiling. Now he had just given me something else to add to my feelings of unease. Not only would I be juggling my household accounts versus an empty purse, but he wanted me to spy on my friends. What if they were planning something more than just an innocent float? But what could that possibly be? Something that would disrupt the parade, maybe. I knew I could never betray them. But if I remained silent and Daniel lost his job? If people in the crowd were harmed? I shook my head. These women would never do anything harmful. They might shout a few slogans, even wave a banner, but nothing that would put others in jeopardy. I decided I would not do my normal thorough investigating on this matter. The less I knew the better. I certainly didn't want to lie to Daniel.

I turned over, giving a deep sigh. Why did life always have to be so complicated? Why couldn't I just be looking forward to the grand celebration like the rest of New York? I snuggled against Daniel, finding comfort in the warmth of his body. He was a good man. A good husband. As he had said, he had never laid a hand on me or our children, never actually ordered me around as he was legally allowed to do. His only worry for me had been for my safety. I closed my eyes and drifted off to sleep.

I was woken by a large weight jumping on me. I opened my eyes to daylight and saw Liam's face, inches from mine. "Is it time for the parade yet?" he asked. "You said we have to go early so that we get good places to watch the ships."

"There's been a change of plans," I said.

I watched his face fall. "We're not going? You promised."

"Hold your horses, young man," I said. "Yes, we are going to see the parade, but even better than standing on the shore—we're going with Papa to watch on a boat."

"On a boat?" His eyes grew wide with excitement. "A real boat?"

"Not only a boat, a police boat," I said. "There. Isn't that a grand surprise? So we'll have a nice breakfast and then off we'll go."

He bounded from the room shouting, "Bridie? Aileen? Guess what? We're going on a boat."

Now that my retainer had kept the wolf from the door for at least a week, I threw caution to the winds and made us eggs for breakfast. Who knew when we'd get another meal if we were out on a police launch? The day had dawned fine with white clouds scudding across a blue sky, but I sensed the wind on the water might be quite chilly. I put on my own topcoat and wrapped a scarf at my neck, then made sure the children were all dressed warmly. Daniel suggested that we leave Mary Kate at home with Aileen, but I thought that wasn't fair.

"She'd want to see the parade with the rest of New York," I said. "Surely there's a corner on the boat for a young woman and a small baby?"

But then Aileen herself decided it for us. "On a boat, Mrs. Sullivan? Oh, that's sure grand and kind of you, but I had enough of boats making the crossing from Ireland to last me a lifetime. I swore never again."

"It's only the Hudson River and New York Harbor," I said.

But she shook her head. "I'll stay here with the baby. It wouldn't be right to have her out in that cold wind all day, and anyway how would you be able to feed her? There would be nowhere to warm up her food."

That aspect of the day had not struck me before. "You're right about that," I said. "So if you don't mind staying, Aileen, I'll make sure you get an extra day off this week to help your family get ready for their parade." I knew Aileen would want to see her father marching with the Tammany brigade.

"All right. That's sounds fair enough," Aileen said, and swept up Mary Kate. "You and me are going to have a grand old time, missy." Mary Kate gave a delightful giggle. I gave her a kiss and off we went.

"I'll go and find us a taximeter," Daniel said.

"Won't that be too expensive?" I asked. "I'm sure they must have raised their rates for the big occasion, knowing how much in demand they will be."

"I do have running money for this assignment," he said. "The federal government understands that I need to move around the city with ease." And off he went. Hiring a taximeter did not prove easy, as the whole of New York was out and about, all trying to get to a viewing spot on the waterfront. In the end Daniel came back with a good old hansom cab and we crowded in, Liam on Daniel's knee and Bridie squashed up against me. As we set off, it dawned on me that we had not had a family outing in a long time. Daniel's new job had kept him away a lot in the nation's capital, and a new baby certainly restricted movement. I glanced at Daniel and he returned my grin. Perhaps he was thinking the same thing.

The cab driver was smart enough to stay away from the waterfront for as long as possible. He took us up Sixth Avenue until he could cut across to the Chelsea Piers on Twenty-Third Street. I looked up, admiring the Flatiron Building as we passed. I didn't think I'd ever get used to skyscrapers—so incredibly high. The last part of the trip became impossible as the cab tried to negotiate through throngs of sightseers, hoping to get to a spot at the waterfront somewhere. In the end Daniel called up to the driver to let us down. There was no point in continuing. The driver agreed. "The whole world's gone mad," he said gruffly. "And what with the streets being closed off for the parades all next week, I don't reckon I'll see a decent fare for a while."

Daniel tipped him more than he should and the man tipped his cap. "Much obliged, sir. You're a real gentleman."

We set off into the crowd. Daniel scooped up Liam and set him on his shoulders. Bridie took my arm as we followed Daniel. It was hard to make any progress as we were jostled around but at last the entrance to the piers came into view. Daniel had to do some rather firm persuading to make it through the last few feet of crowds. In the end he held up his badge and showed it. "If I don't get on that police boat, the parade doesn't start," he was forced to say, and the crowd parted for us.

Then at last we were on the boat. We were escorted to a bench running along the side of the steering house. Daniel settled us there and went off to confer with the various river policemen. I took Liam on my knee. "You'll need to sit still and watch," I said. "You can't go running around and getting in the way of the men trying to do their job."

As I was speaking a hiss of steam sounded behind me and with a toot of the horn the small craft pulled away from the dock. The Hudson River beyond was full of boats of all sizes. We had to negotiate everything from rowboats to pleasure steamers until we were out in midstream and made our way down to the basin where the parade vessels were assembled. We had just pulled up beside the lead vessels when a gun sounded, a great cheer went up from the waterfront, and the tiny ship hauled up its sails.

"I know what that is," Bridie said excitedly. "That's the *Half Moon*, Henry Hudson's sailing boat, in which he discovered the Hudson River."

"I presume it's a replica," Daniel said. "Otherwise it would be three hundred years old and probably not very seaworthy."

We watched the small vessel approaching. The sailors on board all wore ancient Dutch costumes that didn't look suitable at all for manning a ship. Right behind the boat was a replica of the *Clermont*, Fulton's paddle steamer. The wind was gusting and it took the *Half Moon* a while to get its sails adjusted to catch the breeze. When it did, disaster almost occurred. The little ship swerved unexpectedly and collided with the much bigger *Clermont*. A gasp of horror could be heard from the ships and from the nearby waterfront. Our police vessel came up to the boat to inspect the damage. Luckily there was nothing serious.

"It's devilish difficult to control in these conditions," one of the mariners called across to us. "Not sure how we're going to make it all the way upriver."

It seemed the parade had come to a halt before it started, but then a trusty tugboat was called in and, however ignominious it was, the *Half Moon* set out, leading the flotilla of ships behind the tug. The *Clermont* followed and one by one the bigger ships joined the line. First came the US Navy with several giant battleships. Liam was beside himself with excitement.

"Look, Papa, look at their guns!" he shouted. "I want to be on a battleship one day."

Why men are so attracted to guns I'll never understand! I glanced at Bridie. She was huddled in the corner of the seat. "Are you all right?" I asked.

"I'm cold," she said. "Is this going to be all day, do you think?"

Such different reactions from boys and girls! She didn't see anything glamorous in battleships until she spotted the sailors in their dress uniforms lining the upper deck. Then she sat up straighter and smoothed down her hair. I tried not to smile.

After the American ships had passed, our boat circled quickly before the British battleship came steaming toward us. The British sailors, in their different uniforms, stood at attention around the top deck. More cheers came from the banks. Then behind the British, the German battleship. Our boat cut behind this and circled the Japanese naval vessel, then suddenly I felt the engine revved to full steam ahead and we shot forward.

"What the hell?" I heard one of the police mutter.

A small vessel had left the Jersey shore and was making for the battleships. Since the spectator craft had been warned to keep to the shoreline, this was worrying.

"Keep away! Return to the shore!" the bullhorn rang out from our boat. I could sense the tension, and some of the police had their guns at the ready. Daniel was giving commands.

The boat paid no attention to our police boat rapidly closing in. Another warning was shouted, but the small craft didn't move away. It had drawn level with the German battleship. I saw one of the policemen aim his gun. That was when we noticed the boat was flying the Jolly Roger flag.

"It's a pirate ship," Liam said in awe. "Are they going to attack, Mama?"

Before we could reach it, the Jolly Roger flag was hauled down from the small makeshift mast.

"They're taking the flag down," someone shouted.

Then it was immediately raised again.

"It's all right. They are only giving the naval salute," one of the river police commented.

"Cheeky devils," another replied. "Lowering the Jolly Roger. Now that battleship will have to reply."

"What does that mean?" I asked Daniel quietly, not being familiar with ships and their ways.

He was grinning as well. "It's naval law that when one ship salutes the other has to respond in kind." And we saw that indeed a seaman was now working hard to lower the German flag that fluttered from high above the ship. I realized then that it must be a prank, making the giant battleship respond to a tiny tub of a boat.

"It's a bit like making a king salute a mouse," I said, looking at the size of the two ships. Our boat came alongside the little craft and two of the police boarded it. A rope was tied and the pirate ship towed back to the shore.

"College students," Daniel said as he returned to me and we were steaming back to the parade. "Drunken fraternity boys from Columbia, I'm sorry to say. Thought it would be a joke to go all the way down the parade and make all those ships return their salute. Luckily we got to them before they could annoy every nation here."

"At least it wasn't more dangerous," the man beside him commented. "We were warned to look out for anarchist activities. There are factions working to disrupt this whole celebration. Let's hope the next one isn't the real thing."

No sooner was that excitement over than there came a strange buzzing, popping sound from over our heads. We looked up and to my amazement there was a flying machine. I'd read about the Wright brothers, of course, but I had imagined a craft launching into the air for a few seconds. This one was flying like a bird up the Hudson, until it came directly over our boat. Liam was pointing, mouth open in excitement.

Daniel also looked excited. "It's Wilbur Wright," he said. "He had hoped the conditions would be favorable to fly over the parade. Isn't it amazing? Actually staying up in the air that long."

The little airplane turned then and headed back toward Staten

Island, but the cheers from the banks let us know that the flight was a huge success.

"At least nobody tried to shoot at it," one of the policemen muttered. "I've just realized what a hopeless job we have trying to protect a parade against unknown threats. They could strike from anywhere at any time." He turned to Daniel. "I hope you federal agents are doing good undercover work and monitoring undesirable factions."

"Doing our best," Daniel said. "As you said, threats could come from anywhere—a disgruntled Japanese or an Irish republican. This would be an ideal time to make a statement, wouldn't it?"

"Well, at least it seems to have gone smoothly enough so far," the policeman replied. "Apart from a pirate ship and a collision!"

We accompanied the ships up the Hudson until they reached the northern tip of Manhattan, then swung around and made our way slowly back past the motley ships following in the parade, from ferries to paddle steamers to fishing boats to tugs, all adorned with bunting. Finally the last ship was safely past the city with no harm done. We headed back to the dock.

"Day one safely through with only one thwarted pirate attack," Daniel said as he helped me ashore. "Now we just have to get through the next week of street parades equally smoothly and I can take a rest."

We had to walk home, rather than taking any kind of vehicle, as the streets were now so crowded it was almost impossible to move. Daniel lifted Liam onto his shoulders, much to the boy's delight, and forged a path through the crowd while I followed. As we walked I was making plans in my head. Daniel was home; so was Aileen. It would be a perfect chance to slip out again, on the pretext of shopping for extra supplies. I was tempted to go back to Mrs. Belmont's house and see if I could spy through the windows to see if Willa

Parker was hiding there. Although when I considered this it seemed ridiculous. If Willa was hiding at Mrs. Belmont's house, why had she not come down to join in the meeting? She must have known she'd be among friends who would support her whatever her intentions were. But then again, she'd have been among friends at Sid and Gus's house and had chosen not to stay there. And if Willa was not there, then the boy could not have been her son. Everything was so confusing.

My other immediate thought was Mrs. Goodwin. What on earth could she have been doing there? I could not see her wanting to be a goddess on a carnival float. She had never given the slightest indication of being a suffragist, although she had certainly broken new ground as the first female detective in the NYPD. But she had given a false name and a false persona to the group. Daniel's supposition that she was doing undercover police work was probably correct. But why was a float committee being observed? Was there one particular person present whom she was observing? If so, would she tell me the truth?

We arrived home, and I made a cup of tea and was greeted by my baby daughter as if I'd been gone for years. The way she wrapped her little arms around my neck made me realize it would be difficult to sneak away again. And the situation was decided for me when Daniel said, "Molly, can we just have an early snack instead of dinner, do you think? Because I've another surprise for this evening."

"Really?" I looked up.

He was grinning. "I've arranged for us to go to a viewing platform to see the ships all lit up. It will be quite a sight, I'm sure. All those electric lights twinkling in the water."

He looked as if he was a magician who had produced a rabbit from a hat, so of course I had to say that it would be wonderful. Even Bridie didn't protest coming with us this time. We bundled up, braved the crowds, and stood gaping in wonder at the ships on the

Hudson, now all festooned with electric lights. Around us the city also glowed and sparkled with electric lights everywhere. It truly was the grandest spectacle of our age and I felt proud to be a New Yorker, for that was surely what I had now become.

Liam fell asleep on Daniel's shoulder as we made our way home.

"It's been a grand day," Daniel said as we walked up Patchin Place.

I had to agree. If I hadn't been so preoccupied with my task it would indeed have been the grandest of days.

## ≋ Nine ≋

I awoke on Sunday morning eager to get on with my important commission. I had to find Willa Parker before her husband did. And yet it seemed that everything in the universe was conspiring to make sure I was thwarted. Daniel had announced that he had to work and regretted that he couldn't go to Mass with us. He had been more insistent lately that we behave like good Catholics, since we were now raising a family and had to set a good example. (I suspect it was his mother putting pressure on him that brought about this sudden fervency.) I, not the most devoted of Catholics, was happy to skip the service occasionally if something more important came up, thus destining myself to years in purgatory, I've no doubt. And on this day something more important had come up—I had a missing woman to find.

I didn't exactly tell Daniel that we weren't going to Mass, but I didn't say we were either. However, Aileen, raised with the true Irish fear of hellfire if one tiny rule was broken, looked horrified when I said I had other things to do that morning.

"You'll not be attending church, Mrs. Sullivan?" Her eyes darted nervously. "But that's a terrible sin, to be sure."

"I don't think God minds an occasional absence, Aileen," I said, "but do by all means go yourself. I wouldn't like to keep you from your obligations."

"I'll take Miss Bridie with me, if you don't mind," she said, "and Liam too. He should be growing up in his faith. And she shouldn't be getting any heathen ideas from those Protestants she mixes with."

I was thinking that I'd get an hour or so of freedom after all, but then I remembered Mary Kate. I could hardly take her on my sleuthing.

"Could you go to the eight o'clock mass, do you think?" I asked. "I've some things I have to get done today and you'll be gone in the afternoon, won't you?"

Her face lit up. "Oh yes, Mrs. Sullivan. I'll be helping my da with his costume for the parade. Me ma's been sewing away but there is also the banner they'll be carrying."

"Of course. I'm sure it will look splendid," I said and was rewarded with a beaming smile.

"I'll be so proud to see him. And to see Miss Bridie too on her float. I think she'll look a picture."

"No I won't," Bridie said, entering the room to hear this. "Not if they haven't managed to alter my dress properly. I'll be the only one who looks like she's wearing her big sister's clothes. Everyone will notice me and make fun of me."

I put an arm around her shoulder. "Sweetheart, it's going to be fine. When you have the final fitting tomorrow it will all be perfect. You'll see."

She shrugged me away as if she didn't quite believe this. I didn't say any more. I'd noticed it was the way of a fourteen-year-old girl to be either blissfully happy or in the depths of despair. So Aileen went off to Mass with Bridie and Liam, the latter more willing than the former, and I was left at home with Mary Kate. As I looked at her playing happily on the rug I felt a pang of guilt. Was I being a terrible mother by taking a job outside the home and neglecting my children? I tried to tell myself that I was with her most of the time and that she and Liam both adored Aileen, but the nagging feeling would not go away. I resolved to make sure that I gave them enough time and attention when I was home. Since she showed no interest in me at the moment, I got out my pad and pencil and made a list of things I knew and things I needed to know.

Willa Parker, married to a Dr. Parker and living in Philadelphia. Had attended Vassar and then went on to graduate studies at Penn, which I gathered was the nickname for the University of Pennsylvania. (I wasn't too well up on American universities.) What else had I picked up about her? A passionate researcher, according to Miss Johnson. She was continuing her research, even though she was a wife and a mother and her findings had to be published by her husband.

She was supposed to come to New York to stay with Sid and Gus but didn't arrive. Already some things didn't make sense. Why did she want to come to New York? If she was a passionate scientist, why would she want to be part of a street parade, dressed as a goddess? Surely that would seem frivolous and unnecessary to a woman engrossed in her research. It didn't seem from what I'd heard at the meeting that she was active in the suffrage movement. Only Miss Johnson and one other woman from Philadelphia confessed to knowing her. But this Harriet Schilling showed an unwillingness to talk to me, and almost hostility. Had she resented my presence at the meeting? She wasn't the only one who had eyed me suspiciously and questioned why I was there. But what could they not want me to hear or to know about a carnival float? I had seen the plans and the illustrations and they were exactly as Sid had described them: a *Winged Victory* standing in front of an Athenian temple and Mount Olympus. And the live figures were goddesses, draped in white. Perfectly delightful and harmless.

I stared at the sheet of paper in front of me.

*Dr. Parker,* I wrote in big letters. He was the one suspicious character so far. He had followed his wife to New York. But why? If she had told him she planned to stay with friends and be part of a float in the parade, what had made him follow her? Did he suspect she had another motive? Meeting another man, perhaps? Or did he suspect she was trying to run away from him? But then she would surely have brought her son with her, and Sid and Gus were never asked to host a child. My thoughts went back to the small boy I had seen peeking through the stair railings at Mrs. Belmont's. Was it absurd to wonder if he was Willa's son when he could have been the child of relatives or visitors? If Willa's son was staying with her, then why was Willa not doing the same? And if she was, why would she need to hide from her suffragist sisters? Surely she would have joined the meeting and explained to those who knew her that she had changed her mind about a place to stay in New York and accepted Mrs. Belmont's kind invitation.

That led me to another thing that didn't make sense. Willa was originally from New York, so perhaps she was drawn to the celebration in her home city, but then why not stay with family who lived here? I had heard the answer to that—the family was hosting a visiting German ambassador and his wife. But surely there would always be space for a visiting daughter. She could share a room with her younger sister for a few days, couldn't she? Had there been a falling-out with her family? I was glad I'd have a chance to meet this sister tomorrow night and learn more.

So what could I do today? My time was precious and I should not be wasting a minute. I stared down at what I had written on the page. I could visit Mrs. Belmont and find out if the boy was Willa's son, but the guarded look she had given me indicated that she would not want to share information with me until she got to know me better. So it might be wise to come with Sid and Gus to help put the final touches to the float later in the week. It is easier to chat when occupied.

There was Harriet Schilling, who knew her in Philadelphia. I should find out where she was staying and question her again. But Harriet had been unwilling to speak to me to the point of hostility. Was that hostility simply because I was an outsider at the meeting? But then again, so was she. Or did she know something she didn't want to share? Had Willa told her she planned to leave her husband?

That left Dr. Parker himself. I should visit him at his hotel and find out as much as possible about his missing wife. If I presented myself as a concerned friend who was willing to help in any way to find his wife maybe he would agree to talk to me. I didn't relish the task, having witnessed his aggressive behavior, but then I told myself we might have everything wrong. Perhaps the bluster only masked worry. I imagined that Daniel would panic if he thought I was lost in a strange city.

So I would steel myself and go to visit Dr. Parker as soon as the family returned from church. I presumed that he had left the address of his hotel with my neighbors. I glanced at the clock. Eight thirty. Sid and Gus were not normally early risers but I suspected that Cousin Prudence would be up with the lark, and they had Miss Johnson as a guest. I paused to consider her. Such a quiet, mousy little person, the type that was always overlooked. But she did know Willa, or rather, Willa's family. There might be more she could tell me if I asked her.

My mother's instinct warned me that the room was suddenly too silent. I looked up in time to see Mary Kate fully standing, clutching the leg of the side table, which was now teetering precariously.

"Well done, my girl," I said, as I hurriedly crossed the room and steadied the table. "Going to walk now are we?" I watched with anticipation as she let go of the table and balanced on her own with a look of concentration before losing her balance and plopping down no worse for wear on her giant nappy. "Oh well, almost there," I commiserated, scooping her up and tickling her before putting her on my hip and heading for the door. "Come help me do some investigating, then."

I tiptoed across the street and put my ear to the letter box, hoping to hear whether the occupants were up. I was rewarded with a booming voice, somewhere in the background, calling out, "Elena!" in imperious tones and then the sound of feet tapping down the linoleum-covered stairs. So Sid was up and Cousin Prudence was being difficult again. I waited a while before I tapped on the door.

A rather flustered-looking Sid opened it. "Oh, Molly, it's you," she said, giving Mary Kate's hand a loving squeeze.

"I know it's rather early," I said, "and I won't keep you, but I wondered if Dr. Parker had found somewhere to stay and had given you his address."

"He did send round a note," Sid said. "He's staying with a colleague at NYU apparently. Not far from here. Were you thinking of visiting him?"

"I was," I replied. "I need to find out as much as possible about his wife."

A worried look crossed her face. "Do you think that's wise? If he's hired a Pinkerton's man he'll think you are interfering."

"I propose to present myself as a friend of Willa's who is so concerned about her and may be able to help because I know other friends of hers in the city. Anyway, it's worth a try, isn't it?"

"I suppose it is," Sid said. "Won't he recognize you from your previous encounter?"

"That will only add veracity to my story," I said. "It proves I know his wife's friends in the city."

"Elena?" came the voice again. Sid glanced back down the hall, then rolled her eyes. "You're good at solving murders, aren't you? If you want one murder that might be easy to solve I can provide one for you," she said in a low voice. I chuckled.

"I'd better not disturb you now," I said, as the baby began to wiggle and fuss. "Can you put the address through my letter box when you have a moment?"

"Of course." She glanced around. "I'd invite you in, but . . ."

"Oh no. You're far too busy," I said. I gave her a sympathetic smile as she closed the front door.

As I went to walk away I heard the voice saying, "Who was that at the door?"

I didn't hear Sid's reply but then the voice went on loudly, "That immigrant woman from across the street again? Why does she keep coming over here? Is it free food she wants?"

I thought I might join Sid if she was planning the murder of a certain person.

I didn't have to wait long before there was a knock at my own front door. I opened it to see Anne Johnson standing there.

"Elena sends her apologies," she said, "but she is fully occupied at the moment, as you can imagine. She sent me over with Dr. Parker's address."

"Thank you very much," I replied. As she was about to walk away I asked, "Would you like to come in for a moment? A cup of tea or coffee perhaps?"

She stepped into my hallway. "That's very kind of you," she said. "Frankly a moment of peace and quiet would be most acceptable."

I led her down the hall to the kitchen. "I could take you to the parlor and be formal," I said. "But I've got the baby settled in her high chair, and it's warm in here. The mornings are chilly at the moment, aren't they?"

"I suppose they are," she agreed, "although the house across the street is pleasantly warm. A little too warm at times, if you get my meaning."

I laughed as I pulled out a chair for her. "I think Sid and Gus will be ready for sainthood after this," I said.

She nodded. "What a dreadful woman. Barking out commands as if they are servants, or rather as if Sid is the servant. And most impertinent in what she says too. She demanded to know why I wasn't married and if I was one of 'those sort of women.'"

"You should have said it was quite obvious why she isn't married herself," I replied, getting a delighted giggle.

"You're right. But how impertinent. I mean, just because one comes from a high society family does not give one the right to insult other people."

"No, it doesn't," I replied. "Coffee or tea?"

"Oh, tea would be most welcome. I'm afraid the coffee across the street is rather strong for my liking."

"That's an understatement," I said. "You can almost stand up the spoon in their coffee."

I poured her a cup of tea, offering milk and sugar. As she stirred in the latter I asked, "I'm finding everything I've heard about Willa Parker to be quite perplexing. You said that you don't know her personally, is that right?"

"I was quite friendly with her younger sister, Winnie, when we were at Vassar," she replied. "So I did meet Willa a few times, although I believe she only visited home and was no longer living there at that time. She already was gaining a reputation as a brilliant scientist. Terribly earnest. Not the sort of person one chats to. No small talk."

"Was she also a keen suffragist in those days? I got the feeling that the women at that meeting were all for the cause."

Anne shook her head. "I don't think any of us were. At Vassar one is in a bubble, you know. We were led to believe that as educated women we were as good as any man and could do anything we chose. It's only afterward in the outside world that we found that society wants to keep women pregnant and in the kitchen."

"That's true," I said. "So I presume that's when Willa decided to support the suffrage movement."

"I didn't know she had until your neighbors informed me that she would be joining us."

"And presumably you were surprised that she was not staying with her family?"

"I was. But then I learned from her sister that they were hosting important foreign visitors." She helped herself to some more sugar and stirred her tea.

"Are you also from Philadelphia?" I asked.

"Me? Oh, goodness no. I'm from upstate New York. Not far from Buffalo."

"And what do you do now? You said you weren't in a profession."

"Well, not a doctor or teacher," she said. "I am an artist. I illustrate children's books. And I keep my mother company. We lost my father a few years ago and my mother has been overcome with grief."

"I'm sorry."

"So am I. I feel obliged to stay with her, but the longer I stay the more dependent she becomes."

"A tricky situation," I said. "So." I said the word strongly, making her look up. "What do you think could have happened to Mrs. Parker?"

She frowned. "I've absolutely no idea. When we saw the aggressive nature of her husband, I naturally assumed she had planned to run away from him. But if she left her child behind, then that does not make sense, does it?"

Mary Kate chose that moment to drop the rusk she was happily chewing on to the floor with a loud clatter and then looked affronted that it had disappeared. I picked it up quickly before she could begin to scream and turned back to Anne.

"I ask myself," I said, "why did he come looking for her if he did not suspect something was wrong? I understood she had arranged with him to go to New York for a few days. He knew she was supposed to be meeting up with Vassar friends. So what made him come after her?"

Anne Johnson took a tentative sip of tea before saying, "I'm wondering if he had not understood the nature of her visit. Perhaps she had told him it was to see family or old college friends and then he heard she was to be part of a float in the parade. Some men take issue with their wives putting themselves on display. So he came to bring her home."

I nodded. "That does seem a likely explanation. I suppose he could be worried that the women were going to make a spectacle of themselves."

"More than wearing Greek costumes?" Anne Johnson's eyes twinkled. "Come now, Mrs. Sullivan, how could anyone object to a float of Greek myth? And it's part of the carnival parade, not the serious historical one. The floats are supposed to be fun, and ours certainly will be."

"Perhaps he'll tell me why he was so rattled," I said.

Her face clouded. "Do you think it's wise to visit him? He was not the most agreeable of men and would not take kindly to being questioned by a woman, I suspect."

"I'll be tactful," I said. "But I do think it's important that we get his point of view on the whole thing. Perhaps he suspects she has run off with another man."

"He wouldn't admit that to you."

I chuckled. "No, you're right. But one gets a feel from talking to a person face-to-face, doesn't one?"

"I suppose so," she agreed.

"And I hope to learn more when we meet Willa's sister tomorrow night."

"You managed to get a ticket, then?" she said. "I understood they were very much in demand."

"My husband is in charge of security for the event," I said. "He can pull strings."

"That is fortunate for you." She drained her cup and stood up. "I should be getting back. I only said that I was bringing you the address. They will be wondering where I am."

"It was good talking to you," I said. "I never asked, but are you part of the suffrage movement yourself?"

"Oh, most fervently," she said. "I am the secretary for our chapter. I have learned firsthand how impossibly hard it is for my mother and myself in a world ruled by men. They made it impossible for my mother to access my father's bank accounts, would not give her a loan, spoke to us as if we were children. Oh, believe me, I will do everything within my power to get women their rights."

As I closed the door behind her I considered this new version of Anne Johnson—no longer the shy, withdrawn person but passionate and articulate. It is wonderful what a cause will do to a woman. Did Willa Parker also feel so passionately, and—I stopped as the thought entered my head—what did these women hope to achieve by sitting on a float as Greek goddesses?

## Ten

It was with some trepidation that I made my way toward Washington Square and the address on the piece of paper I had been given. Sunday mornings were usually a delightful respite from the bustle of the week in our neck of the woods. In the square there would be students from New York University kicking around a ball or talking and laughing in groups. There would be Italian families with small children chasing pigeons. Our own son certainly enjoyed his outings to this nearby oasis. But today the square was full of out-of-towners and vendors making the most of them. Postcard sellers hawking the official postcards from the parades (made in advance with fanciful drawings), ice cream and peanuts barrows, carts with souvenirs of the city ranging from small versions of the Statue of Liberty to scarves with the bridges on them. Each hawker calling out to advertise their wares competed with musicians of various sorts hoping to earn a few coppers: a violinist playing wonderfully well, a hurdy-gurdy making more noise.

I fought my way across the square until I came to the brownstone that housed the hall of residence where Dr. Parker was staying. My entrance was barred by a frightening old man with a lot of white whiskers. "This is a male house of residence. No women allowed," he barked in my face.

I took a step back. "I am here to see Dr. Parker, whom I gather is staying in one of the rooms, thanks to a colleague on the faculty," I said in what I hoped were frosty tones. "If you would be good enough to tell him that one of Mrs. Parker's friends wishes to speak to him."

The tone softened. "Very good, ma'am," he said. "I'm afraid I can't let you inside—university policy, you understand. But I'll go and see if the gentleman is still in his room and let him know you are here."

I stood on the stoop outside, enjoying the warm fall sunshine on my face. I hoped the fine weather would last for the parades. One never knew at this time of year. I didn't have to wait long before the front door was pushed open and Dr. Parker exited, followed by a man in a brown suit, a fedora low over his eyes. Dr. Parker looked at me hopefully.

"You have news about Willa? She has finally contacted her friends?" I glanced at the other man, wondering who he was and what I should say in front of him.

"This is Jones," Dr. Parker said. "He is a Pinkerton man."

"We're on the case, ma'am." Jones's voice was low and gravelly. "Just you leave it to us. Have you seen the lady?"

"Not yet, I am afraid, but I wanted Dr. Parker to know that we are all working hard to find her. We are all as perplexed as you are."

Dr. Parker heard the Irish tones in my voice and a questioning look replaced the more friendly one. "How do you know my wife? You were not at Vassar with her, surely?"

My brain raced for a suitable answer. Obviously I didn't look like the Vassar type. "I know her family in the city here," I said. "In fact, I'm going to the opening reception with them tomorrow night." This was a slight stretching of the truth but it seemed to work. "My name is Mrs. Sullivan."

"So you're not one of those dreadful women?" he said.

I smiled, fighting back any annoyance I might have been feeling. "I assure you I am not a dreadful woman but one who is concerned about your wife."

"Not half as concerned as I am." He gave a sigh and for a moment looked boyish and vulnerable.

A noisy group of students surged past us. Dr. Parker glared after them.

"Jones, why don't you go on. I'll let you know if this lady has any information of value."

"Whatever you say, boss." The man gave a nod in my direction and strode down the street purposefully, having to dodge several college students walking toward the entrance.

Professor Parker's eyes followed him as he walked away. Then he looked at me in silence for a moment. I believe he was trying to decide whether I would be helpful in his search or if I might be wasting his time or, worse, trying to fleece him in some way. I must have looked harmless because he said, "Is there somewhere we could go to talk?"

"Usually a bench in the park would be quiet and private," I said, "but at the moment it seems half the world has gathered here. There is an Italian coffeehouse around the corner. They might have a table."

"Good. Let's try it."

We didn't speak as I led him around to Fourth Street and into the small coffee shop. There was a table in the window and he ordered two coffees without asking me what I might want. As I stirred in some sugar I asked, "So, Dr. Parker, what did you think your wife might be doing in New York?"

"Doing?" he asked. "She told me a group of former Vassar students would be coming to New York for the celebration. She said it was a long time since she had seen former college friends and she had maybe been too focused on assisting with my work." He paused, taking a sip of his coffee. "I agreed this was true. Of course, she cares for our house and our child, but she is indispensable to me in the lab. She helps with my study of viruses." He looked up. "I'm sure you have no idea what I am talking about. Viruses are recently discovered entities that cause illnesses. They are so small that they can't be seen with the naked eye. Even smaller than bacteria, which I'm sure you know have now been proven to cause all sorts of infections. But now we are discovering that some of the worst diseases that can affect mankind are caused by these viruses." Several patrons in the coffee shop were now studying Dr. Parker with interest as his voice rose and took on the tones of a professor in front of a class. He waved his arms around animatedly. "Of course, being so small, they have been almost impossible to detect, but we are making strides. Take poliomyelitis, for example. You might know it as infantile paralysis—"

"Dr. Parker," I interrupted, "I don't need a treatise on viruses at the moment. We both want to find your wife."

"That is true," he said. "Let's see. She wanted to attend the celebration and take part in a Vassar float in the parade, I believe. However, her sister wrote that it was not convenient for her to stay this week, so Willa planned to stay with some Vassar graduates who are also part of the festivities." He looked at me intently. "Your friends, I believe."

I nodded but did not say more, willing him to go on.

"I received a letter saying that she arrived but I can't discover where she went," he said, his voice strained.

"This must be really worrying for you, Dr. Parker." I gave a sympathetic nod.

"I am out of my mind with worry," he admitted. "I can't think what might have happened to her. She's normally such a sensible woman, so committed to her research, such a good mother."

"She did not take your son with her when she left?"

"No." He sighed. "She offered to but I didn't agree. New York at this moment would be a most unsuitable place for a young child. She left him with our neighbor, who has frequently looked after him while Willa is working."

"What I don't understand," I said, "is why her family is not concerned about Willa's disappearance. You have informed them?"

"I have," he said. "That was the first place I went. Her sister was not very receptive." He drained his coffee. "She suggested that my wife might be taking a holiday on her own."

"Does that seem strange to you?" I asked. "Does she have other friends in the city that she might be staying with?"

He shook his head angrily. "I've been to every house I could think of. To school friends, to the new Rockefeller Institute." His face took on a faraway quality once again. "They showed me around the lab. They have quite a facility and access to a vast number of infected patients. A better setup than our lab at Penn."

"And you thought your wife might go there?"

"Well, the new director was our professor when Willa and I were students. He is a leading expert in virology. I thought she might seek him out." He shrugged. "But he has taken time off for this blasted celebration and no one at the lab has seen Willa." He shifted in his seat. "Look, I shouldn't take up more of your time. What do you think you can do to help find Willa? I have already engaged the services of a Pinkerton man and he has confirmed that she did not stay with the college friends as intended. One other strange thing so far is that none of the women he has mentioned were part of my wife's former circle of friends, as far as I can tell. From what he says some of these women seem to be, shall we say, rather radical in their views. In favor of women's suffrage, you know."

"What were your wife's views on that?" I asked.

"She never expressed the slightest interest. As I told you, her work was her life . . . to the detriment of her home life at times."

"I agree it is a perplexing problem, Dr. Parker," I said. "Believe me, the women with whom she was to stay are doing everything within their power to find her."

He shook his head. "It is just not like Willa. I can't understand it."

"She was happy at home, then?"

"I think so. We were both much occupied with our research; in fact, she has been most beneficial to my own findings. Naturally I would like to have more children. It is not healthy for Charlie to be an only child, but she did not tolerate pregnancy well and fears that more children would put an end to her research." He looked up again. "I have been most tolerant until now, Mrs. Sullivan. But I think it is about time that I finally asserted my authority over her. I did point out that her role is now that of wife and mother and it is my right to have children."

I hesitated before asking, "Have you approached the New York police, Dr. Parker? Is it just possible, given the chaotic nature of the city at this moment, that foul play has occurred?"

I saw his expression change. "Foul play? You're hinting that something terrible might have befallen my wife?"

"I'm sorry, I should not have mentioned it. It has caused you distress," I said.

He was eyeing me intently now. "You're a strange one, Mrs. Sullivan. What is your true interest in this? Has Willa's family asked you to help them? Are you after money? What is your profession and how do you have time to go chasing over the city?"

I hesitated. I couldn't tell him the truth. "I'm a simple wife and mother myself," I said. "And I don't have time to go chasing all over the city, but I wanted to help. That's all." I stood up. "I should go. I have my own family to take care of, but I wish you well, and if you obtain any news of your wife, please do send a message to the ladies she intended to stay with."

I gave a little bow and squeezed past to exit the coffee shop. I confess my heart was beating rather fast. I wasn't sure what I had learned except that she had left her child at home with a neighbor. That indicated that she was not running away but planned to return. So where was she and what had she planned to do? All sorts of wild thoughts were rushing through my mind. She had kept the true nature of the friends she was going to visit from him. Was that because he was against women's suffrage? His tone had certainly indicated that. But what did she hope to achieve by being part of a float in a parade?

Another thought occurred to me. He wanted her to be a wife and mother. She didn't want more children. Was it possible that she found herself to be pregnant and had come to New York to find a way to end the pregnancy without his knowing? But then why not send the telegram home and let him think she was having fun with Vassar friends? The only thing I was now sure of was Dr. Parker had no idea where his wife was.

The sound of bells from Grace Church made me realize that I still had a little time before I had to go home. Time enough to visit Mrs. Goodwin. She and I had worked together on several cases in the past. Surely she could tell me what had made her attend that meeting. Luckily she lived not too far away on Fourteenth Street, so I headed rapidly in that direction, or as rapidly as the crowded streets would allow. I tapped on her door, waited, then tapped again. With a grunt of frustration I realized that the lady was not home. Of course, police detectives worked all hours, as I very well knew. I made for Patchin Place, feeling confused, annoyed, and inadequate. My friends thought I was a good detective, but I had essentially learned nothing so far. I had a horrible feeling that I was going to let them down.

For the rest of Sunday I was tied to the house with domestic duties. Aileen went off happily to her family and I was left with three children, all of whom seemed particularly cranky. Mary Kate, because I had been gone the whole day before, was clingy and whiny. Liam seemed to have too much energy and was rushing around the house like a whirlwind, knocking over the clotheshorses full of drying nappies and making the sort of noises that small boys make when playing. And Bridie was both bored and nervous. Blanche's family was having some kind of reception for the French ambassador, she said, and here she was, stuck in a kitchen with drying nappies. The world was not a fair place. I had to agree with that sentiment. But then she was back to worrying about her dress and whether it had been altered to fit her properly.

"Don't you have homework you should be finishing?" I asked, trying not to sound exasperated. "You said you had a Latin assignment."

"It's not due until we go back to school next week," she said. "I've plenty of time."

I retreated to the sofa in the parlor and tried to read, but I could not harness my racing thoughts. Nothing about Willa Parker's disappearance made sense. If she had run away with another man would she have willingly abandoned her child? I didn't get the feeling that she was too motherly a person so perhaps the answer to that was yes. And if she was planning to end a pregnancy she may not have told anybody, especially not her family. My thoughts went around in circles, but I was determined not to give up. I had taken this case as a paid detective, and I would not let it be a failure.

# ❊ Eleven ❊

On Monday morning I awoke with new energy and new resolve. This evening I was going to the opening reception at the opera house—not allowed to mingle with the dignitaries on the floor, being a mere female, but I would be allowed to watch from the gallery while Julia Ward Howe delivered the poem she had written for the occasion. With luck I would have a chance to meet with Willa's sister and father. Before that I might have time to do a little sleuthing.

My only task for the day, apart from the endless duties of domesticity, was to find something suitable to wear to the opera house. Of course I owned no formal gowns. But I did have neighbors across the street who seemed to have an endless supply of dresses for all occasions that they no longer wore. Gus, or rather Miss Augusta Walcott of the Boston Walcotts, had had an extensive wardrobe fit for high society before abandoning her position and becoming bohemian. These gowns still hung in a spare room wardrobe. Ordinarily I'd have no hesitation about going across the street and asking for a favor. Ordinarily Sid or Gus would have waved at the staircase and said, *Of course. Go up and help yourself.*

But at this moment a dragon lurked at number 10 Patchin Place. I had already heard what Cousin Prudence thought of me. But I needed that gown if I was to meet Willa's family and find out what they knew and why she was not staying with them.

I fed Mary Kate her bread and milk, then I glanced up at the clock on the wall. "What time do you have to go for your fitting, Bridie? You'll need to give yourself plenty of time to get there because everything's so crowded." If I accompanied Bridie to Blanche's house and left her there I might be able to call on Mrs. Belmont, or even find out where Mrs. Schilling was staying. I felt that they both had information that might be helpful to my case.

Bridie gave me a horrified look. "But you're coming with me, aren't you?"

"Do you need me there?"

"All the other mothers are coming." Her voice was close to a wail. "And what if the dress still doesn't fit? You'd be there to tell them and make it right. And then Blanche's mother is putting on a luncheon for us." She grabbed my hand in best dramatic fashion. "Please tell me you're going to come with me."

One look at that distressed face told me that I could not abandon my daughter. Family came first. I managed a smile. "Of course I'll come with you. Let's plan to leave by ten o'clock. And I'm just going across to have a word with the ladies," I said, hoping my voice sounded casual and normal.

Liam sprang up instantly. "Aunt Sid and Aunt Gus. I want to come too!" He was already rushing to the front door.

I grabbed the back of his jacket. "Not this time, my darling. The old dragon who is staying there won't appreciate seeing you."

Liam's eyes opened wide. "They have a dragon staying with them? Can it breathe fire?"

I laughed. "Probably. But it's not a real dragon. I meant they have a guest who doesn't like children. I think it's wise that we stay away until she's gone, but right now I have a question I must ask. You be good and I'll be right back."

"Bridie," I called, "look after Liam and make sure he doesn't try to follow me."

Then I closed the front door firmly behind me, hearing his protesting wails following me across the street. I gave a tentative rap at the front door but before I could knock again I heard my voice being called and Sid was coming up Patchin Place toward me, a basket over her arm. "I've just been to the baker and brought fresh pastries," she said. "You're welcome to join us."

"Oh, no thank you." I waited until she caught up with me. "I might be welcome with you and Gus but not with another inhabitant."

Sid grimaced. "Yes, she is rather awful, isn't she? She absolutely bullies poor Gus and now she's coming up with suitable young men for her to marry. Gus is letting down the family name, apparently."

"Poor Gus. I suppose you can't tell her the truth?"

"About Gus and me? She might die of a heart attack . . . which might not be such a terrible thing." Sid chuckled. "But no, although I'm sure she suspects, judging by the snide remarks."

"Thank heavens it's not for much longer," I said. "I'm glad I caught you on the street, because I was dreading coming in. I only wanted to ask a small favor. I'm going to attend the ceremonial opening banquet at the opera house tonight—"

"But it's only for men, isn't it?" Sid interrupted. "Fifteen hundred men and no women?"

"The floor seating is. But we women are allowed in the gallery to hear Julia Ward Howe read her poem."

"I didn't know you were a fan of poems or patriotism." Sid gave me a quizzical look.

"I'm not, but Willa Parker's family is going to be attending, so I'm going with Anne Johnson, and I hope to find out more pieces of the puzzle."

"Oh, good idea," Sid said.

"So . . . I wondered if I could borrow one of Gus's dresses again. Usually I'd come over and try them on, but I don't want to hear Cousin Prudence commenting that the immigrant woman always seems to be begging for charity."

Sid gave a sympathetic nod. "I do understand. Shall I bring over a few for you to try on? I know you wore that emerald-green one once, and you looked sensational in it."

"Oh yes. The emerald green would be fine, thank you. Could you please hand it to Aileen? I must take Bridie for her final fitting at Blanche's house. I was told all the mothers would be there and Blanche's mother was hosting a luncheon afterward. I couldn't let Bridie be the only one whose mother didn't attend."

"Of course not. But don't worry. I'll find a way to slip across with the dress. And tell Bridie we're looking forward to seeing her in the parade tomorrow."

"And we are looking forward to seeing you and Gus as goddesses."

"Not as much as we are," Sid replied with a wicked grin.

Having sorted out the dress problem without having to confront the dragon I went home and changed out of my shirtwaist and cotton work skirt into something more suitable to meet the mothers of Bridie's classmates. I was well aware that they had much more money than we did in the best of times . . . and this was not one of them. Thank the saints that Sid had given me the retainer so we'd be able to eat for another week and that I'd had a little set aside to spend on Bridie's shoes and stockings. We put these into a bag and took them with us when we set off to brave the crowds. The platform was packed but we managed to squeeze aboard the Ninth Avenue El and rode it up to Lincoln Square, then had a pleasant stroll across Central Park to Blanche's home on East Sixty-Eighth Street. The towering limestone was amid similar mansions in that rarefied part of the city. Here the sidewalks were not teeming with visitors, and a spirit of calm prevailed. Nannies pushed babies in buggies. Chauffeurs stood beside well-polished automobiles. Maids buffed door knockers and swept steps. As we approached Blanche's house we saw a line of automobiles that had drawn up, waiting to disgorge passengers. I saw Bridie shoot me a nervous look that we were the only ones arriving on foot.

"Just remember that you are Blanche's best friend and she'll be delighted to see you," I whispered as we approached the grand front door. And I was right. Blanche and her mother were in the front hall, greeting arrivals. Blanche looked up and gave a squeal, rushing to envelop Bridie in a big embrace as if they had been apart for weeks instead of a few days.

"I've got so much to tell you," she said. "I hope we can find a moment to slip away. That party with the French ambassador. My dear, you would not believe the gown his wife was wearing. And his daughter too. What wouldn't I give to go back to Paris."

Blanche's mother, Lucy, tapped her on the shoulder, reminding her they had more guests. "Hello, Molly, my dear," she said. "Please go through to the library. The dressmaker is there to put final touches."

We did as commanded. Bridie was sent behind a screen to try on her dress. She came out and it was a perfect fit. She looked so relieved I thought she was going to cry. All went smoothly for the other girls. They then put on shoes and arranged the garlands in their hair. Blanche's mother brought in a photographer and they had their picture taken before changing back to their street clothes. A gong sounded to announce that luncheon was being served. The mothers went to the dining room, where a buffet was arranged on the long central table.

"I thought we'd keep it simple," Lucy said, "since we're all so busy this week."

Personally, I didn't think that smoked salmon, ham, cold chicken, and various salads counted as simple, but I helped myself and found a place to sit. Bridie and the other girls had gone off on their own, presumably eating the sort of foods more to their liking.

"Lucy McCormick is so right about being busy this week," the woman next to me said. "Poor thing looks quite run-down. Is there one moment without an invitation or a parade to watch? My dear, I found it hard enough to find the time to come with Helen, but I had promised her. Now I just hope my dress has been delivered for tonight and it fits me."

"Oh, you'll be going to the opening reception, then?" the woman on her other side asked.

"Of course. My husband will be sitting among the men down below but I wouldn't miss such an historic event even if we are banished to the balcony."

Helen's mother turned to me. "Shall you be attending tonight, Mrs. Sullivan?"

"I shall," I replied. "Although like you I object to being reduced to a spectator and not a participant."

"Hear, hear," another woman chimed in. "They make it seem like men are the only ones who planned and executed this celebration. I'll grant that the parade of ships was a male occasion but I'd like to see men know how to decorate floats and sew costumes."

"My husband is attending the banquet on Thursday," the other woman said with a frown, "and it is to be all men. Dining together and congratulating each other. Who ever heard of such a thing!"

I looked around the room at the animated faces. It seemed that no matter what our social status we women were all in agreement when it came to being overlooked or taken for granted. So why was it such a hard thing to convince them that we needed the right to vote?

I appreciated Bridie's friendship with Blanche McCormick, and Lucy and I had become friends of a sort, but I was always aware of the difference in our backgrounds. Lucy had led a sheltered and privileged life, as had most of the women in this room. And, while I sometimes felt embarrassed by the quality of my clothes, I also felt proud of how far I had come. After all, I'd had the chance, if I had wanted it, to be a society wife when Daniel ran for sheriff, and I had hated every minute. I stayed on the edges of the conversation. These women all shared mutual associations and memberships that I didn't, though they were too polite to actively exclude me from their conversation.

Still, I was relieved when the gathering began to break up, and I looked about for Bridie. She and Blanche approached me arm in arm to ask if Bridie might stay the night after the parade. Lucy seconded the invitation so I assented. I rather agreed with Helen that Lucy looked run-down. Her eyes were overly bright and her face rather chalky.

"Are you sure it isn't too much for you?" I asked, laying a hand on her arm. "You look like you could use a rest."

"Just a bit of a cold, I think," she said in a low voice with a smile. "But I had everyone coming so I couldn't really call this off. I'll go to bed right after with a hot drink and skip any more ceremonies tonight." A sad look passed over her face. "Bill would have insisted we be right in the center of things."

Her husband, Bill McCormick, a high official with Tammany Hall, had been murdered just over two years ago. He had many sins to his account and I'm quite sure she was better off without him. But it is the prerogative of a wife to remember only the good. Lucy must have been thinking along the same lines because she smiled again.

"I'm actually quite glad to be out of all that. I'm much more of a homebody. Please let Bridie come to us tomorrow night. We girls have fun together."

"As long as you are feeling up to it," I said. "If you still feel ill, Bridie will come home with no complaining." I shot my daughter a look to reinforce this message. I wished I could return the invitation and have Blanche at our house, but with Aileen in the only spare room with the baby we were bursting at the seams. In Ireland it was common for girl friends to sleep together in the same bed, but Blanche, as a wealthy young lady, would not be used to that.

"Thank you, but I'm sure I will be quite well," Lucy said, immediately contradicting herself by turning away to sneeze, holding her lace-trimmed handkerchief up to her nose. I said my farewells and hurried out of the door. I had much too much to do to come down with a cold myself!

## Twelve

Daniel left in the late afternoon with apologies that he could not take me to the reception himself.

"I'm afraid I have to see to the security of the ambassador at the dinner before the reception as well."

"To which no women are invited," I put in.

"Now, Molly," he said, putting his hands up as if in self-defense. "I'm not in charge of the planning. I just have a job to do."

"As do I," I said. "Thank you for the ticket." I held it up and smiled at him.

He frowned. "I suppose you can't get into too much trouble at a reception with the height of New York society."

"Don't underestimate me," I said and laughed at the expression on his face.

I must admit I felt quite fine as I crossed the little lane to Sid and Gus's just as the sun was going down that night. The day had been clear but a breeze was blowing in heavy clouds that lit up orange and red with the sunset. My normally unruly hair was slicked up and back under a small emerald-green hat that matched the dress perfectly. Only the rather worn cloak I wore against the threat of rain spoiled the look. I was nervous that the dreaded Cousin Prudence would answer the door but Anne opened it with a smile. Though she also had evening silks on, she had chosen muted colors.

"Thank you for accompanying me," she said. "The other ladies have gone out. Augusta declared that she would go to the Hotel Astor and demand that they seat her among all the men."

"I think the banquet at the Astor is not until Thursday," I said. "The German ambassador and his party are dining at the Ritz, according to Daniel."

"Well, then she will get her wish," Anne said. "Won't she be surprised when they let her in."

"Her Cousin Prudence will probably think it was due to her being a Boston Walcott," I said, rather disloyally. We looked at each other and then giggled.

It was not easy to obtain a cab. All the taximeters driving by were full. We almost gave up and walked to the nearest El, but the beginning of a light drizzle put that idea to rest, and luckily a hansom cab pulled up just as I was beginning to despair. We climbed in and were well underway before the skies opened and the streets turned shiny and slick. The electric lights of the celebration had been installed on most buildings on our route. It was a novel experience to be ferried through the streets of a city that was illuminated like a carnival. The rain added to the strangeness as wavering golden lights were reflected from the mirrorlike surface of the wet road.

"I hope this lets up before tomorrow," Anne said. "Won't it be terrible if the parade is rained out?"

"Surely they would have it anyway after so much expense," I said. "But perhaps much of the crowd would stay home."

As we neared the opera house the cab joined a line of automobiles, cabs, and taxis dropping off elegantly dressed patrons. It was a long queue so I had time to inspect my surroundings. An awning jutted out over the pavement, and liveried men ran out with umbrellas so that none of New York's finest were soaked as they entered the building. Despite the rain, quite a crowd had gathered to watch New York's elite enter the proceedings. They were held back behind ropes on either side of the entryway, and a cordon of police and naval men stood between the crowd and the guests. I took my ticket out of my purse and held it nervously. It was clear I would not be admitted without it.

"You know, this whole opera house is here thanks to Mrs. Belmont," Anne said conversationally as we waited to reach the front.

"Mrs. Belmont who ran the meeting on Friday?" I asked, surprised.

"Yes, Elena was telling me. Apparently when she was still Mrs. Vanderbilt the old money wouldn't let her have a box at the old opera house and she funded a new one just so she could have her own box!"

"I find it hard to imagine that much wealth," I said. "No wonder she has the influence to get a float into the parade."

"Yes, she got Vanderbilt money in the divorce and then Mr. Belmont left her his money when he died." Anne's small face became animated as she delivered this gossip.

"I'm surprised that she is a suffragist," I said, "having made her money from her marriages."

"I'm not," Anne said. "I heard she was the force behind those powerful men. Maybe she finally wants to be recognized in her own right. I was a bit surprised that you were at that meeting, Mrs. Sullivan. Elena and Augusta have never mentioned you as a suffragist."

"Well, I have marched as a suffragist," I said with a wry smile, "and even been arrested for it long ago."

"Arrested?" Anne asked. "And you're a policeman's wife? What were you arrested for?"

"For disturbing the peace by marching in a parade," I said. "And I was not yet married to Captain Sullivan." I thought back to that time. "But he did get me out of jail."

"It's always helpful to have a police captain around to do that," she said, displaying a sense of humor I would not have predicted. I decided to take her into my confidence.

"You are right that I was at the float meeting for another reason. I'm a private investigator and Sid and Gus have hired me to find your friend Mrs. Parker." Anne looked at me with such admiration that I immediately felt uncomfortable. It felt strange after so many years to have the words *I'm a private investigator* come out of my mouth. I had been hired on a case, even though my best friends had done the hiring. But until I actually found Mrs. Parker I felt like a fraud describing myself as such.

"Elena and Augusta mentioned that you have solved cases before. Even that they have helped you solve some," she said. "Is that why you are here tonight?"

"Yes," I admitted. "I want to find out more about Willa. It seems so strange that the family have not contacted the police. Perhaps they know where she is."

"And you will be able to find this out by questioning them?" Her voice was full of curiosity.

"I hope to," I said. "It will help immensely if they see me as a social acquaintance rather than an investigator. Do you know her sister, Miss Hartman, well?"

"I used to," she said, closing her eyes as if remembering a long-ago time. "She was very gay and bright in those days. And I, as you may have noticed, am very shy. She adopted me, so to speak, and took me out into society with her." She opened her eyes, and they had mischief in them. "It was quite restful because I didn't need to say a word."

"She is talkative?"

"I don't think she has ever had an unexpressed thought," Anne said with a laugh and then looked guilty. "But she was very sweet and kind to me; please don't think I am insulting her."

"I hope to be able to ask her about her sister," I said. "So it will be very helpful if I can be in a position to talk to her."

"You leave that to me," she said, patting my lap with her gloved hand. "We working women have to support each other!"

Our cab had reached the front of the line and I handed the fare to the driver as we alighted. Mercifully a man with an umbrella stepped out to usher us under the awning. Our tickets were scrutinized by a man at the door before we were admitted to the steamy warmth of the foyer. Once inside we queued again to deposit our wet cloaks with a girl who was handling the coat check. She gave a look of distain to mine as she hung it beside a mink-collared velvet cloak. I personally thought mine had held up a bit better against the rain. There was quite a crowd behind me, and as I turned to walk back into the grand foyer I bumped against a woman who was removing her fox fur cape.

"Excuse me," I said, and then saw that it was a woman I had just been discussing.

"Mrs. Belmont," I said with a nod, keeping my face calm so as not to show how pleased I was. She was just the person I had wanted to meet.

"How lovely to see you." She was the soul of politeness but I could tell she was trying to place me among her circle of acquaintance.

"Molly Sullivan," I offered. "We met at the float committee."

"Of course," she said. "I didn't realize you would be attending tonight." It was clear that meant she hadn't thought I was of the social status to be invited to the event.

"Oh yes, the German ambassador and his wife were nice enough to invite me," I said, wracking my brain to try to remember the ambassador's name. It came to me.

"The Count and Countess Bernstorff are staying with some friends of mine." This was stretching the truth, but I hoped that Anne's introduction would make them friends momentarily. "Mr. Hartman and his daughter Winnie. They are the family of Willa Parker."

"Willa Parker?" Her eyebrows raised in surprise. "She is the Hartmans' daughter? You move in high circles." She studied me appraisingly. "Weren't you asking about her on Friday?"

"Yes, she has gone missing and her friends are trying to find her," I said, throwing caution to the wind. "I wondered if she might have applied to you for help, if perhaps she did not want to return to her husband and wanted a place to stay safely."

"I have never met Mrs. Parker," she said, her voice now cold and distant. "But I hope you find her. How nice to have seen you." It was clearly a dismissal and she turned away.

"Mrs. Belmont." I stopped her with a light touch on her arm and she looked affronted to be stopped in that manner. "There was a child at your house on Friday. Mrs. Parker may be traveling with a child." I left the unspoken question hanging in the air.

"The child was brought by one of the women who came from Philadelphia, I believe," Mrs. Belmont said. "I asked one of my maids to watch the boy while we had the meeting. But as I said, I have never had the pleasure of meeting Mrs. Parker. Have a good evening." She walked away from me with frosty determination.

*The child was also from Philadelphia.* This seemed like too much of a coincidence but I struggled to put the pieces together. Of course, Mrs. Schilling was from Philadelphia. The most logical explanation was that the child was hers. But she hadn't mentioned having a child.

"Shall we?" Anne had deposited her coat and was motioning for us to move out of the foyer.

"Have you seen Willa's sister yet?" I had to lean close to her to be heard in the din.

She shook her head. "I can't see anyone in this crowd, but I imagine we will meet them in the box." I followed her through the throng, peeking through the open door to the floor of the opera house. The stalls were hung with lights in various shades of green, the ivy and cedar of the celebration. Rows of shields from the various guilds had clusters of orange, blue, and white lights. It was a sea of men in black, their faces glowing strange colors in the lights. The ladies were streaming up the staircase to the higher levels, and Anne and I followed. We found our box, a carpeted and velvet-lined space with four chairs and a table with refreshments. Two elegantly dressed women rose as we entered.

"Anne!" the younger one said, coming over to kiss Anne on both cheeks.

"Winnie." Anne's voice was warm but reserved. "Thank you so much for inviting us to your box."

"It was my pleasure," she said. "I'm so sorry we couldn't have you to stay. It is the least we can do. May I present the Countess von Bernstorff?"

"It's my fault you were displaced," the countess said, holding out her hand. Her speech had no trace of a German accent. She had light hair that was stylishly curled, the slight plumpness of middle age, and an ample bosom, well shown off by her gown. "We are staying with your friend. My apologies."

"Not at all," Anne said, shaking her hand. "I am staying with other college friends and am perfectly comfortable. May I present my friend Mrs. Sullivan?"

"Mrs. Daniel Sullivan?" The older woman turned to me.

"Yes," I answered.

"Your husband has been taking such good care of us, seeing to our security."

"And your husband was kind enough to get us tickets." I shook her hand. "Your English is very good."

"It should be, since I grew up here!" she said with a grin. "New York born and bred. But, of course, now that I have married a German man I've lost my American citizenship in the eyes of the law." Her face was serious for a moment and then brightened. "I can still prefer a New York pretzel to a German one though." I smiled at the thought of this elegant woman eating any pretzel at all. "I'm so glad you could join us tonight," she went on.

"Thank you for the invitation," I said. "I believe our husbands are down below in the crowd."

"Yes, we are much more comfortable up here," she said, adjusting her skirt. "No room for our silks down there."

Anne and Winnie took two seats and began to catch up on mutual acquaintances.

"I understand your husband is quite new to his position," the countess said.

"Yes—or rather, the position is new," I said with a little laugh. "The Bureau of Investigation has just been created. Until recently, he was a captain in the police."

"You must have worried about him terribly," she said. "I know that I worry about Johann when he travels to foreign parts. Last year he was almost caught in the middle of an uprising."

"Well, I hope you won't find any uprisings here," I said. "I believe the populace to be quite peaceful. So you grew up in New York?" I asked.

"Yes." She nodded. "Yes, Mr. Hartman is one of my old friends, and I don't have many of those left. I convinced Johann it would be more comfortable to stay with the Hartmans than at the embassy, where everything is so horribly formal and Germanic. I no longer have any family in the city." She fell silent as we smiled at each other awkwardly, unsure of where to take the conversation next. She looked around the huge hall and gave a little wave to a woman across the way.

"Excuse me, I see an acquaintance," she said.

"I do as well," Anne said, rising and motioning to me. "Here, take my seat, Molly." She gave me a little wink as she left the box. I took the seat beside Winnie Hartman, feeling grateful for Anne's help. There was murmured conversation throughout the house, so it was a perfect time to talk. I sat and turned to Miss Hartman, who was studying the crowd below. She was dressed as well as Mrs. Belmont herself, in the latest Paris fashions. Her hair was a flaxen blond, teased into ringlets that spilled around her tiny velvet hat. It had not occurred to me until tonight that Willa came from a very wealthy family indeed. I needed to get some answers from Miss Hartman. It was now even more puzzling that Willa would disappear without contacting her family.

"Do you see your father?" I asked, wanting to begin a conversation.

"Yes, there he is, speaking with Mr. Morgan," she said, pointing. "He is one of his senior bankers." She smiled proudly.

"Anne mentioned that to me," I said. "She said she visited your family when you and your sister were at Vassar with her."

"Yes she did. Do you also know my sister?" Winnie said politely.

"No, I've never met her," I confessed. "But she was meant to stay with two friends of mine, your fellow Vassar alumnae, and of course they feel very worried that she never showed up."

"It's very selfish of her not to let them know where she is," Winnie said. Her calm demeanor surprised me.

"They thought she might be staying with you," I ventured.

"I didn't know she was planning to come into the city at all until her husband called," Winnie said. "There is a little estrangement between my sister and my father."

"I must confess, I am surprised you aren't more worried about your sister," I said, watching her face. "Her husband is scouring the city for her."

She pursed her lips. "If this were the first time, I would be worried, Mrs. Sullivan," she said, "but Willa and her husband seem to have a spat every year." I waited without replying, willing her to go on. "She turns up at our door every time but she won't say a word about why she leaves him," she continued.

"She comes home?" I asked, noticing that Winnie claimed the house for herself, almost as if her sister was an outsider.

"Yes, and brings little Charlie—that's her son—as well. Last year she stayed a month entire. But then Dr. Parker showed up and they went home together. I think she just likes the drama. I'm afraid my mother spoiled her."

"But she didn't come home this time?" I made it a question.

"As I said, that's probably because of my father," she said. "Last year he told her to give up her research and take care of her husband and son. He told her that if she wouldn't do that then she wasn't welcome in his house and her income would be cut off. The university pay is not generous and they would struggle without the extra help."

"And was he serious, do you think?" I thought of my own father, telling my brothers they weren't welcome in the house anymore when they came home drunk and belligerent. With him, that edict lasted only a matter of days. They would come sheepishly back after they had sobered up and he would let them back in with nothing more said.

"Oh, he was serious," she said, nodding. "My father is very soft-spoken, but once he has made up his mind, he has a will of iron. The only one who could get around him was my mother. He even let her call us Willa and Winnie." She laughed. "She told me a third sister would have been called Willow, but she may have been teasing." Winnie's face grew suddenly sad. "Mother was the reason my father allowed Willa and me to study, but now she is gone he says he won't encourage my sister anymore in her foolishness." She flushed slightly. "Please don't think me an awful sister, Mrs. Sullivan. Of course I would be upset if I thought any harm had come to Willa. But she grew up in the city and has many friends here from childhood, and other scientist types who think of nothing but test tubes, as she does. She is probably safely with one of them. Being in the middle of a marital spat is unpleasant."

"I understand," I said with what I hoped was a sympathetic smile. I wanted to keep Miss Hartman talking. "What did you study, Miss Hartman?"

She blushed. "I was not a stellar student, Mrs. Sullivan. I think I would have been happier at a finishing school. But my studies were useful for running a household. My mother died in my final year at Vassar and I took over the running of our house."

Before I could express my condolences, the lights dimmed and raised again. I had never before been to the Metropolitan Opera. People of my social standing did not visit the opera. I took the opportunity to look around curiously. The curtains were open and on the stage, men, some in suits and others in military uniforms, took their seats, shaking hands and even bowing to one another. They were quite dwarfed by a representation of the *Half Moon* on one side of the stage meeting one of the *Clermont* on the other. A celebration banner with the red, white, and blue of the United States hung in the middle.

"Look, there is the count." Miss Hartman pointed out a man onstage, resplendent in a military uniform. "He's very charming in person. It has been an honor to host the count and countess this past week." She sighed dramatically. "I have been extremely busy, but it has been worth it. It can be quite dull hosting New York bankers, but the count seems to know the most interesting people from all over the world." Miss Hartman's wide blue eyes were studying me. With her small features, golden hair, and blue eyes, she was quite a beauty. I wondered why she chose to keep house for her father. With her wealth and beauty, surely she would have had many opportunities to marry. Then I mentally chided myself. Perhaps she valued her independence, as so many of my friends did. She had the running of a wealthy household. Maybe she didn't want to give that up.

"That must be Julia Ward Howe." I pointed to a tiny ancient

woman being helped onto the stage, where a low easy chair was waiting for her. "What a shame she is the only woman on the whole stage. Mrs. Belmont was saying it is a scandal when I was at her house on Friday."

"*The* Mrs. Belmont? Who was formerly Mrs. Vanderbilt?" Winnie asked, suddenly animated.

"Yes," I said simply, not adding the reason for my visit. Let her wonder if my social status was sufficiently grand to be invited to Mrs. Belmont's on my own merit. "I met a Mrs. Schilling from Philadelphia there," I said. "She is a friend of your sister's, I believe."

"Yes, a most good-hearted woman," she said. "I haven't met her, but Willa has mentioned her in her correspondence. Reading between the lines I surmise that Willa takes advantage of her. Ever since Papa stopped sending her money for a nanny, she quite abuses Mrs. Schilling, using her nursery as her own so she can run into the lab and check her precious viruses."

"So they have children who are a similar age?" I said. "I think I may have seen Mrs. Schilling's son the other day."

"Oh no, my dear, that's quite impossible," she said, a shocked look on her face. "Mrs. Schilling's son died two years ago when he was just three years old."

I put my hand to my mouth involuntarily. "How sad! The poor woman."

"Yes, it's abominably rude of Willa to foist her son off on the poor woman, but she said it gives her friend something to do . . . Oh, look." She turned her attention to the front as a men's choir entered and took their places on stage. "I think we are about to begin."

The orchestra began to play "Hail, Columbia," and the audience rose to their feet, adding their voices to those of the choir. Not only the choir was turned toward the boxes but all eyes in the audience seemed to be turned in our direction. I felt distinctly uncomfortable until I realized that they were looking at someone or something right below our box. The velvet curtain at the back of the box swung aside and Anne and the countess entered just as the anthem began.

"It's Vice President Sherman," Anne said in my ear. "He's in the box right below ours."

"The vice president! Of the United States?" I said. "Jesus, Mary, and Joseph!" I took another look around the opera house. The men singing, hand on heart, on the stage and in the seats below me were the richest in New York. They had put on a celebration so grand that even the vice president of the United States had come to take part. Not to mention a Japanese prince and a German count. How wealthy was Willa's father? I wondered. Wealthy enough to have a house on Fifth Avenue. Could his wealth have something to do with his daughter's disappearance?

## ❧ Thirteen ❧

After the anthem finished and the choir members took their seats, a distinguished-looking gentleman gave a grand bow to the vice president and came to the podium. The audience fell silent to hear him.

I must say I was rather amazed that his voice could carry through such a large theater when he gave no sign of shouting. He introduced Mayor McClellan of New York, who asked the Bishop of New York to lead us in prayer. I studied the men on the stage with curiosity. Some, like the mayor, were dressed in well-tailored evening suits. The others wore the military uniforms of their countries, gleaming medals and gold brocade shining in the stage lights. *You've come a long way, Molly*, I said to myself. Who would ever have thought I would be with the members of the four hundred families at the Metropolitan Opera House?

I reminded myself to stay focused. I was here on a case. Of course, the speeches beginning meant I could no longer question Winnie Hartman, but overall I was rather pleased with what I had learned. I knew why the family was not worried about Willa and I rather suspected that Sid and Gus were correct that she did not want to be found. As I thought back on my conversation with

Dr. Parker, I had a guess about her child as well. Dr. Parker had said a neighbor was watching his child. Was it possible that the neighbor was Mrs. Schilling and she had brought his son into the city without his knowledge? The picture I was getting of this married couple, so driven by their research that they neglected their child and alienated their family, was not pleasant. A thought nagged at me. What about my children? Was I doing the same thing right now? I pushed the thought aside.

At first I marveled at how many of the world's leaders were in this room. After all, the men on the stage were wealthy committee members, brigadier generals, European counts, Central American señores, even a prince from Japan. But after a while I confess my attention wandered as man after man stood to give self-congratulatory speeches, describing New York as the center, not just of industry and shipping, but of culture. I couldn't help thinking back to my days living in a tenement. The sight of the workers, dirty from long days of work and skinny from never having enough food, came into my mind. *Who really built this city?* I wanted to ask. *Not you, with hands that look like you've never done a day's work.* I'm afraid I've always been a bit of a rabble-rouser.

My attention was claimed once again when the tiny ancient woman in the easy chair rose and came to the podium.

"Ladies and gentlemen," Mayor McClellan intoned, "may I present Mrs. Julia Ward Howe to read a poem that she has written for the occasion." The audience rose in applause and refused to sit down again but became silent as she laid a piece of paper on the podium and began to speak her poem in a surprisingly firm and carrying voice. Her words, spoken into the intense silence, exhorted the assembly to a brotherhood of man. It seemed to echo the very thoughts that I had just had. For progress to be good, it must be progress for all. At least that was how I heard it.

"So shall all life one promise fill," she ended. "For Freedom,

Justice, and Good Will." There was a moment of silence and then the audience, already standing, erupted in applause and cheers that could not be quieted until the men's chorus rose and struck up an impromptu a cappella version of the Civil War song whose lyrics had made Mrs. Howe famous worldwide.

"Glory, glory, hallelujah," sang every voice in the hall as we reached the chorus, "His truth is marching on."

I looked over at Anne. Her eyes were shining with emotion. It was not a man, but a woman who had given voice to last century's fight for justice. Who knew what we were capable of in this century!

The last two speakers were quite a contrast with one another, although they both seemed to have attired themselves with a desire to see how many medals could fit onto a single man's chest. Sir Edward Seymour, the British representative, brought the greetings of the British king in smooth, posh tones. He was a tall, slim, elderly man with a mustache and beard. The rounded hat that marked him the admiral of the British navy added half a foot to his height, creating an amusing contrast with the next speaker. Prince Kuni, much younger with a smooth, handsome face, wore no hat and was not as tall as me. I guessed by his position as the last speaker that he was the most important man on the stage, a prince of a royal household. He did not look impressed with the proceedings himself but handed a one-sentence statement from the emperor of Japan to Mayor McClellan to read, glowered while it was read, and fairly stomped back to his place. His look seemed to me to say, *This city is a backwater compared to the imperial palace.* But who knows—it was possible he was thinking nothing of the kind. Perhaps the dinner had not agreed with him. The mayor kept his composure and could not refrain from making a few more remarks himself before finally thanking the assembly for coming. The crowd rose to give itself a standing ovation as the men on the stage shook hands and bowed to one another, the curtain then coming down.

"Thank you so much for inviting me," Anne said to Winnie as soon as the applause died away. "That was extremely diverting."

"More boring speeches," the countess said languidly. "My dear, if you knew how many speeches like that I have to listen to."

"How lovely for you," Winnie said wistfully. "I wish I attended so many glittering functions that I was bored of them."

"No you don't." The countess laughed. "Believe me. I would rather have spent a quiet evening in your charming home with your very hospitable father."

"Do I hear my name taken in vain?" The curtain pulled back and a gentleman entered the box with a smile.

"Father." Winnie looked up and smiled back. He gave a slight bow to all of us, lifting his top hat as he did. "Mrs. Sullivan, may I present my father. And Miss Anne Johnson. I believe you may have met before."

"Mr. Hartman, thank you so much for including me in the invitation," Anne said as we rose to face him. He gave another bow.

"I've come to help you down to the carriage," he said to Winnie. "Countess, your husband is waiting downstairs. I believe you have another engagement tonight."

"No rest for the wicked," she said with a sigh. "You see why I am envious of you, Miss Hartman, and your ability to seek your bed at a reasonable hour."

"And I you," Winnie returned. "Actually, I should like to be whisked off to a ball."

"Not a ball, I assure you." The countess laughed again. "Just drinks with politicians." She rose. "I mustn't keep my husband waiting." She held out her soft hand so that Anne and I could shake it in turn and swept out of the box.

"Shall we?" Mr. Hartman offered his arm to Winnie and she stood and took hold of a walking stick I had not observed in the corner of the box until that moment. I also noticed that one foot wore an elegant satin slipper but one had on a large, ugly boot that seemed to have irons going up her leg. She leaned on the stick heavily as she gave her arm to her father and, thus supported, walked out of the box. Anne and I followed. Winnie had to take the stairs slowly, stepping down with one leg and dragging the other after. Her remark about going dancing took on a new significance to me. Of course she would envy the countess, who could go to dances. And did she perhaps envy her sister, who had married and left home while she stayed and took care of their father?

The rain had stopped but the streets were still slick and shiny as we exited the opera house, still following the Hartmans. The crowd behind the barricade was much reduced but some people were still there, waiting to catch a glimpse of a dignitary as they exited. When Miss Hartman had been safely helped into a carriage, Anne and I joined a queue waiting for cabs for hire.

"I had quite forgotten that she was lame." Anne turned to me. "She has such a bubbly personality that one forgets."

"Was it a childhood injury?" I asked.

"Infantile paralysis," Anne answered. "She caught it right after we left Vassar. She was very ill and when she recovered she was left with a paralyzed leg."

I felt, rather than saw, someone's eyes on me and turned toward the crowd. A man in a brown fedora looked away quickly and turned back to the conversation he was having with the policeman guarding the barricade. They must have been quite friendly, because the policeman laughed. I could have sworn I had seen that man before. The figure looked so familiar, but of course it was dark and the reflections of the lights on the wet streets gave everything a strange glow. Then he threw back his head and laughed and I realized where I had seen him. Mr. Jones. I had met him coming out of Dr. Parker's house. This was the Pinkerton man who was on the trail of Willa Parker, just as I was.

I climbed into the hansom cab with a swell of satisfaction. The Pinkerton man had waited out in the cold to catch a glimpse of the Hartmans as they left. Perhaps he wanted to see if Willa would turn up at this gala beside her father. I, on the other hand, had attended the event, even sat with the family. As I had reflected many times, there were places where a woman could gain entry when a man was left outside. Score one for the Molly Murphy Detective Agency! Molly Sullivan, now, I corrected myself, but it occurred to me that the former was a good business name. Daniel would never want the name Sullivan associated with a female detective. If I did decide to open my own agency, I might just go back to being detective Molly Murphy.

I gave my hand to Anne as she stepped up into the cab and turned to close the door. A gloved hand grabbed the door from behind.

"Wait a minute," a deep voice said. "You're not getting away that fast, Molly Sullivan."

I froze for a moment, and then laughed as Daniel's head appeared inside the cab. "Jesus, Mary, and Joseph, you scared me, Daniel Sullivan!" I scolded. "And my traveling companion."

Daniel jumped in. "Sorry to scare you, Miss . . ."

"Miss Anne Johnson," I said by way of introduction. "She is a friend of Miss Walcott and Miss Goldfarb. Meet my husband, Mr. Daniel Sullivan."

"Pleased to meet you, Mr. Sullivan," Anne said softly, shrinking back into her seat.

"Aren't you joining the count for drinks?" I asked.

"No." He shook his head. "I rather suspect that he wants me out of the way for this round of diplomatic meetings. I saw you leaving and thought I would join you. Did you ladies enjoy the proceedings?"

"Very much so." Anne's voice had gained some confidence.

"It was very enlightening," I said. "I met Mrs. Parker's sister and father."

"Oh." Daniel stared out of the window distractedly. "Is she a friend of yours, Miss Johnson?"

"She is the woman that I have been hired to find," I said coldly. "Which, if you remember, is why I asked you for the ticket." I knew that Daniel had been preoccupied these days, but I did not expect him to treat my investigation as a forgettable triviality.

"Oh yes." Daniel gave me his attention, now focusing. I could see he was trying to process how Anne might be involved in my investigation. "And Miss Johnson knows . . ." Daniel began.

"Oh, I know she is a detective," Anne said with an excited smile. "And that she has been hired to find a missing woman."

"Has her family called the police?" Daniel asked.

"No, that's what's strange," I said. "They are unconcerned and say she and her husband frequently have marital spats."

"Do you think her husband has done something to hurt her?" Daniel said gently. "I don't like to mention it in front of your friend, but as a policeman I saw too many women who were hurt or even murdered by their husbands."

"I don't think so," I said and held my hand up to stop the interruption I saw coming, "And not because I am naive and don't think a husband could do it, but because her husband has hired Pinkerton men to find her."

"He might have done that to cast suspicion away from himself," Daniel offered.

"Yes, but wouldn't that just draw more suspicion?" I asked. "As far as anyone knows, Mrs. Parker came to New York and disappeared. What could be easier than waiting until after the celebration and saying that his wife had never returned?"

"Unless she never left," Anne said. "We have only his word for that." We sat in silence, contemplating that possibility.

"If that is true, then I have no chance of helping her," I said. "I choose to believe that she is alive." Several pieces of information came together in one instant and I had a rush of inspiration. "In fact, I have just had an idea of the next place to look."

"You have? How wonderful!" Anne said, her shy face quite animated. "What is your idea?"

"I've just thought of a place that she may be," I said. Both Anne and Daniel looked at me curiously. "And I will investigate tomorrow."

"Nowhere dangerous, I hope, Molly." Daniel's brow darkened.

"Not at all," I said. "And just for that I shall not tell you anything more until I have been there and seen for myself."

"Been where?" Daniel asked, his voice rising slightly, both with strain and to be heard over the noise of the horse's hooves as we turned onto a noisier surface.

"You'll see." I smiled. So Daniel was interested in my investigation again. Good.

## ❧ Fourteen ❧

As late as I had been up the night before, I still had to rise early on Tuesday morning. Even after my late arrival from the reception I had lain awake going over the next step in my investigation. I knew where I should look next, but today I would have no time to do so. Bridie was due at her school early. From there the girls would eat, dress, and be driven uptown to the start of the parade route. She was a bundle of nerves, alternately giddy with excitement and terrified.

"All those people, Mama," she said. "Just think. They say two million people will be watching the parade."

"You'll be perfect," I said, giving her a kiss as I left her outside the school. "Papa will be watching from the Court of Honor and Liam and I will be closer to home."

She bounced rather than walked into her school and I hurried home in time to make breakfast for Daniel.

"Are you sure you don't want to watch from the grandstand?" he asked as he rose from the table. "The German ambassador's wife seemed impressed by you. I'm sure I could get you a seat with his party."

"No thank you," I said, brushing a few stray crumbs from his suit.

"I've been invited to watch with Sid and Gus. They said they have a good viewing spot closer to home."

"Well, keep yourself safe today, Molly." He looked down at me fondly. "The city is full of all sorts of ragamuffins."

"And you think I can't handle a ragamuffin?" I pretended to push him away. "Look who's talking. You are the one putting yourself between the vice president and a bullet."

"Don't joke about that." He was suddenly serious. "It's not an easy place to secure, and it is too easy for anyone to get a gun these days." He stopped as he saw the worry on my face. "But we're not expecting any trouble." He gave me a quick kiss and was gone. *Really*, I thought. *Telling me not to get into trouble when he is the one in the line of fire.* But I knew that my irritation was just covering up a sense of worry. Was Daniel walking into danger?

"I'm afraid we're a rather big party," I said apologetically several hours later to Sid and Gus as we stood in the little court between our houses with Aileen, Liam, and Mary Kate. "I need to bring Aileen to watch the baby. Her father is marching with Tammany, so she won't want to miss the parade." Aileen bobbed a curtsy. She still found the ladies rather grand and had trouble finding her tongue around them.

It didn't help that Sid and Gus were dressed as outlandishly as always, Sid with ballooning blue harem pants and a white silk shirtwaist with bishop's sleeves and a long blue silk scarf, and Gus with flowing divided skirts in the same color. Gus believed in the rational dress movement, and her dress did look easy to move in.

"Of course we have room for our goddaughter and little Liam," Sid said, opening her arms to receive a hug from the little man. I cringed inwardly, hoping he would not leave sticky stains on her pants, and breathed a sigh of relief when the costume seemed no worse for wear. I wondered how their beautiful outfits would fare in the crowd.

"In fact, the best news of all is that we have more room than we thought," Gus said with a wide smile. "Anne is sitting with the Hartmans in the Court of Honor stands, and"—her voice took on a tone of relief—"my dear cousin has been invited by a friend with an apartment overlooking the route to join her."

"So we would not be too squashed," Sid said, the relief on her face matching Gus's, "we had prepared a suitable viewing place for a Boston Walcott, but now we will be able to share it with our Molly."

The torrential rain the night before had left the streets wet. The street was slick under my Oxfords and the awnings jutting out from businesses still dripped water with each wind gust. But, although it was cloudy and a stiff breeze made us shiver, it did not look like it would rain again.

"Thank goodness it's not raining," Gus echoed my thoughts as she stepped around a puddle. "I don't know what we will do if it is raining this Saturday. All our costumes are white organza."

"We should be drowned rats," Sid agreed. "And rather too revealing, I fear." She gave me a knowing grin. "Molly, how did your investigation go last night?" She took my arm to steady herself as we crossed a small rivulet of water coming down from a storm drain and out into the street.

"Her family is not worried," I said, "they think she has disappeared on purpose."

"I understand not telling your family your whereabouts," Sid said, "but why not inform your friends?"

"I have an idea that one friend might know something," I confessed. "Mrs. Schilling is very close to Mrs. Parker. I hope to find where she is staying and ask her more. And there is one other place I think I can look."

"Where?" Sid turned to me with excitement. I was prevented

from answering by being swallowed up into a noisy throng of people, all heading toward the parade and Fifth Avenue. I took the baby carriage with Mary Kate in it, put Liam in front of me with his little hands on the carriage as well, and pushed a route through the throng, glancing back every few seconds to make sure Bridie and Aileen were safely there.

"This is unbearable," Sid said with a groan as we had to stop again in the general crush. "We can't get up Fifth Avenue itself before they close it. The place is a madhouse."

Gus was looking around desperately. "There is no way we can use a taximeter or a hansom cab in this crush, and look at the long lines for the El. We'll just have to walk, but it's a good way. Our viewing place is near Twentieth Street."

"That's an awfully long way for Liam," Sid said. "Should we not see if we can find a cab over on Seventh or Eighth Avenue?"

"He can do it," I said. "I can sit him on the pram if necessary."

And so we set off up Sixth Avenue, battling the crowds coming across our path, all heading straight for Fifth Avenue and the parade route. Cheerful families with excited children carried rugs and baskets. Vendors were also headed toward the parade, stopping to sell postcards or other souvenirs. I noticed people staring at the way Sid and Gus were dressed.

"I expect they are going to be in the parade, dear," I heard one mother say. "They are dressed in costume."

Sid glanced at Gus and smiled.

When we finally reached Twentieth Street, we turned right and headed for the parade route on Fifth Avenue. I wondered where we would find a place in this crowd. The road was not closed yet. Cabs, taximeters, motorcars, and carriages were still trying to get through, although the crowd, now encroaching into the street, was making it difficult.

"Move out of the way," one man called, standing up on the driver's side of his car and gesturing desperately at the stream of pedestrians crossing Twentieth. "I'm trying to get home before this God Almighty parade begins." His admonitions were in vain and he only was able to make the turn by inching the machine forward and forcing the stream of people to go around it, almost hitting several of them in the process.

We reached Fifth Avenue, where crowds were already lining the route.

"Up here, I believe," Sid said, steering us left and halfway up the block. Families had already laid out rugs or pieces of canvas on the pavement to sit on as they watched the parade. People from all walks of life were perched on pillows, milk crates, or even chairs, waiting for the parade to begin. There was little room behind them on the sidewalk. We were pushed against the buildings as we squeezed past the crowd. When Sid finally stopped, I almost bumped into the back of her.

"Here we are!" she called cheerfully. I had to laugh in amazement. It looked like someone had transported a living room onto the pavement of Fifth Avenue. A Turkish rug was laid out with high-backed wooden chairs, a large picnic basket, a small circular wooden table, and even a standing lamp.

Two harried-looking young men were keeping the crowd at bay with some difficulty.

"Wonderful," Gus said, taking some coins out of her purse and walking up to the nearest young man while Sid took a seat on one of the chairs and motioned for Liam to join her. "I'm Miss Walcott," she said, holding out the coins. "Thank you so much." He took the coins and touched his cap.

"Thanks, lady," he said. "The boss said to wait until you got here but it hasn't been easy."

"Well done," Gus said, giving him a warm smile. "Can you and your men come back and pick it up when the parade has passed?" She put another coin in his hand.

"Yes, ma'am, we'll be here." He nodded to her and walked off into the throng. Sid was arranging the items of furniture to keep the crowd at bay.

"What on earth?" I finally got my tongue, stepping onto the rug as Sid motioned to me impatiently.

"Come on, Molly, we have to keep the space."

"A lamp?" was all I could say.

"Well, that is just to be funny and create the right impression," Gus said with a grin as she, Sid, and I took chairs while Aileen seated herself with the baby on a thick blanket and Liam tried to peek into the lid of the large wicker basket. "But as for the rest, what do you think?"

"It's a wonderful idea, but how did you do it?" I asked.

"There is a darling secondhand furniture store just around the corner," Sid said. "We rented the furniture for the afternoon and paid them to set it up here. The shop owner said it was a brilliant idea, and he is going to advertise it for the parade on Saturday."

"I wanted to show Cousin Prudence that we could watch the parade in a most civilized manner," Gus said. "But since she decided not to join us"—she opened the hamper, and Liam's eyes widened—"we will have more for ourselves." She pulled two bottles of cola and a bottle opener out of the hamper.

I rather thought that Cousin Prudence might not have approved of a bohemian living room on the pavement of Fifth Avenue but decided not to say so.

"And then our favorite grocer said he would make us the hamper and have it delivered here," Sid said, opening the bottle Gus handed her and taking a long swig. My friends really did lead charmed lives.

For quite a while nothing happened. Street sweepers came to clean up after the horses as wagons and carriages full of people hurried to get to their destination before the street was closed. After about half an hour, policemen shut the street to traffic, putting up barricades to turn away vehicles. The street took on a festive atmosphere.

The avenue was festooned with red, white, and blue bunting and American flags. Vendors walked up and down selling bottled drinks, cotton candy, and ices. An aura of great expectancy came over the crowd. Then distant cheering could be heard. Mothers grabbed their children out of the road and a hush descended. Some pushcarts snuck through the barricades to take advantage of the crowd and were chased away by patrolmen who then moved the remaining bystanders back from the street.

"They're coming," someone shouted from the crowd. The information spread and the crowd rose to its feet as one, straining to see up the avenue. The sound of a marching band in the distance was coming closer.

"It's just an old guy," a little boy's voice said as an automobile came into view. The crowd around him laughed.

"Hush, that's the mayor," his mother scolded him, and the crowd laughed even harder. It was indeed the mayor. I had spent enough time watching him at the reception to recognize him sitting serenely in the car and waving to the crowd. The mayor's car was immediately followed by the first float. It was massive, with a banner reading THE HISTORY OF NEW YORK. The Statue of Liberty was featured prominently along with a canoe, a steamboat, a wigwam, and a skyscraper.

Behind the float the West Point band marched in crisp uniforms with smart gray-blue jackets and white pants. The music was so loud as they passed us I had to cover the baby's ears, but Liam jumped up and down excitedly, not at all disturbed.

"Shall we eat?" Sid pulled some sandwiches out of the wicker basket and she and Gus began to hand the food around. I was amazed as always by my friends, who seemed to enjoy life at every moment. I caught those around us in the crowd giving some envious looks as we sat with real china cups sipping coffee as the floats passed. Envious though they might be, no one dared to step onto the rug, so we sat in complete luxury.

"Look, it's Indians!" Aileen exclaimed in wonder as the floats came by depicting the first peoples who lived in New York. "Don't they look fancy with their headdresses. Like crowns!"

"I read in *The New York Times* that those are people from the Iroquois tribe," Gus said knowledgeably.

"Well, you couldn't have the history of New York without them, if you think about it," Sid mused. "We are rather late arrivals."

The history of New York paraded by us over the next two hours, albeit a little out of order. There must have been a mix-up when lining the floats up, because although the Indian floats came first as the original New Yorkers, the Civil War veterans somehow marched before Betsy Ross sewing the first American flag. This caused jeers and exclamations from the crowd.

"Haven't studied their history" was one laughing remark. But on the whole the people around us seemed impressed. Some of the floats were so wide they filled the street from side to side. I was worried they would run over anyone leaning out into the street. One had a mountain forty feet tall, strong enough that men walked up and down on it.

We had been watching for about an hour when Liam called, "Look, there's Bridie!"

"Doesn't she look darling," Sid said fondly as the Future Women of New York float came into view.

"What on earth is she doing?" Gus thundered loudly enough for Bridie to look over. The schoolgirls did indeed look darling in their matching white dresses. Some were embroidering, some cooking, one teaching with a slate in hand. One held a baby doll and several were on a higher platform dancing a quadrille.

"I think she's sewing a shirt," I said. "I bet she is glad she didn't have to dance for the whole parade." Bridie held up the shirt and waved it in our direction.

"Sewing," Gus said disdainfully. "As if. That girl is meant for better things." But she smiled and waved at Bridie nonetheless.

"I've worked in a shirt factory," I said with a grin, "and I can tell you we weren't dressed like that."

"The Future Women of New York float should have labor leaders and suffragists on it," Gus said. "Women engineers and scientists, mayors and bishops."

"Yes, but there aren't any women mayors or bishops," Aileen said, her tone somewhat scandalized.

"It would be aspirational," Gus said, waving away this objection, "looking to the future."

"A woman bishop?" Aileen stifled a giggle. "People would throw eggs."

"Will we see your father soon, do you think?" I asked, mostly to change the subject.

"Maybe?" She stood on her tiptoes, looking as far up the street as she could.

"Will he be on a float?"

"Him, a float?" She giggled again. "No, they are marching, army style. And the big Tammany boss is riding along in an automobile."

I wondered who the big boss at Tammany was now. I had stopped paying attention to that part of politics after Daniel had, thankfully, given up his bid for New York sheriff on the Tammany ticket. He had chosen law enforcement over politics definitively after that. It seemed like this new Bureau of Investigation, though it had seemed shaky at the beginning, was really going to be a new form of law enforcement, and Daniel was at the forefront. That made me proud, but also worried. Would that put a target on his back? Would our whole family be at risk?

I brought my thoughts back to the parade. There was a succession of different societies, each accompanying a float, passing one at a time, in uniforms and costumes from their countries of origin. A tassel-hatted Turkish delegation passed and there was a gap in the parade. I looked across the street—and into the eyes of Mr. Jones, the Pinkerton man.

## ❦ Fifteen ❦

The Pinkerton man saw me looking at him and gave a scornful smile, taking a Brownie out of a bag slung over his shoulder and snapping a picture of our party.

"You're wasting your time," I called across the street, although I was not sure he could hear me. "We don't know where she is."

"What's going on?" Sid asked curiously.

"That man is Mr. Jones," I said. "He's a Pinkerton man, hired by Dr. Parker to find his wife."

"And he still thinks we are hiding her?" Sid sniffed. "The cheek! Which man is it?" She peered at the crowd across the street, but a Scottish delegation, complete with bagpipes and men in kilts, had marched into our line of view. The last rank struck up a reel on their bagpipes and for a few minutes any conversation was impossible. When the Scottish party had passed, Mr. Jones was gone.

"How do you know Mr. Jones?" Sid asked, but before I could answer Aileen started jumping up and down and waving.

"Daddy, Daddy! Over here." The Tammany delegation was attracting a lot of attention because they were not only marching with a band but were throwing pennies into the crowd.

VOTE TAMMANY! a big banner proclaimed. The crowd cheered

them on like local heroes and screamed with delight at every shower of pennies that came their way.

The only thing that marred the procession was a mix-up again in the order of floats, so that Tammany was escorting the Discovery of America Dutch float.

"Quite right," quipped one man from behind us, "more Irishmen have discovered America than Dutch have." This comment led to a general laugh. Throughout the parade, though the children were delighted, the adults complained that the Statue of Liberty's torch was crooked, that the floats were too garish, and the men and women on them badly costumed. I was glad that Bridie had passed before these comments started.

I never was able to see which man in the sea of shiny top hats was Aileen's father, but she was so excited and happy that I didn't have the heart to say so.

A stiff cold breeze blew up before the last floats came by. I tired of the spectacle and wished for my own warm parlor. The crowd began to thin out; no doubt many people were having the same thought. Finally the last floats came past. The young men from the furniture store showed up to carry off our campsite, and the employee from the food store retrieved our hamper. The police had opened the streets to wheeled vehicles, but the crush of pedestrians was just too great and cars, cabs, and wagons alike could move no faster than the throng of men, women, and children crowded into the streets.

"Thank goodness we don't have to carry the basket home," Sid said as we were squeezed together between a woman with a child in each arm and her husband pushing another. I carried Mary Kate myself while a now overtired Liam sat in the buggy that Aileen pushed. It was almost evening and, although it was far from sunset, the deepening shadow of the buildings were growing cold and dark.

By the time we reached our neck of the woods with the Washington Square Arch before us, the electric lights had been turned on. Manhattan was once again a fairy village.

I thought with satisfaction of Bridie, enjoying herself with Blanche. What a lovely childhood she was now having, after so many early difficulties and deprivations. Lucy must be feeling better or I was sure that Bridie would have heeded my warning and come home. She might be thoughtless sometimes, but she was always kind.

If I had only had myself to take care of, I would have made a cup of tea and fallen into bed. I had the children to think of though, so I used the stock from our Sunday roast to make a thick beef stew. We were all glad for it with the cold September damp beginning to creep in. The children were already asleep by the time my poor tired Daniel came through the door. I let him eat and tell me about his day.

"So no anarchists tried to murder the vice president, then?" I said lightly as he finished his story.

"Don't even joke about that," he said. "This parade route is a nightmare. To tell you the truth, if someone wants to do something evil, I don't see how we can stop them. We don't have enough men to police the whole city."

"It's good that most people are law-abiding, then, isn't it?" I mused. "We just had a parade with two million people watching and you say there were no major incidents. Perhaps mankind is finally civilized."

"Humph." Daniel reserved judgment on that pronouncement as he tucked in to his second bowl of stew.

"Molly, how is your investigation coming?" he asked as he used a piece of bread to mop up the last of the gravy. "Have you found the missing woman?"

I looked up, surprised. "Are you interested?"

"Yes, you made a good case last night," he said. "If you still believe she may be in danger I could ask some of my police contacts."

"Thank you." I smiled. It was unlike Daniel to take an interest in my cases. Last April I had solved a murder and given him the credit. It was the publicity from that case that helped him get the high position he had now. Perhaps he would not be as resistant to my opening a detective agency as I had assumed. "I'll be investigating a lead tomorrow," I said, following that statement immediately with, "in a very safe and public place." Daniel worried every time I investigated.

"And where is this safe and public place?" he asked with a raised eyebrow.

I hesitated. In truth I had not completely determined my next step. I wanted more time to put together the information swimming around in my brain. But Daniel was looking at me expectantly, so I launched ahead. "Rockefeller Institute."

"What's that?" he asked with genuine curiosity.

"It's a research institute. I learned from the husband that he and his missing wife worked with a Dr. Flexner at the University of Pennsylvania and then from the woman's sister that Dr. Flexner now runs an institute studying viruses here in the city."

"And you think she left her husband to go and visit a male friend alone?" His look was dubious.

"Oh, Daniel, you're so old-fashioned. It's 1909, women can visit a man without it ruining their reputation." He took a breath and I could tell he was going to dispute this statement, so I went on quickly. "Besides, Dr. Flexner must be much older than her if he was their professor when they were college students. Who knows—he is most probably married or bald."

"Which of those would be more off-putting, do you think?" Daniel said dryly, making me choke on my cup of tea.

"Daniel! Go on with ya, you're terrible." I laughed. "I have a theory about this woman's character. It seems to me that she is very focused on her research. I got the feeling from her sister that she cares more for her science than her husband or perhaps even her child."

"God help the human race if more women follow her lead," Daniel said. I ignored him.

"So I thought the best place to ask for her might be with someone in her line of research."

"That's well thought out, my love." Daniel smiled.

"Don't sound so surprised," I said, pushing back from the table and beginning to clear the dishes.

"I'm not surprised." Daniel's serious tone made me stop and look at him. "And I want to ask you for a favor."

"A favor?"

"I know that you are focused on finding your friends' missing woman, but once you have found her, or if you reach a dead end, I would like you to do some sleuthing for me."

"The suffragists?" I asked. "You mentioned this before."

"Yes, but I have heard more since we last spoke. I tried to gather more information myself but I've reached a dead end."

"Because you have no women on your squad." My words were challenging but Daniel just nodded.

"Exactly. I need a woman to learn what is going on." His blue eyes looked at me piercingly. "Are you sure you don't know more than you are saying?"

"I don't," I said. "All I know is that a group of very respectable women are preparing a float for the carnival parade."

"Yes, well, I've heard that Maud Malone is involved," he said. "She is a radical supporter of women's suffrage."

"As am I," I said. "What's wrong with that?" I resumed my clearing of the table, rather more noisily than was necessary.

"Nothing." He held up both hands. "But consider my position, Molly. I can't have an incident when I'm in charge of security."

I relented. It wasn't often that Daniel asked for help, especially with an investigation.

"I'll try to find out what is going on," I said, "but I'm not going to betray my friends."

"Molly—" Daniel began, but I cut him off.

"No, Daniel," I said. "I couldn't find better friends than Sid and Gus. If there is something dangerous going on I will get them out of it and warn you. But if what they are doing is merely inconvenient or a spectacle, I won't betray them."

"I suppose that is fair enough," Daniel said, rising from the table. "And, in return for your help, I may be able to help you."

"Really?" I questioned. "How?"

"Now that the money has started to flow from the federal coffers, the head of the district office"—he grinned and pointed to himself theatrically—"that's me," he continued, "has been granted the use of an automobile for official business."

"Wonderful!" It was lovely to see my husband proud and happy about his job. Also, I reasoned, if the department had money to buy cars, Daniel would not be having more weeks with no pay. We were back on solid ground and I could breathe a sigh of relief.

"I need to go uptown tomorrow afternoon," he went on, "so if your Rockefeller Institute is in that area I will drop you off. Where is it?"

"I'm not sure," I confessed. "But I will find out by the time you come to pick me up."

*I hope it is in the city*, I thought as I cleaned and dried our soup bowls. I didn't think I had ever passed the Rockefeller Institute. I was assuming that if Willa had come here to meet the Flexners they would be close by. But did I really know anything more about Dr. Flexner than that he was at this institute? What if it was miles away, or the wrong direction over in Brooklyn? Daniel wouldn't be able to take me then. I put the final dish away in the cupboard and closed the door with a satisfying thump. That was a problem for tomorrow.

## Sixteen

I was surprised to see Bridie early the next morning, practically running in the front door. "Forgot my schoolbooks," she said on her way upstairs. Her footsteps clattered on the stairs, clomped across the ceiling, and then clattered down. This house was small enough that I could always tell where everyone was by the creaks and rattles.

"You have a minute," I said as she came into the kitchen. "Sit down and have a cup of tea and tell me about the parade."

"It was wonderful!" she enthused and went into a long description of the whole parade route, the applause, and what people yelled along the way, laughing at some of the rude remarks and exulting in the cheers they had received. "It was the best day of my life!"

"And did you have a nice time with Blanche?" I asked.

"Yes," she said, just as enthusiastically. "You'll be so proud of me, Mama. Blanche was feeling poorly after that long day on the float in the open air, so I did just what you do for me. I brought her hot drinks and wiped her head with a cloth and read her a story. And I promised to take our teacher this note from her so Mrs. McCormick doesn't have to go out. She's not quite well yet either."

"Well done," I said, smiling at my little nursemaid, but inside I groaned. Blanche must have caught her mother's cold. I would much rather Bridie had come home than spend the night. I determined to make some chicken soup that night to ward off sickness from the whole family.

"Does your school office have a directory?" I asked her as she put books and the note from Blanche into her schoolbag. "I need to find an address."

"You mean a telephone directory?" she asked. "I'm sure they do."

"I may walk you to school, then," I said. "I need to look up an address."

"Why don't you just call information?" she said.

"Call what?"

"Call information. Blanche and I do it all the time at her house. You just pick up the telephone and ask for information."

"Really?" I must confess that I regarded the telephone as something to be used only in dire emergencies. Now that the police department was no longer paying for ours, I had considered saving the fifty cents a month by canceling the service, but I couldn't bring myself to do it in case Daniel needed to reach me urgently.

"Mama, you're so old-fashioned," Bridie said with an indulgent smile. "I'll do it. What address do you need?"

"The Rockefeller Institute," I said.

Bridie picked up the receiver. "Please get me information," she said into the contraption. "May I have the address and number for the Rockefeller Institute?" She listened and wrote as the person on the other end spoke. "Thank you." She hung up the receiver and handed me the piece of paper. I had to admit I was impressed. It was amazing, the modern world we were living in. "I've been meaning to ask you, Mama," Bridie went on, a note of entreaty slipping into her voice. "Could I give out my exchange number to some of my friends? Blanche calls her friends to see if they're free and arranges outings and such."

This was so unexpected I wasn't sure what to say, so I fell back on, "Let me talk it over with your father." This seemed to satisfy her and she went happily off to school.

I was glad to have the morning to put my house back in shape. I had not had much time to clean with the whirlwind of parades and my investigation. If I began to make money from a detective agency, I mused, perhaps I would hire a woman to come in and do the harder cleaning. *Getting ideas above your station*, my mother's voice rang in my head. Being a mother myself had softened my idea of my own mother. Raising children took the patience of a saint, and neither my mother nor I had been known to be saintly!

I was all ready to go and waiting when a car horn sounded in the court. I grabbed my things and was taken aback by the view of Daniel in a brand-new shiny black Model T.

"Holy Mother of God," I said as I came down the front steps. "From rags to riches!"

Daniel looked hurt. "I have never kept my family in rags, Molly. Don't shout that to the whole street."

I climbed in. "Yes, well, we're living the life of Riley now," I said by way of apology.

He grinned. "Being the agent in charge does have some perks. Now . . . where are we going?" I told him and he reversed down the court and out onto Tenth Street and into the slow flow of traffic around Jefferson Market. It seemed to me that every one of the two million extra people in the city was on the street all at once. At every intersection we had to stop as herds of pedestrians crossed the roads. We crept up Sixth Avenue all the way to Central Park. The flow of humanity finally eased as we turned east. As we neared the East

River, the buildings thinned out. The Rockefeller Institute sat alone, an imposing white building surrounded by lawns.

"Shall I come in with you?" Daniel looked up at the building doubtfully. "It looks a bit like a fortress."

"What official reason would you give?" I asked. "If Dr. Flexner thought there had been foul play he would have reported it to the police." I gave Daniel a quick peck on the cheek and climbed out of the car. "Sometimes an unofficial investigation is best. Besides, you have work to do."

"Very true, I'm afraid." He pulled out his pocket watch and glanced at it. "I have to go"—he hesitated one last time—"unless you need me."

"Get on with you," I said with a farewell wave. "I'll take the El back. It will be faster." He waved back and drove off toward the city. I looked up at the building and took a deep breath. How was I going to get in? The front entrance up marble steps looked imposing, but I saw a few men in white coats entering, so, taking a deep breath, I crossed the drive and mounted the steps.

The door was heavy but not locked. It opened onto a foyer that led into a deep hallway. I could hear voices from various rooms but no one was in the hallway to either challenge or help me. I walked down the hall toward the voices and into a library. Three men, sitting around a table beside the stacks, looked up and one of them rose.

"Can I help you, miss?" he said. The other two men gave each other scandalized looks. I gathered that women were not often seen in such a modern scientific building.

"I'm looking for Dr. Flexner," I said with a confidence that I didn't feel. I gave no other word of explanation. I have found, in these situations, that explanations only make one look weak or uncertain. The men looked at one another again.

"His lab is upstairs," one of them said finally.

"Thank you," I said and strode back out into the corridor.

"Now, wait a second." The first man who had spoken was out in the hall in a flash. "You can't just wander around the building. It's a research facility, you know."

"Of course I know," I bluffed, remembering what Dr. Parker had told me. "I'm looking for Dr. Flexner, who is studying viruses. They are tiny entities that cause disease."

He looked at me with a bit more respect. I decided to reel him in.

"Isn't one called infantile paralysis?" I asked, letting doubt come into my voice.

He smiled down at me. "We call that virus 'poliomyelitis' now." I could tell I had him. Never underestimate the desire of a man to explain something to a woman. "And Dr. Flexner is a great researcher. Let me take you to his lab." Somehow my mention of viruses had proven to him that I was to be admitted to this hallowed ground. He walked me up the stairs to the third floor and down a warren of corridors, explaining all the way what a virus was and how one studied them.

"Well, mercy me," I interjected when he paused for breath. We passed several men coming in and out of labs or offices and they all stopped and gave a second look before going about their business.

"So you have to be careful," the man finally concluded as we came to a halt in front of the lab. "Many of our labs are working with live viruses, and you wouldn't want to take any sickness home to your little ones, would you?"

"Well, no indeed." I smiled at him. "You look familiar," I lied. "I think I may have seen you at a social function with my friend Mrs. Parker. Aren't you a friend of Dr. and Mrs. Parker?"

"Why, no." He shook his head. "I'm afraid you must have mistaken me. I don't know the Parkers. But here is Dr. Flexner's lab." We entered a space that looked like something out of *Frankenstein*. There were long tables with test tubes and large glass balls. A single man in a white coat was heating something over a burner. I almost walked up to him to introduce myself, assuming this must be Dr. Flexner, but luckily, before I did, the man who had escorted me said, "Is Dr. Flexner not in today, then? This lady is looking for him."

"No." The man looked as startled as everyone else in the building to see a woman in the lab. "He is taking this week off to take his family to the celebration."

"Lucky him." The man who had escorted me laughed. "It's nice to be the director."

"Could you please give me his home address, then?" I asked. The man in the white coat frowned.

"I can't give out that information," he said. "Why do you need to see Dr. Flexner?" My time for prevaricating was at an end. I couldn't think of another useful lie.

"I'm looking for a Mrs. Willa Parker," I said. "And I wondered if he might know where she is. She is missing."

"Willa Parker." The man thought a moment. "Did she used to be Willa Hartman? I knew her at Penn. So she must have married George Parker, then. He was here the other day, asking for Dr. Flexner just like you. What do you mean by *missing*?"

"She came to the city for the celebration and has not been seen by her family or friends."

"And you think Dr. Flexner is in the habit of kidnapping married women?" He smirked in a way that made me dislike him very much.

"No, of course not," I said. "But Dr. Parker mentioned that Dr. Flexner was their mentor, so I thought she might have been in contact with him." As I said this, it appeared unlikely to me that she would have come here. I imagined she would have known that every man stopped to stare whenever they saw a woman if it had been the same at the university.

"I'm afraid I can't help you, miss," the man said with an air of finality, "and I really must get back to work, so if you don't mind . . ."

"It's missus," I said, never one to let anyone get the last word. But I had not won this battle. Neither man would give me Dr. Flexner's address, and as I walked back down the marble steps I faced a depressingly long journey back home with nothing gained.

I stopped for a moment on the steps to take in the view. There were no other buildings around and I could see all the way down to the East River. Then, sighing, I started my walk back to Sixty-Sixth Street and civilization. It was a good quarter of a mile until I reached the first houses of the city. These small but neat row houses seemed the perfect place to find an academic. If only I had Dr. Flexner's address. I was sure I must be close. Perhaps I could use Bridie's trick of calling information, but there was no guarantee he would be on the telephone exchange, and if I went all the way home this trip would be for nothing.

I was just crossing the street when a movement caught my eye. I looked back in time to see a brown derby hat before the man who was wearing it ducked into a storefront. Mr. Jones was following me! My heart began to race. How could he have followed me here? After all, I came in a car. As far as I knew, he did not have one. I had not seen a vehicle of any sort following us. Another thought occurred to me. If he had not followed me, he must be following the same lead. Perhaps he was looking for Dr. Flexner as well. I wondered if, as a man, he had had any better luck getting the address out of the men at the Institute.

I walked on as if I had not seen him, but at the first opportunity I turned right. Then, before he had a chance to reach the intersection, I ran across the street, between two houses, and into the alley behind. It was not respectable for a woman of my age to be sprinting and ducking between houses, but there was no one in the street to see it. At first I was glad of that, but as I walked farther down the alley it made me uneasy. Had I lost him? Or was he following me down an alley with no one else around?

I kept going until the alley spilled out onto a street once more. Just as I was about to emerge, a woman walked by. It took me a moment to react, but then I realized: I knew that woman. With my head full of thoughts about Dr. Flexner and Mr. Jones, it took me a moment to place her. Then it came to me. This woman was Harriet Schilling, Willa Parker's best friend.

I ran the few steps between us and touched her on the arm, startling her greatly. She practically jumped out of her skin as she turned in my direction, arms up as if to ward off a blow. Then she froze. She obviously recognized me as well.

"Mrs. Schilling," I said, the words tumbling out in a hurry, "I suspect you are helping to hide Mrs. Parker."

"Of course not—" she began, but I spoke over her in a forceful whisper.

"You should know that Dr. Parker has hired a Pinkerton man who may be following you and he is going to come out of that alley any second."

She turned white. "Oh my" came out as a squeak.

"You are hiding her, aren't you." I made it a statement rather than a question.

Harriet looked up and down the street, obviously flustered. Her attitude told me I was correct. Surely, if she had no knowledge of Willa Parker's whereabouts, she would just calmly continue to tell me I was mistaken.

"If the Pinkerton man sees you, he will follow you to Mrs. Parker," I said. "Is she close? If you know where Mrs. Parker is, we had better get there immediately and warn her."

Harriet nodded and then came to a decision.

"Follow me," she said, quickly striding up the street. She opened the front gate that was only two houses away from us. Willa was so close, and I would never have known it but for this chance encounter! I followed quickly, glancing back every few seconds, expecting to see Mr. Jones emerge from the alley. But we reached the house before he appeared. Harriet knocked loudly and a woman opened the door a few inches. I couldn't see her face.

"Harriet, who's with you?" I heard the woman say.

"A friend, I believe," she said. "Let me in and I'll explain." The door opened and I stepped into a neat, bright living room. The woman standing before me looked very much like her sister.

I held out my hand. "You must be Willa Parker."

## Seventeen

"Shoo Shoo!" A little boy barreled toward us and wrapped his arms around Harriet's skirt. "You're back."

"Yes, my dear." She bent down to give his little head a kiss, then looked up at me. "He calls me Shoo Shoo because he couldn't say Schilling. We've been friends for many years, haven't we, Charlie?"

"Nice to meet you, Charlie," I said. "This is Mrs. Parker's son?" I made it a question and Mrs. Schilling nodded. Here was the mysterious boy I had seen at Mrs. Belmont's house. He gave me one shy glance and hid behind Harriet's skirt. How strange that he should cling to her when his mother was in front of me. I studied Mrs. Parker. Like her sister, her hair was flaxen and her features small. But the resemblance ended there. Her hair was pulled back into a severe bun. Willa's eyes were more gray than blue and hidden behind spectacles. She wore a simple blue skirt and white shirtwaist with worn cuffs, a complete contrast to her sister.

"And you are?" I couldn't tell from her tone if she was anxious or angry.

"I am a friend of Miss Walcott and Miss Goldfarb," I said, seeing her face relax immediately when she heard their names. "You were due to stay at their house and they have been anxious about you."

"Oh, yes, I'm terribly sorry about that," she said. "But I worried that if I let them know where I was, my husband would badger them until they told him."

"But why didn't you just stay with your family?" I asked. "Surely you could have shared a room with your sister if necessary."

She stopped and stared at me. "I'm afraid you have the advantage of me, Miss . . ."

"Mrs. Molly Sullivan," I supplied.

"You seem to know all about my business, and I have no idea who you are." Her voice rose in pitch. "Have you been sent by my husband to find me?" She turned to Harriet. "Harriet, why did you bring her here?"

"I didn't." The room we were in had warm oak floors, a sofa, and two wingback chairs in front of a fireplace. Harriet seated herself on the sofa with the little boy on her lap. She motioned for me to take one of the chairs. "She found me outside and told me you were being tracked by a Pinkerton man."

"It's true," I said calmly. "Your husband hired a detective to look for you. Miss Walcott and Miss Goldfarb hired me to find you first. And, as you see"—I allowed myself a smile—"I did!"

"But why on earth would they do that?" She looked bewildered. "I have never met them."

It was a good point. "My friends feel a great deal of solidarity with their Vassar sisters. And their friend Anne Johnson knows you and was worried as well."

"Oh yes, I remember Anne. She was my sister's age," Willa said.

"They are great champions of women's causes, you have to understand," I went on. "They asked me to find you to ask if you were in any danger or if you needed help to prevent your husband finding you."

"And you are some sort of female Pinkerton?" A note of amusement crept into her voice.

"I am a detective, yes," I said, my temper rising. "And if you are perfectly safe and in no need of assistance then I can go home and report to them that my job is finished." I rose. "And I can point that Pinkerton man in your direction as well so that his job will also be finished."

"Oh, please don't." The note of entreaty stopped me. Willa stood opposite me, twisting her hands. "I do need help. That is, I'm trying to decide what to do and Mrs. Flexner is helping me."

"Do I hear my name taken in vain?" A woman walked into the room wiping her hands on a cloth. She stopped when she saw me. She was a woman, perhaps in her midthirties, with a pleasant face, attired in a simple dress of dark blue.

For a moment nobody spoke. Then Willa said, "Mrs. Flexner, this woman has come looking for me. She is a detective of sorts."

"I've come from her friends, not to harm her," I said quickly to dispel any fears Mrs. Flexner might have. I didn't want to be thrown out of the house by its owner. "They were worried when she didn't show up for her planned visit."

"That was wrong of you, my dear," Mrs. Flexner chided. "You should have let your friends know."

"I started a letter to them dozens of times, but I kept tearing it up. I was afraid that if they knew what I was doing George would badger it out of them," Willa said, appealing to Mrs. Flexner, "and you know I can't face him just yet. Not until Dr. Flexner has had time to consider my position."

"Mrs. Parker was just explaining why she disappeared," I said.

"I'm more interested in how you came to find her," Mrs. Flexner said, looking at me curiously, "if no one knew where she was."

"I heard about the lab from Dr. Parker," I said, noting the way Willa jumped when I mentioned her husband. "That was enough to get me to the general area. Then I spotted Mrs. Schilling." I turned to Harriet. "I had suspected that you had something to do with her disappearance and that it was her son I had seen at Mrs. Belmont's house."

"How on earth did you put all that together?" Harriet said.

"Good Lord," Willa exclaimed. The look of scorn had been replaced with a grudging respect.

"Why did you disappear, Mrs. Parker?" I asked.

"Don't say *disappear*. It is not as dramatic as all that." Mrs. Flexner laughed. "She is not a magician. She has just been staying with us for a few days."

"Why not let your husband know where you are, then?" I asked.

"This is most uncomfortable, standing here interrogating one another," Mrs. Flexner said. "Let's sit. I'll get some cookies and we can chat. I only have a few more minutes before my darling son wakes up and I'll be no more use to anyone."

"Thank you." I smiled at her. "That is so kind."

"I'm a big supporter of women in professions," she said, looking at me keenly. "I would love to hear more about a woman detective." I looked at Mrs. Parker. I wanted to hear her story first. Mrs. Flexner took my meaning and motioned to one of the chairs. "Sit and listen to Mrs. Parker. Perhaps you can help her. I'll get the cookies." She bustled out of the room.

I turned to Willa and she paused for a moment, considering where to start, and then said, "Dr. Flexner is a mentor of mine. He is the director of a new research facility that has been founded here," she began. I didn't interrupt to tell her I already knew this.

"He has the most up-to-date scientific equipment to study poliomyelitis." She paused. "That is my area of research. It is a virus, a small—"

"Yes, I know what a virus is. I've spoken to your husband," I interrupted quickly. These academics seemed to think of nothing but their studies!

"Well, my husband and I are close to a breakthrough," she said. "If I can just find a microscope powerful enough to see the virus I know we will be able to find a cure. But now George, my husband, has decided to accept a research grant from the federal government to study yellow fever, and of course, the lab and all the equipment are his."

"And you don't want to study yellow fever?" I asked.

"Not when I'm so close." Her look turned fierce. "I don't mind having his name on the papers, Mrs. Sullivan. I don't mind that everyone calls it his lab and thinks I just type up the papers. But I will not have him take away my research. It is my whole life!"

"That and Charlie, of course," Mrs. Schilling put in. "That's why I came to help."

"Yes, of course." Willa smiled at the boy warmly, although, I thought, without the passion with which she had spoken of her work. "I tried to convince my husband to continue the polio work, but he refused. I told him that I would be looking for a position in a different lab, then. I suggested that we live apart, just until I make a breakthrough. But he said that if I left his lab he would divorce me and take Charlie away."

"But I understood from your sister that your husband wanted you to stay home as a wife and mother?" I asked, a little confused. "He wants you in the lab?"

"To tell you the truth, it is my research that had led to our discoveries," Willa said. "Without it he would not have had a single paper published. But the university won't give a lab to a woman, or even officially employ a married woman. And since this little one came along"—she held out her arms for her son and he came over to stand beside her—"I have had to take care of him as well as my research."

"Your sister mentioned that your father had cut off his support and you could no longer afford a nanny," I said with some sympathy. After all, I could not be here investigating unless Aileen was home with Mary Kate and Liam.

"Did she?" Willa's lip twisted in scorn. "I suppose she was happy to discuss our family business with a complete stranger, when she knows full well that all of my research is for her."

"It is?" Harriet put in. "I've never heard this."

"And for you too, my dear." Willa looked at her friend with sympathy. "Although I don't like to upset you by speaking of your loss."

"I like to speak my Jesse's name," Harriet said quietly. "Especially with those who knew him. Do you remember your friend Jesse?" she asked Charlie. He nodded.

"You used to love to play with him." A tear trickled down Harriet's face. Mrs. Flexner came back in and set down a china plate with cookies on it.

"Are you remembering your little angel?" she asked when she saw Harriet's face. "Your boys were friends, weren't they?"

"The boys didn't want to be apart for a single day, I remember," Willa said. "And Harriet has been such a good friend to me, Mrs. Flexner. Why, I remember a day when samples came in and I was working around the clock while the virus was still live."

"You researchers!" Mrs. Flexner exclaimed. "My husband is quite the same way. I have to force him to eat sometimes or call the lab and get an assistant to make him come home to rest."

"You looked quite ill that day," Harriet put in.

"Yes, I had worked so hard," Willa said, "and then my nanny deserted me and I couldn't stop so I took Charlie into the lab with me." She looked down at her son. "You were such a little monkey—you got into everything. I had to end up tying you to a table by one leg. By the end of that week, I was so stiff and sore from running around after you."

"I remember," Charlie said with a smile. "You gave me a lollipop." He spoke very well for a boy of five. "And then I threw up."

"Too much sugar, I suppose," said his mother. "Then for some reason you developed an aversion to the lab and absolutely refused to get out of bed to go. I was at my wit's end. But then dear Shoo Shoo offered to let you play with Jesse so I could focus. Do you remember, Harriet?"

"Of course," Harriet said, her eyes now filling with tears again. "That was the last week before he fell ill."

"That was that week?" Willa's eyes opened wide. "My memory is terrible for dates like that. I didn't realize."

"Yes, he ran a fever and his limbs got all stiff, and he stopped breathing," Harriet said and then fell silent.

"I'm so sorry," I said, my heart twisting as I pictured watching one of my children go through the same thing.

"It was infantile paralysis," Willa said, "the polio virus. It was everywhere that summer, as it was the summer my sister had it. Poor little Jesse died and my sister never recovered the use of her leg after her illness. So we are deadly enemies, the polio virus and I. And I will not be deterred from wiping it off the face of the earth."

"I blame myself," Harriet said. "I can't think of what mistake I made. Of course I didn't let him swim in dirty water; he was just three. But perhaps it was the park, or when we stayed with my parents. Or the ham I fed him. It might have been off."

"Don't blame yourself." Mrs. Flexner put a hand on Harriet's shoulder. Just then we heard a noise outside. Harriet and Willa tensed. The door rattled. Then someone pounded on it.

## ❧ Eighteen ❧

"Don't answer it," Willa said.

"Why on earth not?" Mrs. Flexner looked at her in surprise. "My husband has probably forgotten his key."

"A Pinkerton man is looking for Mrs. Parker," I said. "He is trying to find her for her husband."

"Helen?" a voice came through the door. "Are you in? I've forgotten my key."

Mrs. Flexner opened the door. "Oh, Simon," she said as she let in the master of the house, "you would forget your head if it wasn't attached."

"Too true, so I'm glad it is," he said, giving her a peck on the cheek and then looking around in surprise. "Do we have another guest, Mrs. Parker?"

Dr. Flexner, at first glance, did not look like I imagined the typical scientist. He was slim, clean shaven, and quite elegant looking, hair receding but parted neatly in the middle. I took him to be about forty years or more.

"I should be going," I said, feeling awkward with all eyes on me. "I shall tell my friends you are safe, and that is all they will need to hear."

"What does she mean, you are safe?" Dr. Flexner looked at Willa. "Was that in doubt?"

Willa didn't answer but looked at Mrs. Flexner, who said, "Simon, we were going to talk about this tonight but I'm afraid it must come up now. Mrs. Parker isn't here just to attend the celebration. She wants to ask you for employment in your lab."

Dr. Flexner looked startled and then pleased. "You are a brilliant researcher, my dear," Dr. Flexner said. "I would love to have you, but I hadn't heard that George was giving up his fellowship at Penn."

"He isn't . . . That is . . ." Willa stumbled over her words. "He won't, he refuses. But he is giving up studying polio and I refuse to do that."

"I don't understand." Confusion crossed Dr. Flexner's face. "Have you come to ask me to convince him to resume the study? How can I do that?"

"Partially, yes," Willa said. "He may listen to you. But if he doesn't I want to come here without him and continue my work." She looked at Dr. Flexner with a mixture of fear and defiance. "I knew he would forbid it."

"So that is why you pretended to come to Miss Walcott's house and then disappeared?" I was putting the pieces together. "So your husband wouldn't know where you are?"

"If he knew I wanted to talk to Dr. Flexner he would never have allowed me to come," Willa confessed.

"What's this?" Dr. Flexner looked up sharply. "Dr. Parker doesn't know where you are?"

"No." Willa hesitated. "I'm afraid I'm here without his knowledge."

"Really, my dear," Dr. Flexner admonished. "We don't want to be accused of kidnapping. Dr. Parker knows us well. Why would he not want you to come and visit us?"

"I asked her that, my dear," Mrs. Flexner put in, "and she said that it is difficult to speak freely when Dr. Parker is present."

"So you knew about this?" Dr. Flexner looked at Mrs. Flexner.

"I did," she said with some defiance in her voice. "You know I am a supporter of women in the professions, and Mrs. Parker was one of your most brilliant students. You have told me so many times."

"It's true. I think she would have her own lab by now if she weren't a woman, but—" Dr. Flexner began but Mrs. Flexner interrupted him.

"This way you can truthfully tell Dr. Parker you had no idea that Willa was here without her husband's permission," she said. "Now, you and I can discuss that further. But what do you say to her proposal?"

"Do you have a position for me at your lab?" Willa asked. "I have made some breakthroughs that we haven't published yet. I just need a better facility, like the lab you have."

"Without your husband?" Dr. Flexner looked doubtful. "I can't do it if he forbids you. To tell you the truth, it will be difficult"—he hesitated—"even if should your husband agree, to have you in the lab because of your sex. If you were divorced, it would be impossible."

"There would be talk, my dear," Mrs. Flexner said. "I've been wracking my brain to see how we could get around it since I learned of your predicament, and I'm not saying it isn't right for you to continue your research. But, as I have pointed out before, you must think about Dr. Flexner's reputation. We must have your husband's cooperation."

There was a moment of silence in the room as Dr. Flexner considered. The sound of a horse clopping on the road outside could be heard. "If you could convince George, I'd have you both," Dr. Flexner said, coming to a decision. "The other researchers will change their minds when they see how good you are, and of course, they will accept that you are aiding your husband in his work."

"Thank you." Willa was guardedly hopeful. "But George seems

set against it. You know the government is giving very generous grants to study yellow fever, and he wants to take advantage of that."

"I tell you what I'll do." Dr. Flexner came over and took her hands in his. "I will match the research grant that George is getting. I'll write to him myself and I won't take no for an answer. We even have several houses like this one that the institute owns. How could he say no to that? That way you and George and little Charlie here can come and live in New York."

"Oh," Harriet exclaimed, "oh, my dear. What wonderful news for you, but all the way in New York." It was obvious from her expression that she had not thought through this part of the plan, that her friend might be moving away. She clutched the little boy sitting on her lap and he turned and put his arms around her neck.

"Honestly, I don't care where I live." Willa's eyes were shining now. "It's all about the research. Thank you, Dr. Flexner. I'm sure he'll listen to you."

"I'm getting something out of it too." He patted the hand that he held. "You'll show those dolts who work in my lab what real research looks like. We are so close to a breakthrough."

Willa's face broke into a wide smile. "When can we go and see the lab?" she said. "I want to get started right away."

"My dear, the parades," Mrs. Schilling said. "The Flexners have taken the week off and you promised to join me."

"I would not want you coming in right now anyway," Dr. Flexner said. "We have a few monkeys that we have infected and I have a dolt of an assistant who is likely to store his lunch right next to a live virus sample. I wouldn't want you to bring anything home to little Charlie."

"Aren't all researchers like that?" Willa laughed. "I've never known a lab to be any different. But we've always been safe. I'll write to my husband immediately," she added. "It would be better if you make the offer to him in person. Would that be possible?"

Dr. Flexner nodded. "Why don't we invite him for dinner tonight?"

"Not tonight," Mrs. Flexner said immediately. She walked across to an engagement diary sitting on a table and flipped through it. "We are free . . . let me see . . . Saturday night." She turned to me. "Mrs. Sullivan, you say Dr. Parker is in the city. Mrs. Parker, would it be better for you to stay with him? Will he storm over here in a rage when he hears where you are?"

"Now, my dear, George is a good young man," Dr. Flexner said. "Very respectful. I don't expect a rage from him." I caught a look that passed between the women. *Men*, the look seemed to say, *have a very different experience than we do.*

"I think I can keep George calm but I'd rather stay here until we get it worked out, if you don't mind," Willa said. "Once he has made you a promise, he will feel honor bound to keep it."

"I'm not sure he has room for Mrs. Parker or Charlie," I said.

"You know where he is?" Willa asked. "Could you take a letter? It would make everything easier. And I'll write to Miss Goldfarb and Miss Walcott as well, apologizing for distressing them."

"I'll get you some writing paper," Mrs. Flexner said, then crossed to a small writing desk and began to rummage about in it.

"That's one thing I don't understand," I said to Willa. "Why didn't you just stay with my friends in the first place? Or at least come to the house to let them know your plan?"

To my surprise, Harriet answered. "That was my part of the plan," she said, giving Willa a conspiratorial look. "You see, if he believed that Willa was off on a little trip, we knew he would ask me to watch Charlie and I could bring him to the city. If she had just left without warning, he would have used Charlie as a bargaining chip."

"He has used Charlie in the past to get me to come home," Willa admitted. "And he has warned me that if I ever leave him, I will never see Charlie again." I felt a pang of sorrow for her. I couldn't imagine Daniel holding our children hostage to force me to do what he wanted. On the other hand, I couldn't imagine disappearing and causing Daniel such worry. I studied Willa as she wrote. Here was a woman so passionate about her work that she was willing to risk everything to continue it.

"Then, I was to bring Charlie to New York to meet up with Willa," Harriet went on. Her face was full of enjoyment of the scheme. "That day you saw me at Mrs. Belmont's house we had not yet made contact. Willa was coming to the Flexners' to see if they would host her while she was in New York."

"Hide her, don't you mean," Mrs. Flexner laughed. "And I said I would only do it if we found a way to save their marriage." She smiled warmly at her husband. "I'm a big believer in marriage."

"But how does this lady come into the question?" Dr. Flexner turned to me. "And how does she know where to find your husband?"

"I'm a detective hired by some friends of Mrs. Parker," I said. "Hired to find her and ask if she needed assistance."

I noted his look of surprise at encountering a female detective. His eyebrows raised, but to his credit he did not remark on it. Instead he said, "Why was a detective needed?"

"She did not show up to our friends' house; her family did not know where she was. Her husband has hired a Pinkerton man to find her." I counted the reasons on my fingers.

"My dear, you really should have told me." Dr. Flexner turned to his wife with a groan. "What am I going to say to Dr. Parker? That I've been hiding his wife without his knowledge?"

"I'll take all the blame on myself." Willa sat at the little desk, writing as she spoke. "I will say that neither of you had any inkling. And anyway"—she blew dry the first line of link—"my husband and I are two of a kind. If you are kind enough to offer us that position, Dr. Flexner, he will forget about my disappearance entirely."

As she wrote, the little boy Charlie, who had been good as gold for the whole time I had been present, began wandering around the room, picking up objects and exploring them. He picked up the inkwell Willa was using, and her hand closed over his a second before he tipped it over.

"No, my love," Harriet said, going after him. "Poor thing has been cooped up all day," she said to me. "And with that dratted Pinkerton man, I don't dare take him outside now." She left the room momentarily and came back with some paper and a crayon box. "Here, dear, draw a picture for your mother." The little boy lay happily on the floor with the paper in front of him, drawing.

"He really is a darling," she said. "I confess, I didn't think this scheme would result in his moving away from me. Am I to lose my friend and my Charlie?" Her voice was strained and plaintive. Willa looked up from her writing.

"Perhaps you can come with us," she said. "Charlie, shall Shoo Shoo come with us?" Charlie, absorbed in his work, merely nodded. "There! You see, it's decided."

"I'm sure my husband might have other ideas," Harriet said forlornly. "I don't think he would ever leave Penn." But Willa had gone back to writing. It did not take long for her to finish both letters and put them into my hands.

"Please give my personal apologies to your friends," she said.

"You may be able to give them yourself." Harriet gave Willa a look.

"Really?" Willa asked with a small frown

Harriet went on. "You promised you would join us on the float. You can't leave the city until after the celebration."

"The goddess float?" I queried. I still could not quite figure out the connection that Harriet had to the float or Mrs. Belmont. But I had met her at the meeting, and the supposed reason for Willa's visit had been to accompany Sid and Gus in the parade.

"We can't let Mrs. Belmont down," Harriet said. "You may need her support. After all, despite Dr. Flexner's offer, your husband hasn't given his consent yet. What if he refuses?"

"He can't!" It came out as an explosion. Willa twisted her hands with real emotion. "I can't even think about that. Please go, Mrs. Sullivan. I won't have a moment's peace until that letter is in my husband's hands."

I looked carefully before I left the house. There were a few pedestrians, who did not give me a second glance as I opened the little gate and stepped out into the street. Two blocks away from the house I turned west toward the city, glancing behind me to make sure I was not followed. As I started forward again, a man stepped out of the shadow of a building. My way was blocked by Mr. Jones.

His voice was full of menace as he spoke. "Where are you coming from, little lady?"

## Nineteen

"Do I know you?" My tone was frosty.

"Don't play coy with me," he snarled. "You know very well that we met at Dr. Parker's. I suspected that you might be trying to hide his wife and now I have proof."

"You do?" I queried. "What proof? Where is Mrs. Parker?" I looked around dramatically as if expecting her to be coming down the street, then lifted my cloak and glanced beneath. "Not here, Mr. Jones."

"So you do know my name," he said as if he had scored a point. "What are you doing in this neighborhood?" I debated just telling him. Willa was going to tell her husband of her whereabouts anyway. But two things stopped me. The first was that I worried that Charlie might not be safe. What if this detective had been ordered to take the boy back to his father at all costs? The second was my vanity. I had to deliver this letter to Dr. Parker. I did not want to begin a race across town as if Mr. Jones and I were competing for a prize. I pictured us both arriving at Dr. Parker's residence out of breath, trying to be the first to tell him where his wife was. It would be undignified.

"Have you found Mrs. Parker yet?" I decided I could ask questions as well as he.

"Look, lady," he said. "I know you asked at the Institute and I saw you coming from that street. I'm so close, and you're going to show me her house." He crossed the distance between us, and his hand closed on my arm with an iron grip. It had occurred to me that this man might resort to violence and I had been scanning the street for possible means of escape. The street had not been empty, but the children running back and forth between houses and some old women walking by with their shopping had not been good prospects for any help.

He turned me back in the direction from which I had come. We had not gone ten paces when a group of workers heading home for lunch rounded the corner and I took my chance.

"I'm a married woman, get your hands off me!" I said in a thunderously loud voice and kicked the heel of my boot down into his instep. He grunted with pain but did not relax his grip. The men looked up but did not move toward us.

I used my free hand to take a pin from my hair and jabbed it into Mr. Jones's hand as I yelled, "Take your hands off me! Someone call the police!" He jumped back and swore, then raised his other hand to strike me. Now free, I jumped back in time. The men were finally galvanized into action.

"Hey, wait a minute," one said, stepping forward. "What's going on?"

"This man has been following me, and now he is trying to kidnap me," I said. "Call a policeman."

"There's one around the corner," one man said to another. "Hold on to this guy until I get him." Two of them walked toward Mr. Jones.

"Hey, wait, guys, you don't know what's going on here," he began.

"I'm a married woman," I put in. "Just trying to get home in peace."

The men moved to hold Mr. Jones, but he glared at me with pure hatred, and then took off running down the street. Two of the men ran after him for half a block, then gave up the chase.

"Are you okay, lady?" one of them asked.

"Yes, just shaken up," I looked down the street after Mr. Jones. Would he be waiting at the El stop for me? I decided to play the damsel in distress. "I feel like I might faint. Could you possibly find a cab for me?"

"Sure thing, missus," the man in a brown cap said cheerfully, steering me toward a bench, where I half collapsed. Having always been a very sturdy person, I worried for a moment that I was overdoing it, but apparently I was not, because one man ran to get me a glass of water from a nearby store while one of his mates headed to a bigger street looking for a cab. Within ten minutes I had thanked and handsomely tipped the workers and I was on my way to Dr. Parker's.

I must admit that I was quite pleased with myself. I am a big fan of Sherlock Holmes and his mysteries, and, perhaps a little vainly, I found myself comparing my investigations to his. I'm not as clever and I can't tell where someone has been by the mud on their shoes or the type of tobacco they smoke. But, then again, I don't have a Watson to help me, or a housekeeper. And Sherlock Holmes never had to solve a case and be home in time to cook dinner! These rather ridiculous thoughts amused me as I made my way across the city toward Dr. Parker. *This case would be called "The Case of the Disappearing Woman,"* I thought. And I have solved it before the Pinkerton man!

As the cab pulled up at the boardinghouse, I hesitated. Could Mr. Jones have possibly made it here before me? I pictured him running out of the doorway to accost me and accuse me of kidnapping Mrs. Parker.

"Please wait—I'll only be a moment," I asked the driver. If Mr. Jones did show up, help would be close at hand. But, mercifully, I had beat him there. I once again asked for Dr. Parker, and he came out. I thought he looked quite haggard and felt a twinge of sympathy for him. After all, his wife had been missing, and, whatever Willa Parker said, I wasn't sure who was in the wrong in this marital dispute.

"I have a letter from your wife," I announced without preamble and saw his face change. Was that optimism or fear? "She and your son are safe." I fished the letter out of my bag and held it out to him. He tore it open eagerly and began to read. I didn't stop to ask for any thanks or entertain any more questions. The thought of Mr. Jones showing up on my heels kept running through my head. I gave Dr. Parker a nod and jumped back into the waiting cab.

As tired and hungry as I was when the cab pulled up to Patchin Place, I did not turn toward my own door but to Sid and Gus's, eager to share my triumph. I knocked and Sid opened the door.

"Molly, come in. We're just having lunch. Come and join us." I was ushered into the kitchen. I steeled myself for the dreaded Cousin Prudence but she was not there; neither was Anne Johnson.

"Our houseguests are out," Gus said, looking up with a big smile as I came in, "and we have the place to ourselves for a moment."

"I'm sorry to disturb the quiet," I said. "You have had little enough of it recently."

"Nonsense," Sid said, "we were planning on popping over to ask you if you have any more results from your investigation. Have you any news of Mrs. Parker yet?"

I pulled the second letter from my bag and held it out. "I believe she will be accompanying you on the float. But see for yourself what she says."

Gus took it. "This is from Mrs. Parker?" I nodded.

"Molly, you are brilliant! You've seen her?" Sid added. My friends were always too effusive with their praise, but this time I felt I had earned it. I was feeling quite pleased with the result of my investigation.

"I have, and she sends her apologies for worrying you," I said as Gus opened the letter.

"Yes, that's what she says here," Gus scanned down the page. "And, oh good, she says she will see us on Friday for the final float decorations and accompany us as planned."

"But why did she behave in this way?" Sid asked, motioning for me to have a seat and pouring me a glass of water, which I gulped down before replying. "Where has she been?"

"You both know she is a researcher," I said. "Well, apparently she wants to research something different from her husband, but the lab is in his name only. She came to appeal to a former professor of hers who now runs a lab here in New York City. He has offered to find a position for both of them."

"And she couldn't have just told her husband her errand?" Sid asked. "Or her family?"

"Apparently, he has brought her home on previous occasions, and she hoped he might listen to Dr. Flexner—that's the researcher—rather than her," I said, eyeing the cold cuts, cheese, and fruit spread out on the table. "And she was afraid that he could keep her son from her if they quarreled." I was about to relate the role that Harriet Schilling had played, but to my embarrassment, my stomach gave a rumble.

"Molly, join us, you must be starving," Gus exclaimed, grabbing a plate off a shelf and putting it in front of me. Sid loaded it with thickly buttered bread, sliced ham, cheese, and slices of crisp new apples. For a few moments I did nothing but eat while my two friends discussed the historical parade.

"Didn't we have fun!" Sid said. "And wasn't Bridie just darling."

"She would be darling in any situation," Gus said, "but I object to having her mending a man's shirt. Why, Molly has just proven that there are valued women scientists. She should have been in front of a test tube or lecturing to a class."

"Or solving mysterious disappearances more quickly than a Pinkerton man," Sid said brightly. "Or did he beat you there?"

"He did not!" I said with a triumphant smile. "He was close, and he even threatened me."

"He did!" they both exclaimed at once. Then I had to go back to the beginning and recount the whole morning. It was a good feeling to share my triumph with my friends, and, foolish though it was, I even recounted my comparison to Mr. Sherlock Holmes.

"But you do have a Watson," Sid said. "We'll be your Watsons!"

"In this case we were the clients, dear," Gus said, going to a jar on the kitchen shelf and pulling out four ten-dollar bills and handing them to me. "Two very satisfied clients. Let me get something. We have a surprise for you." Sid and Gus looked at one another with conspiratorial smiles and then Gus disappeared from the room and I could hear her footsteps on the stairs.

"It is quite shocking of Mr. Jones to accost you on the street. I'm sure he wouldn't do that to a man," Sid said.

"I don't know," I mused. "Perhaps he would have just punched a man or pulled a knife. And certainly those workmen would not have come to the aid of a man they did not know." I ate the last bit of apple, then grabbed a napkin, even though it was so good I could have licked my fingers. "I think being a woman may be a great advantage in some cases. Those men came running because they believed Mr. Jones was trying to take my womanly virtue." I mimicked a fainting swoon and Sid laughed.

Gus came back into the room, a small silver card-carrying case in her hand. "The case is an old one of mine that I don't use anymore. But what is in it is the surprise." I took it and opened the clasp gently. I pulled a card out.

MOLLY MURPHY DETECTIVE AGENCY, it read. I gasped. This

was exactly what I had pictured. It was as if a fairy godmother had brought my wishes to life.

"We guessed you would not want to use Sullivan," Gus said, "but if you do we can have others made. We only asked for ten of these to see if you would like them."

"I love them!" I said. "Although I wonder if advertising that I am a woman is a good idea."

"As you said, there are certain investigations that a woman can accomplish more easily, or with more discretion," Sid said. "Perhaps you could market your services to women who would appreciate that fact."

"And the exchange number?" I said. "It's yours."

"Yes, I've practiced," Sid said and mimed picking up a telephone receiver. "Good morning," she said in a strong nasal voice, "Molly Murphy Detective Agency."

"You can't answer your telephone like that every time," I protested. "What will your friends think?"

"We'll worry about that later," Gus said, waving the problem away. "What do you think of your cards?"

"I love them," I said, coming around the table to give my friends each a hug. "You are both the best friends that I could have."

"We love hearing all about your cases," Gus said. "It adds some spice to our otherwise dull and conventional lives." I snorted. Their lives were anything but.

"Yes, and on the next case, we must be Watson," Sid insisted. "Your faithful assistants. What will your next case be, Molly?"

At that I had nothing to say. I flushed as I remembered my promise to Daniel. If I did what he had asked, my next case would be investigating my friends.

# Twenty

I let myself in. The house was quiet as I went upstairs. The door of the nursery was slightly ajar and I peeked in. Aileen was lying back on the pillows, asleep, Mary Kate sprawled across her. Liam, who liked to pretend he could read Bridie's books, was fast asleep at the foot of the bed, a huge novel lying beside him.

My heart squeezed with love for these precious children. And I felt guilty looking at Aileen. Watching the children was her job, but she was just a young girl, not much older than Bridie, and she deserved some relaxation herself. Now that my case was successfully concluded, I determined to give that to her. I tiptoed away, not wanting to wake them, went into my own bedroom, and pulled open the drawer that I used to store my own money. I was down to a single ten-dollar bill from the fifty I had begun with. It felt good to put my wages and my new cards beside it. Daniel had chosen to spend his money on salaries for his men, and while that might have been the noble decision, it still galled me that he had not thought of talking that decision over with me. We would have been hungry for a few weeks if not for my money. I needed to have money of my own always, I decided. Money that I made the decisions about.

Would I really open my own detective agency again? I felt one moment as if my mind was already made up. I was good at solving mysteries, I had proven that again and again. I could earn my own money and do some good in the world. A woman could be more than a wife and a mother. But I couldn't ignore the voice in the back of my head. *What about the time you will miss with your children? What if you bring danger to your family? How can you possibly do both things well?* These thoughts alternated in a seemingly endless loop.

I put the thoughts out of my mind when Daniel arrived before sundown for once with the news that he actually had an evening off.

"The count and countess are dining with the mayor," Daniel said. "who has his own security. Although I shall have to be off early tomorrow to be in attendance for the military parade." He sighed. "I'm not sure how we can provide real security when multiple armies will be marching with weapons." He massaged his brow. "The police commissioner has made my job harder by being quite territorial. He told me he has the security for the carnival parade Saturday under control and implied we were not needed at all. But"—he smiled—"on the bright side, I have tonight off. I can spend some time with you and the children."

"And if anything goes wrong at the parade," I said thoughtfully, "it will be his fault and not yours." I said this casually but Daniel knows me too well.

"Do you expect something to go wrong?" he asked. "Because it still would look quite bad for me, no matter what the commissioner does or doesn't do."

"I haven't heard of a thing," I said. "And I'll go to the meeting on Friday just like you asked. But—"

"Hello, Daddy." Little Liam had come downstairs.

"My boyo." Daniel swept him up in a big hug.

"You're home in time to help me with my shopping. Shall we take Liam for a walk?" I said. "Poor Aileen is tired out, and the baby is asleep too. We can be there and back before they wake if we hurry."

I didn't realize until we headed toward the shops how much I missed this. Daniel had been busy so often lately we had little time for walks or outings with the children. Liam walked between us, holding on to both our hands and begging to be swung between us.

"One, two, three, go!" we chanted as he launched himself.

"You're getting too big for that," Daniel said when Liam asked for a third time. "You've wrenched my arm out." We let him go and he ran ahead. He knew the way to the butcher's as well as I did.

I slipped my arm through Daniel's and said, "You might like to know that I solved my case today."

"You did?" Daniel kept walking in silence beside me for a moment. "And is the young woman . . ." He trailed off.

"She is quite all right," I said, "and has written a letter to her husband explaining the situation."

"Molly, that's wonderful!" I realized that his earlier hesitation had been just out of fear of my finding that Mrs. Parker had met an untimely end. I vacillated between finding it sweet that he wanted to protect me and being frustrated that he assumed me to be a fragile female. "Was she hiding at that institute?" Suddenly Daniel's face was alive and focused in a way that I rarely saw. It was the face of a police captain with one of his men, sharing their love of the chase and the puzzle together.

"Not at the institute," I said, happy to share the outcome with him, "but with the Flexners. I was correct that she was asking for their help while she considered a job in New York," I said. "But she was unsure if her husband would approve, so she didn't let him know where she was."

"But he knows now?" he asked.

"Yes, she wrote him a letter with an explanation," I said. "I took it to him this afternoon on my way home."

"You took it to him?" Daniel queried, squeezing my arm more tightly, the police captain having tuned back into the worried husband. "At his residence, I am to suppose?"

"Yes, at the rooms he has rented," I said. "I interviewed him there before." I went on before Daniel could object further, "Outside the rooms. In a safe and public place." I grinned.

"I don't know whether to be impressed or horrified," Daniel said. "Picturing you alone with a man that you thought may have killed his wife."

"He did not seem dangerous," I said. "Quite relieved that I had found her." I had to let go of Daniel's arm and take Liam's hand as we crossed the street. "I suppose," I said when we were safely on the other side, Daniel's arm in mine again, "he will have to let the police know she is no longer a missing woman."

"They will be glad to hear that," Daniel said, "although, given all they have to do this week, they may not have worked on the case very hard."

"That may have more to do with the fact that her family told them she was most likely missing of her own accord," I reminded him. "They are quite important people."

"And you found her," he said, giving me an appraising look. "It's a shame we aren't hiring female Bureau officers."

He was teasing, but I shot back, "Yes it is. I've been realizing there are places that women can go that men can't." I paused and dropped Daniel's arm as we navigated our way around a wooden scaffold, pulling my skirts up to avoid dragging them on the bricks and sandbags sodden with the recent rain. *It would be easier for women to go places without these skirts*, I thought as Daniel easily hopped over a pile of bricks.

"I've admitted as much to you, haven't I?" Daniel turned back and offered me a hand as I stepped over as well. "For instance, since I gave you a ride in my new automobile—"

"The Bureau's new auto," I put in.

"The Bureau's new auto," he admitted, "that I can use whenever I want"—he gave an insufferable grin—"you have to hold up your end of the bargain."

"I will," I said. "I will spend my Friday investigating for you. But tomorrow I am planning on having a rest."

"I envy you," he said. "I wish that I had the same luxury."

"No rest for the wicked." I smiled to take the sting out of my words.

I truly intended to spend Thursday at home in peace and quiet. Bridie left for school at the regular time. I gave the poor, tired Aileen the day off, thinking I would spend a quiet day together with the children. But I had made the mistake of discussing the day's parade in Liam's hearing. The little man begged so desperately to be taken to see the soldiers that we joined the crowds going to watch them. There were more people out than even the day of the historical parade. The average New Yorker must be like Liam, more eager to see the soldiers than to get a history lesson. Since we had no comfortable seating arrangement this time, I tried to buy us seats in one of the private stands, only to find out they were selling for two dollars a piece! We finally stood somewhat miserably under the scaffolding of a building undergoing renovations. I had carried Mary Kate, being doubtful that I could fit a baby carriage through the streets, but by the end of the day I was tired of holding the squirming little girl. Only Liam was happy, since he could climb up on the wooden crossbeams with the other boys and had a good perch from which to see the soldiers march by. The German military was the most impressive by far, the soldiers lifting their legs high in lockstep, even though we were at the end of their route and they must have been extremely tired of marching by the time they reached us. I wondered if they felt, as I did, that they were growing tired of the crowds, the pomp and circumstance, and ready to get back to their normal lives.

Gus greeted us as we entered Patchin Place later that afternoon, Liam running ahead and up the step to our house, Mary Kate asleep on my shoulder, and me with dragging feet. Gus was sitting outside in a flowing Japanese silk robe, cup of coffee in hand. A trio of chairs was set out with a little table between them in the small space between our houses.

"Where are you coming from?" she asked curiously.

"The military parade," I said wearily.

"Oh, that was today?" Gus said.

"Where are you coming from?" Sid echoed Gus without realizing it as she came out of the front door and took the seat next to Gus. I repeated my answer. She made a face.

"I don't see the appeal of sweaty mustached men in uniform," she said. "We had a bit of a sleepy day today."

"I gather Cousin Prudence is not here." I glanced at the house, picturing the lady herself storming out to ask what Gus thought she was doing out in the street in her robe.

"No, she is staying with a friend," Gus said. "Unfortunately only for tonight. She will be back and stay until Sunday. We are taking advantage, as you can see."

"The sun finally came out." Anne sounded joyful and relaxed as she joined us, setting her cup of coffee on the table and shaking my hand. "Hello, Mrs. Sullivan. I hear you found our friend."

"I told you she was a top-notch detective," Gus said with the air of a patroness. "We shall give you a copy of her card to share with any of your friends who need detective services."

"Oh." Anne looked a little taken aback. "I'm not sure that any of my friends are interesting enough to need that sort of service. But thank you again, Mrs. Sullivan. Shall we get you a chair? Will you join us for coffee?" I accepted the offer of a chair gratefully and sat with my friends for a few minutes, enjoying the sunlight and their company, then rose with a slight groan.

"I'm afraid for me it is dinner and then bed," I said. "I'm dead tired after going to that parade." Even in my tiredness I could not forget my commission from Daniel. "Are you still planning on working on your float tomorrow? I'm free if you still want my services." The broad smile on all three faces made me squirm with guilt inside.

"How lovely," Gus said. "We need all the help we can get—perhaps our darling Bridie can come as well. Although I'm afraid we will have to leave dreadfully early."

"Yes," Sid agreed. "We agreed to meet at nine AM, practically the crack of dawn." My eyes met Anne's and we shared a look of amusement.

"That won't be a problem," I said. "Bridie is back at school, but I will be happy to lend my support."

"Wonderful." Sid jumped up and ran into the house, calling back, "Stay there, Molly." She came out with a tray of pastries. "For your dinner. We bought much too much." I took them with a grateful smile but felt my cheeks beginning to burn and a prickle of shame flush through my body. Was I really going to investigate my best friends?

I was met by the sound of sneezing as I returned home. Bridie was home from school and was reading Liam a story, breaking off from her reading to cough and sneeze.

"I don't feel well," she said. "I suppose the parade gave me a chill." I sent her right up to bed, inwardly cursing Lucy McCormick. Bridie was a healthy young girl, not an old lady who would catch a chill. But a feverish cold had been going around the city, and I had no doubt that it had gone from Lucy to Blanche to Bridie.

## ⚙ Twenty-One ⚙

The day dawned with a thick fog that mixed with the smoke from thousands of fires and boilers struggling to take away the autumn chill. The leaves of the trees seemed to have turned orange overnight. My many years living in the city told me that the last warm days of September had gone and that the chill and damp were here to stay.

Bridie stayed in bed and I brought her up some tea with Peruna syrup in it, telling her to get some sleep. Luckily, she did not feel feverish, just tired and with runny nose and eyes. I would not risk sending her out into the cold day. I could tell I had made the right decision because, rather than arguing with me, she went right back to sleep.

Sid, Gus, Anne, and I set off to help with the preparation of the parade float. We did not have to brave the chilly weather in a cab or taximeter, as Mrs. Belmont herself sent her automobile for us. The streets were quiet as the many denizens and visitors rested for the final day of festivities.

"Our poor darling," Sid said when I told them Bridie was in bed. "Should you have stayed with her?"

"Aileen is there, and she's just sleeping," I assured her.

"I hope she'll be well enough to watch the parade tomorrow!" Gus said. "I know she has been looking forward to it."

I'm afraid I was lost in thought and didn't pay attention to the exact direction of our travel, but it was almost an hour before we pulled into a type of yard at the very north of Manhattan, in the area still countrified with small holdings, away from city lights. The yard was a hive of activity. Several giant floats were parked there, and workmen swarmed up and down them adding finishing touches.

It was easy to pick out the Vassar women's float. Not only did it have a giant Greek statue of *Winged Victory* on it, but it was also the only float with women surrounding it. This made me pause. Obviously Mrs. Belmont had the money to hire workmen if she had so chosen. Yet only women, and by the looks of them society women, were doing these final details of construction. If this float was being put together by a volunteer committee of women, there must be a reason.

We got to work immediately, clambering up onto the raised platform, which was twelve feet across and thirty feet long. We lifted tiers of wooden boxes covered with white fabric onto the float to create the different levels on which the goddesses would sit. We attached the marble columns—really papier-mâché painted to look like marble. There were ten of us working to start with, women whose faces I recognized from the meeting but whose names I did not know. One particularly officious woman was handing out assignments and barking orders. There was no sign of Mrs. Goodwin. I wondered if only select women had been invited this morning. Then, as we were taking a small break, quite red-faced from hauling a large box onto the platform and nailing it down, a group of women walked into the yard. It was Mrs. Flexner, Harriet, and Willa.

"Mrs. Parker!" Anne ran across the yard to take both of her hands.

"How lovely to see you. We were so worried about you. Do you remember me? Winnie's friend, Anne Johnson."

"Miss Johnson." Willa squeezed her hands back, her expression a bit embarrassed, as the whole group had stopped to watch. "Yes, you are quite unchanged from our school days. I'm so sorry to have worried you." They approached the float. Sid and Gus scrambled down and walked over to join the newcomers. "And you must be Miss Elena and Miss Augusta," Willa said. "I'm afraid I don't have much of a recollection of your younger selves."

"Well, we are in your sister's year," Gus said. "I'm not sure whether we ever met."

"I have to apologize to you as well," Willa said, "I didn't mean to cause you worry. I just needed some time in which my husband didn't know where I was."

"It was a bit of a scheme, wasn't it?" Harriet said. "I'm afraid I had to tell a few lies myself. But it was all in the aid of my friend."

"And did you get what you wanted out of the whole business?" Sid asked both women. It was Willa who nodded.

"I believe so. Dr. Flexner has offered me a place at his lab and I believe my husband will come around since he is being offered a job as well," Willa said. "Oh, excuse me, this is Mrs. Flexner." Mrs. Flexner smiled and Sid and Gus shook hands with her.

"I was a coconspirator, I'm afraid," Mrs. Flexner said. "But all's well that ends well. We will be able to see much more of Mrs. Parker once she moves back to New York."

"And I shall miss my friend dreadfully." Harriet's face fell. "I can't imagine how boring life will be without her and little Charlie."

"Where is the sweet little boy?" I asked.

"He's at home with my James. I have a girl who comes in when I need her." Mrs. Flexner said. "Now, I believe we have some work to do before the parade tomorrow."

"Are you participating as well?" I asked, surprised.

"Well, I won't be actually on the float," she said, "but I wanted to lend my support today. I am a suffragist, you know, and my husband is very supportive as well."

I looked at the Greek scene taking shape on top of the huge wooden platform. How was this a suffragist message? But before I could ask the question I was put to work by the officious woman, who directed me to attach a flowery bunting along the edge of the wooden platform with tiny tacks.

"Make yourself useful, girl," she barked. "No time for standing around."

"I'll take the other side," Mrs. Flexner offered and we took armfuls of bunting to begin the rather backbreaking task of affixing it to the wooden frame of the platform. Really, I thought, I had plenty of chores to do at home and did not need to be barked at and ordered around. But I reminded myself that I was here to investigate. This was a perfect position. I was partially hidden as I crouched down beside the platform, moving along slowly. I picked up snippets of conversation as I went.

"I haven't mentioned anything to my husband, he would be quite against it," I heard one woman say.

"Mrs. Malone says we must make them listen," another woman said, "and if we have to . . ." She moved off before I could hear the rest of her sentence.

As I made my way slowly to the rear of the vehicle, crouching down to nail in the lower parts, I was quite hidden when I heard Sid's voice above me as she worked.

"Will one of the ladies have the bail money ready, do you think?"

Another voice I believed to be Harriet's replied, "Yes, and they know what station we will most likely be taken to. They'll be there waiting."

"I don't plan on being arrested." That was Willa Parker.

"But the Flexners are supporters," Harriet said again. "They'll be proud if you do. And you want to stay in Mrs. Belmont's good graces."

"Just stay on the float and you should be fine," Gus said. "You can claim you had no idea what would happen."

I waited until I heard them move away before I stood from my crouch and peered over the top of the platform. I pulled myself up onto the float. I was right behind the giant *Winged Victory* statue, and there was a little cavity under its skirt. The silk and gauze were draped over a light wire frame that let in the light, and through it I could see the distorted figures of the women working on the float. The statue's wings were still folded down, but some material with a different texture hung down into the cavity. I pulled the top of the skirt aside and a beam of sunlight came into the dark space. The material hanging down into the skirt was red with giant gold letters sewn on. It took me several minutes of pulling the fabric through my fingers to realize what it said. VOTES FOR WOMEN!

I studied the underside of the figure. There was a hinge that would pull the angel wings open. When they opened, this banner would be unfurled. In an instant I understood their plan. All the dignitaries would be at the Court of Honor stand. I imagined the women waiting until then and unfurling this banner in front of the vice president of the United States. This must be why they were planning to need bail money as well. I myself had been arrested for peacefully marching in a parade for women's suffrage. I didn't doubt that the police would arrest anyone who voiced this point of view in front of the whole world.

It was cramped and uncomfortable under the skirt. Checking that no one was in my immediate vicinity, I slid out and resumed my task of tacking on the bunting, thinking back to the last time I marched with suffragists. The crowd had been angry, men and even women yelling at us to go home and tend to our husbands. It still amazed me that women would be so against other women fighting for their basic rights, but I had seen it with my own eyes. What if this crowd got angry and attacked my friends? What if this started a riot and someone got hurt? I would have to tell Daniel, I decided.

But what would he do? Would he talk to Sid and Gus, or even call on Mrs. Belmont and warn the whole group off? They would know that I had revealed their protest. I would be a traitor to the cause. I might never regain their friendship. I shook my head at the thought, dread in the pit of my stomach as I pictured the hurt in their eyes.

If Daniel didn't get involved himself he could tip off the police. Even worse! I pictured my friends being taken to jail, not triumphant and laughing after a successful protest, but bewildered and frustrated by their ambitions being thwarted before their protest even began.

And didn't I agree with their protest? *After all*, I thought, *in England right now suffragettes are being jailed and force-fed as a type of torture. If women getting advanced degrees and speaking eloquently about their desire to have a say in the direction of the country are jeered at in the press and political meetings, what are we to do? Our desire to be seen as full human beings is mocked. A woman is a person only through her father or her husband, whether that father or husband is an upstanding man or a wastrel and drunk, whether he cares for her tenderly or beats her and leaves her destitute.* I found that I had banged the hammer too hard and broken the head of the tiny tacking nail. Good. I banged it one more time to let out my anger.

*These women are not burning down buildings or shooting senators. They are using fabric to draw attention to a very simple request: that they be treated as equals in their own country.* I finished tacking and stood up, massaging my back from having stooped so long. I chose a side. Whatever the consequences to Daniel's career, I could not betray my friends.

Mrs. Flexner had not been working quite as swiftly as I. She had only three quarters of her side finished as I caught up with her, and we finished the last piece together and rose, Mrs. Flexner also rubbing her back.

"If I had known the amount of manual labor involved I might not have been so willing to volunteer," she said, sharing a smile with me.

I nodded agreement as I put my hammer back into the toolbox. The float was almost finished. It looked quite magnificent. Golden chairs had been nailed down for the goddesses to rest on. A giant peacock with real feathers sat beside a just-painted waterfall coming down from a miniature Mount Olympus, the center of the float. All around the edge, marble columns rose with real silk artfully draped as canopies for the goddesses. And of course, Nike, the goddess of victory, dominated the rear of the platform, towering above the mountain. One hand was demurely on her breast, the other raised with freedom's torch, a flame of red and orange crepe paper spilling up from it.

"I wanted the flame to be real fire," Sid said, hopping down from the side and seeing my gaze. "But the others were afraid that her robes would catch on fire when the wings open."

"Have you seen the wings open?" I asked, not sure how to broach the subject.

"We've tried out the mechanism," she said. "I'm sure they will open."

"I saw what is under the robes," I said, finally.

"Oh, I'm so glad." A look of relief came over her face. "I hate having to keep a secret. Isn't it marvelous?" She looked at me with such trust that my mind was even more made up. Sid would plan something reckless, but not dangerous, and she would not look so innocent if she was planning something dangerous. "I told the group that you would never betray us, but they made me promise not to breathe a word of it."

"And Mrs. Belmont knows?" I asked.

"Yes. She is a supporter of woman's suffrage, but she won't be in the protest herself," Sid said. "Maud Malone—she's another suffragist—helped us plan it, but she won't be in the parade because she has another protest planned in New York next week and she can't go to jail and miss it."

"Go to jail?" I queried. "Are you happy about that?"

"I don't expect it to be comfortable." Sid grimaced, and then a look came over her face that I had never seen before, a look of determination and purpose. For a second she was not the carefree bohemian who flitted through life in a bubble of fun, but someone strong and hard, who knew what oppression was, by both her race and gender. A woman who laughed and played so as not to cry and not to fall into society's trap of hatred and belittling. Then that vision was gone.

"Our committee has promised to rescue us with bail money and croissants," she said. Then, as if the thought had only just occurred to her, "Do you want to join? I can see if we have an extra costume."

"No thank you," I replied. "I must remember Daniel's position and not let him down. But I shall be in the stands cheering you on." But later, all the way home in the car that Mrs. Belmont provided for us, I couldn't help worrying. Would I be bringing my family into danger? Would the suffragists be met with groans and jeers and an indulgent police force escorting them away? Or would tempers flare and violence break out? And, if it did, would I know that I could have stopped it?

I noticed Willa perched on a corner of the float, her legs swinging off, watching the others work. I still had unanswered questions about her disappearance. Although my investigation had been successful and my fee paid I couldn't help being curious. I poured a cup of water and took it over to her. She gave me a grateful nod and downed it.

"I hope you don't hold it against me that I was searching for you,"

I began. "My friends had the best of intentions and only meant to help you."

"I don't," she said, "since it may all turn out well. After all, I had to let my husband know at some time."

"Did you?" I looked at her with curiosity. "Then why disappear in the first place? Couldn't you have begun your work at Dr. Flexner's lab without him knowing?"

"I confess, that was my thought at the beginning," she said. Her voice was flat and resigned. "When I devised the scheme, I thought I might be established by the time my husband found me." She sighed. "But Mrs. Flexner made me see it was impossible. If it were to come out that I was a married or a divorced woman, living on her own and working in Dr. Flexner's lab, everyone would assume I was his mistress. It could ruin his career."

"And are you quite happy to live with your husband again?" I asked delicately.

"Do you mean does he hit me?" There was scorn in her voice now. "Not often. And I could put up with that. It's the research, all my work, published under his name. I won't be dictated to. I must be free."

"Has he agreed to your terms?" I asked. "Will you be joining Dr. Flexner's lab together? What does he say?"

"We haven't spoken," she said. "I want to give him time to think it over. We are going out to dinner with the Flexners tomorrow night after the parade and my great hope is that he will agree."

"What will you do if he doesn't?" I asked.

She shook her head. "I don't know. I can't think of that. But I can't divorce him. He will never let me take Charlie. Even though our son is an afterthought to him. He was fine with me leaving Charlie with Harriet. I bet he didn't even realize that Harriet had brought him here to the city until he got my note."

"I'm not sure he did," I said. "He mentioned his son to me when

I met with him and I believe he thinks Mrs. Schilling has him at her home." There was a moment of silence. "Forgive me for saying so," I said, "but you don't seem like a suffragist to me. I'm surprised to find you involved in a protest like this."

"You'll have guessed that being in the parade was just a pretext for me to come into New York without my husband," she said.

"Yes, but why go through with it now?" I asked. "Especially if there may be trouble."

"I can't let Harriet down," she said, "She's been a good friend to me. The best, really. And, as she says, I need to keep my options open. Mrs. Belmont and the Flexners may be more ready to help a suffragist who has broken with her husband because of the cause than a researcher who just wants to be left alone to get on with her research."

"Perhaps someday women will be able to have their own labs and careers because of protests like this," I suggested.

"Perhaps." She seemed doubtful. "I don't hold out hope. And I notice that you are a businesswoman. Are you planning on joining us on the float?"

"No," I admitted.

"Then I wonder why you are here today?" Her look was challenging. "Are you still following me?"

"I'm here to help my friends decorate a float," I said. "Until this morning I had no idea of the plan to protest. And I had no way of knowing you would be here."

"I suppose not," she said. But her eyes, full of suspicion, followed me as I walked back to rejoin Sid and Gus.

## ❧ Twenty-Two ❧

"Y̲ou will be watching us in the parade tomorrow, won't you, Molly?" Gus asked as we climbed out of Mrs. Belmont's car back in Patchin Place.

"Of course I will." I smiled at them. "With Bridie and Liam to cheer you on." The smile faded as I remembered. "As long as Bridie has recovered. And if you are sure it is safe for them."

"Safe?" Gus looked back and forth between me and Sid, momentarily confused.

"Of course it will be," Sid said. "And Bridie will be proud of us."

"I'm nervous and excited." Anne gave me one of her shy smiles.

The door to their house flew open. "Thank heavens," Cousin Prudence's voice boomed through the court. "I woke to find myself abandoned and the house deserted. I should not have come to this city if I knew I would be treated this way."

Gus gave me a despairing look.

"I think I had better check on my children," I said hastily.

"Traitor," Sid mouthed as I fled.

. . .

That afternoon I threw myself into chores that I had been neglecting, scrubbing the kitchen floor until it gleamed. Bridie got up and ate two slices of toast laden with butter, which I took as a good sign. I bundled Liam up and took him to the park. I dredged filets of fish in flour and fried them along with potatoes until they were crispy and golden. In short, I concentrated on my wifely duties, all to avoid the single question: What was I going to tell Daniel? To my relief and annoyance, the decision was taken out of my hands. Dinnertime came and went with no Daniel. This was not unusual, so it was not until after I had put the children to bed that I started to worry. I lay awake after the house was dark waiting to hear his footsteps, his key in the door. When I did, I breathed a sigh of relief but stayed where I was. And when he tiptoed in and slid under the covers I kept my breathing regular, letting him think I was asleep, and lay beside him listening to the wind whistle outside until I finally drifted off.

I awoke to a kiss on the forehead. "I'm sorry I was home so late," he said, early the next morning. "I was taking care of the ambassador. I'm off again to make sure my men are in place."

"I'll get you breakfast." I started to pull the covers back, reluctant to leave the warmth for the chill October morning.

"Stay." He laid a gentle hand on me. "It's going to be a long day. I'll see you and the kids at the parade tonight. There are tickets to the main stands down on the kitchen table courtesy of the ambassador and his wife."

"Daniel," I began, not sure what I would say. But he took the decision from me.

"Go back to sleep," he said. "I love you."

I lay back, listening to his footsteps running down the stairs and out of the front door, feeling both relieved and insulted. He could not blame me now for not sharing what I knew. But he was the one who asked me to investigate. Had he forgotten? Or did he doubt that I had any information of worth? Most likely he was exhausted by the hours he had kept for the last two weeks.

*I will be glad when this is over,* I thought, as Bridie, Liam, and I made our way uptown late that afternoon, long before the parade was due to start. Bridie had insisted that she was quite well enough to go and I hated to deny her. She did look much better, with just a sniffle and no trace of a fever. With a million extra people still in the city, taxis and cabs were all full and the line to get on the El ran around the block. We finally decided to walk over to Broadway and risk riding the trolley as far as Forty-Second Street. I would be glad to get rid of this nagging worry about my friends and to have the city back to its normal population size. We joined the crowd flowing toward Fifth Avenue and saw that the stands were outside the brand-new library building, completed but not yet opened. It looked magnificent with its steps leading up to grand archways and two proud stone lions guarding it.

I had not seen the Court of Honor yet, and I must admit that it was overwhelming. Columns towered high above Fifth Avenue with strands of lights and swathes of cloth draped between them. A red carpet covered the street between the columns. They looked so majestic, I could imagine a god or goddess of giant size walking between them. But perhaps I had goddesses on my mind because of the suffragist float. Just beyond the columns, the stands on either side of Fifth Avenue were already filling up with people. Police made a cordon around them, checking the tickets of everyone who wanted to enter. Those without tickets were directed farther down the street, where stores and houses were selling places to watch the parade.

"Four dollars for a seat!" I heard one man yell. "That's extortion!"

I showed our tickets to the policeman, who saluted and personally escorted us to the central grandstand. I guessed the ambassador had given us some very important tickets indeed that would place us with the dignitaries. The grandstand was almost empty at this point and we took our places on a long bench a few rows up. I looked behind me and saw benched seating rising at least a hundred feet. At the center of the grandstand, several rows above us, was the vice president's box: a flat stage with more comfortable seating, including gilded armchairs. The late afternoon wind rose, fluttering the flags and bunting, and we huddled together.

"I'm glad Mary Kate is at home," I said to Bridie. "She would be frozen." I looked at Bridie with concern. Was it too soon to have brought her into this cold?

"I'm quite warm," Bridie said, guessing my thoughts. "I'm glad I brought my fur muff."

"How will we see in the dark?" Liam asked, leaning out to peer down the avenue.

"You wait. We're told it will be a light show like no other," I replied. "The whole city will light up."

We amused ourselves commenting on women's hats. Bridie looked for friends in the crowd.

"Julia said she will be here and perhaps Helen." I thought it was quite unlikely that she would see anyone she knew in this huge throng. But as this thought passed through my head, I saw someone whom I recognized. In the stands opposite us across the street, I saw Willa's father and sister. At the bottom of the stands at street level was a little fenced-off area with a velvet rope and some comfortable chairs like those in the vice president's box. Mr. and Miss Hartman were sitting there, talking animatedly to someone I did not know. I watched them for a while until their conversation lagged. I could have sworn that Winnie Hartman looked right me. I rose slightly and waved, wondering if I should cross the street and tell her that her sister had been found. But her eyes showed no hint of recognition and I had to conclude that she had not seen me. She had been correct, I mused. Her sister had been in no danger and had put her friends to considerable trouble looking for her. I had thought her a rather unfeeling sister, I admit, but my investigation showed that she had had this kind of experience with her sister before.

I watched as she took her father's arm and leaned in close to say something. There was obvious affection between them. Willa had mentioned that her impetus for research was to defeat the disease that had robbed her sister of the life she should have had. But looking at the sister, I wondered if she felt the same way. She looked quite content in her position. Spending time with suffragists had made me reflect more on women and society than ever before. Growing up, I would not have thought of myself as on the same side as the wealthy Mrs. Belmont or Miss Hartman, but now I did. After all, did we not all live in a society in which neither hard work, class, nor privilege could keep us from being defined only in relation to the men in our lives? I looked over at Bridie, still straining her eyes to see any of her friends in the crowd. I wondered if it would be different for her generation.

I was deep in thought when a rather rumpled suit and a brown derby hat caught my attention. Across the street, standing in the shadow of the grandstand, was Mr. Jones, the Pinkerton detective, and he was looking right at me. My heart began thumping in my chest as I remembered his rough hands grabbing me. What did he want with me now? Mrs. Parker was found. She and her husband would be reunited tonight, unless she had not told me the truth. After all, I had no way of knowing what had been in that letter. Was Mr. Jones still looking for Willa Parker? He touched his cap and walked up the stairs of the grandstand opposite, taking giant steps from bench to bench. The highest levels of the grandstand were already hidden in shadow, but the man by whom he took a seat looked a lot like Dr. Parker.

We waited as the sun began to set behind the tall buildings, turning the sky red and glinting off the windows across from us. The stands were now rapidly filling as automobiles and carriages deposited ladies draped in furs and men in top hats at the edge of the red-carpeted stretch of the avenue.

"How's my little man?" A deep voice beside me made me jump.

"Daddy!" Liam jumped up and flung his arms around Daniel's neck.

"You're in my seat," Daniel picked Liam up and tickled him, before sitting down with a still-giggling Liam on his lap.

"So you're able to sit with us? How lovely," I said, happily slipping my arm through his.

"I'm sorry I've been away so much," he said. "As it happens, this is a seat with a good view of the whole area and I need to be able to jump up at a moment's notice if there is trouble."

"Do you expect trouble?" I asked a little anxiously.

"I wouldn't have let you bring Liam and Bridie if I did," he said. Then, as if remembering his request for the first time he said, "What did you find out yesterday? What are those women up to?"

"*Those women* are my friends," I prevaricated. "What are you worried that they might do?"

"We heard that there might be some sort of protest, some sort of violence," he said. "What did you find?"

I was glad that he could not see my face in the shadow of my hat. Twilight had come, with the last of the sun's rays now faded until the whole Court of Honor was plunged into darkness.

"I don't believe there will be any violence," I said in a small voice as my stomach churned. I couldn't lie to Daniel, but I couldn't betray my friends. Luckily, at that moment the most amazing thing happened. Someone must have thrown a switch, because every light on the street came on. There were not only the bulbs strung on the Court of Honor, but lights on every building. I am not exaggerating when I say it was bright as day. No one had ever seen the like in the whole history of humanity, I suppose, and the whole crowd rose to their feet as one and cheered. An automobile drove up and the vice president got out, waving to the crowd, and ascended the steep steps at the side of the stand to take his seat. In the excitement of the moment I conveniently forgot to answer Daniel's question. And before he could ask it again, the first float started rolling across the red-carpeted street toward the grandstand. The parade had begun.

Liam had grown weary of sitting on a hard bench, even if the floats were both interesting and amusing. Two hours is a long time for any small boy.

"I need to go pee-pee," he whispered in my ear.

*Jesus, Mary, and Joseph,* I thought. *How are we going to get out of here and where is the nearest lavatory?* Of course, a small boy could do it in an alleyway, but it would be embarrassing to try and squeeze past all those people.

"Can you hold it a little while longer, do you think?" I asked. "If we go now we'll miss Aunt Sid and Aunt Gus, and you'd be sad if you didn't see them, wouldn't you?"

'How much longer is it?" he asked.

"It must be soon. We've already seen a hundred floats or more," I said.

"My behind is also getting sore," Bridie said. Then she peered up Fifth Avenue and exclaimed, "I think I can see them!"

I looked too. And yes, she was right. There came the float, drawn by its six white horses. The backdrop of Mount Olympus with its peacock glowed in the artificial lights. The *Winged Victory* sparkled like white marble, although her wings were still by her sides, not yet spread. The goddesses were tastefully arranged beside their columns. They sat on their golden thrones, one playing the lyre, another examining her hair in a mirror, others chatting. A charming scene.

As they approached the grandstands the goddesses stood up.

"There's Aunt Gus," Liam cried excitedly as he recognized her. "And Aunt Sid."

I grabbed on to his shirt as he leaned forward.

As the float came to a halt at the center of the grandstand the goddesses all stood, taking classical Greek poses. For a moment the tableau resembled the side of ancient Greek pottery and the crowd clapped appreciatively. Then two of the goddesses turned a crank, and the *Winged Victory* suddenly spread her wings. There was a gasp of appreciation and applause from the crowd, and then a second gasp. As the wings spread, the giant banner was unfurled. As I had guessed, it read VOTES FOR WOMEN. At the same time, the goddesses had turned over the sashes they wore. The sashes also proclaimed VOTES FOR WOMEN. They now turned to face the grandstand. Several of them raised signs. In bold red letters they said, WE PROTEST! JUSTICE FOR ENGLISH SUFFRAGETTES. FOR SHAME, SIR EDWARD! ENGLAND, STOP FORCE-FEEDING OUR SISTERS. DEATH BEFORE SURRENDER.

With that they collapsed, one by one, onto the float in a display of mock death.

I could hear murmurs from the crowd around me. Angry murmurs now, as I had feared. A few women in the audience clapped but were quickly silenced. "Disgusting," I heard. "Making a spectacle of themselves. Making it political, and in front of the children too. Lock them up." A whistle was blown. Several policemen were heading toward the float, about to arrest its occupants. But at the very moment this was happening, shots rang out.

# Twenty-Three

Immediately the scene erupted into chaos. Somewhere above my head came the sound of glass shattering. Screams filled the air, their sound echoing from the tall buildings on either side of the street. I had instinctively grabbed Bridie and flung myself over Liam to protect him. When the shooting had ceased I raised my head cautiously. Daniel was no longer beside me. I felt my heart lurch until I saw that he had clambered down onto the street and had joined the policemen who had been guarding the route. Some of these policemen now had guns drawn and were peering around nervously at the stands on both sides, trying to assess where the shots had come from. Between the brightness of the lights there were deep pools of shadow. When I saw Daniel standing there, open and exposed in the middle of the street, my instinct was to yell for him to come back to the safety of the grandstand. Then I realized that this was his job. This had always been his job: to go into danger, to face the shooter, to protect everyone else. I felt proud and alarmed at the same time.

"Let me up. You're squashing me," Liam protested and I realized I was still lying across him. I sat up. Bridie got up too, still clinging to my sleeve. "Is it all right?" she asked. "Is it over? Are they going to shoot again?"

"I don't think so," I said. "See, the policemen have their guns drawn. They'd see where a shot was coming from and be able to grab the shooter."

"Who were they trying to shoot?" Bridie asked, now looking up into the grandstand. "Did they hit anyone?"

"I don't know yet," I said. Some of the people around me had stood up and were looking about them. I too was about to stand up when Daniel called out, "Ladies and gentlemen. Stay calm but keep ducked down until we can ascertain where the shots were coming from and apprehend the shooter." Two of Daniel's men approached him and he pointed up to the stands. "Help the Secret Service protect the vice president." I looked up to see two men in dark suits in front of the vice president's box, shielding him from view, guns drawn.

"From the other side," a man high up in the grandstand shouted back. "A shot went over my head."

"I heard a window breaking above me in the library," another man shouted.

I looked up at the splendid new library building. I hadn't realized there was glass inside those impressive arches.

"Has anyone been shot?" Daniel scanned the tiers of dignitaries. I swiveled around but could only see backs and bonnets as people tried to stay hidden. Since there was no response I presumed that everyone in the stand was safe. At least nobody was screaming or calling for help. Maybe the shooter was playing a stupid prank to scare us, like the students on the pirate ship, and had fired over our heads to cause a disruption. Or maybe he was just a bad shot.

Some of the policemen had crossed to the stands across the street and were already interviewing the crowd in the front rows. I could see someone pointing, and other people who clearly had no idea where the shots had come from. It was only then that I looked at the float. The goddesses had been playing dead as part of their protest and had not dared to move while shots were being fired. Now, one by one, they got to their feet, brushing themselves off, hastily rearranging their costumes in case they were too revealing. I could see them helping each other up, looking around with big, frightened eyes, some laughing nervously, standing in a tight little group and not sure where was safety. I picked out Sid and Gus. Sid, with her usual brave and determined attitude, was standing as protector as she scanned the grandstands and the windows above.

They were all on their feet now. All except one. One woman did not get up. Sid went over to her to help her to her feet. Then I saw her recoil. A hand went to her mouth. She pointed downward. "Over here," she shouted. "Quickly. Over here. Help. This woman has been shot."

Daniel and one of the policemen rushed to her. The woman lay face down on the deck of the float, her arms sprawled out, just as the others had lain in the mock death scene. As I stared in horror I could see a red stain spreading across the folds of her white robe.

"Is she hurt? Who is it?" I heard the words as the policeman climbed up onto the float, then put out his arms to hold back the women who were crowding around.

"Stand over there, ladies. Come on. Move back."

I strained to see who lay there. Most of the women were unknown to me, and with their identical Grecian hairstyles and white dresses, it was hard to tell them apart.

"Stay away, please. This is police business now," the constable snapped. "There's nothing you can do to help her." He beckoned other constables over. One of them climbed up onto the float, knelt, and felt for a pulse. Then he stood, shaking his head.

"Should we turn her over?" he asked. "Or leave her like this until we can get a member of the homicide squad here?"

"Better not to touch her," Daniel said. "One of you go and send a message to police headquarters immediately. Tell them there's been a homicide at the parade. And there are plenty of press photographers in the crowd. Get one of them to take pictures of the body and both the grandstands. Someone has to have fired from the stand on the other side or from one of the windows in that building over there. A couple of you men go and check that out. Get a list of everyone who was watching from each of the windows and see where a gun might have been disposed of."

His voice was loud and commanding enough for me to hear it, but I suppose the scene had grown eerily quiet. One of the men ran off, presumably to summon a detective from headquarters. But I saw another of the constables step up to face Daniel, demanding to know who he was and what right he had to take command. Another constable clearly recognized him and murmured in the first constable's ear.

"I don't care." I heard this clearly enough. "He ain't my boss now and he's no business to be telling us what to do."

"Hold your horses, Constable." Daniel held up a hand. "I agree. A normal homicide is the business of the police and I'm no longer head of homicide. But I'm now representing the federal government to make sure foreign dignitaries are safe. The shooter was clearly aiming at someone important in the grandstand. This poor young woman unfortunately got in the way. So it's up to me to make sure that the shooter is apprehended."

Another man had joined them, looking distinguished in a dark suit and derby hat. I recognized him as one of the organizers of the event. He carried a clipboard with him. "What do we do about the parade, then?" he asked. "We can't keep the rest of the floats waiting indefinitely." As he spoke I realized that I had subconsciously recognized the music of a marching band getting closer. They would be here momentarily and find the way blocked.

"We can't let it go ahead as if nothing has happened," Daniel said. "How many more floats are coming after this?"

The man consulted a list. "Only four," he said. "We're pretty close to the end."

"We can hardly send them back to where they came from," Daniel said.

"I should think not. It's miles, all the way up through Central Park, back to a Hundred Tenth Street. And the streets won't be blocked off any longer. They wouldn't get through." He pushed back his derby to scratch his head. "Nor could we reroute them at this stage. I don't know what to say. I never believed in a million years something like this could happen."

I could tell that Daniel too was perplexed. "This is now a crime scene. I don't like to move anything until the detectives get here," he said.

"I say, you down there," a loud voice boomed from up in the stands. "I think you need to evacuate everyone out of here. None of us enjoys feeling like sitting ducks."

"My wife is a sensitive creature. She shouldn't have to witness this," a closer man joined in.

"I'm afraid nobody can move at the moment, sir," Daniel called up to the man. "But I think you're quite safe now. The police are going through the building opposite and checking everyone on the other grandstand."

"I reckon the idiot has got away by now," I heard someone mutter. "He's not going to stick around to be caught, is he? The police should arrest him for causing a panic." I realized that many in the stands had not seen the dead body. Only those close to the float had any idea that someone had been killed, and I guessed the police would want to keep it that way to avoid a panic.

I scanned the opposite side of the street. The shot had to have come from the grandstand or the building behind it. There had been police constables stationed a regular intervals along the street, keeping the crowd back on either side of the stands, so nobody could have crossed the cordons, come in front of the stand, taken a few shots, and then run off again. The people on that stand were also looking around in confusion. Nobody seemed to be indicating that shots had been fired near them. I did notice the building behind had several open windows. That was the most likely place for someone to have taken a shot and then gotten away. But . . . the shooter had presumably been aiming at one of the dignitaries higher up in the grandstand. I swiveled around to check on the German ambassador, British admiral, and Japanese royalty. They all seemed unscathed. Had an anarchist been aiming at one of them? Or maybe another important figure in the crowd with whom I was not familiar—an industry magnate who treated his workers badly, perhaps.

I directed my gaze to those windows. With the lights so bright, surely a shooter would have had a clear view of the upper rows of the grandstand from any one of them. In fact, it would have been hard to miss a target sitting at that level. And yet glass had been broken above the stand and someone had been shot below it. What could that mean? That the shooter had been so frightened that he couldn't control the gun or that someone had tried to wrestle it away from him when he was discovered in the act of shooting? In which case the police would soon be told about this. My bet was on a disgruntled citizen of one of the visiting countries. Maybe one of the thousands of servicemen in town who did not want to go back to his own country. Maybe someone who had had to flee to America and still bore a grudge about what had happened in his past.

Liam interrupted my thoughts.

"Mama. I want to go to Daddy." Liam climbed onto my lap. "I don't like it here."

"I don't like it much either, darling." I hugged him to me. "But we all have to stay here for a little while."

In what seemed like a remarkably short time, a new police contingent arrived. I was relieved to see that the detective was Lieutenant

Corelli, whom Daniel had recommended for promotion before he left the department. A good man and one who respected Daniel, unlike some of New York's finest. I watched him recognize Daniel and shake hands with him.

"I'm glad to see you here, Sullivan," he said. "They told me some bossy type from the Feds wanted to take over."

Daniel had to smile. "I'm with the new Bureau of Investigation now," he said. "I'm assigned to keep foreign dignitaries safe, and apparently I haven't been doing my job well. There were shots fired and a young woman is dead. So far it seems she's the only one. I'm not sure who they were aiming at, but someone heard glass breaking above the stands. So presumably they were aiming at one of the foreign ambassadors up there."

Lieutenant Corelli walked with Daniel over to the body. The goddesses were now huddled together on the float, as motionless as the tableau they had portrayed before, staring in horror at the woman who lay before them.

"One of the women from that float," Daniel said.

Corelli studied them, hauled himself up onto the float, then knelt beside the body. "I presume on the float they'd have been high enough to get in the way of a shot if it was fired from street level."

"That's true," Daniel said, "But surely someone would have noticed if a shot was fired near them? And there were constables stationed nearby too."

"It's an ugly business when a lady is killed, accident or not," Corelli said. He turned the body over. I didn't recognize her at first, then one of the goddesses gave a cry of horror.

"It's Willa," she said. "Willa Parker."

## ❋ Twenty-Four ❋

The man in the derby hat stepped up to them. "We need to get the parade moving again," he said. "The reputation of New York is at stake. People are getting restless and the marching band will be here any second. They paid to see a parade. And all the rest of the crowds down the street, waiting patiently. The parade must go on!"

Lieutenant Corelli glanced at Daniel. "This is a crime scene, sir," he said. "A homicide has been committed. There is a shooter in our midst. We have to make sure everyone is safe."

"There are only four more floats to go," the man said. "Let's get them through and done with and then we can allow the crowd to disperse. I'd like to play this down as much as possible, don't you see. We don't want it making headlines in the world's press. They already think of America as a lawless place."

"I suppose we could remove the body and let this float move on," Corelli said.

"Begging your pardon, Lieutenant," one of the constables spoke up, "but we were about to arrest these young women for disturbing the peace. They were having one of these suffrage protests, displaying all sorts of signs."

"Quite right, Constable," the man in the derby hat agreed. "They knew full well that such behavior would not be tolerated. We made it clear from the start. No signs of any political, religious, or controversial nature. I want them booked."

Lieutenant Corelli stared up at the float and then at Daniel. His expression indicated that he wished he had not been called to this scene. "Yes, very well, Constable," he said. "Have this float led off to one side. There should be room for the subsequent floats to pass it if they are not too big."

"Right." The constable nodded agreement. "You," he called up to the driver. "Bring the float over to the side down here, past the grandstand. And you women stay exactly where you are. Nobody think of leaving. You're all in serious trouble."

"We did nothing wrong," one of the women exclaimed. "We were expressing our opinion as is our First Amendment right as citizens of this country where all people are supposed to be free."

"Not when it disrupts official proceedings," the constable said. "You knew such protests were banned. You knew darned well and you flouted our rules."

"You've disgraced the City of New York," the man in the derby hat said.

"And we will need statements from all of you regarding the death of this young woman," Corelli said. "One of you must have seen something."

"We saw nothing," Sid said, defiant as ever. "We were busy dying, expressing solidarity with our tortured sisters in England."

The float started forward with a jerk, causing some of the women to lose their balance. I suspected this had been done quite deliberately, the driver obviously not being a supporter of their cause and realizing that he might now be detained for hours with the end of the parade almost in sight. A policeman walked in front of the horses, making the crowd step back until they came to the entrance to Fortieth Street. Here they managed to move the float off the main thoroughfare, allowing plenty of room for subsequent floats to pass. They were now out of the brightest of the lights and I strained to see what was happening to them.

The brass band we had heard approaching was the first to appear. A large float depicting a town square with a bandstand came down Fifth Avenue. The band were dressed in bright red and gold uniforms and all sported exaggeratedly large mustaches. It was a jolly scene but people in the crowd applauded halfheartedly, which must have been discouraging to the musicians. I could see that people around me were still anxious to leave. I would have felt the same way but it occurred to me that I might be of help to Daniel and Lieutenant Corelli. I leaned forward to see if I could observe the goddesses' float. Several policemen were standing beside it, one with a notebook, taking names or statements. Corelli had gone with them, but Daniel stayed close to the grandstand, still alert, his eyes scanning the other side of the street.

Soon one of the constables returned. "We went through the building, sir. Most of it is the bank with offices upstairs. Only one of them was open, with people watching from a window. I got their names and addresses, just in case. And next door is a residence belonging to a doctor. He and his wife and children had all been watching from the dining room window but saw nothing until they heard a gunshot. They confessed they were so fascinated with the horrific spectacle these women were making of themselves—the wife's words, not mine, sir—that they had no idea where the shots might have come from. Somewhere down below, that's all they could say."

"Thank you, Constable," Daniel said. He broke off as the next float came past. This was a true carnival float of circus performers— tumbling clowns, a juggler, a fire-eater, while clowns on unicycles escorted it on either side. Liam perked up when he saw this. Any thought of wanting to go home was forgotten.

"Clowns, Mama," he said and leaned as far as he could as the circus disappeared down Fifth Avenue. How easily the young can forget bad happenings and move on. Luckily, neither Liam nor Bridie had seen Mrs. Parker's body on the float and I determined to keep the day as normal as possible for their sakes.

This float was now followed by a giant boot inhabited by the old woman who lived in a shoe and her children. My children approved of this too, and then the final float was a large fire-breathing dragon and a knight in shining armor. It was most impressive. The way the mechanical dragon moved was almost real. So much thought and creativity had gone into these floats. It seemed horrible that the event was now marred by such a tragedy.

Last of all came another marching band. We waited until it had passed, then Daniel borrowed a megaphone to address the crowd.

"You are now free to leave in an orderly fashion," he said. "We already have the names of everybody who occupied the grandstands. If anyone saw anything that can help us apprehend a killer, please talk to one of the constables as you leave. We apologize that your splendid evening was interrupted in this way."

One by one the rows of people exited in silence. We were all too stunned by what had just happened. When it was our turn I helped Liam to climb down the steps at the side, then stepped out into the street.

"Bridie, hold on to Liam for a moment," I said. "I have to speak to the ladies and see what I can do for them."

She nodded, a worried look still on her face. "Are they really going to arrest Aunt Sid and Aunt Gus?"

"It's only a formality," I said. "I'm sure they'll be given a warning and then released." But I was thinking of those brave women in England who were treated so shamefully, flung into jail and force-fed. As I slipped past the cordon of police I heard my name being yelled. "Molly. Where are you going?"

Daniel reached out to grab my arm.

"I just wanted to see if I could do anything for my friends."

"Your friends are under arrest. Don't interfere. Stay away," he said firmly.

"They're not going to take them to jail, are they?"

"Quite possibly," Daniel said, still frowning at me. "They knew what they were doing, Molly. It was made clear to everyone that no form of protest or political slogan was going to be tolerated. I expect they'll have to pay a fine, maybe spend a night in jail."

"We should do something," I said. "You should do something."

"Molly, I'm an officer of the law," he said. "They broke it and now they face the consequences. All I can think of is thank God you weren't on that float with them. You might have been the one who was shot."

"You think someone deliberately shot at those women because they were protesting?" I asked.

"I don't know what to think yet," he said. "Now, please take the children home. This is no place for any of you. I need to make sure that all these foreign dignitaries get safely back to their embassies or wherever they are staying."

The moment he finished speaking a large man in some kind of military uniform adorned with much brass came striding over to us. "Herr Sullivan, the ambassador's wife is much upset. We have been assured that it would be a pleasant and orderly affair. Instead of this we have shootings. Like the Wild West. This is not good. Please send someone to bring their carriage to this spot."

"I'm afraid this street remains closed, Colonel," Daniel said, "but I will have one of our men escort the ambassador and his wife around the library. The carriages are waiting at the park."

"Humph." The colonel made a disgusted noise. "I knew it was a mistake to come here. You Americans have no sense of order like we have at home in Germany."

He stomped off. Daniel gave me a weak smile and rolled his eyes at the departing colonel before indicating I should go. I hesitated. I wanted to tell him that I knew the dead woman. I probably knew more about her than most people in New York. But I could see that he was trying to handle too many things at once. I took Liam's hand, nodded to Bridie. "Come on, then. Let's see how we get home from here. I suspect we might have to walk, with all this crowd wanting the El and the trolley."

I took their hands and we made for Forty-Second Street.

"That poor lady." Bridie sounded close to tears. "Was she shot because people don't like suffragists?"

"I don't think so, my darling," I said. "I think it was all a horrible mistake. They were aiming for someone else. Someone important."

But as we joined the crowd going around the back of the library I found myself wondering why, out of all the women on that float, someone had killed Willa Parker.

## Twenty-Five

We were all tired and cranky by the time we finally got home. We had stood on the El platform as train after train came by already full or people surged in front of us. I knew that I could walk home the two miles or so from Forty-Second Street, but Liam couldn't and I didn't feel up to carrying him. I had money in my pocket for a hansom cab or even a taximeter but every one that passed us was already full.

I paused to consider what I should do but was buffeted by the crowd of people in all directions and a cold wind that went through to the skin. Liam tugged at my hand and I leaned down.

"Mama, I don't feel well," he said, and promptly threw up on the sidewalk. That, at least, made people give us a little room, and I decided there was nothing for it but to get in the line for the El. I felt little Liam's forehead and, as I feared, it was hot to the touch. I had to get him home as soon as possible. Finally we managed to get into an El carriage and almost couldn't get out again when we came to Tenth Street. As we came up Patchin Place I glanced across at Sid and Gus's house. They might already be down at the Tombs by now, thrown into a damp, dark cell. There were too many men who would love to teach uppity women a lesson and remind them of their place.

I stepped into the front hall wanting nothing more than a cup of tea and a rest but was greeted by howls coming from upstairs. Mary Kate was obviously not asleep. Aileen was sitting on a chair by the kitchen stove. She jumped up as we came in.

"She's been in that sort of mood all day," Aileen said. "I tried to get her down to sleep but she was having none of it. I thought I would see if crying for a few minutes would tire her to sleep." Her face told me that she'd had enough for one day. I thought again that I had been leaving her to do all the household duties an awful lot and she was still a young girl.

"Go and make us both a cup of tea," I said. "I'll take over."

She gave me a grateful little smile. I trudged wearily upstairs, asking Bridie to tend to her brother. Having just recovered, she was the least likely to get sick. I went in to see Mary Kate, held her, and sang to her until she fell asleep from exhaustion. Then I came down and started to warm up the chicken soup I had prepared in advance. I didn't think Daniel would be home anytime soon, and he would probably eat elsewhere, as he had done most of the week. I took a bowl up to Liam in bed but he would not eat more than a spoonful. He was feverish, overtired, whiny, clingy, and obviously upset by what he had seen and overheard on our journey home. "They were shooting at Aunt Sid and Aunt Gus," he said, "and the lady died and there was blood."

I held him close. "I know, my darling. It was horrible, but Aunt Sid and Aunt Gus are safe. And we're safe. And your daddy is in charge."

"He'll find the bad men with guns, right?"

"Yes, he will."

I kissed his hot little forehead, tucked him in, and left him, not feeling as calm as I had tried to sound. I too had anxious thoughts swirling around my head. My friends had probably been arrested and Willa Parker lay dead. And the worst thing was I could do nothing. I had been commissioned to find Willa Parker. I had done that and thought my job was over. Now she lay dead. Was it a just a horrible twist of fate that she was in the wrong place at the wrong time or had somebody come to the parade with the intention of killing her? It wasn't my fault, I told myself, but a thought nagged at me that perhaps she wouldn't have been killed if she'd stayed hidden. Mr. Jones had been at the parade, with a man who could well have been Dr. Parker. Was it possible that her husband had been looking for her and had chosen this very public place to kill her?

"That's rubbish," I said out loud. She was killed by mistake, or, at the very worst, as an act of retribution against suffragists. But the guilt wouldn't go away. Here I was, safe and at home, while my friends were probably in prison by now. But there was nothing I could do. I was stuck here with three children. That was now my lot in life. And anyway, I had overheard their plan for this part of their project. They should have bail money ready. If anything could be done, someone else was already doing it.

I came down and sat with Bridie and Aileen while Bridie told her all the details of the parade.

"Holy Mother of God," Aileen exclaimed. "Thank the good Lord that nobody was shooting at the parade my father was in. Do they know who did it? Was it anarchists? Did they catch the man?"

"Not when we'd left," I said. "The police were there on the spot, controlling the crowds, but they didn't find the shooter. Maybe it was someone in the building behind, although the police were searching up there too. We'll know some more when Daniel gets home."

I'd only just finished this sentence when there was a loud rap at my front door. An authoritative, demanding knocking. Aileen shot me a terrified look. Bridie grabbed at my skirt as I jumped up. *They've come for me*, I thought. *Someone told them that I was at the planning meeting. Someone saw me at the float building and they think I'm one of the suffragists.* But that thought was replaced by a more terrifying one: *Something has happened to Daniel. They are here with bad news.* I took a deep breath as I went to the front door and opened it.

"Will someone tell me what in blazes is going on?" Cousin Prudence was standing there in the dark alleyway, almost spitting fire. "I was told the parade would be over by eight at the latest. Now it is almost ten o'clock and no sign of my cousin and her companion. Have they given no thought to the fact that their cousin may wish to eat a meal at the proper time? They have no servant—which I find quite inexcusable—so here I am, stuck all alone with no food."

The way she was looking at me it was clear she wished to be invited in and fed.

"I'm so sorry," I said. "I'm afraid your cousin and her friend have been unavoidably detained. There was a tragic accident at the parade. One of the members of their float was shot by accident and they have all been transported to police headquarters to make statements."

"Shot? At the parade?"

"I'm afraid so," I said.

"Do they know who was doing the shooting? And why?"

"Not when we left," I said. "It seems likely that the shooter was aiming at one of the foreign dignitaries. There was the British admiral, the German ambassador, and several others."

"Ah, so it was most likely a foreigner, then. Useless with guns, no doubt. No red-blooded American would miss his target. The poor girls must be most distressed. It was presumably one of their Vassar friends?"

"Yes. It was," I said. "Look, Miss Walcott, I'm sorry but I must make sure my children are in bed. I'm still waiting for my husband to come home."

"He's some kind of policeman, I believe," Cousin Prudence said. She paused to sniff. "Was he on the beat this afternoon?"

"He's no longer with the New York Police but is employed by the federal government as head of their new investigation bureau in New York," I replied, a little coldly. "He was responsible for overall security at this event."

"Oh, I see." She looked grudgingly impressed. "Quite an important man, then?"

"Yes. Quite important."

"You did rather well for yourself, then," she said. "Not all immigrants become prosperous so quickly." She tried to peer around me into the house. "A nice little house and a husband with a good job."

This was so patronizing that I felt my hackles rising. "Actually," I said, "the house was mine. I was a successful businesswoman before I married." I paused to let this sink in. "Now, if you'll excuse me. I'm sorry you've been left in the lurch. I'm sure Sid and Gus will be home as soon as they can." My generous side took over. "I could bring you a bowl of the soup I'm keeping warm to tide you over if you like. And I'm sure Sid and Gus have food in their kitchen."

"That's most kind of you, Mrs. Sullivan," she said. "I'd appreciate it. They may have food but I've never had to cook for myself in my life. I moved from my parents' house to my sister's—she did very well for herself. Married well, into the cream of Boston society. And we've always had servants, of course."

"I'll go and get that soup," I said before I was treated to a lecture on the Boston Walcotts. I dished up a bowl, put a piece of bread on a tray beside it and carried it out to her, then across the street, setting it down on their kitchen table. I could see she wasn't happy with eating in the kitchen, but I wasn't about to find a tablecloth and lay the dining table for her. I bade her good night and went home. If my friends weren't let out tonight I'd presumably have to explain what had happened to them, but I didn't feel up to it at the moment.

By the time I returned home Bridie and Aileen had gone to bed. I sat up, checking on Liam every few minutes, sponging his little head with a cloth and making sure his breathing was steady and strong. I always feel anxious when my children are ill. And tonight I knew I could not sleep until I saw Daniel. I heard the clock on a nearby church chime eleven. I was about ready to go and tuck myself in beside Liam when I heard a tap on the front door. Not Daniel. He had his key. Surely not Cousin Prudence again at this time of night. I opened it and Gus almost fell into the front hall.

"Oh, thank God you're still up, Molly," she said. "I've had the most awful time."

I looked around. "Where is Sid?"

"Still locked up. They all are. They were especially hard on Sid. She was rather forthright in her dealings with them . . ."

"She was rude to them, you mean?" I asked with the ghost of a smile.

Gus nodded. "Exactly. She attempted to put them straight on several items of law."

"Well, come in and have a cup of tea," I said. "Or would you rather have a glass of Daniel's whiskey?"

"I wouldn't say no to that," Gus said.

I led her through to the back parlor and poured her a dram of whiskey. She took a sip, coughed a little, but then drained it. "Ah, that's better," she said. "It was awful, Molly. They were so aggressive to us. They told us we were all murder suspects. As if any of us on the float could have shot her. Sid pointed out we were all lying down playing dead at the time."

"Of course," I said. "You were all lying down. I saw you."

"So all they could charge us with was disturbing the peace, but they weren't going to release us until Monday, as they said the judge was off for the weekend and couldn't be reached. They were grinning when they said it."

"So how did you get out?"

"I escaped."

"You escaped from prison?" I looked at her with admiration.

She laughed and shook her head. "We were being marshaled from the court into the women's prison side of the Tombs when a drunken woman was being brought in at the same time. She was screaming, cursing, flailing her arms, and managed to hit a constable squarely on the jaw before breaking free and staggering off. This caused other constables to chase her. I was at the very back of the line. It was quite dark out there. I took my chance and dodged behind a delivery cart, staying there until everyone else had gone inside."

"But won't they have your name and come looking for you?" I interrupted, wondering if she was here to ask me to hide her.

"They hadn't taken all our details yet," she said, "so as long as the other women don't mention that I was there, I should be okay." She still looked so pale that I poured her another finger of whiskey, which she sipped at gratefully before continuing, staring down into the glass. "The murder of poor Willa Parker foiled our plans. Several of our members were not planning to lie down in protest or be arrested. They were meant to follow us to the jail and bail us out immediately. But of course with the murder, the police arrested everyone. So as soon as I got clear I removed my sash hastily and made my way uptown. My first thought was to go to Mrs. Belmont. The police would not accept the bail money that we had ready but perhaps she had enough clout to bail us out. I took the trolley all the way up to her mansion—it took ages, of course, because of the number of people on the streets." She looked up. "And when I finally got to her house I found that she wasn't there. She has gone to her estate on Long Island for the weekend, apparently. I suppose she wanted to be well out of the way if anything went wrong with our protest. She's definitely for our cause but can't be too public about it because of her social standing."

"You could send her a telegram in the morning if they are not released then."

"Yes, I could, although I don't know what good it will do. Sid and Alma Van Horn made it quite clear that we women have plenty of money to bail ourselves out, but they wouldn't listen. We were told that a night or two in jail would help us come to our senses and nobody was going to be released until they had investigated the murder." She covered her face with her hands. "It's all been a nightmare, Molly. All we wanted was to bring our cause to the attention of the public, especially to the British delegate. And now one of us is dead. Poor Willa Parker. I didn't really know her but she was one of us. And she didn't deserve to die." She reached out and took my hand. "You did all that work locating her for us, Molly. And now she's dead. I can't help thinking . . ."

"That we made a mistake in finding her?" I asked. "I've been battling with the same thing. I have to believe that her murder was a mistake, Gus. That someone was aiming for an important person in the stands and somehow the gun went off at the wrong time or the person shooting was unfamiliar with guns and Willa got hit."

"I hope you're right, because otherwise I'd never forgive myself," Gus said. "Did we somehow let the killer know where she was going to be?"

I gave a nod of agreement.

"Her husband," Gus said angrily. "It has to have been her husband. Look how aggressive he was when he came to find her. She was going to leave him and he wasn't having it."

"I believe she was planning to stay with him, and even be the cause of a lucrative job offer for him," I said. "Although, I thought I saw him in the stands across from where I was sitting, along with his Pinkerton detective. I don't know how he afforded it. Seats in those stands were awfully expensive for ordinary people. He didn't seem to be ultrawealthy. Anyway, they have the names of everybody who purchased tickets, and the police were guarding the street so that nobody could walk past during the parade." Even as I said it my thoughts went back to the windows in the building beyond. I had heard that the police had questioned people in that building and had not found anything suspicious. But the roof? Had it been possible to gain access to the roof and then to fire down on the parade? And even with all those bright lights, there had been plenty of pools of darkness where one could hide and slip away.

Gus stood up. "I can't think of anything else I can do tonight. I should go home and pray that Cousin Prudence has gone to bed in a huff."

"She came over here earlier this evening demanding to know where you were and why you had not provided a meal at the correct time."

"Mercy me." Gus sighed. "What did you tell her?"

"That one of your members had been shot by accident and you were all being questioned. I didn't mention the protest or the suffragist part."

"Thank God for that. She's made it quite clear what she thinks about all sorts of unnatural women, including those who wish to intrude into a man's world by wanting to vote."

With those words she headed back across the street and let herself into number ten.

## Twenty-Six

Daniel did not come home until after midnight. I had been lying in bed, trying to sleep and worrying, when I finally heard his feet on the cobblestones and then his key at the front door. I can't tell you how many times I had lain awake like this, holding my breath until he came home. I suppose it is the fate of a policeman's wife.

I listened as he took off his coat and then crept up the stairs. He sat on the edge of the bed to take his shoes off.

"Did they find the shooter?" I asked.

"Molly, you're still awake at this hour?"

"I couldn't sleep. I was too worried."

"You didn't have to worry about me," he said.

"I always worry about you, but I was more worried about my friends, hauled off like common criminals when they were expressing their right to peaceful protest."

He let one shoe fall to the floor with a clunk. "Molly, we've been through this before. It was made quite clear that no form of political or religious protest would be tolerated at the parade. Your friends knew that, took the risk, and received the consequences. And it was lucky they were all taken to the courthouse, as they were all in one place to be questioned about the murder. And lucky that Corelli is on the case. He's a good man."

"So have you made progress?" I asked.

"Not really. There was such chaos with all those people trying to leave the scene at once that I presume the shooter could have hidden under the stands, slipped into one of the buildings, and disposed of the gun."

"I presume they searched the building across the street, including the roof?" I asked.

"I'm sure they did," he replied, removing his shirt and hanging it on the back of the upright chair.

"And what ideas do they have about who the shooter was aiming for, because—"

"Molly, I'm dog-tired and in no mood to discuss a case with you."

"But I could help, you see."

"No, my dear. This is a case with significant international importance. I'll have the embassies of half the world breathing down my neck in the morning and I need to get some sleep. So if you don't mind." He climbed into bed, gave me a peck on the cheek, then turned away from me. "Good night."

I couldn't say any more but lay there fuming for a while before I tiptoed into Liam's room. His forehead was sweaty and cool, a good sign. I climbed into my own bed and drifted off to sleep.

In the morning I awoke to the sound of bells. I had completely forgotten it was Sunday. How quickly a week had passed. How many things I had learned and seen . . . and all for nothing, it seemed, since I had not prevented a woman from being killed and Daniel was not willing to listen to the facts that I had learned. I gave a long sigh. I supposed I could see his point of view. The shooting most likely had nothing to do with poor Willa Parker. It would turn out to be some sort of international intrigue, someone making the most of a crowded, chaotic scene to attempt to assassinate a person of importance. It had happened enough before in other countries, and to our own president not so long ago. I had been there, in the Temple of Music at the fair in Buffalo, when President McKinley had been assassinated and I had played a small part in bringing that person to justice. How long ago that seemed now. Almost a different lifetime.

A loud wail from across the hall made me push these thoughts aside and go to my daughter. Daniel, it seemed, had already gone back to work. If this new job was always going to be so demanding, I wondered if he'd wish he was back with the New York police, or that he'd taken the police chief job in White Plains and spent his days with shoplifters and lost dogs. I retrieved Mary Kate, who stopped crying the moment I walked into the room, took her downstairs, and set her in the high chair while I prepared breakfast. Liam bounded down the stairs not fifteen minutes later, his nose snotty and eyes bright, but full of energy and with no trace of fever left. I took him back upstairs to rub Vicks on his chest and bundle him in warm clothes just in case, but my fear left me.

All the while my thoughts were going a mile a minute. What was happening with my friends? What was Gus doing to release them? And had anyone told poor Willa's husband and family about the loss of their loved one?

As soon as everyone was fed, washed, and dressed I was about to go over to Gus's house to see if there was any way I could help. Aileen came down the stairs at that moment with her bonnet and shawl on. "I'll be off, then, Mrs. Sullivan," she said.

"Off?"

"That's right. It's Sunday. I told you I'd like to go to church with my family as it's the big Tammany mass at the old cathedral. I mentioned it when we were at the parade watching my father walk past."

"Oh yes. So you did, Aileen. I'm sorry. I've had so much to think about this week that I can't keep my head straight. And you'll go home with your family, then, for your afternoon off?"

"I will, if you don't mind," she said, looking at me with big, hopeful eyes.

I smiled at her. "Of course. Enjoy your time and your family."

She smiled back. "I don't know about that," she said. "My little brothers are always fighting and my mam is always scolding them, but I love them all the same."

I gave her a hug and off she went, leaving me trapped with small children and no way of being useful to anyone involved in yesterday's tragedy. At least that gave me an excuse not to go to church! I left Bridie in charge for a few minutes and went across to see Gus. Liam was annoyed at not being allowed to come.

"Not this time, my darling." I kissed the top of his head. "They've a lady with them who doesn't like little children and Aunt Gus is very, very busy. I'm not going to stay."

"I could play with Aunt Sid," he said.

"Aunt Sid is away from home at the moment." I didn't go into more details but hurried across the street.

"I won't keep you, as I'm sure you're busy," I said when Gus opened the door, "but I just wondered if there was any news?"

Gus shook her head. "I've heard nothing from Sid. I've been to the telegraph office and sent a telegram to Mrs. Belmont but haven't had a reply. I suppose it takes a while to get to her estate. I think it's on an island. How annoying of her. Just when we need her most. Still, I don't suppose there is much she can do if the judge is not in town until Monday morning. Poor Sid, stuck in that hellhole. Poor all of my sisters. It's just not fair. I think I'll write a letter to the *Herald*, but I bet they won't publish it. 'Just some silly woman who doesn't know her place!'"

"Augusta?" came the imperious voice from the back of the house.

Gus looked back and sighed. "Obviously the eggs weren't cooked to her liking. Thank God this damned festival is over and she'll be going home. I feel like the maid and the cook. So has Daniel found anything out about Willa's death?"

"Not when I last spoke to him, or at least nothing he's shared with me."

"I hope he does find out who killed her," Gus said. "If it was someone who is against our cause we'll find him and make him sorry for his actions."

"You don't want to end up jailed in earnest this time," I said.

She nodded. "True."

"Augusta!"

Gus sighed. "Duty calls." And she shut the front door.

I spent the morning catching up on household chores, darning Daniel's socks, and watching the children. Bridie was unusually quiet.

"I think I'll go upstairs and work on my Latin homework," she said.

"Are you all right?" I asked.

She nodded, then said, "I'm just really upset about that lady yesterday. She wasn't doing anything wrong and yet someone killed her."

"I know. It is upsetting," I said. "But we must assume it was just a sad accident that she was killed. The shooter was aiming for someone else. One of those foreign bigwigs."

Bridie nodded. "But the women were already lying down," she said. "It wasn't as if she got in the way."

I realized she was right. They were already lying down when the shots rang out. "That's true. Perhaps the gun went off at the wrong moment. Perhaps the person had never handled a gun before. Or just fired randomly for some reason." *Were they all lying down? Or had some women flung themselves down only when the shots rang out?* Gus said some of them had been planning to stay standing. I tried to think back to the scene just before the shots had rung out but found my memory a blur.

"It seems so wrong," Bridie said. "Aunt Sid said she was a female scientist and she was doing important research into stopping infantile paralysis. Now who will do that?"

"You're right," I said, feeling too tired to find any consolation. "There are so few female scientists in the first place, and if she could have found a way to wipe out poliomyelitis, wouldn't that have been wonderful? She was so passionate about it, having seen what it did to her own sister."

"Maybe I should be a scientist," Bridie said. "As well as a writer. And maybe an actress in moving pictures."

I had to laugh. "It's good to have big dreams," I said. "You don't have to decide for a long while yet. Now go and finish that Latin homework."

I watched her go, thinking about myself at her age. I'd been taking lessons with the young ladies at the big house, and their tutor said I was a clever girl and could make something of myself. Then my mother died and I had to become the mother to my young brothers, so no more schooling. I'd always regretted it, although, as Cousin Prudence had pointed out so rudely, I had done quite well for myself with my limited education.

Daniel arrived home in the middle of the afternoon. I was in the back parlor alone for once. Bridie was still at her Latin homework or upstairs reading, Mary Kate was napping, and Liam was in the kitchen making a complicated building with his blocks. Daniel sank down into the armchair. "Am I glad to be home," he said. "I don't suppose there's any tea?"

"I can make some in a jiffy," I said. "Bad day?"

He nodded. "I have been on my feet for two weeks now, at the beck and call of every visiting nation to this country, and today I have had them all, one after the other: the Japanese officials demanding a written apology from the mayor and the president, the

British delegation berating me for allowing wild women to insult them and hint that the British government is in some way not civilized, and the Germans . . . have you ever been shouted at, at close quarters, by a German general with bad breath? How I personally had endangered the life of the German ambassador and his wife by not doing my duty. Why had I not thought to check the pockets and purses of every member of the crowd before they were allowed into the stands? In Germany there would be no such mistakes. Anybody who looked like a criminal or an anarchist would have been hauled off to jail before the celebration began."

He looked up. I nodded sympathy but couldn't resist saying, "Instead a group of innocent women were hauled off to jail for expressing their rights."

"Oh, come on, Molly." He smiled. "You know taking them to the courthouse was only to send a message that the organizers of the parade were taking their job seriously. It was a slap on the wrist, that's all."

"Two nights in jail is a slap on the wrist?" I demanded.

His eyes shot open. "What do you mean?"

"That the women have been given two nights in jail, the police claiming that the judge is away until Monday morning. You know my friends, Daniel. They are educated, upper-class women. Can you imagine them crammed into a cell with drunks and prostitutes?"

"But surely one among them could have had the funds to post bail?"

"Sid tried that but they refused. It was quite clear that they intended to humiliate and punish. Gus managed to escape and is trying to contact a powerful benefactor to whom these thugs will listen."

"Gus what?" Daniel's eyebrows rose. I hesitated. Perhaps I should have kept that information under my hat. But I forged ahead.

"She slipped out of line and escaped, which does not say much for the efficiency of the New York police last night."

Daniel sighed. "I'm going to ignore that piece of information, since I am no longer with the police. But I don't know if I can interfere, since I am no longer employed by the city of New York. I don't think it would be taken well. You might be surprised, but I am entirely with you on this."

"On giving women the vote?"

"Well, perhaps I wouldn't go as far as that . . ."

"And why not? You know your wife. Am I not a rational person, able to decide what is good for my city and country? As someone who gives birth to citizens, am I not entitled to have my say about who runs the country?"

Again he hesitated. "I suppose you do have a point," he said. "But in our case we would discuss matters of voting and I would take your concerns into consideration before I voted."

"Then vote how you wished anyway," I shot back angrily. "Daniel, what this says is that women are lesser, not as important as men, not as smart in making decisions."

"Well, men do control all the money," he said. "We are the ones who drive commerce, man the armed forces, and sign treaties."

"Did it not occur to you that there might be fewer wars if women signed the treaties?" I asked sweetly.

"Most women would swoon at the mere mention of the word *war*," he said.

"Women only swoon because their corsets do not allow them to breathe properly," I retorted. "We are kept imprisoned by our clothing, Daniel."

"You're not." He grinned.

"And never intend to be."

"Now, good little wife, are you going to make me that cup of tea or what?"

"If you're not careful you'll get it over your head," I retorted as I stalked out into the kitchen. That was the problem with men.

Daniel was more tolerant than most husbands, but he still saw the role of women as keeping the home and waiting on their men. I wondered if that would ever change or if it was built into the fabric of the male.

After he'd had a cup of tea and a slice of soda bread he gave a sigh of content. "Now if I can have two minutes' rest before I'm back facing the firing squad again," he said.

"Has any progress been made?" I asked. "Have they found the weapon? Or come to any conclusions about where the shots were fired from?"

"I have been so occupied in fending off important people that I haven't had time to confer with Corelli, but he knows his police work. He'll find out if anyone can. Frankly, given the number of people we're dealing with I wonder if we'll ever find the culprit."

"Don't you think that's strange?" I asked. "As you said, there were so many people. Everyone packed in close together, people leaning out of windows. One of them must have seen something, heard the shot as coming from close to them or above their head, and yet nobody has come forward with that information."

"They are checking on the verification of those looking out of the windows," Daniel said. "But so far they all seem aboveboard. Only a limited number of people could get into the upper rooms of a bank or the doctor's residence."

"I did mention the roofs," I said. "Someone could have accessed the roofs from a fire escape, couldn't they?"

He nodded, looking doubtful. "I didn't get a chance to examine the body, but a rooftop would be a long way away for a shot to be fired. To me, it seems more possible that someone could climb up the framework at the back of the opposite stand while all eyes were fixed on the parade, maybe try to fire when he was perched in a precarious position, which would account for a broken window and the shooting of the woman on the float. I suppose by now they'll have found out more about the unfortunate young woman and notified her next of kin, but after that it may well be case closed."

"I could be of help, if you like," I said. "I happen to know—"

Daniel held up his hand. "Oh no, thank you, Molly. I can't have you getting involved in any kind of criminal case. In any case, what could you do that a trained detective could not? It seems clear to me that a person shot wildly and happened to strike one of the young women. Let's not talk about it anymore. But I am concerned with Miss Goldfarb and the other young ladies. From what you have told me they are from some prominent families. I hate to think of them in jail until tomorrow. I must go out again and I'll see if I can do anything to release your friends. Don't save any dinner for me. I may have to dine out." He got up and headed out of the room.

I knew I should be grateful that he wanted to help my friends, but I was still angry. "How hard it must be for you," I called after him. "Attending banquets all the time while your wife and family barely have enough to eat. Might I ask when you expect to be paid and give me the housekeeping money you owe me? That soda bread and tea was bought with money from the investigation you don't want me to share with you."

He turned back and put an arm around me. "Don't think I enjoy this, Molly. I scarcely get to eat because I'm constantly making sure nobody poisons the guests of honor. And I may have good news tomorrow. Someone from the Bureau is coming up to meet me. They were notified about the shooting attempt and want to hear my version of it and what could have been done to prevent it. I fear I'll be in the hot seat. But the man may be bringing my pay packet."

"I'll believe it when I see it," I said.

# Twenty-Seven

The next morning life resumed its normal pattern. Bridie returned to school. There was the Monday clothes washing to be done. Aileen was helping me hang sheets on the line when Gus arrived with the good news that Sid and the others had been released. Mrs. Belmont had returned from Long Island and had immediately used her influence, not to mention her automobiles, to have the suffragists transported from the Tombs. Sid was now at home, recuperating with a cup of coffee. I immediately left Aileen to finish the laundry and went across with Gus.

Sid was sitting at the kitchen table and did indeed look pale and hollow-eyed.

"It was awful, Molly," she said. "None of us slept a wink. We were crammed, several to a cell, with the most disreputable of women. The smells, Molly. You would not believe the nose could endure such things. And only enough space for one or two of us to lie down on the hard bench at a time. I tried reasoning with the guards but they were quite stony-faced, with hearts of ice. One of our lot, a sweet, quiet girl called Lily Prentice, became quite ill. We tried to get medical assistance for her but it was refused. Mrs. Belmont was horrified when we told her and will make sure heads roll." She took a sip of her coffee.

"Oh, thank God for coffee. I dreamed about this all night. I do have to thank your Daniel, Molly. He came by to ask how we were being treated, and the jailers treated us much better after that."

I would have to thank him for that. For all that Daniel and I were fighting, he still had tried to do something for my friends. I looked around. "Where is your cousin, Gus?"

"Claims she has been so shaken by these strange occurrences that she must have her breakfast in bed. Two lightly boiled eggs and a thin slice of toast with the crusts removed. The worst of it is that she was supposed to leave yesterday but insisted on staying until Sid was home."

I gave a sympathetic smile, then looked around, remembering. "Where is Miss Johnson? Has she gone straight to bed too?"

"Yes. And once she has caught up on some sleep she is planning on going straight home," Sid said. "She said she had had enough of New York and wanted to be safe and secure in her own home. She said it was a mistake to think we could change minds about the future of women. As long as men are in charge they'll never want anything to change. She was quite discouraged, poor woman." She shared a glance with Gus. "Mind you, that prison was enough to shake anybody of a delicate constitution, and coming on the heels of watching one of our members shot . . . well, it was more than most people could take." She turned to me. "Has your Daniel been working on the case? Have they arrested a suspect yet?"

I shook my head. "It's not for Daniel to investigate," I said. "He's no longer a member of the New York homicide squad. And he has been fully occupied with fending off complaints from the various embassies about not protecting their dignitaries properly."

"As if Daniel could have foreseen that something like this would happen," Sid said indignantly. "It must have been really well planned for the shooter to get past that police cordon and take aim without being spotted."

"I agree," I said. "I wondered if the shooter was actually up on the roof opposite and then escaped over rooftops. It's so easy to do in New York—in fact, I've done it myself."

"I don't doubt it." Sid exchanged an amused glance with Gus. With some coffee in her she was beginning to regain her spark.

"So I expect all the women were devastated about one of their own being killed," I said. "Did any of them think this was a deliberate act against suffragists?"

"Obviously we were all shaken by it," Sid said. "But it wasn't as if any of us knew the woman well. Gus and I know her sister, Winnie, of course. In fact we were quite surprised when she and that Harriet woman joined our group for the protest. We hadn't actually asked suffragist sisters from other cities to come and join us, although Maud Malone might have rallied them."

"I spoke to Willa Parker on Friday and she said the parade was just a cover for her real reason for coming to New York," I said. "She was thinking of taking a research position in the new Rockefeller laboratory. She was quite passionate about her research into viruses."

"Viruses?" Gus looked confused. "What in tarnation are they?"

"Organisms smaller than bacteria that can make us sick, so I gather," I explained. "She was particularly investigating what causes infantile paralysis, or rather, polio."

"That would certainly be a useful discovery if she could find that and then tell us how to prevent the disease. I think we all know someone who has been left crippled from it," Gus said. "Of course, her sister was stricken with it, wasn't she? And didn't her mother die of it?"

"She did," I said. "Was Mrs. Schilling on the float with you? And arrested? She must be quite devastated by her friend's death."

"She seemed stunned, as if she couldn't quite believe it," Sid said, "but we were not in the same cell so I didn't have a chance to speak to her."

"I presume someone must have notified Willa's husband," I said. "I thought I saw him there at the parade."

"Really?" Gus looked at me. "Why wouldn't he have come forward when he saw his own wife killed?"

"I don't think that many people even realized that someone had been killed," I said, "let alone who it was. Many people just saw police swarm the float and might have assumed that was because of the protest."

"Oh, the poor man," Gus said. "What if he was there and didn't realize what he witnessed? He'll be crushed when he realizes his wife has been killed."

"Will he?" Sid asked. "From what Anne said he liked to control Willa. He'll be annoyed there is nobody to starch his shirts. Oh, and to do his research for him."

I looked up, processing this.

"It was clear she was the brains; he was the journeyman. She conducted the groundbreaking research and he took credit for it."

"Yes," I said. "It did seem to be that way. And their poor child. He will be left motherless. Although Mrs. Schilling has been looking after him, so I suppose she will continue to do that."

"A horrible business," Gus said. "I almost wish we'd never agreed to take part in the parade. It's done no good and a lot of harm all around."

"We have to keep fighting, dearest," Sid said. "No matter what the cost."

Gus sighed. "I suppose you're right."

"I should go," I said. "I left Aileen hanging sheets on the line. Life has returned to normal for the Sullivan household."

"Let's hope it returns to normal here too." Sid glanced up the stairs. "It can't come soon enough for me."

I left them and went back to my chores. I was just setting out cold beef, cheese, and pickles for our lunch when Daniel came home.

This was so unexpected that I looked up nervously. "What's wrong?" I asked.

"I thought I'd just pop home with the good news," he said. "Mr. Adams from the Bureau is here and has come with our back pay. It is now deposited in the bank, so we can all breathe a sigh of relief."

I went over to him and wrapped my arms around his neck. "Oh, that is good news. Thank you for coming home to tell me. And thank you for checking in on my friends in jail. They're home now and Sid said your efforts were helpful."

"I'm sorry you had to go through this, Molly," he said. "I feel terrible you had to use your money for our household. I should have told you what I was doing. It's not right to keep things from you."

"No, it isn't," I replied. "I don't want to be treated as the little woman who needs protecting. I'm your partner, Daniel, through thick and thin."

He gave me a look of such tenderness that it melted my heart. "I married the right woman, Molly," he said.

"You'd have had a much easier life with Arabella Norton," I couldn't resist replying, referring to the woman who was his fiancée when I had first met him. "You'd have lived in luxury and not had to worry about the odd penny coming in."

"But she would have expected to be that woman you despise. The one who wants spoiling and protecting," he added. He glanced at the kitchen clock. "I should be getting back to work."

"You don't want anything to eat? A cup of coffee?"

Daniel shook his head. "I must go. Mr. Adams from the Bureau was not very complimentary about my achievements. He said this attempted assassination has made the country look weak in the eyes of the world. He said there are already those in Congress who were not keen to fund this new Bureau of Investigation and will now clamor to defund it. So my job's on the line, Molly. If I don't find the culprit and get this smoothed over I'll be looking for work."

"That's not fair!" I retorted. "You're really good at your job. How could you possibly have known that someone was planning to attend with murder in their heart? If you want someone to blame, then the New York police should have noticed a person with a gun. So should people in the crowd. I know all eyes were fixed on the parade, but if someone next to me reached into his jacket and took out a gun, I'm sure I'd have seen it." I stopped, thinking. "I'm no expert on guns, but it must have been quite a big one with a long barrel to shoot with any accuracy from that far away."

Daniel nodded. "I haven't had a chance to examine the body yet, or to talk at length with Corelli. When we last spoke nobody had come forward to report seeing anything suspicious." He sank onto a kitchen chair. "I have a horrible feeling we'll never know. I've tried to work with the various embassies to see if they had picked up any hint or threat. My first choice would be the German ambassador."

"Really?" I queried. "I met his wife, remember. She's American and I like her. Would someone really be shooting at him?"

"He's known to be a shifty character," Daniel said, and went on, "A little bit of a spymaster, so we're told. But whom could he have antagonized? And then the Japanese prince was there, and the vice president. So the shooter could have been targeting anyone. I told Commissioner Baker that it was impossible to secure this location."

He gave me a hopeless look.

"Perhaps you are approaching this the wrong way," I said. "My old mentor, Paddy Riley, said you should always start with what you know. And what we know is there was one victim, Willa Parker. Somebody killed Willa Parker. So was that by accident when they were aiming for someone else? Or was it by design?"

"A suffragist? Unless somebody had brought a gun in case he met a suffragist, he must have been aiming for someone else and hit her by mistake. But who? The bigwigs were in the upper levels of the stands. Even someone with horrible aim couldn't miss by that much, unless they were in such a precarious position that they couldn't aim properly."

"They did aim upward at least once," I said. "Remember the window glass was broken?" A chilling thought just struck me. "You and I were seated at the bottom of the stand," I said. "Perhaps they were aiming for you."

"Me?" He looked up, startled.

"Perhaps someone thought you were too close to something they didn't want disclosed. You have been spending lots of time with the German ambassador."

He thought for a moment, then shook his head. "That's ridiculous, Molly. Nobody even knows what I do now."

"The whole German contingent seemed to know."

He paused again. "No, I can't believe that."

I took a deep breath before saying, "Then we have to consider that Willa Parker may have been the intended victim."

He considered this. "You're suggesting that someone killed one of those women on purpose? In the middle of a parade? Why? Who would want her dead? Why not kill her in her own home?"

"Because they could get away with it in the chaos of a parade?"

He went to stand up again. "I'll have to speak to Corelli. Maybe he's found out a little more about her by now."

"You could let me help," I said. I was about to tell him what I knew when he cut me off.

"Oh no, Molly. This is a homicide, a police matter. And the police are under some pressure over it. It turns out that her father is an influential man, a member of the Hudson-Fulton committee."

"I know," I said, "I've met him."

His jaw dropped open in a most satisfying way. "You know Mrs. Parker's father? How?"

"I was with his daughter in her box with the German ambassador's wife. That was why I asked for the tickets." I watched him struggle to process that.

"Willa Parker's father is the same man that the German ambassador is staying with?" Daniel said. "Mr. Hartman? I've met him too." He began to pace. "So—" he started, stopped, paced some more, and then said, "How on earth are you involved in this? Why did you want to meet Miss Parker? Wasn't it about a missing woman?"

"Willa Parker is the woman I have been investigating, the one who never showed up at Sid and Gus's house," I said. "I told you that when you accompanied me home from the opera house."

He was staring at me now. "Willa Parker is Mr. Hartman's daughter? The daughter of a very wealthy man? And one connected with the Hudson-Fulton committee and the German ambassador? That puts an entirely new spin on this whole thing."

"That is what I have been trying to tell you," I replied.

"And you have information about her?" he asked.

"Are you sure you don't want a police constable to come and take my statement?" I couldn't resist saying. "After they have exhausted all their other leads?"

He was not amused. "Don't be foolish, Molly. The Bureau is going to want to get involved in this too. It could be an international incident. Any little information you might have will be helpful."

I stayed silent.

"So what information do you have?" he asked in a softer voice. "It could be very important."

"I have a little information," I said.

"Good." He nodded at me encouragingly. "Anything your little investigation yielded would be helpful. Don't worry how inconsequential it may seem to you."

"Well, I know her profession . . ." I said. He nodded, encouraging me to continue. ". . . why she disappeared, and where she went, who she stayed with, where her husband is staying, the name of the

Pinkerton detective who was following her, where her son is, who her best friend is, and why her family is displeased with her. Is that enough to be getting on with?"

He gaped at me. His comment about my "little" investigation had been the last straw.

"Let me get something," I said and ran upstairs to grab the little gold-colored case. Coming downstairs, I opened it and offered one of the cards to Daniel.

"The Molly Murphy Detective Agency has all the information you need," I said, "and is available for hire."

## ❧ Twenty-Eight ❧

There was silence for a moment. Daniel glared at the card in his hand. I waited for the explosion. To my surprise, he burst out laughing.

"I should know better than to ever underestimate you, Molly," he said. "'Molly Murphy Detective Agency.' Where did you get these?"

"Sid and Gus had them made for me," I said, completely flabbergasted by his response.

"And Molly Murphy? Are you not Molly Sullivan?" He raised his eyebrows.

"Well, yes, but I didn't think you would want your name associated with a woman detective." I took the card back and carefully replaced it in its case. "I haven't made my mind up about the agency's name yet, to tell the truth."

"But you have made your mind up about the agency," he stated.

"Yes, I have," I said. "I've decided I want to have my own money and my own profession."

He looked hurt. "Haven't I been able to provide all these years? We've never been in desperate need." I raised my eyebrows and he said hurriedly, "Except for the last few weeks, and you can't hold that against me."

"It's not about holding it against you," I said. "It's not about you at all. I want to have my own money that I earn and control my own life. I like solving crimes, and I'm good at it."

"But Mary Kate and Liam—" he began in protest but I finished his sentence.

"Will be well taken care of," I said, "I have Aileen, and Bridie is a good helper. After all, have they really been neglected while I investigated Willa Parker's disappearance? Haven't I proven I can handle both?"

"You really know all about Willa Parker?" Daniel asked. I was aware he was steering the conversation away from my detective agency but I let him. Let him take some time to think about it. At his heart he was a good man who wanted me to be happy. I thought time would be my ally.

"I do," I replied, then gave a rather cheeky grin. "What is it worth to you?" I was teasing, of course. If Daniel was in trouble I would move heaven and earth to help him. But he was paid for his efforts. I wanted him to think of my efforts as just as valuable.

"I don't think I can pay a woman detective for information," he said. "What would I list it as in my expense ledger?"

"Mrs. Goodwin is paid, isn't she?" I challenged. That opened another avenue of thought for me. I would have to go and see Mrs. Goodwin. I had assumed she was at that meeting to find out what the suffragists were up to. What if she had been there for another purpose? Perhaps she was on the trail of a murderer.

"Yes, she is," he admitted grudgingly. "But she is a legitimate member of the police department."

"The Bureau must admit that it sometimes takes a woman to investigate a woman's life. There are spaces that men just can't understand."

"You may be correct, but you can't expect me to hire a female detective to the Bureau," he said.

"Not yet," I admitted, "but you must have a fund for informants and consultants. You can pay me out of that." He considered it.

"That might be possible. Ten dollars plus expenses?" he ventured.

"Sid and Gus gave me twenty," I challenged.

"Miss Goldfarb and Miss Walcott are not the federal government," he countered. Now it was my turn to consider.

"I accept," I said and shook his hand. I was not naive. Both Daniel and I were playing a little game. I would have helped without money, just because he asked me to. On the other hand, I suspected that Daniel would pay me out of his own money before he would try to justify paying a woman detective with Bureau funds. So, in effect, I would be paying myself. But I was already invested in this mystery. Willa Parker had died after I had found her. Now I felt it was my job to find her killer.

"Cross my palm with silver," I said, holding out my hand, "and I can share what I know with you." I watched, satisfied as he opened his wallet and counted ten dollars into it. Of course, I would use the money to buy our dinner, but it would be my money I was using!

Dinner made me think of the food I had set out. "You must be hungry," I said. "Have something to eat and I'll tell you what I know, and we can start our investigation properly." For once there was no splutter at the sound of "our investigation." Perhaps this time Daniel was truly going to treat me like the equal I was. We sat and ate and I filled him in on the steps I had taken to find Willa Parker. My thoughts darted back and forth trying to make connections. I told Daniel that I had seen Mr. Jones at the parade and thought he had been with Dr. Parker. Then I had to go back and describe my encounter with Mr. Jones outside the Flexners' house. I thought of glossing over Mr. Jones's nastiness, knowing Daniel would not be happy to hear of my being in danger, but decided to tell him the whole truth. Mr. Jones had been at the parade. Daniel had to know how threatened I had felt to understand that he might have posed a danger to Willa.

Predictably, he swore when he heard that Mr. Jones had laid hands on me, then examined me with some pride as I described how I had used the workers' presence to escape.

"And what did Dr. Parker say when you told him you had found his wife?" he asked, mopping up the last bit of pickle with some bread.

"I didn't speak with him at length," I said. "Just handed him the letter, said it was from his wife, and went on my way. I didn't want to risk Mr. Jones catching up to me."

"So you don't know for certain what was in the letter?" Daniel said. "Do you think that Mrs. Parker was truthful on the whole? Is it possible that the letter did not contain the hope of a reunion, but a message that they would never be together again?"

That possibility had not occurred to me. "Mrs. Parker said she was arranging a reunion, and she even set a date with the Flexners, but no one saw what she actually wrote, so what you suggest is possible. I didn't know her long enough to see if she was a truthful person," I said.

"And we know that she made a false plan to come to your friends, so she was not above lying when it suited her," Daniel went on.

"That's true," I said, though privately I thought that Willa had not struck me as a liar, just someone in a difficult situation. I myself have been known to stretch the truth to get out of a corner. "I suppose the next step is to speak to Dr. Parker. I wonder if he even realizes that the woman killed in the parade was his wife?"

"If he was there, wouldn't he have realized?" Daniel said. "How could you see your own wife killed and not come forward? If you had been on that float I would have been down there in an instant."

"I know you would." I smiled at him fondly. "But I have a theory that some of the watchers had no idea that a woman had been murdered. I thought I saw Dr. Parker at the far end of the grandstand. At least, that is where I saw Mr. Jones, and I assume the man he was with was Dr. Parker. But it was quite far away, and the scenery of the float would have blocked the view of the body. I think people in those parts of the stands assumed that the parade had been stopped because of the protest and the gunshot and have no idea that someone was killed."

"Let's find out together," Daniel said. "I will tell Corelli what you've discovered and offer to accompany him to break the news. I'll tell him you are coming along as a friend of the victim." Would wonders never cease! Daniel was not hesitating to include me in an investigation. A warm glow of happiness bloomed in my chest, despite the dire nature of the murder we were discussing. I was being treated as an equal.

Not wanting Daniel to change his mind, I put on my hat, spoke to Aileen about the children, and reminded her not to let Liam out into the cold, and we were out of the door on the way to Dr. Parker's rooms within half an hour.

"No motorcar today?" I said as we came out into the bright sun of the court.

"Several of my men are helping the Secret Service with the vice president as he goes further up the Hudson," he said. "I wanted them to be mobile so I'm back to my own devices for a few days."

I hooked my arm through his as we started toward Jefferson Market.

"We should speak to Mrs. Belmont," I went on, "and the Flexners. They were acting as her patrons and in on the scheme." We passed the Jefferson Market building and headed toward Washington Square. "If Mrs. Schilling has been released from jail she will have told them the sad news by now." An image of Harriet telling little Charlie of his mother's death swam into my head unbidden and gave my heart a squeeze. "And of course, Dr. Parker will want to be reunited with his son."

"True." Daniel frowned. "It was not right for them to help hide a son from his father in the first place. They could be charged with kidnapping if they don't come forward."

"Dr. Flexner was entirely ignorant of the scheme and aware that it put him in a bad light," I assured him. "He suggested that Willa inform her husband of her whereabouts immediately. That's why I carried the letter."

"A man I approve of, then," Daniel said, stepping gallantly over a puddle and saving my skirts. "It's not right for adults to use their children as pawns. But you said you didn't read the letter, so you are not sure what is in it?"

"I didn't," I admitted. "It was sealed."

"Somehow I don't think that would stop you, Molly." Daniel laughed. "You would have found a way to read it if you wanted."

"Well, at the time I was running across town as fast as I could to beat Mr. Jones," I admitted. "And just wanted to do my job and get home." I wondered for a second if I had gone too far in mentioning my job. But Daniel did not flinch.

"So we have no way of knowing if that letter really contained an offer of reconciliation," Daniel said, "or if Mrs. Parker wrote it merely to put off the Flexners, who wanted her to reconcile with her husband."

"That's true," I agreed. "She would have had to be a good liar to sit there writing a letter calmly and hand it to me without batting an eye while telling us she was writing to arrange a dinner with her husband for Saturday night."

"That seems a long time to make the man wait, if he had come into the city looking for her," Daniel mused. "This was on Wednesday that you saw her?" I nodded.

"Mrs. Flexner was not available to host the dinner until that day," I provided, "and Mrs. Parker did not seem to want to be alone with her husband."

"That in itself is suspicious," Daniel said.

## Twenty-Nine

I stopped as we reached Sixth Avenue. It seemed a normal Monday morning, with the traffic returning to its usual patterns. Street vendors were out, their carts avoiding the puddles and the dripping awnings from last night's rain. The celebration, it seemed, was over.

"I know you have told me that the husband is always the first suspect in your murder investigations," I said, "but why kill her at a parade in front of thousands?" It seemed strange to be speaking of murder in the bright, breezy sunlight of the afternoon.

"Perhaps there was no way to get her alone," Daniel said. "Perhaps the letter said she never wanted to see him again."

"Perhaps," I mused, "although that would ruin all her plans. Dr. Flexner couldn't have a married woman work at his lab without her husband's permission. If you think about it, Willa Parker had more motive to kill her husband than the other way around."

He looked at me. "That is rather dangerous, Molly. Talk of murdering husbands."

I grinned at him. "Not my husband. But a widow could work without a man's permission."

"Anyway, that is not what happened," he went on. "Willa Parker is dead. Her husband is the first suspect. If not him, then who?"

"One theory is that she was in the way of a bullet meant for someone else. After all, the vice president and foreign dignitaries were right behind the float." I held up one finger. "The second is that it was her husband"—a second finger—"the third"—I held up a third finger and paused, considering—"someone shooting at suffragists who is unhappy with protesting women."

"Who just happened to bring a gun with him in case there was a woman to shoot at?" Daniel raised his eyebrows.

"There may be men who walk around carrying guns." As we turned left on Bleecker Street I had to pick my way through a puddle, lifting my skirts.

"Now I'm picturing a Wild West sheriff with a gun strapped to his belt." Daniel laughed.

"Or a man like Mr. Jones who has a dangerous job." That sobered him up. I could tell we were both thinking of my encounter with that man.

"Don't forget the women who were on the float," Daniel said. "They are the most likely since they were standing right next to her. Women can commit murder as well."

"They weren't standing, if you remember," I said, "They were lying down on the float pretending to die."

"Not all of them," he said, "Some still stood with signs, I think."

"It's hard to recall exactly what happened before the shots rang out," I admitted. "But there is one reason I don't think it was a woman on the float. They were all arrested immediately after the protest and searched. If it was one of them, what happened to the gun?"

"Good point." Daniel nodded in agreement, then sighed. "I'm afraid that automatic pistols are becoming too easy to obtain. Some of them are so small they can be easily concealed and used to fire multiple bullets."

"But a gun would have been discovered when the police searched the women," I reiterated.

"Absolutely," he said, "but didn't Miss Walcott tell you she escaped through the darkness and never went to jail?" I looked around to make sure no one had overheard that remark, but luckily there was no one near us on the sidewalk.

"So it's possible that someone else might have done the same thing," I mused. "But very unlikely. I met all those women and they seem like very earnest, good people. An automatic pistol seems more like something a spy would use."

"You're thinking of my ambassador," he said just as we climbed the steps to the police headquarters. I had been in the headquarters on Mulberry Street many times before but this was the first time since Daniel was no longer with the force. In the past, the desk sergeant would chat with me cheerfully or wave me up to Daniel's office. But now the sergeant nodded cordially, if a little stiffly, to Daniel and said he would see if Lieutenant Corelli was available.

The lieutenant came downstairs with a cheerful welcome for Daniel. If he was surprised to see me he didn't let it show. Lieutenant Corelli was still a young man, with a full mustache and kind eyes. He was dressed in a brown suit with well-polished brown shoes. I knew from Daniel that he was newly married, but this was clearly not the time for congratulations.

"My wife knows the address of your murdered woman's husband," Daniel said without preamble.

"Does she now?" Corelli raised his eyebrows. I confess I blushed slightly, hoping he didn't think I had had an assignation with this man. But then he would hardly think Daniel would be involved.

"I am a friend of two women with whom she was supposed to be staying," I said. "And her husband gave them his address in case they heard from her."

"So the woman was missing before she was murdered?" Corelli's eyebrows got even higher.

"I think you had better hear what my wife has to say," Daniel says. "She has a lot of information about the woman."

"Let's go to my office." Corelli ushered us upstairs. I saw the desk sergeant take note and guessed that we would get a warmer welcome the next time. Corelli was calm and thorough, taking notes in a small notebook as I told my story. I did not mention that I had been hired and portrayed it as happenstance that I ran into Harriet Schilling near the Rockefeller labs, and thus found Mrs. Parker.

"And what took you to that part of the city?" Corelli, having been trained by Daniel, was too sharp to let anything slip by him.

"I was checking to see if Mrs. Parker had visited the lab," I admitted. "Having heard that Dr. Flexner was her mentor."

"I can see that there is more to this." Corelli looked at me with undisguised interest. If I had not been Daniel's wife, I rather thought I might be the primary suspect. "Thank you, Mrs. Sullivan. That is most helpful. We can go and inform the professor of the sad news immediately."

"And we would like to accompany you, if you don't mind," Daniel put in. "I, in my official capacity, and my wife—" He broke off.

"Your wife has taken an interest," Corelli supplied, still looking at me curiously.

"Just so." Daniel nodded. I was beginning to feel out the rules of this game. I would be accepted as an investigator, and perhaps even valued, as long as we pretended that I was merely Daniel's wife. Society, and the police department, were not yet ready to handle another female detective. Very well. I would play by those rules if it meant staying in the game.

I smiled at Corelli. "Lieutenant, have you recovered a gun?"

"No, not a sign of it," he said. "We have taken the float to a storage yard and there was no gun evident. But we think we know the weapon. The wounds on the body—oh, excuse me, Mrs. Sullivan—" He broke off, clearly wondering if he had offended my sensibilities.

"My wife is tougher than she looks; go on, Corelli," Daniel said.

"The wounds on the body are from a small weapon, a pistol perhaps."

"A Browning? Or Luger?" I asked, thinking of the German ambassador.

"Or a Colt," Corelli said. "We still have to examine the bullets. But something small."

"Then the shooter must have been close, or else not cared who he hit," I mused.

"Yes." Corelli nodded. "The accurate range on those is less than fifty yards. You say you saw her husband at the parade?"

"I believe I did," I said. "I saw a man who looked like him. But he was across the street in shadow. I'm not sure I would have thought it was he had it not been for the investigator going up to him."

"The investigator." Corelli consulted his notebook. "Mr. Jones, a Pinkerton man."

"Yes," I said. "He was hired by Dr. Parker to find his wife."

Corelli closed the notebook. "I think it's time we ask Dr. Parker some questions."

There was a different reception for us at Dr. Parker's rooms than the one I had experienced as a lone female. The three of us were ushered into a kind of shared parlor and Dr. Parker was called.

"Can I help you gentlemen?" he said warily as he entered. "I heard you were looking for me."

"We have some news for you," Corelli began. "I'm Lieutenant Corelli from the New York Police Department. This is Agent Sullivan from the Bureau of Investigation." But Dr. Parker did not seem to take in the introductions. He stared at me instead.

"You brought the letter from my wife," he said. "I haven't heard anything since then. Where is she?"

"I'm afraid we have some very bad news, Dr. Parker," Daniel said. I noticed that Corelli let him assume the lead, a habit he had picked up in the years when Daniel was his captain. "Perhaps you should sit down."

"What?" Dr. Parker jerked his attention back to Daniel, clearly struggling to take in what was happening. "I'll stand. Just tell me."

"I'm afraid your wife was shot during the parade on Saturday." Daniel said. "She did not survive the shooting."

"The shot? During the parade?" Dr. Parker pulled his hands through his hair. It stood up and made him look insane. "I was there. Some crackpot shot at the vice president. Are you saying he shot my wife?"

"Yes, I'm afraid so." Daniel's voice was calm but professional, the voice of someone who has had to give bad news often. "And we have to ask you some questions about it."

"Questions?" He gave a bitter laugh. "That's all I have. Ask this woman—she seems to know much more about my wife's whereabouts than I do. Are you sure you are not mistaken? Perhaps it was some other woman. Perhaps she decided not to attend the protest and she is somewhere safe." He bent over double, clutching his head again, and groaned, "Charlie, what will I tell him?"

"Charlie is safe," I said. "And I know where he is."

"What?" His face tightened in confusion again. "My son? He is in Philadelphia with the wife of a colleague."

"Charlie is with Dr. Flexner and his wife. The neighbor brought him to the city at Mrs. Parker's request. I thought the letter told you," I said.

"But I received a letter from Mrs. Schilling only yesterday, after I had written to give her the address of these rooms," Dr. Parker said, with the professor's air of someone explaining something simple to a recalcitrant pupil. "She assured me Charlie was well and told me not to worry. She did not indicate that she was not at home."

"Did you check the postmark?" I asked. "I assure you that I saw Mrs. Schilling, Charlie, and your wife together on Wednesday afternoon at the Flexners'. Mrs. Parker was seeking employment in Dr. Flexner's lab."

"So that's what this was all about." Dr. Parker began to pace. "I knew she was unhappy with the thought of changing our research. You remember I mentioned she might run to Flexner over it. But the lab said he wasn't in. Was he hiding her? And did he think I would approve and let her work in another state?" Was that a flash of anger I saw in his eyes, or was I just looking for the signs of a husband from whom Willa had had to flee?

"Dr. Flexner had no idea that you weren't informed," I said. "And I don't believe that Mrs. Flexner realized you did not know Charlie's whereabouts. She doesn't seem the type of woman who would approve of separating a man from his son. She encouraged Mrs. Parker to communicate with you and wasn't happy until she had sent you that letter. The plan was for you to come to dinner on Saturday." There was a silence. Dr. Parker looked at Corelli and then Daniel.

"I'm sorry," he said. "And you are?" It was as if the last minutes had not happened. I had seen great emotion do that to a person in the past. Corelli patiently introduced himself and Daniel again.

"And you are investigating her death?"

"We are investigating her murder," I said.

He took a great breath and became very still.

"Yes, of course," he said. "I'm sorry for my outburst. It is just such a shock. She did tell me that all would be revealed on Saturday. Her letter said she was safe with friends and she would send me a note with her whereabouts. But she didn't mention Charlie."

"We can have a policeman collect your son for you if you like," Corelli said.

"No, there's no room for him here." Dr. Parker's gesture took in the boardinghouse. "If I could have the Flexners' home address, I will visit with them there and we can decide together the best course of action. As the lady says"—he indicated me—"they are good people. I highly respect Dr. Flexner. It was a good plan of my wife's to get him on her side. It would probably have worked." He gave a bitter bark of a laugh. Corelli handed me his notebook and a pencil. I wrote down the Flexners' address, tore out a page, and handed it to Dr. Parker, glad that I had committed the details to memory.

Daniel and I locked eyes. He asked the question we were both thinking. "Dr. Parker, if you were worried about your wife, why did you choose to attend a parade on Saturday?"

"Well, I," he began and then spluttered, "You see, Jones said—" and then stopped. "I am the victim here," he blustered suddenly. "My wife has been shot. Why am I being cross-questioned?"

"Do you know why your wife was involved in a suffragist protest?" Corelli asked, changing tack smoothly. "Did she have suffragist sympathies?"

"My wife cared about two things: her research and her family," Dr. Parker said. "She had never expressed an opinion on suffrage, or spoken much about her Vassar days, until a few months ago when she spoke of reuniting with some Vassar friends and participating in this blasted parade."

"So you knew she was planning to be on a float in the parade?" Daniel asked.

"That was what she told me," he said. "Although it seems everything else she told me was a lie."

I suddenly put it together. "So you went to the parade to see her," I offered. "To see if you could spot her on one of the floats. But why was Mr. Jones there? Was he to follow her after you had spotted her?"

"Is it a crime to want to see my own wife?" I noticed he did not answer the question.

I wanted to press him about Mr. Jones, but Corelli was there before me.

"Mr. Parker—" he began.

"Doctor," the man immediately corrected.

"Dr. Parker, do you own a gun?" Corelli asked.

"What?" Dr. Parker looked both affronted and afraid now. "I most certainly do not."

"We will be looking into that," Corelli went on. "And talking to Mrs. Parker's family." He cleared his throat and continued in a solemn tone, "And while I am not officially cautioning you yet, I advise you not to leave the city."

Following his lead, we swept out of the boardinghouse, leaving Dr. Parker gaping after us.

## Thirty

"That made him sweat a bit," Corelli said with a grim smile as we started back to the station. "I don't think he is telling us everything."

"Poor man." Daniel shook his head. "He's just learned that his wife has died. But I got the same feeling." I did too. I had no love for the professor. He had been extremely rude to my friends. But was he the cause of his wife's death? Had we just seen a man devastated by his loss, or one putting on a show?

"Lieutenant." I walked beside Corelli so I could lower my voice. "Can you tell by the wounds whether the shot came from above or below?

He looked at Daniel, I suppose asking permission to discuss the case further with his wife. Daniel nodded and Corelli said, "From below."

"So Dr. Parker could have approached the float in the darkness and fired from street level," I said.

"Exactly." Corelli nodded. "And when an estranged husband is on the scene of a murder, he is going to be our main suspect. But we do have to proceed with caution."

"Why is that?" I asked. At first Corelli walked on in silence, giving no response. I suspected, nice young man though he was, that he was not used to sharing police theories with women. "Lieutenant?" I gave him a bright smile and made my eyes as big and curious as possible, a proven technique for eliciting information and sympathetic treatment.

"It's Mrs. Parker's father. As I said before, he's quite a wealthy man. He may not want the family mired in scandal."

"So you would just stop pursuing the case? Or look elsewhere for the murderer?" I let my shock show.

"No, of course not," Daniel said, jumping to Corelli's defense. "But the department will need solid evidence before proceeding."

"Like proof that he had a gun," I mused, something tickling the back of my brain. Somewhere I had just seen guns that might fit the bill—where was it?

"In fact, I'm headed to the Hartmans' this afternoon," Corelli said. "To speak to them more about their daughter."

"Could we accompany you?" I asked.

Daniel was already shaking his head before the lieutenant said, "No."

"I'm afraid I couldn't bring you on official police business, Mrs. Sullivan," Corelli said.

I took a breath to remind him that that was exactly what he had just done when Daniel forestalled me. "I'll go along if I may, Corelli; as part of the Bureau it is my responsibility, and we should coordinate our efforts." He looked at me and winked out of the sight of Corelli. *Then I'll come home and share my information* was the unspoken message.

Something had changed in me. I no longer wanted these schemes, to be relegated to Daniel's news and accept my role as a woman who had to hide my knowledge. I took a breath to speak, but at that moment a brilliant idea occurred to me, so I returned Daniel's wink.

"I'll see you at home, then, shall I?" I said. "Thank you, Lieutenant Corelli."

He stopped walking and solemnly shook my hand. "Thank you, Mrs. Sullivan. Your information was very helpful. We thought Dr. Parker was in the city, but we had no address."

"I'm sure you would have discovered it without me." I gave a generous smile. "I hope someday soon you and Mrs. Corelli can come to dinner with us."

That was the right thing to say. Corelli had all the pride and embarrassment of a newly married man. He flushed and glowed at the same time. "How nice of you to offer," he said. "That would be wonderful." And with one final handshake, he and Daniel walked up the steps to police headquarters while I walked around the corner. As I got out of sight I began to walk faster, fairly sprinting toward home. In Patchin Place I headed, not for my own house, but for number ten and rang the doorbell.

At first the door opened just a crack. Then I heard, "Oh, it's you, Molly." The door was flung back to reveal Gus in a long silk robe, a novel in one hand. "We're having a bit of a lazy day. Sid is still asleep."

"It's Miss Johnson I wanted," I said. "Is she still sleeping as well?"

"No, she's up," Gus said. "And entertaining Cousin Prudence. What are you up to, Molly?"

"I want to go and see the Hartmans," I said, "and bring them my condolences. And, of course, Miss Johnson knows them much better than I."

Gus looked at me appraisingly. "You're investigating. Excellent. This will cheer Sid up. Can we come along? We're extremely helpful."

"I have to get there right away," I said. Her face fell, and I added hurriedly, "But I promise to come back and tell you all I know. After all, it was you and Sid who hired me in the first place."

"And we'll hire you again to find her killer," she said. A worried expression crossed her face. "Do you think we caused this somehow by looking for her? Should we have left well enough alone?"

"I've been wondering the same thing," I said. "And that's why I'm not going to stop until I find out who did this." Time was growing short. "I really am in a hurry," I said, and to her questioning look I added, "I want to get there before Daniel and the police, and they are on their way, or will be in a minute."

"I see." A grin spread across her face. "Triumph of the woman investigator."

"Something like that," I said. "Can I speak to Miss Johnson?"

Gus ushered me into their parlor, where Cousin Prudence and Anne were sitting. They were not talking and I wondered how much of our conversation they had overheard.

"Mrs. Sullivan again," Cousin Prudence said, nodding at me without deigning to rise. "How nice to see you up and about, paying calls and fully dressed." She gave a pointed look to Gus in her silk robe.

"Nice to see you, Miss Walcott," I said politely and then turned to Anne. "Miss Johnson, would you consider paying a call on Mrs. Parker's family with me? I want to express my condolences."

Anne fairly jumped out of her seat. "Let me get my hat," she said, disappearing from the room in a flash.

"It's rude to go empty-handed," Cousin Prudence sniffed. "Why, when my Aunt Alba died, every woman who brought their condolences to Uncle Edgar brought some homemade cakes or pastries."

"That was because they all wanted Uncle Edgar's money," Gus said, taking an enormous bite of an apple as she sat on the settee and picked up a book. "And the pastries were made by their cooks, which we don't have. You could take some apples, Molly." She gestured to a large basket of apples on the counter.

"You can't take apples." Cousin Prudence was incensed. "They can afford their own apples." If Gus was trying to drive her away, I believed she had almost done it. Why was Cousin Prudence staying on? The parades were over. What was there to stay for? "I am afraid I will have to tell your father that you have become very wild," Prudence went on, shaking her head sadly. "You should have a cook and know how things are done in proper society."

I suddenly had an uneasy feeling. Was Cousin Prudence here to spy on Gus? For years Gus had acted as if her family had no influence on her, but Willa Parker's death had made me wonder what a family might do to rein in one whom they perceived as letting the family down. But these thoughts were swept aside as Anne reentered the room.

"Shall we go, Mrs. Sullivan?" And we hastily departed before Cousin Prudence could offer any more advice. Gus followed us to the door and pressed an unopened tin of imported biscuits into our hands.

"Don't tell Cousin Prudence, but she's right," she whispered. "You can't show up empty-handed." And thus armed with biscuits we hailed a cab and set off.

"We could easily have walked up Fifth Avenue," Anne said as we rounded the park. "Are you in a big hurry, Mrs. Sullivan?"

"I confess I am," I said.

"Are you using me to do your sleuthing again?" Anne smiled to take the sting out of her words, but her eyes were tired and a little wary. "That didn't have a good result the previous time."

"Do you blame me for Mrs. Parker's death?" I asked, a little stung. "I merely found her for her friends."

"No, I didn't mean that," she hastened to reassure me. "How could it be your fault? It was a terrible accident that she got in the way of that bullet. I only meant that she might still have been hiding and not at the parade at all if she had not been found."

"You mean if I had not found her," I said. I had a feeling of déjà vu. Here I was, once again in a cab, wondering if I should take Anne

Johnson into my confidence. She had been helpful the last time, but a doubt gnawed at me. What did I really know about her?

"Gus said you will be going back home as soon as you are rested," I ventured.

"Yes, my mother will already be wondering where I am. And I am to give an update on the demonstration to our local chapter of the WSP."

"WSP?"

"Woman Suffrage Party; I think I mentioned I am the secretary. There is a debate in our ranks over whether to continue engaging in these flamboyant demonstrations or to more sedately prove our worth in letter-writing campaigns and intelligent discourse with our local politicians."

"And, after your ordeal, will you recommend the latter?" I offered, thinking that this shy woman would surely prefer to sit home and write letters. She surprised me by shaking her head.

"The way they treated us in that jail," she said in a voice that was choked with emotion, "like we were naughty children being punished." She shook her head. "That's what will happen behind closed doors. We are never taken seriously. We must take our fight to the streets."

"My husband thinks it is possible that Mrs. Parker was shot by someone who opposes the suffrage movement." I wasn't sure this was true but I wanted to see her reaction. Her eyes blazed even more fiercely.

"They will not cause us to back down, even if poor Mrs. Parker was a martyr to our cause," she said hotly. There was a moment of silence in the cab. Then she continued. "To be honest, Willa would be a strange martyr for our cause. I am not sure she was a very vocal supporter."

"She wanted to be able to work in a lab without her husband's permission, I believe," I said.

"Yes, but I can't see her marching for it," Anne offered. "I believe that was Mrs. Schilling's passion, and Willa just went along to please her friend." That raised more questions in my mind, but the hansom cab was pulling up outside the Hartman residence. I paid the driver as we climbed down, the emptiness of my purse reminding me that I needed to ask Daniel for household money. I was going to save the money I earned rather than spend it!

Anne presented a card to the young maid who answered the door and we were shown into a rather grand parlor.

"Anne, how lovely of you to come," Winnie Hartman held out her hands to grasp both of Anne's. She looked at me as if trying to place me. In my blue wool suit and sensible boots I might not have resembled the woman dressed in Gus's fashionable clothes at the opera house.

"And you remember my friend Mrs. Sullivan from the other night." Winnie's face cleared as she placed me. I held out the biscuit tin.

"I'm so sorry to hear about your sister," I offered.

"Oh, Mrs. Sullivan," Winnie said, "how nice of you to come. You were right the other night. And I feel dreadful for all those things I said about poor Willa. Her life was in danger and I accused her of being selfish." She dabbed at her eyes in what seemed to me a rather theatrical motion. In all aspects she looked like a person playing the sister of a murdered woman. She was dressed all in black with a tiny, rather pretentious veil. I rebuked myself for being uncharitable. She had just lost her sister and people grieve in different ways.

"You were not wrong, Miss Hartman," I assured her. "I was able to find your sister and she was perfectly safe."

"You were?" Winnie's eyes glistened with tears in her otherwise composed face. "The police have been able to tell us so little." She rang a bell and the maid appeared. "Could you ask my father to join us, please?" she said to the maid. "He will want to hear this," she said to me in way of explanation. "Won't you have some coffee while we wait? Anne, would you pour it?" I was aware again of the brace on Winnie's leg under her fashionable skirts. What would it be like to need help to move around your own house? I have always taken my own sturdy legs for granted, even been proud of my ability to walk far distances. A disease had robbed this woman of that possibility. No wonder her sister had felt so passionately about finding a cure.

Anne poured coffee with cream and sugar. "Dear Anne," Winnie said. "You and I were best friends at school. Why has it taken this tragedy to bring us together again? You must promise to come and stay soon."

"I will," Anne said in her quiet voice.

Mr. Hartman entered. I wasn't sure whether I should rise to meet him, but Anne stayed seated, so I did too. Like his daughter, he did not seem to recognize me from our brief encounter at the opera house, but he nodded politely as Winnie murmured our names to him.

"Miss Johnson," he said to Anne. "I believe you knew my dear daughter Willa."

"We did," Anne said. "I'm so sorry for your loss." I noticed that Willa was his dear daughter again, the arguments of the past forgotten.

"Mrs. Sullivan says that she saw Willa before it happened," Winnie put in. "She knows what she was doing in the city." He looked at me expectantly. Winnie motioned for us to retake our seats and they sat as well, looking at us eagerly.

"She was visiting friends." I chose my words carefully. "An old professor and his wife. She wanted to find employment in their lab."

"Was she going to leave George?" Winnie asked. "Is that why she disappeared?"

"I don't believe so," I said. "I think she wanted employment for both herself and Dr. Parker. The Flexners thought it wouldn't be respectable any other way."

"The Flexners?" Winnie asked again. She and her father made an interesting contrast. He was quite taciturn, and as I had noticed at the opera house, she filled every silence with conversation.

"That is the lab director and his wife. She was staying with them. I believe she was only in the parade as a favor to Mrs. Flexner and her friend Mrs. Schilling."

"Mrs. Schilling is the woman I was telling you about," Winnie said. "I've read so much about her in Willa's letters I feel that I know her."

"Mrs. Schilling is the one who has the boy?" the father spoke now. "My grandson?"

"Yes," I answered. "She was caring for Charlie while Willa came to New York. The police have sent someone over to the house to find him and let his father know where he is."

"I would like to see him," the father said. "You seem to be heavily involved in this. Can you find a way for us to see him?"

"I'll do my best," I said.

"No one has told us anything," he went on. "Why was my daughter there? She is not a suffragist, nor does she care for costumes and frippery. That parade is the last place I would ever expect to find her. In fact"—his voice was tense with emotion—"I saw it happen from the stands and it never occurred to me that the woman who lay there on that float was my own daughter."

"I was there as well," I offered, "with my husband, and saw you and Miss Hartman."

"You should have come over to greet us," Winnie said. "We could have found you a seat by us."

"You were up and down yourself," Mr. Hartman added. "Why, when the shooting started I couldn't see you anywhere."

"I left my seat to wave to the German ambassador and his wife. I spotted them up on that dais and I was trying to get their attention. But he was in earnest conversation, speaking to the Japanese prince's attendant. They were exchanging addresses, political sorts of things I suppose," she said. I noted that the ambassador had been speaking to someone from Japan. Daniel had mentioned a possible exchange of plans for a battleship. Could this be how this type of spy work was done? At a parade where no one would be paying attention?

"So we were, luckily, out of the line of fire," Winnie went on, "but I hurried back to you as soon as I could, Father. I will never forget that moment, will you? Anne"—she turned to her—"I didn't see you, but you must have been there, weren't you?"

"I was on the float," Anne said. "I was one of the goddesses."

"You were involved in that disgusting spectacle?" Mr. Hartman's voice rose.

"Now, Father." Winnie put out a hand to calm him down. "I'm sure my good friend has a reason, don't you, Anne?"

"Well . . ." Anne, shy at the best of times, struggled to come up with the words. "We try to protest peacefully for the right to vote. But in England, the women who are protesting—"

"The suffragettes," Winnie put in.

"Yes," Anne said, "they are being jailed and force-fed. And our government is hosting Sir Edward and the English navy. We thought attention should be brought to it."

"Sir Edward is a perfectly decent man," Mr. Hartman said, his harshness mitigated by his daughter's warning glance. "You can't hold him responsible for the actions of the whole country. Women are too emotional. This is why it is best to let your opinions be tempered by your husband and father. They can take them into account in a reasonable way as they cast their vote."

"I have no husband or father," Anne said and a silence followed.

"Mr. Hartman, did you catch a glimpse of the shooter?" I asked. "He must have been somewhere near you for the bullet to hit the glass behind the stands."

"I didn't," he said, "or of course I would have told the police, but there was so much movement everywhere I doubt I would have noticed."

Just then the maid entered again. "There are two men here to see you and Mr. Hartman," she said softly to Winnie. "One of them is a policeman."

"Show them up," Winnie said, "and please ask the ambassador and his wife to come down. They may wish to speak to them before they depart."

"They're still here?" I asked as the maid left the room.

"Yes, Miss Luckemeyer . . . that is—I mean, of course, Countess Bernstorff—is an old friend and she has been a comfort during this time." Mr. Hartman's voice sounded soft for a moment. "And her husband had a few more matters to attend to before they return to Washington, DC."

Footsteps sounded in the hall and two men were shown into the room. My back was to them and I didn't turn around.

Mr. Hartman rose and walked over to them.

"I'm so sorry for your loss," Corelli's voice said. "We came to assure you that we are doing everything we can to find your daughter's killer."

"Thank you." Mr. Hartman's tone was formal and a bit wary. "We are here at your service if we can help in any way." He shook hands with Daniel next. "Are you involved in the investigation as well, Mr. Sullivan?"

"Well, my primary job has been to keep the ambassador safe"—that was Daniel—"but I feel responsible for the safety of all at the parade, and so want to make sure we find your daughter's killer. May we ask you a few questions?"

"Yes, of course," Mr. Hartman said. "Please come in. Let me introduce my guests. They may have some information as well since they were at the parade."

I turned to face the two men. "Oh, hello, Daniel." I nodded pleasantly. "And Lieutenant Corelli as well." I smiled. "What a surprise to see you here."

## Thirty-One

Before Daniel could reply, Count and Countess Bernstorff entered the room. The countess went immediately to Mr. Hartman. "Johnny," she said, "do they have news on your daughter?"

"Sullivan." The count nodded to Daniel. "Are you involved in this thing?" His German accent was light and cosmopolitan.

"I'm heading the investigation," Daniel said. "This is Lieutenant Corelli from the New York police. He has some information and some questions for you."

The parlor, a very feminine room obviously designed for a small group of callers, now felt overcrowded. Winnie gave instructions for more chairs to be brought in.

Mr. Hartman sighed and sat in the wingback chair that Winnie had vacated. "We only have questions. I have no idea where my daughter had been, who she was with, or why she was in the parade. You might ask this lady here"—he gestured at me—"she seems to be some sort of female investigator."

"Yes, I have her information already," Daniel said with a wry look at Corelli, who shrugged. "Perhaps I could ask you about Mrs. Parker's marriage. Was it a happy one?"

"Oh yes," Winnie said. "They were very well suited, both academics." I gave her a hard look. This was not what she had told me as we sat at the opera house. Then she had spoken of their fights and Willa's attempts to come home and bring her son. Was this Winnie not wanting to speak ill of the dead or was there something to cover up here?

"When Mrs. Parker was reported missing by her husband, did that cause you any alarm?" Corelli asked. "He came to the police about it. I believe he also came to you?"

Again, it was Winnie who answered. "My sister had so many friends in the city, we were certain she was with one of them and had just forgotten to write to him, or her letter had gone astray. She could be a little muddleheaded, my dear sister. Just like so many brilliant academics." Again she held a handkerchief to her eyes and dabbed them.

"So you would be surprised to hear that Dr. Parker was at the parade as well, in the vicinity of his wife when she was shot?" Corelli asked, watching closely for their reactions.

"Really?" Winnie asked. "I had no idea. Although he may have known Willa's plan to be in the parade and wanted to support her."

"Is he a supporter of woman's suffrage?" Daniel asked, and Winnie flushed red.

"I didn't mean that at all," she said, "he would not support that." She looked at her father a little fearfully, but it was the count who spoke.

"What a disgrace that was," he said sternly. "Word of it is already in the papers in Germany, and there are articles about the disrespect shown to the dignitaries and even your own vice president."

"I am sure my daughter was unaware of what those women were planning," Mr. Hartman said. "Let us forget all about it, so as to not sully her memory. I believe this lady"—he gestured to me again—

"has the address Dr. Parker is currently staying at and the one of my grandson. My intention is to bring them both here so that we can decide what to do next."

"It's what poor Willa would have wanted," Winnie said, now allowing a real tear to roll down her face. I gave Daniel a meaningful look. It seemed to me that Willa's death was fortunate for her family. They were remaking her in their image to be the daughter they had wanted. And it appeared that if her husband had had any part in her death, they were not interested.

"I believe," Corelli said, flipping through his notebook, "that your daughter was a scientist of some type at the University of Pennsylvania?"

"My daughter was a loving mother," Mr. Hartman said with an air of finality, "who supported her husband in his scientific career. Much as my other daughter supports me." He gave Winnie a fond smile. "Every man should have a feminine face to come home to after the harshness of the masculine world." This seemed a deliberate misrepresentation. I had just informed him that his daughter had been seeking employment in a research institute. But whether he had not been listening or was deliberately refusing to believe it, I couldn't tell. I wondered what it would have been like for Willa to grow up in this family. Mr. and Miss Hartman acted as a single respectable unit. Winnie obviously loved to keep house and give parties. I had a pang of sympathy for the daughter with a burning passion for academic study who clearly was always made to seem an outsider in her family home. It made more sense to me now why Willa had not chosen to stay with her family when she came to the city. Her father would not have approved of her seeking employment, or of her thoughts of leaving her husband.

The more I thought of it, the more I respected Willa's plan of action that at first had seemed foolish and not well thought out. Mrs. Schilling clearly was her only true friend: willing to not only take in little Charlie, but bring him to the city, presumably leaving her own husband to his own devices while she did so. In her, Willa had received a love and devotion that was absent in this family or, as far as I could tell, in her husband. And Willa, as driven as she was, must have returned it, or else what had she been doing on that float?

I'm afraid I lost track of the conversation as I had this insight. I brought myself back to the scene at hand.

"But surely," the count was saying, "an anarchist must have been trying to shoot one of us, or even your vice president, and Mr. Hartman's lovely daughter was the innocent victim."

"If so," Daniel said, his tone measured, though I saw the stress in his expression, "the person chose to use a small pistol and was a terrible shot. From the bullet wounds—excuse me, Miss Hartman, for mentioning such an indelicate subject—it seems the shooter was close to Mrs. Parker. A pistol of that size could hardly shoot accurately more than fifty yards."

"Were they shooting at the protesters, then?" Countess Bernstorff asked. I wondered what her views on women's suffrage were.

"That is one possibility," Daniel said, "but no one knew about the protest until it happened. Someone would have had to already have the pistol on them."

"This is very bad, Sullivan." The count shook his head. "I thought your men had this under control. This looks like American lawlessness."

Daniel flushed. "If you remember, sir, I strenuously argued with the commission against having the Court of Honor in such a wide-open place. It was impossible to protect from all angles."

"I did not hear your objections," Mr. Hartman said, a little too loudly. "And I was in every committee meeting."

"What I don't understand," Corelli said, his voice also calm, trying to defuse the situation, "is why the shooter would choose such a small weapon. As Agent Sullivan says, the site was indefensible. A rifle fired from any of the windows across from the grandstand would have done the job. So why a pistol, and why haven't we found it?"

"Well, you haven't found it because the shooter disappeared into the darkness of night," the count said.

"I don't think so." Corelli shook his head. "Remember that the police and agents were already on the scene. Everyone close enough to have fired a shot was questioned and searched. We have evidence it was fired from close to your poor daughter."

"Someone on the float, then," Mr. Hartman conjectured. "One of those degenerate women."

Anne bristled at that, but Mr. Hartman didn't glance her way and had clearly forgotten that one of those women was present.

"That is the most obvious explanation." I decided it was time to add my voice to the mix. "But there is one problem. All the women on the float were immediately arrested and booked. The police searched them all. So where is the gun?"

After that there was silence. Mr. Hartman cleared his throat. "That is your department, Lieutenant. If there is nothing else I can help you with?"

"No sir," Corelli said. "We will be releasing the body after the coroner's inquest."

"Agent Sullivan, isn't your new Bureau in charge of political crime like this?" the count spoke up.

"Yes, that is one of our duties," Daniel said gravely, "And I assure you we will find who killed Mrs. Parker."

Winnie gave a sob and raised her handkerchief again.

"Then I suggest you go and do it." Mr. Hartman stood up. "We are distressing the ladies." The interview was at an end. Daniel and Corelli shook hands with Mr. Hartman and the count and left.

"I'm afraid we must be going as well," Count Bernstorff said. "We are due in Washington, DC. We only stayed because Jeanne wanted to see if we could be helpful in the matter of your daughter."

"And you had those meetings with that Japanese man," Jeanne said hotly, a little stung.

"True, true," the count said placatingly. "I had business as well, I admit. But now we must be going." They rose as well.

"We are all packed, if we could request that your chauffeur drive us to the station," Countess Bernstorff said. A fond look passed between the countess and Mr. Hartman, but I think I was the only one who noticed.

"Yes, let's have your bags brought down. Excuse me, ladies." Mr. Hartman nodded to us and the three of them exited.

Anne and I stayed with Winnie for a few more minutes, letting her talk about her dear sister. I had real sympathy for her, having lost my own brothers, and I understood the complicated emotions that can arise when a sibling whom you fought with is gone. *Don't speak ill of the dead* is what I was always taught.

"She was so passionate about her work and those little viruses," Winnie said with a chuckle that was also a sob, "I wonder if she ever gave us a thought."

"But she did," I offered. "I didn't know your sister well, but in the short time I knew her, she told me her passion for science was born of a desire to prevent others from suffering the same affliction as you." I glanced at the brace on her left leg, whose metal outline was visible through the fabric of her skirts. She shifted in the chair and smoothed the fabric.

"Thank you for saying that, Mrs. Sullivan." Now her eyes were bright with real tears. "I don't think I had realized that." She cleared her throat. "I get along quite well, though. I hope you don't think of me as an invalid."

"No indeed," Anne said with a smile. "It's obvious that you run this house beautifully."

Whether it was the talk of viruses or the exertions of the day, I suddenly felt overwhelmingly tired. A knot of pain began to throb in my temples. We made small talk for a few more minutes and then left, choosing to walk back now that I was not in a hurry to beat Daniel there. The sun was out, however briefly, and I thought it might clear the chill that I felt settling in my bones. Both of us were quiet, lost in our own thoughts.

"Will I see you again before you go?" I asked as we rounded the corner into Patchin Place.

"Oh, but you must come in," she urged. "You promised Sid and Gus." A gust of wind raced down the narrow court and I sneezed. I was about to make an excuse when the door to number ten opened and Sid popped her head out.

"You're back," she said. "What did you find out?" She beckoned us inside. "We're being quiet," she said in a low voice. "Cousin Prudence is taking an afternoon nap." Her look told me she was anxious not to awake that lady.

"When is she going?" I asked in a similarly low voice. "Wasn't she just here for the celebration?"

Sid shrugged and gave me a look of desperation. "We're not sure. One does want one's house back."

"I should be packing myself," Anne said. "You've been such lovely hosts."

"Oh, I didn't mean you, Anne dear," Sid said hurriedly. But Anne was already heading upstairs. Sid led me into the parlor, where Gus was clacking away on her typewriter, a frown of focus on her face. She stopped and smiled when she saw me.

"I'm writing an editorial to the paper," she said. "On the disgraceful treatment of our sister suffragists. The First Amendment guarantees the right to free speech and assembly!"

"Molly has just come back from the Hartmans'," Sid said. Then, turning to me, she asked, "What did you find out? Do you know who killed poor Willa?"

"More to the point," Gus said dryly, "did you get there before Daniel and the policeman?" She knew me very well.

I gave a sly smile. "I was waiting in the parlor when they arrived."

She chuckled. "Good girl. Now, what did you learn?"

"Not much, I'm afraid," I said. "The family doesn't want her husband investigated. I think they are afraid it will cause scandal. They believe it is anarchists that were shooting at one of the dignitaries."

"Where would they have been shooting from?" Sid asked. "Wouldn't we have seen them?"

"My dear, we were lying down with our eyes closed," Gus said. "We wouldn't have seen anyone."

"Yes, I had forgotten that," Sid said. "It was all so chaotic. But the other women on the float might have seen something, the women who were still standing with banners. I don't see how someone could have gotten close enough to shoot without one of them spotting him."

"Unless it was a rifle, shot from a high window?" Gus made this a question.

"It wasn't though," I said. "It was a small gun. The shooter must have been quite close."

"Do the police have the gun?" Sid asked.

"No, they can tell from the bullets in the body," I said. "The police are quite puzzled that they have not found the gun. They searched everyone that was in the area."

"Impossible," Gus scoffed. "It was chaotic—someone could have slipped away."

"Hmm." Sid was thoughtful. "I'm not sure they could. There was a whole line of police. They would have seen someone trying to run away."

"They didn't search us," Gus said. "The women on the float itself."

"Yes they did," Sid said. "As soon as we got to the police station a woman matron made us all undress." She shuddered.

"Well, they didn't search me," Gus said defiantly. "I got away."

I looked at her with a mixture of fondness and exasperation. "Well, Miss Augusta, then I suppose you are our prime suspect!"

## Thirty-Two

They both chuckled.

"Someone very close to the float, or on it, shot Mrs. Parker," I said, sobering at the thought. "Did any of the other suffragists get away as you did, Gus?"

"I'm not sure," she said, but Sid shook her head.

"I would know," Sid said. "We were all there."

"So all the suffragists were searched," Gus said. "And anyway, where would any of us have acquired a gun? It isn't a normal thing for a lady to be carrying around."

"I suppose we could have nicked one from Mrs. Belmont," Sid said. "Or an axe or broadsword, for that matter."

"That's right." I suddenly remembered. "The wall of guns at her house. Why, anyone at that meeting could have taken one."

"I suppose we need to find out if one is missing," Gus said. "Mrs. Belmont has been away from home and might not have noticed. I doubt she goes into her armory on a daily basis anyway."

"Is she back now?" I rose. "I should go and see." But as I rose I felt the room swim around. Little black dots swam in my vision and I sat back down again quickly.

"Molly, are you all right?" Sid was at my side. "Your face has gone as white as chalk." Her hand found my forehead. "And you're quite warm."

"I think I might have caught what Liam had," I said. "It was inevitable, as I was his nurse, I suppose. Luckily, neither he nor Bridie seemed to suffer from it too long, but I do hope I don't give it to the baby." I wondered if I could rise without the room swimming around. "I should leave before I get you both sick," I said, rising and steadying myself on the chairback.

"Nonsense, we are never sick," Gus said, brushing off my worry. "But you should get some rest." She turned to Sid with a delighted smile. "We can sleuth for you. We are going to a meeting with Mrs. Belmont today and will ask her to check for that pistol."

"That way you can rest and feel better," Sid said.

"I thought you were supposed to be hiring me to find the murderer, not the other way around," I said with a weak laugh, an ache beginning behind my left eye.

"We are honorary members of the Molly Murphy Detective Agency, after all," Gus said, adding, "It is our exchange number on the card."

"Very well, I would appreciate that," I said, giving in. "I am sure that Mrs. Belmont doesn't want to be visited by the police or connected with a murder investigation in any way, so you would be doing her a kindness as well."

I had to lie down as soon as I came home and surprised myself by sleeping the afternoon away. When I woke I asked Aileen and Bridie to warm up some leftovers from the icebox for dinner and went back to sleep yet again. When Daniel came home, I managed to sit down to dinner with the family but could only eat a few bites.

"We picked up the Pinkerton man for questioning," Daniel said as the children went upstairs to get ready for bed, for once eager to share the details of an investigation with me. "He insists he was only paid to find Mrs. Parker and had no idea about the murder. He also has a very different recollection of your encounter."

"I bet." I managed a smile. "Did he know you were my husband?"

"He did not." Daniel smiled back. "According to him, a meddlesome woman got herself into trouble with some ruffians and he rescued her from their clutches."

"Well, that tells you how truthful he is," I said. "I would not trust his account of anything. But I can't think of a reason why he would kill Mrs. Parker. Unless he was paid to do so by Dr. Parker."

"Which is quite unlikely," Daniel said. "I've known some Pinkerton men myself and, while they are ruthless in their investigations, they are not paid killers."

"I agree," I said, "as much as I would like him to be the killer. He is a very unpleasant man."

"I suspect you would like to put all unpleasant men in jail." Daniel's booming laugh went right through my head and I winced.

"Did you find anything out from the Hartmans that we were not able to?" he asked. I was surprised it had taken him so long.

"Miss Hartman is hard to decipher," I said. "She seems devastated by her sister's death, but in a very theatrical way. She is very friendly and talkative, but I feel she is hiding something beneath all that."

Daniel nodded. "And?"

"She was on the scene," I said, "But she did not see her sister. According to her, she was not aware that her sister was going to be on the parade float at all."

"She could have crossed the street with a concealed gun, hidden behind the float, and shot into the stands, narrowly missing her own father," Daniel said. I felt he was being sarcastic but ignored the sarcasm.

"When murder is committed with a gun, we have to look at women suspects, but I don't think Winnie could have done it because of her leg."

"What about her leg?" Daniel asked.

"Well, the polio she had paralyzed one of her legs. She wears an iron brace. You wouldn't have noticed, as she was sitting, but she can't move very quickly."

"Heaven's above, Molly, how do you know the woman's life history?" Daniel gave an exasperated laugh that came out as a bark.

"I sat with her at the opera, and she is hardly a closed book," I said. "I hope for the state of the Union that she is not privy to any government secrets, because she surely would have shared them with the ambassador and his wife. I learned about her home life and growing up, her illness and her mother's death."

"She is the younger sister?" Daniel asked.

I nodded.

"They are a very wealthy family," he said. "That kind of wealth can be a powerful motivator." I shook my head.

"As I say, she can't move very swiftly and relies on her father," I said. "If she was involved there would have been an accomplice." There was a knock on the door and I struggled to my feet a little wearily.

"Are you feeling any better?" Sid said as I opened it to find my two friends on the front step.

Gus handed me a strange-looking flask. "Mrs. Belmont said she is sorry you are ill and had her cook make you a restorative with real lemons from her conservatory. She grows them year-round, apparently."

"We didn't want to disturb you, but she insisted it is better when hot, and it is very hard to argue with Mrs. Belmont," Sid said. "It's in a Thermos bottle, which apparently keeps things hot." She paused, then went on, "Plus, we have news." Her eyes lit up as she said it. "Mrs. Belmont is missing a Browning pistol from the display in the armory. Oh, hello, Captain Sullivan," she said as Daniel came into the hall behind me to see what was going on. "We have been sleuthing for your wife."

"And bringing her something to help her feel better," Gus added hurriedly. "And we'd better let you shut the door and get her out of the wind. Drink all that tonight," she said, nodding at the Thermos, and they started back across the street.

"What did she mean about feeling better?" Daniel asked at the same time that I said, "A gun is missing from Mrs. Belmont's house." Then we both said, "What?"

I got a mug from the kitchen and poured some of the liquid from the Thermos. It came out steaming hot and smelled sweet and tangy. I took a sip. It was sweetened with honey and something I suspected was rum.

"This is very good," I said, taking another sip.

"Are you not feeling well?" Daniel asked. I nodded.

"I have Liam's cold," I said. "I slept part of the day away, but I should probably drink this and go back to bed. It's just a cold, I'm not dying," I added as a look of concern crossed Daniel's face. "And Sid and Gus brought us some interesting news. A gun is missing from Mrs. Belmont's armory. That's the room we had our suffragists' meeting in. So any of those women could have taken it."

"That is a clue I will follow up on tomorrow," Daniel said, rising and kissing my forehead. "But you should sleep. You are feverish. You shouldn't have been up at all."

"Pshaw," I said. "As if a woman can take to her bed for just a cold." But, in truth, I did not feel well and I was not sad to follow Daniel's advice and go back to bed.

The wind picked up and, although the night was not rainy, it had that damp, foggy chill that penetrates to the bone. I was rarely ill and, like many people blessed with an excellent constitution, I was a terrible patient when sick. Bridie and Liam had both suffered through this cold almost cheerfully, enjoying my extra attention as I brought them pepper tonics and wiped their brows with a cloth. They were brave little soldiers. I, on the other hand, would not accept help, but tended to myself with a very ill humor. Daniel tried to minister to me, wiping my head with a cloth as I had for the children, but I grumpily said that it hurt my head even more to be touched, and turned to the wall. I was not worried for myself but for Mary Kate. Her last cold had been in the summer, when the hot weather could help restore her breathing and I could dress her in little clothing to bring down the fever. If she became ill now, I feared the cold might penetrate to her chest.

I couldn't help but feel angry at Lucy McCormick. She should have known to keep Blanche from company when she was sick. This was 1909, after all, and we knew that illness passes from person to person. And this fever went from Blanche to Bridie to Liam to me. It was only a matter of time before it passed to Mary Kate. It was most irresponsible of a mother to expose other children to her daughter's illness. I supposed that, since she could afford doctors, medicine, and good food for Blanche, the thought of a winter cold did not frighten her as it did me.

I have found that, when ill with a fever, my thoughts pain me, throbbing along with my aching head, spinning around in circles. And that night the circle of thought kept coming around to this web of sickness. I pictured the sickness like little devils jumping from one person to another, gleeful at the injury they inflicted. My anger at Lucy grew. I thought of a few choice words that I would say if I confronted her, then I reminded myself what a good person she was and how kind she had been to Bridie and our family. I forgave her, sure that she had not meant harm. After all, I had often sent Bridie to school with a cold or a cough, not wanting her to miss her lessons. *Every family has their little secrets,* I thought. Then I thought once more of how my head hurt and my fear for Mary Kate, and the whole train of thought began again, as if it were a real train on a circular track I could not escape. Pain, fear, anger, forgiveness. *Every family has their little secrets.*

I was about to finally drift off into sleep when a different thought occurred to me. This thought was so unexpected and strong that I sat upright in bed and let out a gasp.

"Are you all right?" Daniel said sleepily, turning to see me.

My head was throbbing in pain and feverish, and my heart was pounding along with the sudden insight that shook me like a lightning bolt. "Daniel," I said, "I know who killed Mrs. Parker and why."

# ॐ Thirty-Three ॐ

We did not have a long conversation that night. Daniel believed I was feverish and made me take some Peruna tonic and two aspirin tablets. My head was hurting so badly that I didn't argue, but when I woke the next day, miserable with aches and catarrh, but no longer feverish, I did not forget my insight.

It is to Daniel's credit that the next day he did not dismiss it, as I'm sorry to say he had in the past. He had begun to take me a bit more seriously. It didn't hurt that his reputation was on the line. I had Aileen bundle up Mary Kate and Liam and take them for a morning walk, hoping that the baby would not get sick. Bridie had already left for school when Daniel and I sat at the kitchen table. I told him again my conviction, and even in the light of day, it still made sense to me. But in order for him to understand I had to explain again what I had learned of Willa's relation with her family and husband, her research and her single-minded focus on it, and what I had learned at the Flexners'. When I had finished he nodded gravely.

"I think you're right, but if so, we have a problem."

"I know," I said. "How could we ever prove it?"

"And what happened to the gun?" Daniel said. "If everyone was searched and none was found?"

"Do the police still have the float?" I said. "It must be somewhere there."

"I'm sure they have searched the float, Molly," he said. "They're not amateurs."

"Still," I said, "I would like to see it for myself. I have an idea."

"Of course you do," he said. "Let me tell Corelli, and his men can check for it."

I half rose from the table. "I prefer to look for myself," I began, but a wave of fatigue washed over me and I sat again. I was in no condition to be traipsing around the city.

"Tell Corelli I believe he will find the gun somewhere inside the large sculpture," I said. "The killer left it there after they shot Willa from under the skirts of *Winged Victory*."

"Under it?" Daniel queried.

"Yes, I have been under there myself. There is enough room for a person to be concealed, and folds and folds of material in which to hide a weapon. The wire structure is very intricate. The police would have had to dismantle it to find a pistol in there."

"I'll go down to the station myself right now, and you go up to bed," he said. "If we find the gun, we may be able to take some fingerprints from it."

I wanted to protest, but I was in no shape to. *Count your blessings, Molly*, I told myself as I slowly made my way up to bed, feeling dizzy with just the exertion of climbing the stairs. *Daniel is on your side and now you have the police doing your bidding while you lie about in bed.*

It is strange how sometimes we have a certainty of an event, or a series of events. I'm not usually prone to religious thoughts, except perhaps when passing a church and feeling a bit guilty about how long I have been absent. But illness will do strange things to you. My reconstruction of the murder could just be a theory created from a fevered brain, but deep down I had the conviction that it was not. I knew that the police would find the gun right where I said it was. What worried me was that there was no way to prove who the killer was, nothing to link them to that gun. So, while Daniel rushed across the city looking for physical evidence, I lay back trying to devise some scheme by which I could entrap a murderer, and quickly, before all the suspects left the city. I had to give up. My head was heavy and it hurt to hold it up. Bridie and Liam might have bounced back from this illness quickly, but it had hit me hard. I dozed and woke. When I was awake enough to consider anything, I considered how fickle illness was, sparing some and bringing others low. It seemed like an act of God, but I didn't believe in a God who would cause suffering. Anyway, if there was such a God, I couldn't choose to worship him. Would I ever cause my babies a moment's suffering if I could help it?

"It was there, right where you said." Daniel's voice woke me from sleep. I was momentarily disoriented, not being used to sleeping during the day. Daniel standing over me and the light coming in the window seemed incongruent with me being in bed. I could hear the children downstairs. Bridie's voice floated up. I must have slept a long time.

"In the *Winged Victory* statue?" I queried, sitting up. My head did not spin as I did so. Perhaps I was on the mend.

"Yes, but well hidden. I had to get under it and push through the folds of fabric inside the bodice. It was an ingenious hiding place."

"I was under there when I helped with construction, and no one knew I was there," I said. "That's what made me think of it. One could fire a gun through that fabric and be perfectly concealed."

"And the dignitaries?" Daniel asked. "Were they part of the plan?"

"I think they were," I said slowly, "in a clever way. The first shots made everyone duck and run for cover. That way poor Mrs. Parker could be shot and everyone could believe she was not the target."

"Except you." Daniel smiled at me fondly.

"I have been lying here thinking about how we can prove it," I said seriously. "We have a murderer who is willing to take bold action. I think we can use that to set a trap."

Two days later I took a deep breath as I stood outside of Mrs. Belmont's house ready to put that plan into action. No one could refuse an invitation from Mrs. Belmont. It was essential, I had told Daniel as we hatched our plan, that Mrs. Belmont be our ally.

That is what I had counted on when I approached her with the idea yesterday. She had admitted me to the house, out of curiosity, I believe, when I sent up my new card and a note saying it was about Willa Parker's murder, also returning the Thermos bottle and thanking her for the cold remedy she had sent to my house with Sid and Gus. As always, the name of Augusta Walcott opened doors for me. I had warned Daniel to stay away. The police or Bureau arriving at Mrs. Belmont's house would cause talk, whereas I was just another female caller. Yet another way in which it was helpful to be a female detective.

Mrs. Belmont remembered me and took in what I was telling her amazingly quickly. She really was a remarkable woman. She agreed to be a part of our plan, and it was due to her influence that everyone concerned with Mrs. Parker was gathered here today when they had intended to be scattered to the wind. Everyone's plans to board trains back to their homes had been stopped by the expediency of an invitation from Mrs. Alva Belmont.

We gathered once again in the armory. The tables were laid out much as they had been on the day of the meeting. The late afternoon sun streamed in the window, turning the suits of armor blood red. Every woman who had been on the float was there, as well as Mrs. Belmont, presiding over the meeting, and the Flexners, who had attended at my request. Willa's father and sister were also included. It was my idea to choose Mrs. Belmont's house for this little operation. My theory was that Corelli would have a hard time enticing this whole group to the police station, but nobody refuses an invitation from Mrs. Belmont. The second part of my plan also required a private house rather than a police station. That was the part I was not as confident about. I confess I may have taken the idea from a Sherlock Holmes novel, but it was the only way I could see to catch this murderer.

Sid and Gus waved as I entered. To my surprise, Cousin Prudence was with them, standing by a table laden with pastries, helping herself. I walked over to Sid and asked in a low voice, "Has she not gone home yet?"

"She is chaperoning us," Sid said in a pained voice. "Do you think I could use one of the weapons in this room to murder her?" I stifled a laugh and gave a commiserating smile.

Dr. Parker was seated at the front with little Charlie on his knee. My heart broke for the little boy who had lost his mother.

"Mrs. Sullivan, what a sad day." Mrs. Flexner came up to me and shook my hand solemnly. "Can you tell us why we are here? Do you know what happened to Mrs. Parker?"

"That is what we are here to find out," I said. "Lieutenant Corelli from the police will no doubt tell us more about the case."

"We are done with the police after how they treated us," one woman said hotly.

"Now, ladies, we've been asked by Dr. Parker and Mr. Hartman to cooperate to find out who shot poor Mrs. Parker." Mrs. Belmont rose and took a position at the front of the room. "The lieutenant is going to tell you all about it."

Corelli stood up, looking a little nervous. I suspected he would rather be addressing a room full of convicts than suffragists and society women.

He cleared his throat. "We think that someone shot Mrs. Parker on purpose," he said. "With the gun that is missing from that spot right there." He pointed, and the whole room swung around to see the space left on the wall by the small Browning. "Since all of you were in this room before the murder, you might have touched it for quite an innocent reason, so we need to take your fingerprints."

"How do you do that?" Anne Johnson asked, a little fearfully.

"It doesn't hurt," Corelli assured her. "We just place your fingers in ink and examine the patterns. Every finger has a different pattern of swirls."

"I'm sorry, I don't see how this will help us find my friend's killer." Mrs. Schilling was tearfully sitting right beside Dr. Parker and little Charlie.

"You see," Lieutenant Corelli said, "we have found the gun." And he pulled it out with a dramatic flourish. Even though I had helped to plan this meeting, I thought he was being a little overdramatic. "Now, have you ladies heard of fingerprints?"

"Of course we have, Lieutenant, don't speak to us as if we are children," Mrs. Belmont said frostily. "The murderer will have left their mark on the gun. Are you saying we are suspects in this murder? Have you forgotten I was not in the city at the time?"

"No, ma'am," he said quickly, "but your fingerprints are the most likely to be here since it is your gun in your house. We need to know which are yours so we don't mistake them for the killer's."

"Presumably your fingerprints are all over it as well," Mrs. Belmont said dryly. "Since you are brandishing it around my armory."

"I am holding it by the barrel with a cloth, Mrs. Belmont," Corelli said. "And the fingerprints we need are on the handle."

Daniel and I exchanged a swift glance. We were bluffing here, and we hoped that no one guessed the truth. I waited tensely for someone to raise an objection.

But instead Gus jumped up. "I'll go first. I want to see this for myself. Will I see my own fingerprints?" She stepped up to a table in the front that had a tray with ink and white paper cards.

"Yes, miss," Corelli said. "In black and white." Gus dipped a finger in the ink and exclaimed as she pressed it down. "Oh, yes, I see the swirls. Fascinating." Sid wanted to go after that and compare her fingerprints with Gus's.

"Be careful, miss," Corelli warned as she waved around her inky fingers, "you'll mark your dress." Sid drew on her upper lip with her forefinger, creating a debonair mustache and causing Gus to go into peals of laughter, before cleaning off her hands and sitting down.

I was thankful to the two of them. The tension was eased and everyone in the room lined up to have their fingerprints taken. After Sid and Gus, Dr. Parker, Anne Johnson, Harriet Schilling, Mrs. Belmont, and even Cousin Prudence all put their fingerprints onto little white cards, Dr. and Mrs. Flexner followed them, as did the Hartmans.

Daniel casually leaned against the door at the back of the enormous room. If anyone tried to leave, he would know.

"I don't see how my fingerprints could possibly have gotten onto a pistol since I have never held one in my life," Winnie protested. "But I suppose we must do our duty. Really! You would think we were suspects in my own sister's murder."

"Ridiculous," I heard Mr. Hartman mutter to himself, but the spell of Mrs. Belmont was over the whole gathering. No one would dare refuse her anything.

When all the fingerprints had been taken and fingers wiped clean, refreshments were served.

"You should make sure to take those down to the police station right away," Daniel said to Corelli in a bullying tone. "You can't just leave evidence out in a private house."

"You're not my boss anymore, Agent Sullivan." Corelli's voice was low but carrying. "I have to get the fingerprints of all Mrs. Belmont's servants for comparison. Her underbutler is out until six, so I will be waiting here awhile. Unless you want to stay and supervise."

"That is your job, as you have pointed out." Daniel's voice was scornful. I was afraid they were overplaying this scene, but the other occupants of the room politely went about their own business as Corelli put the fingerprints into a folder and the gun carefully into a cloth bag, then placed both gun and folder in the drawer of a small secretary desk in the corner of the room.

The Hartmans, Dr. Parker, and Mrs. Schilling sat down on some comfortable chairs arranged around a fireplace in the enormous room. They clearly had to decide what to do with Charlie. If Dr. Parker took the job in the city, the Hartmans would be able to be a part of the child's life, but Charlie would be ripped away from the life he knew and from Harriet Schilling, with whom he had spent almost as much time as with his own mother. Mrs. Schilling, of course, had no legal say in the matter but did add to the conversation. I stood along the wall, near enough to hear, appearing to study the scrollwork on an ancient dagger.

"I think it would be a shame for Charlie to lose his mother and his home all at once," she said. "Dr. Schilling works late hours at the lab just like you, Dr. Parker, and he doesn't mind a bit if I look after Charlie while Willa works at the lab." She reddened, realizing what she was saying. "I'm sorry, it still hasn't hit me that my friend is gone. While you work at the lab, Dr. Parker. He's very welcome."

Charlie seconded her words by hiding behind her when his grandfather called him over.

"Now, Charlie, come to see Aunt Winnie," Miss Hartman called enticingly, holding out her hands. "Would you like to come and see your aunt more often?" The poor boy looked quite stricken and shrank closer to Harriet, who put an arm around him comfortingly.

"Leave it, Winnie," Mr. Hartman growled. "The boy doesn't know us. And I blame you for that, Parker. You would have been welcome anytime. I can't understand why you shunned us."

"Excuse me?" Dr. Parker looked more confused than angry. "Willa told me that we were not welcome. She said you had cast her off. And when you no longer helped us with the nanny, what was I to believe?"

"I never said you weren't welcome," Mr. Hartman said. "I stopped paying for a nanny to help you take control in your own household over my headstrong daughter. She should have been home looking after her son and giving me more grandchildren. I didn't want to provide her the means to ignore her duties."

The two men looked at each other as if each was appraising the other for the first time.

"I'm afraid my wife was not above telling lies to get her own way," Dr. Parker said with a sigh. "Nothing could come between her and her research. I regret that we have been estranged." And the two men shook hands. It struck me how differently Dr. Parker behaved around other men. To Sid and Gus and me he had been a bully, emotional and threatening. To Mr. Hartman he presented himself as a rational and somber man of science.

"So will you be taking Dr. Flexner's offer of a job in the city?" Harriet Schilling's voice was light but I could see the hand she had around Charlie shaking slightly.

"I want to stay at Penn," Dr. Parker said. "I'll hire a nanny myself, of course, now that my Willa is gone." Harriet stirred slightly. "But I would appreciate if you would stay a part of Charlie's life." Dr. Parker looked at Harriet, who smiled back at him. "And I wonder, Mr. Hartman," he said to his father-in-law, "if we might spend the school holidays with you so that Charlie can get to know his grandfather and aunt."

Mr. Hartman nodded gravely and Winnie beamed. "We would love that, wouldn't we! Charlie, we are going to be great friends! You can come with us to the summer house. We have a pony you can ride. You are going to love it!"

So it seemed that everyone would be getting what they wanted. The Hartmans would have their grandson back as part of their lives; Harriet would still be a part of his life, although she must miss her friend terribly; and Dr. Parker was reunited with his wealthy father-in-law and could continue his research.

I had observed that conversation unnoticed. As the men shook hands and the party broke up, Winnie making her slow way out, dragging one leg behind her, I wondered. Which of them was desperate enough to get what they wanted that they would have been willing to kill?

Anne Johnson came up to Winnie before she could reach the door.

"I'm going back home, so I don't know when I will see you again," she said in her soft voice. "It was so nice to renew our acquaintance, even under such tragic circumstances."

"We were great friends at Vassar, weren't we?" Winnie sounded wistful. "Being in this room full of women reminds me of it. We certainly got up to lots of mischief and had great fun."

"They were the best days of my life," Anne said simply. I imagined her college days, full of promise and friends, as compared to her current life, working quietly at home to support herself and her mother. I wondered if she felt life had cheated her. I felt blessed myself. I had not had the privileged life of a Vassar girl. I had had to work hard for everything I had. But now I had everything I had ever wanted. A comfortable home, a good man as a husband, children I adored, and perhaps even a career I could be proud of.

Dr. Parker spoke to Dr. Flexner in low tones before he and Harriet left together with Charlie in tow, looking like a little family. I wondered how Dr. Schilling would feel about that, or if he was so absorbed in his studies he wouldn't even notice. I had never met the man but from Harriet's description had formed an impression of an owl-eyed academic.

Some of the suffragists were making plans for a meeting later that week, planning a protest campaign against their treatment in jail.

"We can host at our house," Gus was saying. "If we all fit in our little parlor." Sid still had the ink mustache on her face, whether by choice or because it would not come off, I did not know.

"What about Thursday?" one of the women said. "Maud Malone is going to protest at Bannard's political rally and we can all go together to get her out if she is arrested."

"Will they let her in?" another woman asked. "Aren't those things all grave-faced, black-suited men?"

"Yes," the first woman replied. "And she's planning to wear schoolgirl white. We're not sure what will happen, but Mrs. Malone is a force of nature."

"Splendid idea," Gus said. "Now, we must get back and help my cousin pack. She is going back to Boston today." The force with which she said it made me think that Cousin Prudence would be on the train to Boston whether she liked it or not.

Slowly, with many thank-yous to the hostess, the group broke up. The last of the women left.

Daniel, Corelli, and I came together wordlessly. Now it was time to wait.

I took my place behind the suit of armor, enjoying, I must admit, the theatrics of the situation. I sat on a little stool, aware that we might wait for hours. Daniel and Corelli disappeared into shadows in the corners of the room.

And we waited. From my perch I could see through the large windows into a green space beyond. A tall tree was losing its leaves in the stiff breeze, and they fell like a brown and orange shower as the tree swayed back and forth. I could hear the sigh of the wind coming through the house and the drip and tap of a radiator. Below us and far away were the voices of the household staff carrying on with their day and outside the purr of automobiles and clickity-clack of carriages. The sounds were soothing. I was glad I had chosen a hard stool rather than a soft chair or I might have fallen asleep. Gradually the tree became gray as the light outside faded. The shadows in the room lengthened into a gloomy twilight.

Then I heard a rustle: a very faint noise, almost a disturbance of the air rather than a noise itself. There was no creak of a door, which had been left open as enticement of our little mouse into this trap, but the slight tap of a soft slipper. Then nothing. I was just wondering if I had imagined the tap when there was a smooth, low sound—a drawer being opened. Then something being removed. *Wait*, I told myself. *Wait until we are certain.* I counted to three and then laid my hand on the electric light switch on the wall beside me and pressed it. Light flooded into the room and into the startled face of Harriet Schilling.

## ॐ Thirty-Four ॐ

She had the gun in one hand and was wiping the handle with her skirt. She froze, momentarily blinded by the harsh light, and then started for the door.

"It won't do you any good wiping off the fingerprints," I said mildly. "The police have already developed them. They're back at the station."

"I wasn't—" Harriet looked down at the gun in her hand as if it would give her an explanation for her presence in this room. "That is to say, I'm interested in the collection of fingerprints." She was babbling now, unable to talk herself out of this predicament.

"Why were your fingerprints on the gun, Mrs. Schilling?" I said, walking toward her. "Wasn't Mrs. Parker your best friend?"

"Oh yes, she was," Harriet said, putting the gun down on the desk. "I loved her, you see. We were like a family. Willa and me and our boys, Charlie and Jesse."

"That's your son, Jesse," I said. "Who died of infantile paralysis."

"He died of polio." Harriet's voice was harsh. "That's the name of the virus; the one Willa was studying."

"And you blame her for the death of your son." I wanted to keep her talking as long as possible. This had been the theory that had come to me in the night when I was feverish myself.

"I didn't at first," Harriet said. "I accepted her love and sympathy. Willa was my best friend. Charlie was like my son too, a child to fill my heart after Jesse's death left it empty. My husband threw himself into his work to forget his grief, so their friendship meant everything to me."

"You were willing to help her in any way," I said. "You even left your husband alone to come to the city to care for your friend's child. That is much more than most friends would do."

"I loved her," Harriet said simply. "And I didn't understand viruses then. I didn't know that the samples Willa worked with in the lab might make her sick, that they might make little Charlie sick, that he might bring that sickness home to Jesse. I didn't know that what was a little fever in Charlie could be death to my son. But now I do."

"You must have learned that quite recently," I said. "Or you would have never helped her come to New York."

She nodded. "Mrs. Flexner was talking about her husband's research, how careful he must be not to bring sickness home to his family, and suddenly I knew. Willa had killed my son. She had exposed both children to the virus so she didn't disrupt her precious research. And I saw it in her eyes; she knew what she had done as well. She had known since it had happened and never told me."

I wondered what I would have done in the same circumstance, pictured seeing Liam's little face as he breathed his last breath and knowing that my friend had been the cause. I looked at her with sympathy, and she went on.

"I thought we would always be a family. Our husbands had their own world, their scholarship and positions at the university. But we had each other. Even after I found out about Jesse I tried to excuse her."

"Then you found she wanted to move to New York," I guessed. She nodded.

"I thought the whole thing was a ploy to gain her husband's attention, to get him to promise to let her continue her research. But then I realized she was serious about moving. She would have left me and taken Charlie with her. I was just a convenience for her. I felt like such a fool." I heard something new in her voice, a jealousy I would have expected from a lover, rather than a best friend. Willa had been this woman's lifesaver. Clearly when her affection and support were withdrawn Harriet saw no way to go on. But why resort to murder?

"I couldn't let that happen." She turned to me with pleading eyes. "I'm not a bad person. I did it for Charlie. I had to do it in such a way that no one would suspect. I had to be free to go home with him. I knew his father would be happy to let me care for the boy with his wife gone. I'm a lot smarter than people give me credit for. I remembered the guns in this armory and contrived a reason to visit Mrs. Belmont and speak about the float. It was easy to sneak in here and steal the gun. If it was missed, who would think of me?"

"No one did think of you," I said, "because we all thought you were Mrs. Parker's best friend." She winced at that but went on. She seemed eager to show me how clever she had been, eager to tell someone what must have been occupying her every thought since it happened.

"I realized on the day we decorated the float that no one would see me under the skirts of the sculpture. I could take my time and shoot at close distance. It only remained to convince Willa to join the parade. Right up to the last minute she tried to beg off—she was never a suffragist. But I finally convinced her that appearing to be one would help her in the eyes of the Flexners and Mrs. Belmont and she agreed to come. Then all I had to do was fire over the heads of the dignitaries to make everyone duck down and shoot"—her voice broke but she cleared her throat and went on—"shoot Willa." She looked at me defiantly. "So now you know, Mrs. Sullivan. Will you tell others? Will you deprive little Charlie of the one person who loves him now that his mother is gone?"

I hesitated, wondering if I could get her to keep talking even longer. She took my hesitation for a denial and went on in a colder tone. "I shall leave this room now. You can come after me if you like, or try to accuse me, but I shall deny everything you say. It will be your word against mine."

"I'm afraid not, Mrs. Schilling." Daniel chose that moment to step out of the shadows. She jumped convulsively at the sound of his voice coming from the depths of the room, saw him walking toward her, and turned to flee. Corelli emerged from behind a screen and stood in the doorway.

"Harriet Schilling," he said. "You are under arrest for the murder of Mrs. Willa Parker."

All the fight went out of Harriet as she saw that she was trapped. Corelli did not even handcuff her but kept a firm grip on her arm as he steered her through the house past the eyes of curious servants and to the police wagon that was waiting outside.

Daniel and I were invited into Mrs. Belmont's sitting room.

"So, your ruse paid off, Miss Murphy," she said as we were seated. "And presumably Agent Sullivan and the police will take all the credit."

"It's Mrs. Sullivan, actually," I said, glancing hastily at Daniel and blushing.

"I'm confused," Mrs. Belmont said, looking between us. "Your card said Murphy. I have a very good memory."

"Yes." I was unsure of what to say. Unexpectedly, it was Daniel who rescued me.

"That is my wife's professional card," he said. "For her detective agency. You can understand why it is advantageous for people not to connect us when she is working on a case."

"Hmm." Mrs. Belmont frowned. "I thought I was speaking to a Miss Murphy. I feel a bit deceived."

"Well," I improvised, "you have gone from a Vanderbilt to a Belmont, and no one would doubt your worth. Why can't a woman have a professional name for her business? When I first started as a detective I used a man's name and pretended I was just his secretary because no one would hire a woman."

"And you think it will be different now?" she asked.

"I do," Daniel said firmly. "In fact, she is an official consultant for the Bureau on this case."

"Very well," Mrs. Belmont said, "perhaps the times are changing. In the future, you will please not try to deceive me."

"The future?" I asked.

"I will keep this card," Mrs. Belmont said, "in case I have need of you. A woman detective who can pass in my society might be a very useful person to know." She looked me up and down appraisingly. "Although you may need to borrow clothes from whoever lent you some on the night of the opera. This will not do for higher society."

"One of my advantages," I said, surprised at my own boldness, "is that I can enter any level of society. I come from Irish peasants and I've lived in tenements. But I've also stayed at the finest houses and lived on Fifth Avenue." I grinned at her. "And yes, I borrow dresses from Miss Walcott and Miss Goldfarb when I need to."

"Very well," she said with an air of dismissal, "Detective Murphy or Mrs. Sullivan, whichever you are, I will keep your card."

"Thank you, Mrs. Belmont," I said. We rose and turned to go.

"Oh, Agent Sullivan," she called just as Daniel reached the door.

"Yes, ma'am?" he answered.

"As my husbands learned to their advantage: a wife with brains can be the making of a man. Hold on to this one."

"Yes, ma'am," he agreed. "I will."

"Let's catch a cab home," I said as we came out onto the pavement. "I'm exhausted."

"Well done, Molly," Daniel said, taking my hand and squeezing it. "We would never have caught her if it weren't for you."

Those words caught me so off guard that my eyes filled with tears. How long had I been waiting to hear them?

"Thank you" was all I could think of to say. I was not used to praise and I confess it embarrassed me a little. "Corelli has his confession," I went on, wanting to change the subject. "He will be happy."

"And the city can rest assured that no anarchists are running around shooting at dignitaries," Daniel said.

"Or passing on battleship plans," I added.

"Now, I'm not so sure about that," Daniel said. "My sources think the German ambassador is up to something. We will be keeping an eye on his activities." He stepped out into the street to hail a cab and we climbed in. I let out a sigh as I sat down. All that waiting and the drama had left me exhausted, not to mention that I was not completely recovered from my cold.

"Do you really think his wife would scheme against the United States?" I asked, resuming our conversation after we had sat in silence for several blocks. "After all, she is a New Yorker herself."

"Wives don't always know what their husbands are up to," Daniel said. He gave me a pointed look. "Nor husbands their wives."

"And look what it leads to," I said. "Loneliness and murder. I don't want that for us, Daniel. I want us to be each other's support always."

"To be honest, you have really helped me this month, Molly," he said seriously. "I was brought up to think it was impolite to involve women in money matters. I was trying to shield you by not talking about salary and income."

"But I do the shopping, so I become quite aware when there is not money in the tin," I said dryly.

"That's true." He nodded. "I realized I was treating you like a child with pocket money. But when we were in trouble, you were able to figure out a way to keep us going. You're strong, Molly."

I laughed. "You've always known that, Daniel—I've never pretended to be a wilting flower in need of protection."

"Yes, but I thought if I could give you everything, you wouldn't need to be strong anymore." He hesitated as if thinking how best to say this, "I thought you would want to be a flower if you could, if I could give it to you. But you don't want that, do you?" He gazed at me with such understanding that I felt truly seen.

"No," I said, "that's not me and it won't ever be. I'm a fighter and a worker. I need things to do and causes to fight for. And work that means something to me."

"Then we have a use for the ten dollars that the Bureau is paying you," Daniel said as the cab pulled up beside Patchin Place and we jumped out. "We will have to go to the printer's shop and have more cards made for the Molly Murphy Detective Agency."

## Epilogue

Two weeks later

Mrs. Goodwin's house was not far from my own. I walked there, wanting to clear my head and take advantage of the clear late October day. It was chilly but the sun felt good and the breeze was fresh. I felt I had lately become too dependent on cab and car rides. I used to walk everywhere because I could not afford to hail a cab. But I had reminded myself that one got a different view of the city by walking and I should not get out of the habit.

I came on a Sunday afternoon, reasoning that it was the most likely time to find a police matron home. I knew that I could find her at the police station during the week when she was not undercover, but this was not an official visit and I wanted to conduct it in the more pleasant surroundings of her own home.

She opened the door herself, and if she was surprised to see me, she did not show it. "Mrs. Sullivan, come in," was all she said. She invited me into a small parlor. It was plain and purposeful, quite like the woman herself. The window gave a good view of the street in front, which I thought was a good idea, given her profession.

"How is Captain Sullivan?" she asked as we sat down.

"Very well, thank you," I answered, "although not Captain Sullivan anymore, but Agent Sullivan of the New York office of the new Federal Bureau of Investigation now."

She nodded. "I have heard of that. Some men at the station thought it wouldn't last, or at least wouldn't operate outside Washington, DC, but if Captain Sullivan is in charge it has a good chance of succeeding."

"Thank you," I said. "This parade business was its first test and I can't say it worked seamlessly coordinating with the police, though it did help that Daniel was a former police officer."

"Well, you can't expect New York officers to be very happy to have federal men in their city." She laughed. "And how are you, Mrs. Sullivan? I heard that your family is growing."

"Yes, I have a little girl who is almost a year old. My Liam is five and my oldest girl is a young lady."

"And are you quite happy being a wife and mother?" Her steady eyes appraised me thoughtfully. "I remember you as quite a good detective."

"Can one be both?" I asked seriously. I could hear the voices of children in the house, whether her children or grandchildren I did not know. "That is what I came here to ask."

"I have been able to manage it," she said, "with the help of my mother. Do you have someone to watch the children?"

I nodded. "Yes, I have a helper, and now the baby is eating normal food, so I can leave her for longer periods of time."

"Then I believe it is possible. Are you thinking of joining the force? Have you come for a recommendation?" she asked. "I have had to fight to gain my opportunities, but I will help you as much as I can."

I shook my head. "Not the force." I pulled out one of my cards and handed it to her. "I am reopening my detective agency."

She studied it. "Will this be for domestic cases only? Pilfering maids and philandering husbands?"

"I hope it will be for all sorts of cases," I said. "The Bureau hired me to find Willa Parker's murderer. And I did." That got her attention.

"That was not reported in the paper." Her voice was mild but there was a challenge in it.

"Are all your triumphs reported in the paper?" I answered the challenge. "Or do your male superiors take the credit?"

"I'm afraid you are correct," she said. "I keep hoping for that big case that no one can deny I solved. Hoping that they can no longer deny I am a detective."

"Well, I will hope for something more modest," I said with a smile. "Hope that I can help support my family through my agency. I suspect that someone else will take the credit."

"And how did you come to solve Mrs. Parker's murder?" Mrs. Goodwin asked. "The papers said it was a good friend of hers. Some called her a husband stealer and suspected she had done it out of passion gone awry."

"It was out of a passion," I said. "But not for the husband—for the child, and for her own child who died as a result of Mrs. Parker's negligence." I gave her a longer explanation and quite enjoyed telling her about my ruse to catch Mrs. Schilling and seeing the approbation in her eyes.

"Now I see why you were the perfect person to solve it," she said. "I'm not sure a man could understand that motive."

"Yes," I said, "I had very little hard evidence. The answer came to me as the result of a fever. Is that too ridiculous to say?"

"Not at all," she answered. "Women make strong detectives because of their ability to sense things for which at first they have no actual proof. I think that the reason why a woman sometimes succeeds where a man fails is because she is more strongly endowed with this intuition."

"That has been my experience," I said.

"So what did you come here to ask me?" she said forthrightly. I took a breath and sat up a little straighter. I could not help but have a great respect for this woman.

"Two things. The first is to ask you to pass on any business that comes your way that calls for a private detective," I said, "and for the discretion of a woman."

"I can't give you any police work," she warned, "but if I come across any private parties wanting to pay, I could pass that your way." She looked at the card again. "I see you have gone back to your maiden name."

"Just for the agency," I said. "Just so it is not connected with my husband."

She rose and put the card in a little holder for the purpose on her desk. "And the second thing?"

"We couldn't acknowledge each other when we met at Mrs. Belmont's house and you were Mrs. Smith," I said.

"Yes, I appreciate you not giving me away." She smiled. "I was there on business, as you have probably surmised."

"It is just curiosity," I said, "but I wondered why you were there. Was it because of rumors that a suffragist protest was planned?"

She waved away that supposition. "Not at all. It wouldn't bother my captain if some petticoats upset the British ambassador. Let the higher-ups and the politicians worry about that."

"Then why?" I asked. "If you can say."

"I'll tell you," she said, "because you know the ladies, and I clearly can't go undercover with them when you are around. I think this time a more direct approach is called for."

I looked at her without understanding and she went on.

"I'm investigating two women that you know well: Miss Elena Goldfarb and Miss Augusta Walcott."

# Historical Note

The Hudson-Fulton celebration was a real event that unfolded exactly as we have described it, minus the murder. The *Winged Victory* float was our invention, but most of the other details of the parades were drawn from newspaper accounts, including the naval parade nearly coming to disaster as the *Half Moon* struck another vessel, the flyover by the Wright brothers' plane, and the first-ever total illumination of New York City with electric bulbs.

# Acknowledgments

As always, our heartfelt thanks to Kelley, Katie, and the whole team at Minotaur for allowing Molly to flourish for so long. And a big thank-you to the best agents in the universe, Meg Ruley and Christina Hogrebe at Jane Rotrosen Agency. Finally, we owe a lot to patient husbands who understand that we have to phone each other every single evening and chat for an hour.